A MAN WITHOUT TALENT

BOOK TWO

DAVID COTTER

Copyright © 2024 David Cotter

Cover art by Daniel Burgess

The content contained within this book may not be reproduced, duplicated, or transmitted without direct written permission from the author or the publisher.

Under no circumstances will any blame or legal responsibility be held against the publisher, or author, for any damages, reparation, or monetary loss due to the information contained within this book, either directly or indirectly.

Legal Notice:

This book is copyright protected. It is only for personal use. You cannot amend, distribute, sell, use, quote, or paraphrase any part, or the content within this book, without the author or publisher's permission.

Disclaimer Notice:

Please note that the information contained within this document is for educational and entertainment purposes only. All effort has been executed to present accurate, up-to-date, reliable, complete information. No warranties of any kind are declared or implied. Readers acknowledge that the author is not rendering legal, financial, medical, or professional advice. The content within this book has been derived from various sources. Please consult a licensed professional before attempting any techniques outlined in this book.

By reading this document, the reader agrees that under no circumstances is the author responsible for any losses, direct or indirect, that are incurred due to the use of the information in this document, including, but not limited to, errors, omissions, or inaccuracies.

CONTENTS

1. Rootless — 7
2. The House at Oranswell — 165
3. Party's Over — 495

FROM: TO-EM-MEI'S "THE UNMOVING CLOUD"

The clouds have gathered, and gathered,

and the rain falls and falls,

The eight ply of the heavens

are all folded into one darkness,

And the wide, flat road stretches out.

I stop in my room toward the East, quiet, quiet,

I pat my new cask of wine.

My friends are estranged, or far distant,

I bow my head and stand still.

T'ao Yuan Ming. A.D. 365-427 From *Lustra,* 1916

1

ROOTLESS

TUESDAY 29 DECEMBER 2015 01:16

This life is unbearable.

My body feels crushed and broken, my lungs deflated, muscles wasting. I feel that I have been stretched so thin that there is nothing left of me. I feel that I could implode at any moment.

This morning when I left my apartment to go to work, I looked out the window and saw seven lanes of traffic jamming the road travelling south, which was not a one way road. I would have to find another way out of our area.

I put on my mask, went down to the car, and drove south instead of north. The car windows were caked with frozen grime, and the world outside was misty with exhaust fumes. Apocalypse was upon us.

I drove a ways and turned left, then found myself in what looked like another immovable traffic jam, so I did a *diao tou*, and headed back to our area along the bike lane.

I decided to walk in. I just couldn't bear to fight with the traffic any more. There were police at our intersection directing the traffic now. When I got to the corner down toward the secret junkyard or military base or whatever it is that shuts us into this corner, a couple of *ge mer* in a big green Toyota Land Cruiser turned the corner revving and accelerating as though to hit me. I didn't budge but stood my ground. I was ready to bash their car with my computer. They were laughing it up, thinking it was great fun to buzz a *laowai* like this.

I was in my office by about five past nine. There were Chinese teachers in a classroom, updating records. I stayed away from them. I couldn't find my *cha bei*, but then it appeared on the table in front of my nose. I called in Zhang Yang and Sammy to show them a photo of the traffic. Chen Xi and Tan arrived about ten minutes later.

Chen XI phoned to tell me we need more audits–not company audits, but proper education audits. She called Alice in and now they are talking about this right in front of me. It is another *ma fan* to deal with, this *tebie taoyan* official.

Tan is also in this morning, because they need the buyers to write up something to protect us against the way they have broken up the payments. Fan is in the office now, chatting with Chen Xi. Things continue to be complicated. Tan and I have been getting along very well all morning. We talked about travel, and different countries, and we talked about psychology. Tan asked me to show him the basics of boxing. I got him to stand up, and showed him the basic stance and movement. After a while Chen Xi stood up and showed us what she understood of what I had taught him. She was cute and adorable, and we all laughed, and felt relief for a while.

These are my only friends now, the only two people outside of my family who love me. Tan wants to go for a massage with me someday. The best time for him would be around eight, after Davey is asleep. Tan and I went outside for a talk, and I found that with a little help from our translators we were able to communicate very well. The five million deposit is non refundable, so I am confident the deal will go through. Also, Chen Xi thinks we will have the next five million by Thursday.

They have cancelled the meeting for tomorrow to announce the handover because of conflict between Xu and Fan. Fan seems to have been drunk last night, maybe because Xu is pushing him a bit. Xu is a direct investor, but Fan is not. The investment group is invested in a number of very long term projects, but Aihua is the only investment that might be immediately profitable. Yesterday Xu went to YDL and rented a 200 square metre HQ with very little concern for the cost; demonstrating to me their seriousness about taking us over–there would be no hitch. It was just a hell of a lot of paperwork and worry. I went back to the office after lunch to support Chen Xi as best I could. It's not like there's much I could do, but as her muscle I thought I should be present.

At 3 pm I got in the car to collect Davey. The feeling on the road was weird and aggressive. It is a hard world here in Beijing. One of the other parents from Davey's class gave me some air masks for Davey. I watched Davey from outside of the gates, and it gave me an uncomfortable feeling. He was mostly on his own, playing in his own world.

Once, he was standing behind another little boy, and suddenly his face twisted in rage and it looked like he smashed the boy on the back. I don't think he connected; he was just practising rage. I feel that my influence may cause this, or that there is a genetic predisposition to rage in my blood.

Davey and I drove home. He was tired, like he was ready for bed. I tried to get him talking, but couldn't interest him. I got very angry at another car, and I started growling you fucking asshole and Davey said daddy don't be like that. I felt ashamed of my inability to control myself.

We got home and went up to the apartment. The new air cleaner had arrived but was still in its box. Lin was still sick so she had not had a chance to tidy up. As soon as I walked in she asked me to go to the supermarket. I was bordering on being short tempered, but then just went ahead. When I got back I tidied up, and set up the new air cleaner.

Lin made fried rice for dinner, and then we watched the end of Toy Story. While Davey had a bath I played Don't Starve again and was eaten twice by spiders. When Davey wanted to play Don't Starve I was no longer in the mood.

Davey and Lin went to bed. I was reading about Chief Joseph when I heard screaming from Lin's room. Lin had left Davey alone in his room because he told her in Chinese he was hungry, and that if she didn't get food for him he would kill her. Lin feels that since she was away Davey hates her, and this is why he is cruel to her now. I tried to tell her that I did nothing to turn him against her, that I told him she was sick and that we needed to be tender with her.

He was quite upset. I don't think he felt comfortable with what he said to her, that it scared him a bit. I went back to bed, and read a bit more before falling asleep. I felt sick, congested, and claustrophobic.

When I woke up, Davey and Lin were up eating breakfast. Lin told me that Davey had woken at 4:30 and not gone back to sleep. Davey came in wearing a new sweater, chatting to me sweetly, being very good. He got his other new jumper to show me how he could fold it up nicely then showed his mom how nicely it was done. When Davey is sweet he is the most charming little boy in the world. We had a couple of squabbles while Lin was in the hospital, but for the most part we were loving with one another. When we get this all business over with, I hope to be able to focus more on helping Davey and dealing with my own emotions.

Chen Xi, Tan and I took Chen Fu out for lunch at the Muslim place. We all loved the *yangrouchuan'r*. Chen Xi told Chen Fu that we would give him a million for the selling of the school. He was happy though he didn't show it.

When we got back Fan Cheng said hey I thought you used to be taller than me but it seems you are shrinking. I wanted to punch the fucker in the nose but thought better of it.

I see a message from Lin telling me Davey is sleeping. I am exhausted, don't want to go home. I need to rest.

BAJIAO NORTH ROAD, BEIJING, CHINA • -5° MIST AND FOG

WEDNESDAY 30 DECEMBER 2015 00:27

When I woke up at 4:30 to go to the toilet I noticed that the air seemed clean. I looked at the air quality app, and saw that although Beijing was still 195, Gucheng was 25. I went around and turned off the air cleaners. It was a relief to be rid of the jet engine whir. I am worried about the renovation pollution in our apartment, so I opened the windows a bit. I lay down and tried to sleep.

Lin came in. She touched me. It was nice, but it is my peculiarity that I can't feel sexually attracted to someone that I see as hurt.

When I got up to make coffee I noticed that the air quality monitor was still showing a high reading for renovation pollution in the apartment. I didn't want to get one of these inside air quality monitors. If we open the windows, the PM 2.5 comes in; if we close the windows, the poison builds.

I talked to Lin about moving to Rome– I could teach English there. I suggested that Davey wasn't getting the best education he could, and Lin was upset about me criticising China. She may be right. Last night Davey said he hates Beijing. I apologised to Lin, and I told her that I would miss Beijing, that part of me still loves Beijing even if now I appear angry all the time.

I asked Lin to get a professional in to do a reading of the renovation poison in the apartment, and we agreed that if it was too high, she would take Davey away while I stayed in Beijing beside Chen Xi until the sale went through. Lin suggested that she take Davey north to *Heilongjiang*, but I didn't think it was a safe place, even with her family there. I thought we should just sell the apartment. Lin didn't want to, but the pollution would be an issue for the next 10 or 20 years.

Davey cried out again when he woke up, and Lin went in to him. I was brushing my teeth, and my gums were bleeding heavily. When I went out to Davey he didn't react to me being there at all. Eventually I made a joke about sloppy Joe socks, and he cracked a lovely smile. A few minutes later he got angry because the backpack of his Buzz Lightyear was broken. He wouldn't accept that we couldn't fix it; hit out at his mom. I felt angry at Davey for a flash, and I criticised him, but then my heart went softer and my head wiser. I told him I could fix the backpack with a rubber band, and that when I did this it would be cooler. He agreed to this, and calmed down.

Lin served us coddled eggs. I told him that we were having a problem with being angry these days, and we needed to help each other not to be angry, because it is not good to be angry. I told him that the other day when I got so angry in the car, he told me don't be like that daddy, and I stopped, because he helped me. I told him we have the problem of being angry, but it isn't good and we need to help each other. He agreed to this, and we shook hands. I told him that if ever we felt angry and we needed to stop being angry, we would give mommy sloppy Joe socks and call her Sloppy Joe. When Lin tried to dress Davey he resisted trousering, and they got angry at one another, but then I pulled Lin's sock to make her Sloppy Joe, and we both had a good laugh.

The drive tested my temper with the obscene selfishness, arrogance and stupidity of my fellow sapients; the six lanes of traffic waiting at a single turning lane, cars continuing to the top of long queues of cars waiting in line. I honked, I swore, I sighed. Davey sat beside me saying nothing.

After a while Davey asked me why the cloud was following us, and I told him that this was because it was so big and so far away, and compared to how big it was we were barely moving. I told him that when I was the same age as he was now, I asked my dad why the moon was following us outside the car windows, low behind the trees near Flin Flon. I told Davey that when he grew up he wouldn't remember many things from when he was younger but the things he did remember would be very important, they would be golden. I told him that Dad was a scientist who studied the earth, volcanoes, and rocks, and that he could tell me why things were as they are.

The traffic became increasingly difficult, and we went quiet, and then Chopin came on and I turned it up because I really needed to calm down. There were so many things that I wanted to tell Davey, to have him remember as clearly as I remembered the afternoon in my grandfather's back garden, and then the evening, when he told me the story of Icarus.

We got to the kindergarten, and Davey didn't want to get out of the car. When we went in he was pulling down his eyes the way he does when he is ready to cry. I sat down and held him to me and gave him a kiss and told him he needed to go. A happy little girl came through and a lady in a nurse's outfit asked me if he didn't want to go in because he hadn't been to kindergarten much lately. I insisted on him going, and though he didn't cry he also didn't say anything, not even goodbye to me.

I only started this diary entry before Chen Xi, Tan and Fan arrived at the office. Chen Xi started printing up contracts for Tan to take to some government office after they were countersigned by Chen Xi and Fan. After Fan and Fred leave to see the new HQ space in YDL, Chen Xi sits in silence, listening to the clicking of my two fingered typing.

I was reluctant to go home. I felt weak, that I wasn't able to carry the burden.

When I got home, Lin was making gingerbread cookies with Davey at the kitchen table. I felt depressed at the sight of the messy home, the closed windows, whirring air cleaners, and the half mad – half depressed eyes of Lin and Davey.

I asked Lin about dinner and she had no idea. I said I couldn't do it, I was afraid I would cook something and Davey wouldn't eat it, and she said she was afraid of this too. I started to complain, but then tried to turn it into a joke, saying I wanted to come home to a clean and tidy house, and her cooking dinner with a lovely smell, and I would come through the door saying, honey I'm home.

I apologised for being grouchy and went to the grocery shop. The air was very dirty. There was no fresh milk, only the one jug I had been refusing to buy for the past week. Every piece of ugliness in Beijing, every lack of convenience, had begun to feel like a personal slight.

I cooked vegetable soup, and Lin went out to buy milk from the other supermarket. I played with Davey, but it made me tired. Davey didn't like the soup I'd made. It wasn't great, to be honest.

Lin told me the reading for renovation pollution is high unless we open windows. We are damned if we do and damned if we don't. I can't break ranks and be routed. We will need to withdraw together in an orderly fashion.

We watched *Despicable Me* after dinner. The AQ level got up to 500, after which number it can no longer be read. I told Lin I was tired and couldn't breathe, that I needed to go to bed early and alone.

I went to my room and shut the door. Davey took ages to get to sleep. I read about Chief Joseph and the Nez Perce. None of us can expect justice.

BAJIAO NORTH ROAD, BEIJING, CHINA • -4° MIST AND FOG

THURSDAY 31 DECEMBER 2015 00:48

Yesterday the weather was beautiful, and it lifted everyone's spirits. I saw a few Foreign Teachers, and the vibes were not good. Chen Xi and I cleaned up our office, and then went for *yangrouchuan'r* with Tan. I spoke only Chinese. We were light hearted and sincere. A crowd of HQ staff came in and Tan ordered *yangrouchuan'r* for them.

I had noticed that Chen Xi sent me my next share of the payment. I was grateful and relieved to have received this money. Of course I will have to make sure that I receive the next payment. It is a lot of money, but I have no pension.

I put Tinder on Lin's phone, and then plopped down on the sofa beside her. She was shocked, and then she laughed, and we had a jolly time swiping left and right.

I put blue cheese on nacho chips. We lay together watching *Toy Story 3*, me on the floor at Lin's feet. I was ready for bed, for a few minutes on my own.

I feel guilty about this. I am a selfish person.

Davey and I wrestled in my room. Then, Davey started in that he wanted to sleep with me. I carried him to Lin's room. He was cruel to Lin. I could tell that Lin was hurt. I told him if he didn't go to sleep, Lin would come in and sleep with me, and we would lock the door. He called me a little baby, which had become his go to insult. I told him that he will have to sleep on his own soon enough. I shut off the lights, and listened at their door for a few minutes to see if he kept at Lin.

My gums are bleeding. I need a check up.

I went to my office at YZ. I was only there a couple of minutes before Chen Xi and then Tan came in. I made us tea and we talked about driving long distances without stopping. We talked about God is Love and the *Spiritus Mundi*. It was improving my Chinese to chat with Tan.

Fan came in and we confirmed details of the big meeting on the fifth. I drank a lot of *hong cha* this morning and my stomach was rumbling. I had only one slice of toast for breakfast. I hope to have lunch with Chen Xi today. It is clean at the moment, 87. Of course the WHO advises that nothing above 25 is safe. Still, for us this is a nice day, but I don't think it will last. If and when it shoots above 200 I will just go and get Davey.

This December has been by far the worst month that we have experienced in Beijing, worse than any February. It would kill me to keep worrying about my business collapsing because of foreigners running from the pollution.

BAJIAO NORTH ROAD, BEIJING, CHINA • -5° MOSTLY SUNNY

MONDAY 4 JANUARY 2016 01:15

I woke up at five. The air was clean with a cool north wind, so I turned off the air cleaner. Davey was sleeping with me. I had kept him covered all night. He had been whimpering during the night, and this made me sad.

I looked at property in Ireland, and saw that we could probably afford something. I drank my coffee and Lin lay on the sofa. I suggested we sell our apartment but Lin wasn't keen on this, even though she didn't think we should live in Shijingshan. We got nowhere. We agreed that we should live somewhere that had a good school for Davey. It will take time to get our money out of China, and Davey doesn't need to start school for another year or two, so we had time to figure out what to do.

It was difficult getting Davey out the door. First, there was the mandatory I'm not going to kindergarten, and then he lay down limp while I forced on his shoes and his jacket. We walked to the car together, me holding onto his hand though it was pulled up into his jacket sleeve. The car was filthy. The drive up Shijingshan Lu was awful, stuck behind giant trucks crawling along. When we got to the top of the road, we saw there was a traffic accident slowing everything down at Wukesong. Guy with half a head, five fingers curled up, reaching for something.

I got Davey to the kindergarten without much trouble. When I arrived at YZ Chen Fu said nothing to me. Chen Xi was an impatient bitch, but I realised she was sick, overworked and exhausted. I asked her to have lunch with me. We went to Haosaozi. She told me not to feel sad about leaving Aihua. We walked back toward the school and she saw someone from her government party so we had to hide in an alley, as she had told her party that she was not in the country now. When we came out of the alley, we saw Fred, and he asked what we were doing in the alley.

At the office I organised some hot water for Chen Xi and some tea for me. I signed a bunch of papers for Li Miao, then I gave Fan the key to my office. I began to tell him that after tomorrow I wouldn't be here but he could always get in touch with me if he wanted any help or advice. Chen Xi stopped me in the middle of what I was saying.

Tomorrow I will speak at the meeting after Chen Xi, and then I will make sure to meditate every day, stop drinking, cut down on meat, walk 10 km every day, and go to the gym as often as possible. I will work on my old poems.

BAJIAO NORTH ROAD, BEIJING, CHINA • -1° MOSTLY SUNNY

TUESDAY 5 JANUARY 2016 AT 05:47

After I got home yesterday, Lin and I went to get the car washed. It had that ghostly, dusty colour of Beijing smog. As they finished up, one of the washers asked Lin where is he from? She told him I was from Yingguou, because no one had heard of Ai-er-lan. Can you understand him? Do they speak English in England?

Davey shook his little fist and said I hate kindergarten. I asked Lin to take him to kindergarten today. I felt emotional about leaving Aihua, and Lin comforted me when I cried. As she and Davey were walking out the door I criticised him about something, but then, still in the same grouchy voice I said give me a kiss I love you, and he laughed and gave me a kiss.

I walked into WS. On the way, I saw many things that I should have had a camera to catch. I got to WS a bit early, and wandered around. I felt sensitive to what people said, what they thought of me. Things started promptly and Chen Xi gave her speech. At the end, people were crying. I felt a bit weepy, so it was hard to start. At one point I became misty eyed, and Chen Xi sighed and looked up to heaven though she had been bawling only moments before. I told of my dream about being a ghost moving around the centres. Sarah translated for me, and Chen Xi tidied up her translation. I walked home, free at last.

It was a blue sky day. In Beijing, if it is clean, it doesn't matter about anything else, you are happy.

BEIJING, CHINA • 0° MOSTLY SUNNY

WEDNESDAY 20 JANUARY 2016 07:25

Lin dropped me off at YZ on her way to get Davey. I went down the hall and found Chen Xi training Fan and Rita, their GC lady, in my teaching theory.

We went to the Muslim for lunch, and ate *latiaozi*. Chen Xi's new haircut suits her well. I hope it is a positive first step toward a new life for her. She told me that we would probably receive our money today, and that she would be totally finished with Aihua after that. While she waited for Tan, we talked about old times, and about how Fred would cope with running the foreign side of Aihua.

We also talked about how to get money out of China. She advised against gold. She planned to transfer it to a stranger in Hong kong. She seems convinced, and she has always come through before.

We will stick it out in Beijing over the Chinese New Year, but then go somewhere the weather is not so evil.

BEIJING, CHINA • -3° MOSTLY SUNNY

THURSDAY 28 JANUARY 2016 01:11

Lin booked our flights to Thailand. We will leave on the 18th and return on the 28th. I hope we can bear it until then.

Davey kept saying how he loved us more than his toys, and his vitamin candy, and the moon and the world and his dirty socks. After a while I became dizzy with how much he was talking.

When I got up to make coffee the air was very polluted and I wasn't sure if we should take Davey to kindergarten, but Lin was adamant that he should go. Nothing I could say would convince him that it was a good idea to go. There were not that many students there, and the teacher told me that a lot of them were sick. Davey began to bawl when I made to go, and I had to agree to have a little talk, as he put it. He would not be convinced. I knew taking him home with me wasn't a good idea. I felt guilty about leaving him at this crappy, low level place, and suspicious that they weren't treating him well. Eventually Song Nainai took him with her. When I got home and told Lin about Davey crying, she wasn't overly sympathetic. She just said kids are like that.

I need to use my time wisely now. We have a lot of money, and a lot of opportunity, but the value of the RMB is going down, so I need to be careful. Hopefully Lin and I can change some money to USD next week.

I want to buy a small place somewhere, and live a while in the west while Davey goes to kindergarten. Then I can live a proper life full of pushups and meditation, keep writing my diary and even taking on *The Time Machine*. For now I'm preoccupied with getting our money out of China.

BEIJING, CHINA • -4° MOSTLY SUNNY

FRIDAY 29 JANUARY 2016 AT 01:19

Yesterday I did push ups, and a fifteen minute unguided meditation. I changed into my outfit and did a special cleaning, while Lin booked us rooms at Centara, and ordered bikinis.

After dinner we watched *Atlantis*. Then Davey and I played a game with Lego people where we took turns sliding a coin to knock over the other's Lego people. It took a bit of work to convince Davey not to cheat, but eventually he got it and we had fun.

I suggested to Lin that each evening before bed time we should consciously try to wind down the tone, and speak in slow hypnotic voices. That morning Davey and I had another little talk at the kindergarten piano before he went in, and then all the kids came out to see him. Maybe going to this kindergarten will teach him to be humble. As I left he called and waved, and the other kids waved and said bye bye uncle.

I was full of plans as to how aspects of our lives could be made more organised and systematic–collecting recipes and making grocery lists, for instance– would open up more room for us to live creatively. I had an outline of the time machine story:

- Background (abbreviated personal history)
- Discovery (of time machine)
- Gear (description of machine and suit)
- First forays (journeys)
- New focus (undoing of wrongs)

Meditation, laundry, lemon tea. Shadow boxing and yoga. Humbly tending to the cleanliness and order of our living environment.

BEIJING, CHINA • -6° MOSTLY SUNNY

SUNDAY 31 JANUARY 2016 00:33

We walked to the top of the watchtower at Laoshan. I told Davey how when I was a kid I started a fire in Edworthy Park. He wanted to hear more stories about bad things I'd done so I told him about when I took my dad's car and drove through the Rocky Mountains with no money. I didn't tell him about the LSD.

Lin seems distant but I know that she is committed to our family and to giving Davey the best future that we can. Compared to Chinese love, all the rest is cotton candy.

Davey fell asleep and I went out to the living room. Lin was taking tablets for her headache. I hadn't expected a cuddle or anything, but I'd wanted a chat. She said she had a sore head, and went to bed.

We had to be up early to take Davey to do the fox dance on TV. I noticed that Lin had slept on the sofa.

Lin told me that she was having breakfast with some of the other parents. I was a bit disappointed, because I had wanted to talk with her about her avoiding me.

BEIJING, CHINA • -13° MOSTLY SUNNY

TUESDAY 2 FEBRUARY 2016 01:00

Yesterday when I sat down with Lin to go through the things we had to do she yelled at me that I would be unable to get money out of China. She went to Pullman's for a drink without me.

I went out for a walk, and brooded on how Lin has been behaving toward me recently. She is on Wechat with the other kindergarten mothers, but if I ever speak with her she closes up, tries to keep away from me. I went back to speak my mind, and started a big fight. Lin threw her phone to the ground and it broke. She kept speaking to me in Chinese, with this fucking *tingbudong* bullshit, and it drove me berserk. I told her she was ugly to me now, and that I hated her. She said that when I left she would lock me out, that this wasn't my apartment. As a foreign person I have no rights in China. She threatened to take Davey away from me, which is another thing she could easily do.

I went out and got a beer, and wanted to smoke. When I got home I told Davey that the family was broken. It hurt him, and he cried hard, but I thought he needed to know the situation. Lin wanted to turn him into a typical Chinese kid. She didn't want to sell this apartment because she wanted to keep us stuck in China, where she controlled everything.

I felt ugly and disgusting, of no interest to anyone. I had a crappy sleep.

BEIJING, CHINA • -4° MOSTLY SUNNY

WEDNESDAY 3 FEBRUARY 2016 AT 01:09

Yesterday I was too upset to draw my thoughts in for meditation so I went out to start up with Lin, and we dug ourselves deeper, became meaner and meaner. It was incredible how we could say such cruel things to one another. We broke apart in rage a few times, and Lin threatened to leave. We said more awful things. Lin packed.

I asked her to come sit at the table. It was hard for us to speak. We moved toward the idea that we could just stop fighting and remain together peaceably for the sake of Davey. Lin came to me and held me and started to cry, said she was sorry. We lay down and we had no one but each other, our little family. When we collected Davey we told him we would never fight again.

Coffee, Facebook. Lin prepared sea cucumber, which I ate between sets of pushups.

BEIJING, CHINA • -4° MOSTLY SUNNY

THURSDAY 4 FEBRUARY 2016 AT 00:39

At the HSBC we went straight into an office, where Lin was told that she would be able to get dollars by evening, and that money from the sale of our apartment could be transferred out of China upon completion.

As we were leaving HSBC, the lady official asked me some questions about Aihua, and I started blabbering. When we got into the cab, Lin was laughing at me, saying I have such a big mouth, and how I am so happy and excited when I have a chance to blabber.

Over barbecued fish at Wanda's she told me that she would be going out for lunch in Chaoyang on Thursday. For a moment I was crushed, but also humbled and elated.

We cuddled with the window open. The sun was shining, and cool air caressed Lin's legs, smooth and warm against mine. I peeled, cut and boiled the potatoes, and then I went under the sink and opened the pipes to scoop the congealed fat out of them. It was filthy, horrific. I thought I'd closed all the pipes, but when I gave a final wrench something sharp slid under the cuticle of my thumb nail. The whole time I was fighting with the pipes beneath the sink, Davey was trying to get my attention, and I was short with him.

I stopped working on the pipes, and started to worry about the swelling on my thumb. We went to the emergency room at Chaoyang hospital. When we got home, Lin tried to work on the pipes without having any success. She called a plumber to come in the morning.

In the morning I cleaned Lin's boots while she was putting on makeup and the plumber had his machine sucking the fat out of our pipes.

It is a hard compulsion I carry, a hard road I walk, but there is a sublime intensity in this pain that I crave. I am content with Lin as the object of my slavish adoration, submission and servitude, resigned to her leaving to return, to her being alive out there without me.

BEIJING, CHINA • -2° MOSTLY SUNNY

FRIDAY FEBRUARY 12, 2016

I woke up to the smell of coffee and news that gravitational waves had been detected. Davey whispered to me if mommy makes you coffee will you get up and I said yes. He went out and told Lin I would get up if she made me coffee and she said tell silly old daddy I already made him coffee. I talked about gravitational waves while eating my cheese toast and sea cucumber with Davey.

We drove to Chen Fu's place by way of Shougang. The house was crowded, and Davey was shy at first, but by the time we were ready to leave, he was inviting Chen Fu and Hulaoshi to visit so they could play with his toys.

At lunch I drank *baijiu*, and this gave me the taste. I started on the beer. I felt comfortable, and able to communicate easily in Chinese. I was quietly proud of myself for having Aihua done with.

After dinner Chen Fu was keen on getting us out of there. I

was drunk and started crying about my dad dying. He asked someone to get me a tissue.

FEBRUARY 14, 2016

I lay down beside Lin on the sofa, full of love. She said it was Valentine's day tomorrow so she would go to Chaoyang for dinner. It was as if a *poignard* had pierced my heart–I was amazed by how deeply she understood me, how she had become what I had dreamed.

I gripped her desperately, pressed my head to her breast, and bleated I love you. I felt so hurt and alone and alive. Be careful what you hope for in youth, because you may just find it in middle age. I was stunned by the intensity that had been brought to bear upon me. To be crushed with such mercy was an amazing gift.

16 FEBRUARY 2016

My heart is big with contentment and peace. I am happy and at ease. I never dreamed that I would find this easy feeling.

I don't want Lin to be the old socks at home, something that I caught and kept at home to cook dinner and clean up. She is the beating heart of our family

There were ambiguities to our relationship, its intensity and tenor, which others found difficult to understand–I was scared to think that I could lose her, but didn't believe that I would.

SATURDAY 20 FEBRUARY 2016 00:49

We travelled by boat taxi from Krabi to Centara under pillars of cloud such as I had never seen before.

The room was close to the beach and the lobby. I started in on the beer in the fridge, and supplemented it with my tea jar of whiskey Coke. I played some Bowie for Davey. We walked along the beach to the buffet dinner. The food was good, and we ate a lot. Davey was afraid of the long gold fingernails of the Thai dancers, and said they were witches.

I dreamed that the Shijingshan education commission took all my money and Chen Fu couldn't help me. I heard Davey telling Lin he didn't want to tell her his dream because it was so bad it would give her bad luck. There was a good king who had a white heart, and then he became a bad king with a black heart. He said that when he was a bad King there was a monster who was friends with him, and he was ugly.

There were monkeys on the deck. One of the monkeys took Davey's water wing and started to chew it up. I opened the door to scare him off, and one of the other monkeys bared its teeth and made a move toward me. Lin threw out some nuts, and then a whole swarm of them were grabbing our shoes, our shorts, our underpants. One started to open the front mosquito screen, and I chased him off.

Under a fire-red sun I filled the jacuzzi, and we all got in. Lin went to shower, and Davey asked me why I had to be so tough on him. I told him that if I didn't care about him I would just let him do whatever he wanted, but I want him to grow up to be a cool and smart guy, so I wanted to teach him how to behave.

He pointed at a little gecko crawling up a pillar and asked me what they ate. He got out of the pool and I helped him put on his penguin blanket. He sat on the sofa and told me again about his dream, but this time the man was a husband, not a king. He had a beautiful wife who loved him. He was good and he loved his wife, but then he turned bad. When he turned bad he was ugly, and it was scary. He spoke so sincerely that it felt like a very deep conversation, as though we were emotional peers.

When I lay down to sleep Lin slept at the other end again. Davey and I had a long talk. I told him how I regretted fighting with my dead father and mother, and how this regret passes when I think of the two of them looking down on Davey, sunshine dragons who live in his heart and can shoot sunshine to blow apart shadows and monsters.

22 FEBRUARY 2016

More weird dreams. Renovations were being done in the basement of 26 Westview Drive, where my mother died. The basement was being divided into apartments. I remember thinking this was a good idea because it would bring in money. I can feel dream images floating around me: Lambrina, Paul Glenfield, Chapin. Deane.

I thought about Deane last night. What a terrible thing to die so young. I thought about how scared he must have been for those tens of seconds. Did he have time to think I am going to die? Telling my poor dad over the phone. I didn't beat around the bush. Dad, Deane is dead. What? he replied, incredulous. No, decisive. Is he hurt?

My poor family. And of course, behind it all, beggaring belief, my poor mother, who I treated so badly as she died, who loved me as much as Lin and I love Davey, and who I couldn't give an inch to.

25 FEBRUARY 2016

When we got back from dinner I let Davey watch *Wreck it Ralph*, and I drank Bacardi in the hot tub alone. When she tried to go to bed, I started another savage and evil fight. I couldn't live up to my end of the bargain, couldn't not bring up the French boyfriend. I put words that would hurt me in her mouth and she disdained to take them out. I finished a beer, and three bottles of spirits from the mini bar. We beat one another, and I threw a drink. Davey was sobbing and begging us to stop. Eventually we all fell asleep, but when I heard Lin get up we started up again, which ended with her leaving.

When Davey woke up he and I went for breakfast but we didn't eat much. We were going to look for Lin, but it seemed pointless, so we sat on the beanbags on the beach. Lin came out from between palm trees in her bikini and hugged Davey and kissed him. I sat Lin on a beanbag and sat in front of her and told her that Davey and I couldn't live without her. She started crying. She had a goodbye letter for me and I begged her to stay.

After breakfast we went back to the room for a shower and a rest. Davey and I went swimming, and Lin joined us. Davey was wearing a big smile.

27 FEBRUARY 2016

A hotel worker gave out sling shots to keep the monkeys at bay.

We walked the beach, and sat at the end of the blue floating pier, lifted and dropped by the waves. At the buffet Davey cried and screamed until they found us seating outside. Dinner was rock lobster, and red curry with lychee and duck. A bird girl danced to bells. By the time the fire dancers finished Davey was exhausted. On the walk back I joked about plucking stars for them, playfully putting this heaven-fruit in their mouths.

28 FEBRUARY 2016

I do not recommend flying on a Chinese tour group plane. Davey and I were fighting as we boarded, and I spanked his bottom after he punched me in the face. We were seated in three different rows, so I sat on the arm of Lin's seat and wouldn't move. Some Chinese dude pushed past and started screaming filth at me. Lin argued with him, and I flicked his nose. He and Lin exploded in Chinese curses. It was becoming a kerfuffle. I picked Davey up and made like we were going to get off the plane. I was fed up with this asshole saying fuck my mother so I flicked his nose again.

After we got seats together I had a tiff with the guy seated ahead of me who tried to recline his seat down on my knees. Davey fell asleep almost immediately, so I had to stand for a few hours. Davey wet himself, and when we started to descend he woke up and went berserk about having no trousers. We were all drifting in and out of sleep on the cab ride home.

TUESDAY 1 MARCH 2016

Lin so cool and distant, my perfect, beautiful girl, as if designed to match my aesthetics.

We lay in the dark and discussed the night I turned evil in Thailand. I couldn't explain how this happened, how some monster could step into my body and take over my actions. Of course there was the drinking. Also, I had to consider that while my perverse drama might have healing power, the pain that I pushed beneath the drama rose up as resentment. I pushed Lin to be someone cold and distant in my drama, and then that night I believed that she was that person, of her own accord, and I became resentful of her doing the things I pushed her to do to satisfy my dream.

Lin was relieved to think there might be an explanation for this monstrous behaviour, a possibility it might be brought under control. because if we were at least aware of it we might be able to control it. We laughed about the guy's shocked expression when I flicked his nose on the airplane.

I will meditate. I will study, tend a garden, listen to Zen wind chimes, and keep myself calm.

WEDNESDAY 2 MARCH 2016

After the first time Davey woke up choking, I was more adamant than ever that we needed to leave Beijing. This made Lin angry. At the bank she said I had Hulk eyes.

We drove to kindergarten in silence. Davey gave out a little sigh as we arrived. He told me his teachers lied to us and that they were actually mean to him. He told me he was scared because there were so many kids crowded into the room, and I could relate to how he felt.

Lin is worried that our fights are making Davey feel unsafe. I think we could buy a home somewhere in the west with what we have now.

WEDNESDAY 2 MARCH 2016

48 hour pollution yellow alert

Davey has woken with an old man's cough. His snot has flecks of blood in it, as does mine.

At the kindergarten gates, Bonnie talked to Lin, and said that recently Davey had been defiant, refusing to obey directions, and being confrontational with other kids. Some of the little girls came over to chat with me, and I joked with them. Davey came over and warned: Don't be too stupid, Daddy.

Thinking we should go north to have Lin's parents change some USDs for us. We need to change as much money as we can as quickly as possible, and then we need to head to Europe, to prioritise Davey's health.

FRIDAY 4 MARCH 2016 06:53

It was another tough day stuck in the house.

Davey asked Lin why he was feeling tired all the time. Even with all of the air cleaners running the pollution readings were too high, and it was difficult for Davey to breathe.

Lin phoned emergency, and they said they would call us back. After 15 minutes a British lady called. She was emphatic that we should take Davey to a hospital immediately.

MONDAY 7 MARCH 2016 AT 22:52

When I went to the passenger door Davey moved to the driver's seat. We went back and forth until I pulled him out of the car, towards the kindergarten. He pulled back against me, so I had to drag him. When we got into the kindergarten, he grabbed onto my legs and refused to let go. I pried him off and tried to leave, but he sobbed and screamed so I went back to him. I picked him up and carried him somewhere to sit down. He was unable to catch his breath. Kids gathered around to watch Davey cry. Bonnie and the headmaster looked at me. I told Davey that I wouldn't take him to see the world now because he was such a baby. I tried to put him into one of the baby classes. I took him upstairs and then I just left.

I was ashamed and upset. Lin said that tomorrow she would take him in. This made me feel like she thought the problem was me. I thought they were turning Davey into a Chinese kid, alien to me, that I was being sidelined somehow, while my son became something other to me.

When I walked in the door, I said I need to talk, Lin, I don't want to fight but I need to talk now. She said wait until I finish the dishes, and didn't even turn around. I said I want to talk now. She came over and when I started she let out a disgusted sigh. When I complained, she narrowed her eyes in a threatening fashion. We decided to get divorced. The fighting was just too much, it never stopped.

I tried to phone her parents but called her sister. I told her I will leave Davey to Lin, that I won't look after him any more. I will go to Europe on my own, and will leave the apartment to her, pay her 10000 RMB a month.

Or maybe I would take Davey with me, and leave her here alone. When I didn't love Lin she was good to me. Now that I loved her, I felt that she had no respect for me, that she made everything ugly and nasty. I insisted this was not my fault, that I was happy with my family, and that it was the only thing in the world I cared about, but felt all I got in return was criticism and disrespect.

But of course it was me; it was my fault. I have never been able to sustain a relationship with anyone. Everyone has cut me out of their lives. I wanted to redeem myself with my love for Davey, but felt like I'd failed this intention too.

WEDNESDAY 9 MARCH 2016 04:00

The street was full of people watching me. I got back in the car and pulled an aggressive u-turn. I was a creature of rage. Lin sent me messages, and it sounded like she wanted to reconcile, but I thwarted her efforts.

I got the subway to Sanlitun, made eye contact with some black guys, scored some hash. When I got home I started work on the time machine.

WEDNESDAY 9 MARCH 2016 22:55

Hoots. To avoid jumping into the words as though into the abyss. If I could just sit at the edge of them as at the edge of a pool, rather than diving into the tar and gasoline fumes. Gulls were flying, flapping then. Picking him to tinsel pieces. Wee. Yellow beaks, she wrote in the poetry class when we had to write pieces in one another's style. I was but a boy.

The Good Ship Stonehead is the time machine. Hoots is the time machine. Opening up alternative universes is to live without consequences.

. . .

FRIDAY 11 MARCH 2016 23:13

I woke up very early yesterday, and again today, and worked on the time machine story. It is starting to unfold beyond my comprehension. I need to be studiously mean in my exposition of the workings of the machine.

I worked on the story for most of the morning. Lin took Davey to kindergarten, and when she came back I kept writing. I read it to Lin at one point and she seemed to think it was good. I smoked too much and started to get groggy. Davey noticed the pipe before he went out, and tried to suck from it.

Finlay appeared in my dream last night. On a bicycle, goatee gleaming, eyes a-twinkle.

MONDAY 14 MARCH 2016 AT 07:28

He told me he would kill himself and I wouldn't have a son. He told me to take him home and he would tell mommy to kill him. He paused a moment then and told me it wouldn't be mommy's fault he was dead, because he would tell her to kill him. I listened to him carefully and told him I hoped he wouldn't kill himself and that I would be very sad if I didn't have a son. Unfortunately, I still didn't have money for the rides.

I smoked a bowl and moved the story along. I walked to Bajiao to meet Chen Xi. When I got home, I talked to Lin about going to Ireland, and she cried, but wouldn't say why. I don't think she wants to live in Ireland.

WEDNESDAY 16 MARCH 2016 23:47

We went to collect Davey for his last day at kindergarten. Lin doesn't support our move to Ireland, but she can't provide an alternative. She worries that if Davey doesn't learn Chinese in the first couple of years he will never be able to.

TUESDAY 22 MARCH 2016 00:24

So many dreams last night. Hard to describe. Feeling the time machine story, a sensation of planning, and gathering ideas.

Meditation, hygiene, work on the story. Lin tidying up for her parents' arrival. She has let her family know that she is leaving for Ireland soon, and they are worried about her.

SATURDAY 26 MARCH 2016 22:45

I woke up alone and worked on the story. Lin stayed the night with Davey at the place she had rented for her parents, and then they went to the Zoo in Da Xing.

I didn't enjoy the work I was doing on the story, wasn't confident in the quality. It has such a stoned and crazy tone.

Lin called me to come for lunch, and I met them at the little restaurant down the road.

After lunch, everyone came back to our home, and it was difficult. I didn't feel comfortable with her parents sitting in there.

TUESDAY 29 MARCH 2016 00:32

My rage is animalistic and overwhelming. Davey came in and said Daddy why are you so angry? I am disgusted with how I behave when we get into these situations.

Lin brought up our big row in Thailand, and then it happens again. I just don't know how to control the worms creeping around in my head, heaping up a seething hill of grievances.

I couldn't sleep because of my self loathing. I remembered all the ugly things I had done and said to Lin and Davey. I don't know why I am so. I feel desperate enough to consider counselling or medication.

Lin got up early and made me a pot of coffee. Davey came in and cuddled me. I sat there feeling how I don't deserve such a loving family. It occurred to me that they have no choice but to love me. I need to stop abusing their dependency.

SATURDAY 2 APRIL 2016 AT 00:34

The subway was crowded, and we changed onto line 10 at Guomao. This area has eclipsed Sanlitun as the cool neighbourhood for foreigners now. Lin told me that this is where she usually meets her French friend, and this made me feel insecure. There was a lineup at the French embassy, but we were treated courteously. Her French friend had told her that he could help her, and I'm glad she didn't need the help.

Down the road we found a nice coffee shop and bakery. Lin was looking gorgeous, and I felt exquisitely insecure. She wasn't talking again, like the night at Sanlitun, and I was cringing. She told me that she would come and meet her friend on Sunday here. I took some photos of her, for my lonely Sunday evening. We walked around all over the place, and I felt so uncool. I said her French friend would be more decisive in taking her somewhere. We were leaving China in a week.

MONDAY 4 APRIL 2016 00:41

I asked Lin if she was still going out tonight, and she said she was. My heart sank, because I wasn't in the right headset, but I didn't make any waves. We had a cuddle, and this got me into the right frame of mind.

Davey and I went down to see her off in a taxi. Then, we watched *Hotel Transylvania*. It took a long time for Davey to get to sleep. At one point he said, you are the best daddy in the world, even if you always fight.

After Davey was asleep, I worshipped photos of Lin, and drove myself insane. When Lin finally got home, I greeted her at the door, and had a cup of tea ready for her. I was so happy to see her.

I want to write the time machine story. I should mention in the introduction that some of the writing was done while travelling and that the time machine has a way of distorting the mind.

FRIDAY 8 APRIL 2016 02:41

The drive to Davey's last day at kindergarten was a nightmare–six lanes of traffic in either direction and not a policeman in sight.

We will be leaving for Ireland on Sunday. Lin has agreed that we can sell the apartment.

SATURDAY 9 APRIL 2016 00:52

Everything is so much easier when you don't smoke, especially flying. The Tinder deal Lin made with me was great motivation.

While we were at the restaurant, I became quite stressed out that Chen Xi had not called. I was sad to think I was losing my oldest and closest friend.

At Moshikou I walked up to the Chen family home where I had spent my first days in China. I had a sweet and tender chat with Chen Fu.

Chen Xi messaged me to say she and Tan were having a fight. I suspected they were fighting over her being in contact with me.

We leave for Ireland today.

MONDAY 11 APRIL 2016 12:00

Davey and I went for a walk down Grafton Street at 6:30 am. The rain had stopped and it was a fresh morning. It was nice to hear seagulls. I got Davey to give a fiver to a homeless guy.

TUESDAY 12 APRIL 2016 12:00

The hotel called us a cab, and we went over to the next place north of the Liffey, not far from the Ha'penny Bridge. The driver called it the Italian quarter. It doesn't suit us though—it's a place for young people.

The car insurance girl said there was no way for me to get insurance without a full licence. The accountant told me that whatever I do I will have to prove where the money came from. We should move to Galway. Dublin is too hectic.

WEDNESDAY 13 APRIL 2016 03:25

We walked along the river run through Eve's and Adam's from bend of bay to swerve of shore, bringing us back to Howth Castle and Environs. It was nice to be out that early; the sunrise stroked the slow river pink and orange.

The taxi driver took us to the police station at Sandymount to deal with Davey's passport and the driver's licence. The tide was out so far it stretched to the beginnings of my memory. You couldn't see water's edge, only sand forever. I was walking into eternity along Sandymount Strand. Ineluctable modality of the visible. That if nothing more. Thought through my eyes. So many people out jogging or walking dogs. Davey and I walked a long ways toward the sea with me carrying him on my shoulders. Lin said she finally felt hope, said this is Ireland, her eyes agleam.

We walked back to the police station. A lovely wee lady gave us directions. In the station, the big guarda told me I will need proof of residence to get the passport and driver's licence.

FRIDAY 15 APRIL 2016 08:09

We were an hour and a half early for the train to Galway, and there were no lockers. Lin stayed with the bags, and I took Davey for a walk. I pointed out St Michan's, and told him about Lord Lietrim. I left Davey with Lin for a few minutes and slipped into the pub next door for a pint of Guinness: smooth, creamy and not bitter at all.

We checked into the Connaught Hotel, then went looking for a place to eat. It was bright, cold and windy. Lin was concerned about the Irish cold.

I woke up at 5:30, and felt trapped because we were all stuck in the one room and I couldn't get up to have coffee or write my diary. I looked for places to rent in Galway.

SATURDAY 16 APRIL 2016

Hobos

We took a cab to the place in Knocknacarra. It was perfect, across the road from a forest. But many people had viewed the apartment already. Davey and Lin went across the road to have a look around the playground. There were kids playing football, although it was rainy and cold. The lady showed me around the house. Then she started to talk about references and my work. It felt awful, like applying for a job. Everyone had said it would be difficult to find anything in Galway, but I thought they had been exaggerating.

We had a walk down the shopping street, which was even livelier than Grafton Street, then went down to the Spanish Arch and sat by the sea.

We moved to the Atlantic View bed and breakfast, a dreadful little room with one bed, which we changed for another dreadful room with two beds and no windows. Only Davey was in high spirits.

SUNDAY 17 APRIL 2016

Drums in the night

When we went for a walk down the main shopping street I encouraged Davey to give money to the buskers. My right hip was in agony, and I felt crippled. I was hobbling.

Throughout the night drunken orcs roared and crashed around outside our rooms. When I mentioned this to Davey, he laughed and said he had been watching them through the Venetian blind.

At the next place the rooms had big windows looking down on the beach at Salthill. I bought a ready-made lasagna for dinner. Davey has never tried that.

MONDAY 18 APRIL 2016

It was great to see waves and rocks again. Walking along the beach made me think of my dad, of Deane, and of Danny too.

Lin was impressed by the houses, and I told her that if we sold our Beijing apartment we could buy one of these. She said she would be OK with that, and I kissed her.

TUESDAY 19 APRIL 2016

We walked down to the Spanish Arch, watched some buskers playing the King Louie song from Jungle Book. The feeling at the Arch was amazing, like a 60s flower power thing, all the young people tattooed, the boys shirtless, guitars everywhere. A swan approached us. I told Lin it was welcoming her to Galway.

I called a load of places, and set up a handful of appointments. I changed clothes and put on my new sunglasses. I gave Lin a kiss and went to kiss Davey but he told me to take off my glasses first because he didn't want to kiss robot daddy. I walked to the place in Knocknacarra. It is near a creche. I will take Lin to see it tomorrow morning at 9 am.

SATURDAY 23 APRIL 2016

After we ate the potato and leek soup I made, I went back to the supermarket for alcohol. I am tired and dirty. There are so many things here that I am not familiar with. It is exhausting having to deal with Davey around the clock.

WEDNESDAY 27 APRIL 2016

I can hear the cooing of a pigeon. It is quiet and peaceful. I am happy to be up early and alone, with my family safe upstairs.

I went into the back garden, and pulled out some weeds. I imagined my time traveller gardening in different geological eras.

Davey was excited to play with the plump, healthy cat who came along. The cat made himself comfortable in the house. When it was raining, he sat on the front porch. Davey insisted the cat was homeless, but his plumpness indicated otherwise.

THURSDAY 28 APRIL 2016

I continued to tidy up in the back garden, pulling out weeds and sweeping the cement. The sound of the broom on the cement reminded me of Dergmoney and the horses when I was a kid.

Lin didn't have a great sleep. She is bored and alone, like my mother was in Calgary. We need a car, and something for Davey to do.

FRIDAY 29 APRIL 2016

I hadn't really wanted to spend so much money, but we decided to just go ahead and buy the Santa Fe. It will immediately improve our lives.

We walked down Shop Street–the sun was shining, and there were muscular low clouds moving overhead. The band was playing I Shall Be Released. We got Davey a toy knight and a Minotaur.

Lin and I back and forthed about Ireland and Beijing. It is easier to feel part of the community in Beijing– you just walk out and there are all the kids and families. I was happy that even though it was lonely for Lin she still recognized the benefits of living in Ireland. It has been so long since I have felt angry.

We will get a car. We will get Davey into play school. We will make friends.

SATURDAY 30 APRIL 2016

We got a bus into Eyre Square, and then a taxi to the Hyundai dealership. On the bus, I suggested we might consider running a sort of high class bed and breakfast. Lin thought it was a good idea. We could do up a brochure and market it in Shijingshan.

Our taxi driver was a nice old man, and he told us about the dawn chorus.

SUNDAY 1 MAY 2016 08:56

Yesterday was misty, drizzly. We walked down to the water, found a fairy forest. We walked through it amazed; Lin said she didn't feel trapped any more.

Davey was asleep in Lin's room. He had been scared in the night. I told Davey about Yeats's Irish magic, that in the evening he should imagine a big dog beside his bed who would fight away ghosts, monsters and bad dreams. Davey said he would imagine a wolf.

MONDAY 2 MAY 2016

The bank account requires an electricity bill. Electricity requires a bank account.

THURSDAY 5 MAY 2016

The money hadn't even gone through, but they gave us the key anyway, and let us drive away.

. . .

FRIDAY 6 MAY 2016

The Galway Street Band playing right in front of us, bare feet on the cobbles. Chen Xi sent a message saying she'd bought a house in Bray. Lin and I agreed to sell the apartment in Beijing to buy a better house here.

SATURDAY 7 MAY 2016

We drove to Connemara. The car was wonderful to drive. Lin and Davey turned back, and I walked up to the top of the mountain. It was difficult going, and I was worried that I wasn't up to it. My heart was hammering and it was hard to get a breath. I sent photos to Chen Xi, Lin and Facebook. There was a day when this would have been a private thing.

I wanted to get back to Lin and Davey quickly, and I felt a lot of energy, so I half skipped and half ran back down. I had a cup of tea and a sausage roll, and we fed sparrows that had no fear.

On the drive home the moon roof was dappled with rain. We stopped at Joyce's and got a big chicken, and put this in the oven. I drank some whiskey, and sat in the back answering Facebook messages while Lin and Davey played Don't Starve.

. . .

MONDAY 9 MAY 2016

We aren't doing very well here so far. Davey needs to play with other kids. I can't focus. Davey is always with me, always talking in the background. I want to read, to meditate and do yoga, but it seems I am responsible for Davey around the clock.

TUESDAY 10 MAY 2016

Rising housing prices in Ireland. Maybe another cultural revolution in China.

FRIDAY 13 MAY 2016

It has been tough going recently. Our whole lives–all of our habits, routines, structures, and systems have been overturned, and we are having to build all of these things from scratch. Maybe that is why we have taken such pleasure in little rituals connected to our life in Beijing.

SATURDAY 14 MAY 2016

We went to the walled garden at Coole Park. There were so many families sitting around having picnics that it was hard to imagine how this would have once been a quiet and lonely place.

We walked through the Seven Woods. The forest was thick, but the walk was on a road, and kept ending in parking lots. We walked back down to the top of Coole lake, saw a swan. Davey was tired so I carried him on my shoulders.

The visit had been disappointing. I had been hoping to feel something Yeatsian at Coole Park, but the only thing I felt was a sense of a degraded world. Davey kept calling Lady Gregory Aunty Gregory, so that was one good thing. I told him how when this house was standing there were no cars and people travelled by horses and carriages.

SUNDAY 15 MAY 2016

Bathing with Yeats

Each poem is a little world. I put the book down (in a puddle, as it turned out) and relaxed. I am fat now, but didn't feel revolted by myself this morning.

Lin told me she is bored. I don't know what to say. The garden is starting to spring up with flowers. Chen Xi called and I chatted with her. I think Lin was jealous.

Soon we'll have a bank card, and then we can put the money belt away.

. . .

MONDAY 16 MAY 2016

I dropped Davey off at play school, then went home, read more of Yeats' *Recollections*, and went for a walk in Barna woods. I felt so happy it was frightening. I thought about the time machine, and felt confident that I could write this story. If only I could dictate while walking. All the ideas I had as I walked disappeared before I could recall them.

Lin was in a bad mood, and I was disappointed, because I was so happy. I got angry with Lin because she complained about living here too much. I got the idea into my head that she wanted to keep the place in Beijing so she could be close to the French guy.

TUESDAY 17 MAY 2016

I dreamed I was at my dad's house–a mix between the Westview Drive, Lasquetti, and the Denman bungalow. There were children there. Sam and Ralph arrived, and they ignored me. The children made a mess with some green stuff, and when Netty and my dad got home I worried they would think I did it. Netty walked past me haughtily, and she was very big. Dan, who had arrived shortly after me, left. I thought about telling Lin to come over, but I didn't. My dad fell down. I rolled him onto his side, lifted him up and hugged him. I was worried that he would be scared when he woke, and struggle and attack me like Netty said he did in the hospital when he died. But he was peaceful and calm, and

I explained to him that he had fallen down and bumped his head.

THURSDAY 26 MAY 2016

Davey's teacher told us he'd been rough with a boy who wouldn't call him Monster Dragon. She said the name thing was an issue, and that Davey must be made to understand that they would call him Davey at school.

Later when I saw him with his shirt off, the sight of his skinny torso drenched me in tender sorrow.

FRIDAY 27 MAY 2016

Davey hit another kid. When I asked him about it he told me he was talking to Broanagh about Mr Mojo, and how Santa Claus and he and his daddy were rebels. At Joyce's I got beer for me and wine for Lin. We sat in the back garden drinking and listening to music. After dinner, I still wanted to drink, so I went back to Joyce's.

SUNDAY 29 MAY 2016

On the Aran Islands there was a guy on the dock who had a horse and cart for hire. His horse was Johnny Cash, and needed loads of encouragement. The driver was Andy. He'd lived in Boston for some years, lost his leg there and came back. All the islanders talked Irish among themselves. Dun

Aongus was not a let down, like Coole Park and the Cliffs of Moher. We went down to the rocky shore, where there were seals. It was a bit like Lasquetti, but different.

Davey and Lin went up to bed, and I delved further into *A Vision*.

THURSDAY 2 JUNE 2016

We looked at a few schools, and settled on Bushy Park, which had more outdoor space than the others. The principal was a nice fellow. They taught Irish, but only as a subject. As a Catholic school they did teach religion, but I was assured that this wouldn't be a problem. I told the principal about how my father had to wait in the coal shed when they had religion classes at his school in Glenties. The principal told us they had a place for Davey, and that we could bring in the application form tomorrow.

When I went to pick up Davey at the kindergarten, I saw a note on the door saying one of the kids had head lice. When I talked to the teacher she told me it was one of the little girls. Then, she told me that Davey had been hitting other kids, and that even the little girls were backing away from him. I was upset to hear this. I criticised him in the car. We collected Lin and dropped her off at the gym.

MONDAY 6 JUNE 2016

Ray and I sat in the back garden while the kids played. At noon, Ray and Ivy got ready to leave. It felt a bit sad when they left. It had been nice to see them, and by the last day I felt comfortable with them but I'm not good with people, and I don't have friends. I wish I had treated them better, but I can't put my finger on anything I did wrong.

Lin is awake, but she hasn't gotten out of bed. Davey is still sleeping. We need to book our flights back from Beijing to Galway, and I need to help Chen Xi with her lawyer.

I had been thinking about writing a letter to Ralph but I don't feel sorry for my behaviour toward that bunch–all of whom have treated me badly–especially Netty and Sam.

FRIDAY 10 JUNE 2016

Roundstone was beautiful, with clouds capping the mountain tops. Someone said something to me in Irish, and I regretted not having even a little bit of it on me.

We walked across rocky green cow pastures to the third beach, where we all took off our shoes. I waded up to my knees. In this most beautiful place I seemed to have escaped time. I had no craving, I felt no hurry, I was happy to be exactly where I was.

We sat in front of a hotel restaurant, had a pot of tea, some mussels, fish cakes and salmon. The clouds were high above and wild.

TUESDAY 14 JUNE 2016

I talked to Chen Xi about the survey report for her house, and agreed to write two letters for her. She advised me how to get into Tan's good graces.

I had a dream in which there was a baby with Zika Microcephaly. His siblings had hung him at the door. I was with Davey. I wanted to help the child, but I noticed there was blood around the child's head, and I didn't want Davey to see something that disturbing, so I left it.

THURSDAY 16 JUNE 2016

I went out and drank beer. Willow had replied to my post with the horse, so I wrote a long note about how I hope we could still be friends. After dinner, I felt lonely, so I called a lot of people on Facebook messenger, but no one replied. Eventually I got through to Greg and we had a bit of a chat.

I felt embarrassed about all of the desperate messages I sent. I put on Facebook the word why. The morning brought messages, but not from Ralph or the Chambers Clan. Tony Murray predicted my downfall from too much free time.

. . .

WEDNESDAY 22 JUNE 2016

We parked and got out to look at the waves. There was a dead seal lolling in the water, turning over this way, then that.

Lin had a fight with Davey. After she pushed him down he said no mother would do that to her child. He learns from what we say. When they went to bed, she asked him if he forgave her, and he said nothing. Lin and I agreed that we must be clear that there will be no violence in the family. Davey's constant challenging of our authority and lack of respect is wearing us down. Going out the door, Davey whispered to me that mommy said he wasn't her son, and that she had hit him in the face.

The Euro was plummeting, and I assumed that the value would bounce up again after the vote to remain. I told Lin to go ahead and change the rest of our dollars, but thankfully she only changed half.

THURSDAY 23 JUNE 2016

I was surprised to learn that there had been a leave vote. It didn't sound good for foreigners in the UK. Chen Xi will lose a lot of money. Most of our money hasn't been changed to Euros yet, so if anything we might make money on the dollars we have left.

FRIDAY 24 JUNE 2016

The continued unfolding of the news about Brexit made me feel sick in my stomach. I advised Chen Xi not to buy a place in London. Sterling is plummeting, and she has changed all of her money to sterling.

SATURDAY 25 JUNE 2016

Chen Xi might just stay in China. I'm not sure that I will be able to sort anything out with Tan.

I still haven't gotten past rewriting the first six or so pages of the story. It is very enjoyable to write without marijuana, to be so clear and careful.

MONDAY 27 JUNE 2016

Chen Xi called and told me that Tan went in with a knife and told them he would kill himself if they didn't make the last payment that day. Chen Xi will pay this money into our account when we get to Beijing, and then she will help me change this to USD through the HK underworld. This is a relief, and a windfall.

We drove to the arts and crafts place in Spiddal. We got a slate thingy for Tan, to thank him for the trick with the knife.

TUESDAY 28 JUNE 2016

I talked to Chen Xi about getting a surrogate mother to carry a child for her. It seems this is best done in America. I spoke with Hannah about it, and she gave me the name of the place she dealt with.

WEDNESDAY 29 JUNE 2016

Travel is hard work. At the train station Lin went to get some gifts, and I took Davey to get me a pint of Guinness, but they wouldn't serve before 10:30 so we walked over to the park and sat there. By the time we got into Paris, we had been on the road for twelve hours.

THURSDAY 30 JUNE 2016

Once we got on the plane, we still had to wait on the tarmac, but I was in a good seat with no one in front of me, so I was OK. The plane was full of Chinese people. I got two vodka and tomato juices, and then a cognac. Davey watched *The Good Dinosaur* and I watched *DeadPool*.

Beijing was hot, and I was sweaty and uncomfortable. As we got to the Fifth Ring Road, the traffic became ridiculous, and I began to curse. The apartment looked great at first glance but there were problems. The windows hadn't been opened in a long time, and it smelt like chemicals. There were insects in the bucket under the sink and on the floor in my room. The window in my room wouldn't work.

We got a cab to the Muslim place for dinner. We had two bottles of beer and tried to be happy. I had a battle with the cab driver. We got some milk, some water and a watermelon at the supermarket. I chatted with Chen Xi. She sent me photos of our wedding pictures, because Tan had insisted she destroy the originals.

I turned on the air conditioner and slept until I heard Davey and Lin. Lin began to flounder, and she went to bed.

I couldn't sleep with Davey chatting, so I got up and made coffee. In Ireland it was time for us to be in bed.

FRIDAY 1 JULY 2016

The Tucson was very dirty, and compared poorly to the Santa Fe. We ate *baozi* and noodles in the Dongbei restaurant across the road from the Muslim. Tan and I arranged to meet up at Pullman's for *pu'er cha*.

We went out for dinner with Li Yue. She was a good friend to Lin, and she seemed to like us. It would be nice if she could come and visit us in Ireland. After we dropped Li Yue off Davey played with other kids outside our building. Beijing was good that way.

Just as I was getting into bed, Chen Xi called to list the ways I could ingratiate myself with Tan. I seemed to have just got to sleep, when Davey came in, shining and beautiful.

SATURDAY 2 JULY 2016

Pu'er cha with Tan

After I registered with the police we got the car washed. Drivers seemed to be cutting me off more than usual.

I went to meet Tan at Pullman's. He is a warm and funny person. I think we had a nice talk. My Chinese was good enough to keep the conversation going for two and a half hours. When I went up to pay I found that the tea cost almost eight hundred–I had only brought three hundred with me, and I hadn't brought my card. This made things awkward, as letting Tan pay defeated the purpose.

SUNDAY 3 JULY 2016

Davey came in about six, full of beans. I gave him the iPad, then made some coffee and wrote in my diary. Looking through some old entries, I saw how much stress the selling of the school was.

We went to the 99 Yurts for a massive feed of lamb. Chen Xi and I had to be cool with one another so that we wouldn't upset Tan. It was a pity that we couldn't just have a nice chat, and that I had to say everything in Chinese. Tan was very good with Davey, and Davey glowed when he looked up at godfather Tan.

We went up to the apartment, and the cleaning lady was still there. The basin was full of dead insects. We identified where the insects were coming from, and I threw out the bag of rotten rice. Lin went and got some bug killer. When she got back, Davey and I went out and watched the old people dancing. I danced a bit too, while Lin sprayed the apartment.

When we returned from the real estate office people started coming to view the house immediately. I went out for a walk, and when I got back people were still piling in to see the apartment.

We had just settled down to watch *Castle Transylvania 2* when Lin got a call saying someone wanted us to come over and sign a contract to buy the apartment. It was about 8 o'clock, and the apartment had only been on the market for a couple of hours.

We went to the office despite Davey's protestations. They tried to negotiate price, but I told them they were not in a position to negotiate. Davey played with a laser pointer, and we teased a little boy with it out the window.

The apartment was sold. We were a bit melancholy about selling it but knew it was the right thing to do.

WEDNESDAY 6 JULY 2016

I met Smart at Yonganli, then went down to the toilets at the Jianguo hotel, and smoked a bit off the end of my key. I got the subway back to Bajiao, and Lin collected me at the bridge near the station.

While Lin made dinner I had a smoke and read the opening of my story, and then read it out loud to Lin. I was happy with these first pages. I went and got some beer.

Chen Xi was trying to figure out how to reduce her losses. She had transferred all of her money to Sterling just before Brexit. She would lose a lot of money transferring back.

THURSDAY 7 JULY 2016

I am listening to cicadas.

I spent yesterday hungover. I couldn't remember much of what happened the night before, had no recollection of getting home. Not great for a guy of my age. I never seem to learn. I didn't even bother saying I will never do that again. I lay in bed, still quite drunk, and didn't get up. Lin took Davey to kindergarten. Davey was good with me, but Lin was disgusted. She went out, saying she wanted to do some girl things. I read the story straight through without stopping to eat.

I agreed to meet Chen Xi at Pullman's. I felt confused and messy, uncomfortable driving–I'd been honking like a big cannon and needed to tone that down before I got murdered. At Pullman's we drank lemon tea beside the big windows. Chen Xi was angry at Britain.

FRIDAY 8 JULY 2016

I was loathing Beijing, the hot and sticky, cottony white pollution.

Too much hooting whilst working on my story made me confused and messy. I posted three sections on Facebook. The response has been hard on my ego–only two comments and a couple of likes. I got a laugh react from Greg, which I'm not sure is good or bad.

Chen Xi came over and we looked at houses in Ireland. She liked Wicklow. I was a little out of it from too many morning hoots. I went out for a walk, but it was so hot and polluted that I came home gasping and panting.

SATURDAY 9 JULY 2016

I took the story down. By the time Rob Warman phoned I was so drunk I was slurring.

It is still grey and ugly outside. I am fat, unhealthy, and uninspired. The dope is keeping me low. I lost feeling for the story after putting it online.

SUNDAY 10 JULY 2016

Putting the story up on Facebook has made me lose confidence. When Chen Xi arrived Davey was screaming crazily as I pushed him out the door of the apartment. I was not only a bad writer, I was also a bad father.

Chen Xi straightened Davey out. I went to the supermarket for lettuce, cucumbers and milk. I had become a grouchy *laowai*; it was hard for me to control my face, especially when I'd had a few hoots. I huffed and puffed and muttered at the till. Lin and I roared at one another. I went to my room to smoke dope and read the story.

Davey had a bath. Lin brought him into my room in a blanket. I sat beside him, astonished by his laughing face.

I should throw this dope out the window.

THURSDAY 14 JULY 2016

Getting off the subway there were no more random hellos called out to you in the streets, no whispered *laowai*, or people pointing you out. These days only a few stare downs from Chinese men. Tensions in the south China sea.

Back to the time machine. I did good work yesterday, and started to tidy up the narrative structure.

Nice terrorist truck. Turkey coup. When I finished writing, we drove to a place where they sell *guzheng*. We decided on the most expensive.

SUNDAY 17 JULY 2016

I have mostly finished the story. I will have plenty of time to tidy it up, and fill it out.

I smoked a lot of hash, drank a lot of coffee, and my ass was sore. I called Lin, but couldn't reach her, and this got me worried about them being kidnapped or something. I went over to the little supermarket, got two tins of beer, and drank these quickly on a bench outside.

When I got home I tried again, but she was powered off. I sent her a load of angry messages, and she called me right back shouting. We had a big fight. Davey was crying, trying to keep the peace.

THURSDAY 21 JULY 2016 05:00

I hope we can get out of Beijing soon–there is a hell of a lot of packing and shipping to be done. Very bad vibes from the security guys working on the road. I don't want to get murdered just as I'm about to escape.

SATURDAY 23 JULY 2016

Terrible big fight

I shouted at Davey. Lin tutted, and we began to poke one another. She said I wasn't a good father. We shouted and roared. Davey cried and held onto me saying don't leave daddy. I was dripping sweat; so very ugly. She told me that she didn't love or respect me. We roared in the parking lot. Davey was in hysterics, and I howled after her as she walked away. Unspeakable. The whole world was teetering this way and that.

I called Li Yue, and I could tell that Lin was with her. I lay in bed, and told Davey to be nice to me because I was sick. I sent messages to Lin saying I had given Davey to Wulinlin the yoga girl because I was in the hospital for a heart problem.

Chen Xi called, and I told her about my fight with Lin, then we talked about other things. We worried about the instability in the world. What was a safe currency to hold? What was a safe country to live in? Lin came home with Li Yue. Tomorrow I will buy Davey a toy car.

I dreamt that Oliver of Swan Training had put a two million RMB price on my head. I woke up at about 5:30, and didn't sleep again. I read the news. The world is in a dreadful state. It doesn't seem that anywhere is safe.

. . .

SUNDAY 24 JULY 2016

When Lin came to me first thing in the morning for a cuddle she didn't say anything about the day before.

Sunday of emptiness.

MONDAY 25 JULY 2016

Reading David Foster Wallace's Good Old Neon made me lose confidence in my story, just as *House of Leaves* did. One more weekend before we're back in Dublin.

TUESDAY 26 JULY 2016

Lin will return mid September to complete the sale of the apartment. Life is looking up. The world is falling apart, but we are in a good situation. I want to live long enough to get Davey started in life, do some good in the world.

WEDNESDAY 27 JULY 2016

Chen Xi wasn't sure about buying a house. Of course, I wanted her in Ireland so I could look after her.

THURSDAY 28 JULY 2016

Good Old Neon makes me feel I should give up, but it also gives me ideas. I dreamed the jade stones we bought were covered in mud and filth, but we were able to wash them off.

FRIDAY 29 JULY 2016

Davey didn't want to leave Beijing. Lin said he told his teacher he didn't want us to sell our apartment.

After dinner we went out for a walk. Davey rode his bike, and Lin and I walked round and round the water place. Lin assured me it was right for us to move.

I dreamed I was hanging around some offices when Chen Xi told me Tan was going to buy a school in partnership with Fred or James or someone. I was shocked and upset.

SATURDAY 30 JULY 2016

All of our things are gone with the shipper. It feels like a relief to be rid of so much stuff.

The *Ayi* arrived to clean up. Lin went for a Guzheng lesson while Davey and I drove around Laoshan. Davey said he didn't like Barna Woods. I saw a mother punch her little son in the face, and then drag him roughly by the arm.

After dinner Lin and I were on the verge of another fight. I felt hot and tired. Spending the whole day with Davey was hard. Davey talks to me about his lego game while I try to write this. I told him to let me finish, and he went away briefly before coming back and telling me more.

SUNDAY 31 JULY 2016

Davey and I drove around Laoshan, listening to Pink Floyd. Davey said, that's pretty good guitar, huh? Not as good as Phil Lynott though, hey?

TUESDAY 2 AUGUST 2016

I couldn't sleep, was worried about the flight, about someone reclining a seat in front of me. I didn't think I could bear it. In the morning Lin told me she'd got good seats, with no one in front of us.

I have started thinking about prostate cancer. I can't bear to think of not witnessing Davey grow up.

WEDNESDAY 3 AUGUST 2016

Last morning in Beijing.

We dropped Davey off at kindergarten. I was nervous letting him go in. I was still worried we wouldn't get out of here in one piece–that I would crash the car, or be attacked by some road rage guy with a knife.

I walked around the community. I felt some regret that we were leaving, but couldn't see any reason to ever return to Shijingshan.

When we collected Davey, Bonnie Laoshi kissed him good-bye, and one of the parents rubbed his cheek. Davey gave Zhang Yu Ti a big hug. In all likelihood we will never see any of these people again. When Davey got into the car he was happy to see Red Skull.

Eight and a half hours to Helsinki, and then another three and a half to Dublin.

THURSDAY 4 AUGUST 2016

Sitting in the toilet of the hotel room in Dublin to write, a cup of instant coffee beside me.

At customs a young person behind the counter was rude to a Muslim guy, telling him he was not making any sense. Your mout' is movin, but yer sayin nu-in.

I felt repulsed by Dublin. Lin asked how rainy Galway would be, and I could tell she was feeling the same way. It's hard to know where else we might live.

. . .

FRIDAY 5 AUGUST 2016

I could tell that Davey and Lin were happy to be back in Galway. Davey had brightened up as the cab passed Joyce's, and he realised where we were. There were spiderwebs all over the car but no giant spider nests inside. The back garden had gone crazy, and there was alien growth coming out of every nook and cranny. I had been looking forward to a proper cup of tea for a month.

I let Davey play *Don't Starve*, and Lin unpacked. I brought out two lawn chairs and drank a Hen's Tooth beer in the back garden, with Chen Xi on wechat. Tan had said he didn't want to stay in touch. I was not bitter–I could afford a bigger heart now we were back in Galway.

SATURDAY 6 AUGUST 2016

Lin had a bad dream, but wouldn't tell me about it. In the morning she told me someone she didn't know had been strangling her.

SUNDAY 7 AUGUST 2016

After breakfast I went back into the garden and pulled out the plants that had grown up between the patio blocks. Davey played lego behind me, and Lin cleaned the house.

We went out for a drive. Lin looked so sexy I imagined everyone who saw us had their minds blown. It was windy, and the sand whipped our faces.

TUESDAY 9 AUGUST 2016

Another horrible fight

I don't feel like writing today. I don't know how we can ever get things back to the way they should be. There were so many horrible, unforgivable things said.

It was me doing the strangling in her dream.

Poor Davey stuck in the middle, and us tugging at him and using him as a weapon. I thought this would never happen again.

Lin was making dinner, I was having a beer in the garden. Lin kept telling me that I should cancel the viewing on Thursday. She said she didn't like the house we were going to view. She kept pushing, and I told her to shut the fuck up. Next thing she's banging her head off the wall and slapping her own face. We dug ourselves deeper and deeper. I took all of our papers and documents, and her bag, and locked it in the car. I told her no matter what happened I would always hold a little piece of hate for her in my heart.

Davey was crying and begging us to stop. I kept drinking, and got meaner. I finished the Bacardi, then started on the

Irish Mist. Lin scratched my face, and I dragged her by the arm out of the bed and toward the stairs with Davey hanging onto her other arm. She said she wouldn't leave. She wanted the police to come.

WEDNESDAY 10 AUGUST 2016

I tried to cuddle Lin, but she was stiff and prickly.

Dropping Davey off at summer camp he looked so little. My heart was swollen with love. I had to walk swiftly to the car so that no one would see me crying.

Lin and I drove into town. We said nothing, but I couldn't help sighing and taking deep breaths. We stopped, and I tried to talk with Lin, but she was sharp, so I stopped trying.

THURSDAY 11 AUGUST 2016

Working on the story it was easy to feel I could push through to completion. I felt limitless possibility in what I could do with the story, that the time machine was a metaphor for fiction, or even language itself.

FRIDAY 12 AUGUST 2016

I immediately wanted this weird house built in 1964 on one acre, with its little rooms and its forested southern end. A stream ran along the eastern edge of the property. We saw a big frog , and the biggest blackberry I had ever seen, beside an otherworldly butterfly. I made the guy an offer on the spot, and this annoyed Lin.

I woke up worrying about the house–it needed so much work, and if there ever was a haunted house, this was it.

MONDAY 15 AUGUST 2016

At Oranswell we started in the garden, and then found a tree with big apples in the woods. I thought about how I could tidy this forest up–leaving the perimeter dense so that no one could see that inside was a magical place. The house had a library where Davey and I could do our homework.

Chen Xi sent me a message to tell me they had made an offer on a place in Bray. She said Tan likes Ireland.

TUESDAY 16 AUGUST 2016

The agent selling Oranswell told me that four other people were considering the property. I offered more. Lin was very annoyed by this.

I saw some Facebook posts about break-ins in Knocknacarra and Moycullen. The house in Oranswell is way out in the country. Between burglars and big black spiders, Oranswell could turn out to be heavy. I thought about making the upstairs impregnable.

I read a post by a monk on meditation. He suggested we can distract the monkey brain from its chatter by giving it a job, such as a deliberate focus on breathing.

SATURDAY 20 AUGUST 2016

The story detoured to Olly's room, where he was making clocks as if in preparation for an expository conversation with the time traveller.

SUNDAY 21 AUGUST 2016

I woke up worried about lead paint and pipes and asbestos and damp and infestations.

MONDAY 22 AUGUST 2016

I called Tony, the agent for the house, and told him we'd transferred the money, and hired Susan as a solicitor.

Arrived at the house in Oranswell we could hear the sound of running water in the garden. The stream beside the house was high, and suddenly I was worried that it could flood some day.

. . .

FRIDAY 26 AUGUST 2016

I was reading and writing my way to Lord Leitrim.

It was windy at Blackrock. We sat on the rocks, and then I lay back and looked up at the sky. Davey lay back and I put my arm under his head so we could both just lay there looking up at the sky.

SATURDAY 27 AUGUST 2016

A glimpse of Lin putting on her makeup. It was thrilling to be reminded that this exquisite woman was way out of my league.

SUNDAY 28 AUGUST 2016 05:42

Too many vivid dreams to recount. In one I was on a ship with Colin. I told him I would get a black and white sheepdog. He told me I shouldn't talk in front of the guy we were sitting with. The pizza delivery guy was late, and we decided not to take his pizza until he told us he had a flat tire. In another I was with Lin and Davey. It was raining heavily, and I looked across the watery yard at the stairs leading up to the house we had just bought. The stairs collapsed, and the stone artwork crumbled.

When I got off the phone, Lin criticised my immodesty. I had been on the 50 foreign teachers, 200 Chinese staff rigamarole. I need to be humble. I noticed when I started that rigamarole JB became a bit cooler. When I got off the phone, Davey said he wanted us to go back to China so I could still be the boss of Aihua.

After dinner, I read through the documents Susan sent. I needed to check the planning permissions around the house. Apparently surveyors are insured if they make a mistake in terms of the house's structural integrity.

TUESDAY 30 AUGUST 2016

We hired a couple of builders, Kenneth and Cyril, to help us with the house at Oranswell. We will have to replace the floor to install a radon barrier and under floor heating, as well as all the windows, electrics, plumbing, and the asbestos roof, and pump insulation into the walls.

The teacher seemed a bit cool when we picked up Davey. I asked Davey and it seems that he had some trouble with another little boy. I worried about him getting off on the wrong foot here.

We drove back to Oranswell and I gave Davey some big blackberries. I sat with Cyril and Kenneth, going through plans and drawings. Later I found Davey and Lin in the little forest. Lin was beaming. She was happy with how bright it was inside.

Davey was excited to tell me about *Paw Patrol*. I felt bad about being grouchy with him at the park. I promised to be more gentle.

THURSDAY 1 SEPTEMBER 2016

Lin had to give fingerprints to the *gardaí* for her residence permit. She was nervous and cute.

When I got home, I tried to talk to Lin, but Davey wouldn't stay away. Lin and I had a short, sharp fight, with Davey crying and all.

After dinner, we went to Silverstrand. The wind was strong. We sat in the car and watched the big waves breaking.

Chen Xi needs me to scan a document proving that her money is clean. Susan hasn't mentioned any such requirement to us, and now I am worried that this will become a problem.

FRIDAY 2 SEPTEMBER 2016

I am still a bit drunk. It took me a while to patch together how I got home, but I remember most of the night except for the stamp on my hand.

Evan, an old Aihua teacher, sent me a message asking me to meet up with him, Max and Kevin. I went out totally certain that I would only have two drinks, or four at the most, and I guess I had five before the lads even arrived. When the lads arrived, I ordered a round of Redbreasts, and started blathering. Two other ex-Aihua teachers arrived, fellows who had not completed their contracts, and had implemented midnight getaways. We walked down the road, lively as the lads will be. I think I had a Big Mac, and then got in a cab. I remember talking to a black guy about Libya and Gaddafi. I think we were even parked out front still talking. I have a sore and foggy head.

Davey is quiet in the bed beside me.

SATURDAY 3 SEPTEMBER 2016 06:30

The sky becomes blue, the hangover is mainly done.

Listening to Kate Bush, Wild Man, made me weepy, and I messaged Dan. I also sent apologetic messages to the lads, just in case I had done anything awful.

At Blackrock we saw a dead shark rolling in the water at the edge of the beach. The wind was strong and the waves were big.

WEDNESDAY 7 SEPTEMBER 2016

Another night of vivid dreams. We were driving around Nose Hill in West Calgary–it was badlands like around Drumheller, but to get there we had to walk through a house that we could never manage to get out of. Then Lin and Davey were gone and I was trying to find a way out through another old house. I saw through a window Scarlet and all her friends on the front lawn of Dergmoney. I had no trousers on, so I found an old towel and wrapped it around me before I went out to the garden. The girls were gone, so I went up to the house to find some trousers, and I found Warnock smoking hash. I asked him for a hoot and he organised it, but left as soon as he handed it to me.

THURSDAY 8 SEPTEMBER 2016

More dreams, but they elude me now. I think they might have been about cooking.

Lin got a muffin, and Davey fed this to the seagulls, gathering a crazy mob around us. Lin mentioned that China was going to stop people from getting money out through Hong Kong, so we went home immediately to transfer money.

FRIDAY 9 SEPTEMBER 2016

I remember only one bit from last night's dreaming–I was looking into a restaurant, and saw a dog protruding from a picture frame. The dog wiggled out of the frame, hanging from one foot for a moment. I thought the dog was going to need saving, but he got away OK.

Yesterday was a depressing day. It rained and rained, and the wind was strong. I saw severe weather warnings on Facebook. The doctor called and told me that my test for prostate cancer had come back high. We arranged for me to come in on Monday for a rectal examination, and referral to a specialist.

I saw Facebook pictures of Ralph sailing in the Strait of Georgia with Dan. There was a message from Scarlet asking him to come out and see her in Ireland. Seeing their obvious happiness hurt me. I dug deeper and saw photos of them with Netty and what appeared to be her new man, which clogged my heart.

SUNDAY 11 SEPTEMBER 2016

The waves were huge. I need to watch waves closely for the next part of my story, when the traveller goes back to the time of the Vikings.

TUESDAY 13 SEPTEMBER 2016

A ceiling of bubbly, bluish cloud extends above the bright line of the horizon.

THURSDAY 15 SEPTEMBER 2016

We signed the contract to buy the house at Oranswell.

Chen Xi received the contract for her house. She will arrive in Dublin around the same time Lin returns, so that I can collect them both at the airport.

SATURDAY 17 SEPTEMBER 2016

We waited with Lin at the station, and when she got on the train we waved to her through the window.

At a restaurant nearby, Davey and I ate sausages, bacon, black and white pudding, egg and toast while I exchanged messages with Lin.

MONDAY 19 SEPTEMBER 2016

Lin called us on wechat while I was getting Davey into his school uniform. We didn't talk for long; Davey didn't know how to deal with it, so he was shy, and kept making funny noises, and trying to touch Lin through the screen.

WEDNESDAY 21 SEPTEMBER 2016

Chen Xi arrives Saturday; Davey and I will collect her in

Dublin. She was annoyed with me because I'd forgotten some details from Kenneth's report.

Researching what Viking Dublin would have looked like, wandering through it. Setting for father-son conflict.

When Lin called Davey continued reading Dr Seuss on the iPad while we talked, so I took it from him. He hit me, I hit him back, and then he tried to bite me. Lin said goodbye, and Davey and I had a big fight. Afterwards we drove to Blackrock, and sat on stones as the water lapped. He sat on my knee, and we were happy.

I feel so tired. I hope I can keep it together. Davey and I agreed that we won't fight today.

THURSDAY 22 SEPTEMBER 2016

Terrible sleep–Davey kept waking me with a knee in the spine, or a fist in the face, or whatever. I had a dream about driving a car too fast through a crèche.

We went to the circus. It was raining heavily. We parked along the promenade. The circus tents were empty, thrumming in the storm. Circus people were struggling to keep the big top together. A girder crashed at Davey's feet. The wind was howling and the rain was vertical. We got into the tent and sat down. I got popcorn. I let Davey ride the pony. It was three euros for two loops, and the guy couldn't crack a smile. Davey insisted on cotton candy, and we almost had a row, but then I just went and got it. I also got gummy bears. The show began, and there were dancing horses, a clown, aerial acrobats, and a strong man. Davey's trousers were soaking from the rain, and he sat on my lap. The intermission came after an hour, and Davey and I left.

FRIDAY 23 SEPTEMBER 2016

Lin is in Heilongjiang. I worry about her being kidnapped.

SATURDAY 24 SEPTEMBER 2016

We parked at Dublin airport, got a bus into Dublin, and walked down Grafton Street past Trinity. Davey wanted a sausage, so we got a full breakfast in Eddie Rockets. Then we walked to Bruxelles and took a photo of Davey with Phil Lynnot.

Chen Xi arrived without incident. As we approached Galway, the rain lifted, and a golden sky of clouds appeared.

Davey and I haven't eaten vegetables for three days. I need to make sure he has a shower, and get something for his lunch tomorrow. I feel pressure to look after Chen Xi as well as Davey.

SUNDAY 25 SEPTEMBER 2016

We showed Chen Xi the house at Oranswell, and she seemed impressed. Then we went to the Clybaun, and she booked a room.

After lunch, we went to Blackrock; it was cold and windy, but once we got there it felt warmer when we saw all of the people swimming. We went up onto the diving platform, and then sat on the rocks. It was windy, cloudy, and bright all at once.

Chen Xi helped Davey make the lego wagon while I warmed up the leftover soup, and made toast and jam. I gave him raspberries and grapes, then turned on the dishwasher, and took out the garbage. When Chen Xi completed the lego wagon, I drove her back to her room.

WEDNESDAY 28 SEPTEMBER 2016

Lin says we won't be able to change the money for the apartment to USD. We will need to use Chen XI's friend again.

Chen Xi and I had lunch at the Clybaun. Chen Xi cried about how I cheated on her with Grace, and how soulless I had been during my drug taking years with Molly. I felt sorry that I had hurt her.

She had been complaining all day about how dirty our place

was, so we went into town and bought new bedsheets and cleaning products.

THURSDAY 29 SEPTEMBER 2016

In Beijing, Lin was having a tough time at the taxation office, but she managed to come out with the document we needed.

I felt grouchy with Chen Xi as we walked through town. She always bumped into me when we walked, and was always scolding me about this and that. I tried to suppress these feelings. We put on some laundry and Chen Xi cleaned around the house. After we collected Davey we went to the playground. I left them and walked once around the park to clear the mess in my head. Being with Chen Xi and Davey all day long I hadn't had a minute with my own thoughts. I need to start doing meditation again. I got back to the playground just as it started to rain, and found Davey and Chen Xi taking shelter under one of the climbing towers

SATURDAY 1 OCTOBER 2016

Chen Xi was packed and waiting in the foyer. After breakfast, she did some laundry, and tidied up around the house.

We drove to Ashford Castle. The drive through the grounds was brilliant; I knew this was the sort of place that Chen Xi loved. We parked and had a cup of tea, and then it started to rain and we huddled under some trees. I drove back the other way, west of the lakes, through tiny cart roads, across the weirdest landscape.

Lin had landed, and was on the bus to Galway. After dinner, Davey and I went to get Lin. I parked behind the bus station, and found her wandering the roads with two big bags. When we got home we laughed and joked, and then Chen Xi went to bed.

Lin slept with Davey and I slept alone. Later, Lin came to me.

WEDNESDAY 5 OCTOBER 2016

Chen Xi and I walked on a hill looking over Galway. Her delight at discovering a blackberry bush momentarily transformed her into a little girl.

FRIDAY 7 OCTOBER 2016

At Oranswell I walked the perimeter, thinking about the book *Gardens Awakening*, trying to listen to the land, and transmit intentions. There were two partially burned candles on the lawn, near some rampant mushroom piles. Someone had been performing witchcraft. I will likely follow some of the advice from *Gardens Awakening*, just for the psychological comfort of having the spirits of the land on my side. It's not like I believe in this sort of thing, but I do have moments when a sense of supernatural creepiness crawls over me.

Lin played Guzheng; I got a cup of tea and went to work on the story.

TUESDAY 11 OCTOBER 2016

I got Davey dressed and drove him to school. It was another misty morning, with crazy crashing golden light breaking out of the clouds.

I have to get another blood test for prostate cancer. Thinking about the needle gave me a bad feeling last night.

We paid for the house, and now need to set up bank accounts, credit cards and insurance.

At Oranswell the trees were turning colour. I went into the forest and found some old McDonalds wrappers, so I will have to build a fence and hedges. I want to get a formidable dog, but don't want to chase off wildlife. I noticed that the farm behind us was more intensive than I had thought. The cows were in their sheds, and they were lowing loudly. The stream looked dangerous for a kid.

We went to Barna. Davey ran over to where I was sitting on a bench to put down his leaves and plants before going back to see the dogs that Lin was petting, but Lin had finished seeing them and was on her way back to us. Davey started crying, saying go back go back, get them to come back. I became frustrated and began to scold him. He was screaming and I was holding his wrists tightly. When I let go of him, I pushed him over with my foot. As we walked away I said very mean things to Davey, that seeing such bad behaviour made me want to leave the family. Lin went off on her own, and I ordered Davey back to the bench. He was still crying heavily. I asked him why he wanted to ruin the family, and I wouldn't let him touch me. I knew I was being cruel and cold but I couldn't help myself.

An old lady came along and she was like an angel. She had seen Davey screaming, and I apologised for Davey's behaviour, but she said ah no, he is a wonderful boy. He is just beautiful, I love his lovely brown eyes and his lovely skin. She was so kind. Davey played with her dog, laughing sweetly. I chatted to the old lady for a while, and then she went on. I hugged Davey, and apologised, and told him I love him and that nothing would ever ruin the family.

I felt bad about how mean I had been. Lin came back and we walked on. Davey said you know in my *Growing in Love* book there was a picture of a boy kicking a girl that we weren't supposed to colour because it didn't show a loving heart.

FRIDAY 14 OCTOBER 2016

I watched Davey through the window of the classroom explaining to a little girl the lasers on the clay thing he had made. It had many lasers and was very formidable. Only Black Bolt could destroy it.

We drove home past the house at Oranswell, and I explained to Davey that this was our house now, and that this would always be his house.

We signed the deed, and Susan gave us the keys. When we got home, I put lasagna in the oven, and opened the champagne. I felt drunk and happy immediately.

SATURDAY 15 OCTOBER 2016

At the new house there were hundreds of dead flies up in the bedroom; huge apples dripping from the trees.

SUNDAY 23 OCTOBER

More strange dreams. In the first one I was in a public toilet, covered in shit. I had taken off my clothes and the door of the cubicle was glass. Chen Xi and some other Chinese girls came to my rescue.

In the next I owed money to a drug dealer, who was threatening me over the phone. I told him I would have the money with me. There were several dreams about finding accommodation, and then one where Lin left with Davey because my long hair looked so silly. I phoned her mom, and got a weird message.

MONDAY 24 OCTOBER 2016

Lin got angry because I said taking Davey to *Hēilóng Jiāng* was dangerous, given that her cousin had recently had his eyes gouged out, his head cut off and stuck on a pole. She said she had to go, and that if I wanted she could go alone and I could keep Davey with me.

SUNDAY 30 OCTOBER 2016

Chen Xi is moving out of her London house, going back to China.

WEDNESDAY 2 NOVEMBER 2016

Reading *The Orkneyinga Saga* evokes dreams of a group of tall ghosts pushing through the woods.

FRIDAY 4 NOVEMBER 2016

I dread the weekend. It is draining to spend the whole time focussed on Davey, but if I go off on my own, I feel guilty for abandoning Lin. I feel that Lin has been impatient with me recently, and I worry that we could have an argument. Obviously I am doing something wrong.

Dealing with this problem is probably more a question of managing how I feel than organising what I do.

MONDAY 7 NOVEMBER 2016

When Davey and I got to school he told me he didn't want to go in because Victor and Mikhail were bullying him. I told him to either punch one in the nose like a crazy guy, or just keep his distance from them. I told him to let me know how things went. I'm sorry he has to go through this. I know it damaged my character.

I walked around the house at Oranswell. With the leaves fallen it was easier to get an idea of what was going on.

When I got home, Lin had moved the lego from the table and things seemed better for that. We read about the biopsy. It sounded terrible. Not to even mention the fear that they will find cancer.

I played a little bit of guitar and went for a walk to the forest, past the church. It was a beautiful morning, and it felt great to be out. I tried to think about the story, but the fear of what they would be doing to my insides tomorrow was too much.

After meditation I bought a longsword from Swords of the West.

TUESDAY 8 NOVEMBER 2016

It was dark and rainy. The other guys seemed a lot older than me. I asked reception if I could be put under but she said no. Lin arrived like a blast of sunshine.

We had to wait about an hour and a half before they called me through. The nurses knew I was nervous, and the wee lady who took me through led me by the hand.

The biopsy wasn't pleasant. At one point I thought I might need to scream, fight the pinch gun out of me.

A guy acting like he had a knife or something in his pocket held open the cab door for Lin and I, said there were assassins in the hospital who wanted to kill him. It was raining heavily, and I was starting to feel uncomfortable between my legs.

I lay down in Lin's room with the door closed. Davey was good to me, and left me alone. I had trouble sleeping, so I got up and watched TV, an American action film that consisted entirely of people getting shot in the head.

When I woke, I saw Trump had won, and the USD had plunged again.

WEDNESDAY 9 NOVEMBER 2016

The shock of reading that Trump had won the election made me worry for the future. It was rainy and depressing. Lin wasn't in a great mood. She said she felt trapped, that it was a mistake to sell the place in Beijing.

It felt like I was re-enacting family history, taking Lin from her home, her language, stranding her here on this strange little island. We haven't managed to make any friends. I hoped we might in our new house, but I know I said that about Davey starting school.

THURSDAY 10 NOVEMBER 2016

I managed to use a bit from Sandymount Strand in *Portrait*. The story is moving along.

We walked into town and saw four swans land in the river. The tide was high, and the water was dark and deep. Davey gave the busker a euro.

Reading the essay on Death in *A Vision* put me to sleep.

FRIDAY 11 NOVEMBER 2016

I found the passage about Vikings in *Ulysses*, although I'd thought it from *Portrait*. I used this for a scene on Sandymount Strand before moving the traveller back to Dublin.

Chen XI is excited about the prospect of being in her new house in Bray before Christmas.

MONDAY 14 NOVEMBER 2016

Looking up at the super moon; the sky is clear for the first time in a month. Yesterday was dreadful.

I had a shower, then asked Lin to come lie with me. She started crying, and fled downstairs. I saw that the ejaculate in my hand was blood red.

When I came downstairs, Lin told me we had missed the parent-teacher interview. I was upset that this made us look like irresponsible parents. I drove to Joyce's and bought some whiskey and coke. I sat down and drank this at the table. Lin and Davey sat with me and I started to fight with Lin. Then she started to drink whiskey too, and we decided to get drunk. Davey drank coke. We got in the car and I cranked up Led Zeppelin Rock'n Roll, and we drove like crazy hillbillies to Joyce's for steaks and beer. We drove home blasting Whole Lotta Love. We ate our steaks and laughed and drank. Davey drank Cidona. We ate a whole pack of mince pies. We listened to gothic death metal and I posted two Tristania songs on Facebook. I played *guzheng*, and then filmed Lin playing, put this on Facebook too.

When we went up to bed, I dug out the old sword and Davey took this into his room with him. I reminded Davey about the Yeats Magic, about imagining a big dog by your bed before going to sleep.

WEDNESDAY 16 NOVEMBER 2016

Davey says he feels different today from how he felt yesterday, because today he is five. Lin came in and lay beside me, and I opened Davey's presents for him.

THURSDAY 17 NOVEMBER 2016

I thought of making the Masai appear riding whales.

FRIDAY 18 NOVEMBER 2016

Outside the sky is black and clear, and I can see Orion standing straight upright. Davey and Lin are still asleep.

Almost finished the first dreaming-back. For the Cú Chulainn bit I read some of Yeats' plays–*At the Hawk's Well of Immortality,* The wearer of the *Green Helmet* is declared the Champion of Ulster *On Baile's Strand*; redeemed by *The Only Jealousy of Emer*, and Comforted by *The Death of* ....

SUNDAY 20 NOVEMBER 2016

The sky is dark, and full of stars. Orion is standing on the roofs of houses across the way.

I am happy with how I got Larry back to the mead hall in Dublin to meet Silva. When Lin got up she pointed out the ice on the roof of the car.

Lin made porridge, and seemed a bit short with me, and we could have got into a row, but I went out for a walk instead, down to the forest past the church.

It was cold and foggy. When I got down to the water, it was still. There was a heron standing on the rocks.

MONDAY 21 NOVEMBER 2016

At Oranswell I started snipping. I opened up the stone stairs that face the farm, and a second view of the stream.

Davey said he liked the garden now. Davey and Lin snipped at the long grass while I sawed down big branches of an evergreen that was pushing over the birches.

WEDNESDAY 23 NOVEMBER 2016

I put out some bird seed at Oranswell, and got to work pulling out branches and piling them at the back of the property. Lin and Davey puttered around snipping things while I dragged out the wood.

More dreams. A big Native guy joking with me about being a tough guy. Then he came up to the apartment where Lin, Davey and I were staying and insisted I kill him. He started to push Davey and wave a knife around so at his instruction I cut his throat a few times. Somehow it became Donald Trump that I had killed. A lot of the dream was me anticipating spending time in jail. The other dreams involved Netty.

THURSDAY 24 NOVEMBER 2016 AT 12:00

The sky was dark and star filled.

I took Davey to school, then drove to the house at Oranswell, the sun still low through the trees. I met the farmer who owns the cows out behind us, and we chatted over the stone wall.

Davey played quietly while we talked with his teacher. She said he was intelligent, and good with language. She said he was a nice boy too, well behaved and well mannered.

SUNDAY 27 NOVEMBER 2016

My head hurt, and I was grouchy with Lin and Davey. I apologised for being so mean. It is this bloody nagging headache that makes me cranky.

The sky was beautiful over the Burren; Lin took photos out the car window. When we got home, I went up to my work room and drank cider and tried to figure out how to get some dope. I wanted to go alone to a castle for a few days to finish up the story. I played guitar, then went downstairs and made brandy and port.

I will go up to Omagh to get some of Scarlet's homegrown. Warnock was working as a Wildling in *Game of Thrones*. Scarlet planned to avoid the impending end of the world by going to sea.

Davey came in and tried to talk to me, but I sent him away.

MONDAY 28 NOVEMBER 2016

I'm looking forward to the drive to Omagh.

I am close to wrapping up the Cú Chulainn bit. Then, I will only have one part to complete.

Lin and I talked about missing China. Galway is so grey and dark in the winter, and it is hard for us to make friends here.

When I went to get Davey I felt distant from the other parents. I felt Aaron was being cold to Davey, and his mom seemed cold to me. In the car, Davey told me he wanted to go back to kindergarten in China.

Lin was upset that Davey was still scared to sleep with her because of a dream in which her face was grey.

TUESDAY 29 NOVEMBER 2016

I set off for Omagh. At Tuam I stayed on the N17. I stopped at Glencar Waterfall for a piss, and posted a photo of Benbulben on Facebook. The GPS took me through Enniskillen. Tyrone, with its green, rolling hills, is Narnia and The Shire. Scarlet was good to me. We admired the view from her house, looking down at the river from the top of a hill. We went to Willow's place. Holly, John, Troy and Warnock's two girls were there.

We drove back to Scarlet's place, and she organised some dope for me. I got more than I had expected, and it was of a nice quality. She invited me to stay on, but I didn't want to leave Lin and Davey alone at night. The GPS took me south through Monoghan. The trip home seemed longer than it was, driving down the dark roads with the lights of oncoming vehicles in my eyes. I stopped for a sandwich and another coffee. I followed behind slow cars most of the way. Once I got onto the motorway at Athlone things went more smoothly. I got home before nine, and Lin made me fried rice. She was upset because Davey kept telling her he was scared of her when he remembered his dream of her face turning grey.

WEDNESDAY 30 NOVEMBER 2016

The marijuana weighs heavily upon me. I have a lot. I want to calm down, not make every day an all day marathon.

THURSDAY 1 DECEMBER 2016

Chen Xi knew right away that I had been smoking marijuana. She said she could smell it through the phone. Lin had a smoke with me in the back, but she didn't like it. I read the story while Lin played guzheng.

SUNDAY 4 DECEMBER 2016

The dope makes my writing unclear and my mind muddy. I'm lost in the story. The Irish history bit is good, though it needs more quotes from Irish literature. The most daunting bit is my own life.

MONDAY 5 DECEMBER 2016 04:59

I drank quite a bit last night, and I don't remember going to bed. Davey slept with me but I don't remember us agreeing to it. I think he just snuck in. I discovered little bottles of 8 percent Guinness scattered about.

Yesterday's story-planning–what happens next. I put down dates like anchors. I hooted while writing, and I'm not even sure if I had breakfast. I don't think I did. At Oranswell I fed the birds and walked in the clearing. When I got home, I drank and worked on the story while Lin made dinner. I don't remember going to the supermarket again for more beer, but apparently I did.

I am falling apart.

TUESDAY 6 DECEMBER 2016

Lin and I went to B&Q to look at garden things. We will get some gravel for the paths. We stopped at Joyce's on the way home and I got a couple of the strong bottles of Guinness. I drank these while trying to write, but nothing came out. Lin made a fire.

WEDNESDAY 7 DECEMBER 2016

It felt as though my muscles were decaying. I have been pushing hard at the story. I need to go to the gym but am driven to finish this part that I am working on.

THURSDAY 8 DECEMBER 2016

I worked on the story for a while, but then I just stopped, unable to do any more.

I feel run down. I'd love to finish this story but this big jar of marijuana is a problem. I wish I could just go easier on it, but I have it in my head that I need it to push through to the end. I am nearly there, but I also get the feeling that I am moving too quickly. My body feels wrong. I'd like to get back to a normal life. It's difficult living like the undead. I should give Lin the rest of the weed to hide away from me, but I'd be happier to do that after I finish the story.

FRIDAY 9 DECEMBER 2016

Chen Xi arrived for the day. We went to Susan's to get the keys to her new house. We had a cup of tea while waiting for

Chen XI's bus home. Davey and I got some Turkish delight at the Christmas market.

We said goodbye to Chen Xi. Tan dictates the shortness of the visit, and there isn't much we can do about it.

When I got home I told Lin that the story I am writing now is about when love breaks and dies in a family, and how sad that is. Lin pointed out that when I am smoking dope I don't fight with anyone.

SUNDAY 11 DECEMBER 2016

I finished the story. I will let a few people read it, then send it out to publishers.

MONDAY 12 DECEMBER 2016

Chen Xi is having a hard time. The visa situation is not easy, and apparently the Chinese government has the cooperation of foreign companies to track down people who have taken money out of China. We talked about the possibility of losing money. The wheel of fortune goes up, and it goes down.

TUESDAY 13 DECEMBER 2016

I went to Oranswell and had a toot in Lin's Zen room, then went out to the clearing. Two little birds criticised me for not leaving them any food over the weekend. When Lin called me to come and get her, I was in her room again smoking dope. I felt more comfortable in the house now that I knew it had insurance.

WEDNESDAY 14 DECEMBER 2016

Gardening dreams under a big full moon. Yesterday I finished the dope and read a bit of the story. I felt a loss of confidence.

FRIDAY 16 DECEMBER 2016

I woke up at about two and read my phone until nearly four. Once the marijuana is gone the good sleep is gone too.

MONDAY 19 DECEMBER 2016

Davey was so funny, telling me how he was going to stay awake and see Santa. He is such an enthusiastic little guy.

I went to Oranswell, and laid out some peanuts for the birds. I snipped and pulled away dead wood to make the circle clearer. It felt like more editing.

Going to get the results of my biopsy. Some people don't take treatment until the cancer is aggressive, because the treatment makes you impotent, and incontinent, so that you need to wear a piddle bag around your ankle.

I am afraid.

TUESDAY 20 DECEMBER 2016

The doctor told me I don't have cancer. I was over the moon, and I was grateful for everything.

When we got home, I spoke with Chen Xi about her kitchen. What she wants is awkward, and she was impatient with me.

I want to change how I live. I want to take more time for myself. Lin and I don't both need to spend all of our time with Davey.

THURSDAY 22 DECEMBER 2016

We drove into town. There was an amazing rainbow up above us, the most pronounced rainbow I had ever seen. The water was a beautiful blue-green, with white waves breaking across it. We parked at the top of the bridge, and walked into town. We looked around for a present for Lin, but couldn't find anything she wanted.

It is raining now, a gentle song. I have a nice feeling about this Christmas. We will give Davey a magical feeling that he will always remember.

SATURDAY 24 DECEMBER 2016

Christmas morning, down at the dining room table with Lin and Davey. Davey has just opened his presents. After breakfast, I put together the lego. My buttocks were sore by the time I finished.

TUESDAY 27 DECEMBER 2016

After Davey fell asleep, Lin came in and visited me. We talked about the next couple of weeks with Davey off school, and how to deal with this time. We agreed we should use this time as an opportunity for us to set habits, and create a tone of calmness and positivity.

I woke up at 5 and read the BBC's depressing take on the new year. I wouldn't care if this wasn't the world Davey will need to step into.

WEDNESDAY 28 DECEMBER 2016 07:15

Still dark. Davey is downstairs watching Peppa Pig, and Lin

is probably at the Clybaun. I will have to make some breakfast for Davey.

Last night Davey had wanted me to lift him off the bed, and carry him down to dinner. He was pushy, so I ignored him. When I went downstairs he followed me aggressively, so I slapped him on the head. When he tried to hit me back, I whacked his bottom a few times. Lin was pissed off.

I poured myself a glass of whiskey, and Lin and I kept squabbling. I drove to Joyce's for more booze, and when I got back things got nasty. She threw things, and punched me, and I slapped her twice. Davey was screaming and crying. Lin left with her passport, swearing that she was finished with me. Davey and I stood around while I finished off the booze, and then we went up to bed.

I don't know how this is going to go.

THURSDAY 29 DECEMBER 2016

Happy again

Lin had been at the Clybaun. I asked the lady at the desk if I could phone the room. When Lin answered, I asked her if we could come up and she said we could.

We sat for a while in Lin's room, and she gave Davey a bath. We went to Salthill, and walked to Blackrock. It was a beautiful day, with the sun blasting down through clouds, creating ladders up to heaven. After we walked, Davey played in the sand.

Everything is going to be OK, so long as the world doesn't fall apart on us.

SUNDAY 15 JANUARY 2017

I dreamed that I bought a giant new house and Ralph and Sam visited. We had an argument and they stormed off. I followed, begging them to return.

MONDAY 16 JANUARY 2017

Relieved to have signed the contract for renovations on the house at Oranswell. It will be ready by August.

TUESDAY 17 JANUARY 2017

Yesterday morning I didn't feel so good about the story. I think I will need to drop the bit where I have tried to integrate Deleuze and Guattari on Nomadism.

Lin said she feels trapped. I feel she is living with me because she has to, but secretly detests me. Lin wouldn't back down, and then she took off. I took Davey to the diving board. When we went back to the car Lin was there. The fight got bigger as we drove home–she wouldn't back down an inch, or even deny that she despised me. I dropped them off and went and got some beer.

THURSDAY 19 JANUARY 2017 06:15

Out in the back garden for a hoot, the sky a clutter of stars. Lin just came to me, and she was very sweet.

Yesterday I got up at 4 to drive to Omagh. I drove the whole way in darkness. I saw a fox run across the road, and I called Davey to tell him this. I took a couple of wrong turns getting to Scarlet's place. She made me avocado and toast. Her boy, the younger one, Troy, was there, and we chatted a bit about his school. I had a wee hoot, and became chatty. We went to Willow's house, and I put on John's green wellies and went out with Scarlet to shovel some horse shit. Then we got Willow and went for a bowl of soup and a coffee. They talked about Ralph and Sam. They were both kind to me, and positive about Lin and Davey. I talked about my story, and about Ralph.

After we finished lunch, we walked back to the car. Willow held my arm and Scarlet's arm. Scarlet gave me some dope, and I set off for home. The GPS wanted me to return through Athlone, but I forced on to Sligo. It was beautiful coming in through the mountains to Sligo listening to GusGus with a nice buzz on. I ate junk food, and drank coffee. There was a traffic jam outside Galway, as darkness fell.

When I got home I opened a strong Guinness. Davey was full of beans. Lin said to me, he loves you so much.

SATURDAY 21 JANUARY 2017

It is 5:07. Lin and Davey are asleep. The moon is very small. When this moon disappears, it will be Chinese new year. Lin will go to London then.

SUNDAY 22 JANUARY 2017 AT 12:00

The marijuana makes my head feel like it's stuffed with cotton wool. On the way home I got a couple of beers. I sent messages to people asking them to read my story.

MONDAY 23 JANUARY 2017

Emailed the story to Muriel, Hannah, Adele, Tony, Greg, Dan and Jim, and booked our Learner's Licence tests.

WEDNESDAY 25 JANUARY 2017

I haven't heard anything back from the people I sent the story to.

THURSDAY 26 JANUARY 2017

I have been feeling tender toward Lin these past few days. Yesterday she was sick and I cuddled her to make her feel better. Today I cuddled her because she is sweet and tender.

I worked on the Battle of the Somme part. Then, I sent the revision to the people I'd sent it to with an explanation. I got a message from Greg saying he was enjoying the story. He is only at the discovery of the Time Machine though. I chatted with Tony about the story. I hope he will read it this weekend. It would be a dreadful disappointment for the story to remain unread.

FRIDAY 27 JANUARY 2017 05:46

Stars in the cold sky. It is the morning of Chinese New Year's. The year of the chicken is auspicious, especially with work starting on the house yesterday.I stopped at Oranswell and met Padraig. He was taking out the shelves from the library so that they won't be damaged during the work. Tomorrow Lin goes to London until Tuesday evening.

SUNDAY 29 JANUARY 2017

Davey and I drove Lin to the bus station. She seemed angry with me before she got out of the car, though I didn't think I'd done anything. Davey asked her why she was going alone.

I feel sad, old and alone, lost with Lin not here, heavy because I haven't heard back from any of my readers. I think the story is good , but it's possible that it isn't. That would be a hard blow, but I guess it wouldn't be the end of the world. I still may hear something back from them, but I have to be prepared to not hear anything, or to not hear anything that I want to hear. Perhaps the story is too convoluted, or circular, or, I don't know–too something.

Davey is quiet down in my room. I will make him some scrambled eggs, and then I'll prepare his lunch.

MONDAY 30 JANUARY 2017

No messages or anything from Lin, but she is to be home tonight. Received a cryptic message from Greg. He just quoted a phrase from the story, zero moral gravity, and put a flexed bicep beside it.

WEDNESDAY 1 FEBRUARY 2017

I read through the contract or whatever it was that Chen Xi sent me from whoever it was.

I played guitar, and then Lin and I went for a walk at Salthill. It was windy and wavy. Lin said I was like the sea, sometimes peaceful, and sometimes furious.

We met Tom at Oranswell. Padraig continues to tear out floors and walls.

It was cold and rainy when we picked up Davey. He had been given the Charlie Bear to take home because he was patient. I told him patience was the greatest virtue.

THURSDAY 2 FEBRUARY 2017

Yesterday I finished the second edit of the story, and then sent it out to all of the people who are reading the story, along with an aggressively arrogant introduction–something about errors being volitional. Fionna wrote back a peeved email, and none of the other readers answered at all. I am not worried though, because I know the story is good. I have no doubt about its quality. The question is how to publish it.

It's hard to know what to do with these early mornings once this story is done.

FRIDAY 3 FEBRUARY 2017

Not working on the story first thing in the morning clears time to pull up the socks on the personal organisation front.

I went to Oranswell, and started a pile of deadwood in the centre of the apple trees. After dinner I went back to Oranswell. The sun was going down, and the sky was orange. I went into the garden and just stood there looking. I went into a trance. It was like standing in God's holy fire. I saw that lights were on in the house, and I went in and turned them off.

SATURDAY 4 FEBRUARY 2017

He pulled a wishbone with his mom, and he won. He wished for a black dragon. I told him the black dragon could appear at any time, though maybe not until he was as old as me. He was excited, and he believed all of this. I saw a cloud that looked like a black dragon, and we said that this was the black dragon spirit arriving to begin watching over Davey.

I went into the garden and started tidying the trees and the space between the trees. I felt like a ranger. The sun came right into the garden around noon. It was magical. Everything was luminous. I realised I should put a sundial in the centre of the garden. I could identify the solstice and equinox, mark them with big stones. I pruned the cherry tree. When I am working on the garden I feel very peaceful, very Zen. I am able to get right into it and forget about myself. Lin and Davey don't seem to get it, and from Lin's reaction I gather she feels I am becoming obsessive about the garden. Still, it is cool to have a temple to the goddess of time. Working in the garden feels like doing the story. There is the same ordering, tidying energy. I am thinking about what will go in the library, to make it a temple to education and learning. Globes, busts, books, maps, charts, swords, masks, a telescope.

My life is becoming my dream. Everything has fallen into place. I entertain the thought of my father as a guardian angel for our family now, making everything turn out.

I am certain my story is good, and worth publishing.

MONDAY 6 FEBRUARY 2017

It seems strange that no one I sent the story to has said a word. I don't know what to think. The people I gave the story to aren't bad people who would like to keep me down. Either it is too long, or too hard to read, or there is something about it that is upsetting to these readers.

TUESDAY 7 FEBRUARY 2017

I feel lost. Not having the story to focus on leaves a giant void in my days. Kelly Pitman sent a message saying she would start reading but it would take her a long time to finish. I guess the rest just gave up on reading it. Is it too boring?

WEDNESDAY 8 FEBRUARY 2017

Davey and Lin play with a neighbourhood cat that has wandered into our kitchen. We will have animals at Oranswell. Davey will be at the Bushy Park school for eight years, and then high school for another six. We will live at Oranswell for at least that long.

THURSDAY 9 FEBRUARY 2017

A message from Kelly Pitman. She doesn't understand why I asked her to finish the story. I am puzzled. Is the story too personal, too painful, too messy?

FRIDAY 10 FEBRUARY 2017 06:32

The moon looks down–black clouds moving across it.

Lin and I went into town, and walked up and down the main strip. It was very cold, and the only busker out was the one brave and true Galway man with his banjo. I was thinking about the future, about my library in the new house. It might not be easy to get my book published. I could invite artists and poets to the house, and let them stay, make connections, accumulate enough *guanxi* to get the story published.

SATURDAY 11 FEBRUARY 2017

I need to bring back the passion I felt when I was writing the story. The new house and its library might help with that.

I'm afraid of running out of money, but we must let Davey have a good, stable childhood, and then see what happens. Once we are settled at Oranswell, it will be time to look at other ways of earning money. We could rent out rooms, Lin and I could look for some easy-going work to supplement. We could grow our own food, that sort of thing.

I don't know what will become of my story.

TUESDAY 14 FEBRUARY 2017

Davey said I am a lazy daddy who doesn't work. I was upset, and I tried to justify myself to him. Of course I talked about the book, though I'm glad I haven't started spending the royalties from its publication yet.

In the car, Davey started up about a treat. I was patient to begin, because I had expected this. He said awful things to me: he would throw tomatoes in my eye, I would have to leave and he would get a new daddy. I got angry and said mean things. I stopped the car and told him to get out. I couldn't stop myself, or the part of me in charge didn't want to stop myself. When we got home, I went up to my room and closed the door.

Davey came to me and apologised, and I apologised too. He gave me a Valentine's day card he'd made for Lin and me. I got a few daffodils from out front for Lin's flower vase.

THURSDAY 23 FEBRUARY 2017

At Salthill the day was fresh, the waves long and slow. Birds were picking at the material that had been lifted by the tide, and whenever a wave stretched across the sand they flew up and then back down as it retreated, a beautiful dance.

SATURDAY 25 FEBRUARY 2017 07:08

Birds singing. There is rain on the window, and heavy cloud, but it looks like it might lighten up.

I got an email from Greg telling me he had finished the story, but nothing else. It is clear that the story doesn't work. I don't get it; but will have to accept it. I replied to Greg's message, trying to explain to him how I found the story's failure disturbing not just because of vanity, but also because of the difference it implied between my perceptions and the perceptions of other people. When I read the story, I felt that it was funny and exciting. That other people didn't feel that way made me worry about my grip on reality. I asked Greg if he thought the story salvageable. Told him I had time to dedicate to rewrites if it is possible to save the story, to make it publishable….

SUNDAY 26 FEBRUARY 2017

Fluffy clouds in the distance, a bird singing. I received a message from Greg, and he didn't answer any of my questions. Can it be that bad? So bad that he can't say a word about it?

WEDNESDAY 1 MARCH 2017 07:14

I have been awake since five in my room beside Chen Xi's in the Uppercross House Hotel in Rathmines. I am to help Chen Xi today, but I also want to get home. I hate to be away from Davey and Lin.

Chen Xi was in a bad mood because she thought people had been rude to her at the airport. All she gets from Tan is pressure and opposition. We went to her house and met Donal and the countertop guy. Donal introduced Chen Xi to some of her neighbours.

THURSDAY 2 MARCH 2017

We called the gas and electricity companies and set up direct debit for Chen Xi on her accounts. We drove to Bray, but found that her bank account hadn't opened yet because she didn't yet have the bills from utility providers giving her address. We went to a mobile phone shop, and bought cleaning things. Donal arrived with the new appliances. On the way to lunch Chen Xi became shouty, and I shouted back at her. She started crying. She stayed quiet during lunch. On the way to the next furniture shop she asked me to call a fertility clinic in America, but it was too early their time.

I couldn't sleep. I felt angry with the people I had sent the story to. I tossed and turned, thinking about unfriending them on Facebook, or abandoning Facebook altogether.

FRIDAY 3 MARCH 2017

It has been raining non-stop for a couple of weeks. It is like we are living under water.

I sent emails to California Fertility Partners, drove Chen Xi back to her B&B. It was bucketing. I felt sad leaving her there on her own in the pouring rain. I drove home through flooded roads.

I went to bed and read *Time Travel*, by James Gliek.

SATURDAY 4 MARCH 2017

We sat in the car with rain drumming down on us. The fertility clinic had told Chen Xi that she was too old to provide eggs for a baby. She had bought the house in Bray with a child in mind. Now she'd bought a house that was too big for her, and she didn't feel like she belonged in Ireland. I stroked her back and tried to encourage her, but there wasn't much I could say.

Lin was tender with Chen Xi, and I was happy to see she had such a big heart. She later said Chen Xi had always been the strong girl, and she didn't know how to act when she saw her so hurt. We tried to get her to stay with us, or at least let me drive her back to Bray, but she wouldn't have it.

SUNDAY 5 MARCH 2017

Lin called her parents. Her mom and dad have been fighting, and her mom can be violent. Ancient resentments simmer, then boil over.

MONDAY 6 MARCH 2017

I am becoming an alcoholic. I got beer and Southern Comfort from Joyce's. Lin was playing lego with Davey. Scarlet called on Messenger and we chatted but I was messy drunk. I shouted at Davey. I felt unhinged, shocked by the prospect of our money not being limitless.

TUESDAY 7 MARCH 2017

Lin brought home a flyer seeking host families for a language school, and this gave me a bit of hope that I might be able to teach English again. We could be a host family, and recruit Chinese students for summer camps, that sort of thing.

WEDNESDAY 8 MARCH 2017

I had weird dreams, one of which woke me with its tension. I was sneaking through houses in a Canadian style neighbourhood, searching through fridges for booze to steal. I found a weird bottle of something, and snuck away through the alleyways.

TUESDAY 14 MARCH 2017 06:01

The dawn chorus is a raucous delight. The sky is dark and cool. I heard Davey whimper during the night, went in to him and gave him a sip of water.

At the NDLS office the guy asked me what I do, and I started in on my fifty foreign teachers rigmarole.

SATURDAY 25 MARCH 2017

I still want to know if Greg thinks the Time Machine story can be made to work.

MONDAY 27 MARCH 2017

I have become anxious about my ability to protect Lin and Davey. I feel weak and sloppy. I need to go to the gym.

I feel bad about leaving Lin and Davey alone, but Chen Xi needs me too.

TUESDAY 28 MARCH 2017 07:05

The renovations at Bray seemed to have been done poorly. We couldn't turn on the cooker or the hob. I called Donal and wrangled with him. Eventually he came by and sorted out some of the problems.

Back in town we went to the Horseshow House. I explained to the barman that this was the first place I'd ever been drunk, at 13, spewing honey'd whiskey into the Irish mist.

Chen Xi and I talked about Aihua, how lucky we were to be out of it, about Tan, how he can't tolerate her being friends with me, about Lin, how lucky I am to have her.

WEDNESDAY 29 MARCH 2017

Town was buzzing. We wandered around looking for a sushi place Chen Xi remembered, and a grouchy cloud settled on me. We walked to a place in Temple Bar, but it was crap. We walked to a place on Capel Street, but there were no tables available. We became grumpy with one another. We argued, then sat on the bridge. We went for a pint at the Turk's Head. I told Chen Xi I was sorry for being grouchy. We walked back to the rooms and said good night. I didn't sleep well. I have been worried about all of the money I'm spending recently.

THURSDAY 30 MARCH 2017

After breakfast we drove to the bank. Chen Xi's account still wasn't open. We went to her house and took measurements for beds. Back at the furniture shop she selected beds, a dining room table, and bar stools. I drove Chen Xi back to Bray. She said she would get a bus home from there. I felt bad leaving her alone, but it was nearly rush hour, so I went on.

FRIDAY 31 MARCH 2017

The sky is full of white and purple clouds.

Lin booked tickets to China. I worry about her taking Davey to Heilongjiang. It is so wild.

SATURDAY 1 APRIL 2017

I have been writing this diary for two years, logging what my days were like, and how one day followed another, to prove that all of this actually happened.

THURSDAY 6 APRIL 2017

I stopped at Oranswell and had a walk around. A lot of the trees have blossoms now, and rosebuds are beginning to appear on the trellis structure. One of the workers seems to dislike me, but I should not be so sensitive, always assuming it's about me.

I made a fool of myself on Facebook. I called Kelly an asshole, then said I love you. I chatted with Greg, and had a brief chat with Dan. I don't think I'm so good with Dan anymore. Lin made Miso soup. I was drunk and stupid. I nearly crashed the car going out of our lane. We parked on Threadneedle Road and walked down to the diving board. On the way back, I had a fight with Davey. I felt uncomfortable in my heart because I made such a fool of myself on Facebook. Lin drove home.

SUNDAY 9 APRIL 2017

Two years off cigarettes, one year in Ireland.

MONDAY 10 APRIL 2017

Lin and Davey leave for China today. I am filled with dread whenever we do anything different. I am a fearful person.

I pray they will be safe.

They will be in transit for 20 hours. I will follow on the 19th.

TUESDAY 11 APRIL 2017

I couldn't sleep. I have a pain in my chest, a sore heart that is not figurative. I have a wetness in my throat and a battery taste. I don't know what's wrong with me, but it isn't good.

I had followed the GPS to avoid the first toll gate, and went through a police stop. The policeman asked me where I was from, and I went into the rigamarole: a difficult question to answer; Tanzania, China, Canada, Ireland? He told Lin I was confused. Thankfully, he didn't ask for licences. When we got to the airport, Lin checked in and we ate McDonalds. We said goodbye at passport control.

I picked up a frozen pizza and three tins of beer at Joyce's, sat in the backyard drinking beer and read Facebook, something about an airline pulling a passenger off a flight because they had overbooked. Once you enter an airport you are in a dystopian space with no human rights. When I went up to bed, I felt awful, I guess from sitting all day. I took two painkillers, then another. The house was eerie and wrong without Davey and Lin. I tossed and turned. I was scared I might die in the night.

I think I should go to the barber. I look silly with long hair.

THURSDAY 13 APRIL 2017

I drank while I chatted with Lin. She said Davey's Chinese isn't great.

I woke at two and read an article on Facebook about how reading Facebook decreases quality of life.

FRIDAY 14 APRIL 2017

I chatted with Lin. She was at Zhang Yu Ti's apartment. Davey didn't pay any attention to me, and Lin was cranky. Zhang You Ti dashed across the screen and called me Poopy. Her mom laughed at my beard, and Lin told me my haircut was crap.

North Korea is threatening nuclear war. Heilongjiang is right beside the North Korean border. If I said this to Lin, we would fight.

TUESDAY 18 APRIL 2017

I took photos of everything in case we were robbed. It was good to be on the open road. I stopped at the service station near Portumna, had a sub, and got some coffee. When I got to Dublin, I went on a mission to Oliver Bond Street where I was arrested years ago. It is a sort of Chinatown now. It is certainly not as rough as it was. I got instant coffee, whitener, and tea, a little bottle of whiskey and some Sprite.

I went to Grogans and sat down beside a table full of old Grogonians. I drank whiskey and Guinness. I was laughing at their jokes, and they included me. One of the guys looked like Brendan Behan. I told them my grandfather had been a friend of Brendan Behan. Then I started blabbering about 50 foreign teachers. I left not a moment too soon. I don't like sleeping in a strange bed. They always smell a little off.

WEDNESDAY 19 APRIL 2017

I had a window seat. I was amazed to see so many wind turbines between the UK and the Netherlands. I found my gate for Beijing, got a croissant with cheese, and a bag of liquorice. After a glass of wine and an aperitif I watched *Dr Strange*. I stood for a while. My back was sore. I watched *Twelve Years a Slave*. I had to turn it off during one of the whippings. It was too cruel.

THURSDAY 20 APRIL 2017

I am in a suite in the Marriott Hotel in Beijing. Lin and Davey are asleep in the other room. I had three or four hours' sleep after 24 hours awake, and am now on my second cup of instant coffee. I finished the entry for the 19th, although it is hard to tell where one day ends and another day begins.

At the airport a young *laowai* advised me to ignore the taxi guys. I thought about saying I am *Beijingren* but didn't bother. I lined up at the rank, got a cab to Shijingshan. The cab crawled along the Fifth Ring Road. It took an hour and a half to get to the Wan Shan Hotel. I inquired after Lin, and they sent me to the third floor. Davey ran to give me a hug, and Lin gave me a kiss.

We packed up their things, and got a cab to the Muslim restaurant. We had a few dishes and a couple bottles of Yanjing. Then we went to the Police Station so I could register. We had to wait for it to open at two. A crowd had gathered, and we were all eyeing the door. We squeezed in, shoulder to shoulder. It was something out of Kafka, only with more smells. The counters were swarming with peasants. Stern cops behind glass. They asked what we needed, then sat chatting, ignoring us, without giving back the passport sitting right in front of them.

We got a cab to the next hotel in *Dongzhimen*. I began to fade on the way through *Gongzhufen, Xidan, Tiananmen*. I kept falling asleep and waking with a jolt. Lin told me she'd already paid for four days at the next hotel. I was sulky, because we hadn't even seen it yet.

The hotel was grim. The street was under construction and we had to drag suitcases through building rubble. Reception was on the 3rd floor. The girls behind the counter acted like the police in *Shijingshan*, chatting among themselves while we stood in front of their desk. It was a *Hebei* person's idea of what a good hotel should be–a large buffet hall, a conference room of Chinese workers diligently listening. Davey and I went up to the room. It looked nice, but smelled of cigarettes. Lin tried to cancel the room. I was beginning to hallucinate from lack of sleep. The young lady continued typing while lending half an ear to Lin's complaints. I jumped in wild-eyed and blazing, and we got our money back.

Sitting on our suitcases amidst building rubble outside, we decided to go to the Marriott. My spirits lifted. I pushed two armchairs together for Davey's bed, then crashed. Lin came in later but I couldn't even open my eyes.

FRIDAY 21 APRIL 2017 07:02

We are in the Marriott Hotel in Beijing. We are on the 19th floor. Big windows and a spectacular view.

We were entitled to an evening buffet, so we sat down. There were several bottles of hard liquor. I had Kalua, rum and

Malibu mixed together. Then, I got the lady to make me a martini. This was the first time I enjoyed a martini. I was loud and happy, the life of the buffet. Lin warned me not to wind up with a headache, so I made the martini my last drink.

Lin ran me a bubble bath and Davey got in with me. Davey slept between us. He was laughing in his dream.

SATURDAY 22 APRIL 2017

We are in Swissotel. Davey is watching TV, and Lin is saying goodbye to her crappy friend from Shandong. I am wrecked, having had a feed of martini.

The view here is majestic on a day like this—we can see the mountains to the west through the clear blue sky.

When Lin was signing in, I thought the staff were rude, so I criticised them, and we got an upgrade for my efforts. We went upstairs and settled, and Lin's friend came up. I didn't like her from the get go. Lin and she went for lunch, and Davey and I followed. Davey was angry because we didn't order the chicken he wanted, and he threw his chopsticks. I tried to pull him out and he held onto the table so I pried his fingers free and pulled him down the road, where I spanked him angrily. Then he said just kill me, I want to be dead. I felt so bad. I still needed him to understand that it was wrong to throw chopsticks. When he eventually agreed it was wrong we went back to the restaurant. He was exhausted.

Later Davey and I went out for dinner at the bar downstairs. I had a martini and he had a cheesecake. We walked up to where The Den used to be. On the way back to the hotel, I saw Lin's friend leaving the building with a boy, and no Lin. She tried to hide from me, and when I got to the hotel bar I saw she had phoned Lin twice after seeing me. I had a martini and tried to call Lin but couldn't reach her. I had another martini then went up to the room. I sent insulting messages to Cherry Dou Dou and Li Yue. I also sent angry messages to the little bitch from Shandong. I emptied the mini bar. Eventually Cherry Dou Dou brought Lin back. Lin was so drunk she could hardly stand, and when she got in, she puked and puked. I feel awful about the things Davey has been exposed to.

SUNDAY 23 APRIL 2017

Yesterday there was amazing *doujiang* at breakfast, and I drank gallons. Lin and I were hung over, moving as though through honey. I sent Cherry and Li Yue apologetic messages. We took the subway to Silk Street. We looked at Chinese ornaments. I wanted jade dragons, dragon masks, vases, bowls, and tea cups.

WEDNESDAY 26 APRIL 2017 07:25

I am drinking Nescafe 2+1 in our room at the *Mudanjiang* Holiday Inn. My nose is stuffed from the dust, so I no longer notice that the room smells of smoke accented by a layer of perfume.

Yesterday after breakfast we hung around the room, because once we left we'd be out on the street until we got to the airport. After a shower I jumped up on the ledge of the big window and waggled my naked body at the whole city. Lin and Davey were in hysterics. The flight wasn't bad. I read more of *Sapiens*. *Mudanjiang* airport was appalling. Our taxi driver seemed half comatose, and ferried us through a wretched city full of potholes, police in armoured trucks, cranky citizens.

The hotel had no restaurant. A crappy little Russian shop sold Russian beer. We sat at what they called a bar and ordered french fries and onion rings, cooked by invisible chefs in a dark hall. I tried to joke with the server, but she was having none of it. When we finished I ordered cognac and took it up to the room.

THURSDAY 27 APRIL 2017 01:04

We are in an even crappier hotel in *Lin Kou*. So far, this adventure has been a nightmare. I feel like Eustace in *The*

Voyage of the Dawn Treader. We rented a car and drove to Lin's hometown. I put on a 70's playlist.

We found Lin's brother's home. The electricity was out and I was already tired of it all. We walked to the little park nearby, where I was swarmed by a gang of Chinese guys who thought I was Russian. We walked up through the town to the police station, and Lin updated her identity card. We walked back to her brother's place, then got a taxi into town for *huoguo*. The driver was blabbering something about Russia while crunching on an apple–when he was done he opened the window beside me and tossed it past my face.

Lin's sister's husband sat beside me at dinner; he pushed me to drink, and clung to my shoulder, blabbering in my ear the whole night. Later, he touched Davey's penis, as they all seem to do around here. Davey had fun running around with his cousins. He started to use more Chinese. Everyone kept giving him treats. Lin's brother gave him beer and he got a bit drunk.

We went back to Lin's brother's place. The electricity still wasn't working, and our phones ran out of power. We shuffled into the dark room with the *kang* and tried to sleep but it was too uncomfortable for me. I was allergic to the pillows. I had a fight with Lin, and stood for a few hours. I got diarrhoea and had to hover over the squat toilet in absolute blackness. The next morning I woke up shell shocked. I stared up at a centipede with elbows and even a face. Lin's sister-in-law brought breakfast and spread it out on the *kang*.

We had a walk with Lin's mom, her sister and brother in law. The place was so poor. We passed over a rickety bridge. A venomous yellow pool of poison ran alongside the river. Later we went for a drive with Lin's mom to gather dandelions for dinner in a landscape like the foothills west of Calgary, but this is the Alberta in which Spock has a goatee. We saw sheep, and were told to watch out for ticks.

We have rented a hotel room in *Lin Kou*. It is crap, but at least there is no *kang*, and there is electricity.

FRIDAY 28 APRIL 2017

I didn't sleep well. I am too soft for the hardships that Lin's family take for granted.

We met them for dinner. Dinner was tripe, duck heads, and croakers. We took a family photo, and Lin was happy. Lin's dad was old and tired, a Zen master of indifference.

I was getting sodden on beer. Lin's brother in law pulled his chair closer to Lin's sister, put his hand on her shoulder and asked me, is this how I should do it? He was joking about how attentive I was to Lin, placing the choicest morsels on her dish. I said yes, and gave Lin a kiss on the cheek. Lin pushed me away, scandalised. Her mother shrieked with delight; her father smiled with satisfaction.

After dinner the kids went out, and I followed them around the square. Davey likes his big cousins and he is possessive of Liu Hao. He let me follow, but got angry if I interrupted and told him what to do. The square was lively with dancing, tai chi, and families strolling. We said good night and went back to our hotel. I find it difficult to be here. Davey has family here, but this isn't somewhere I could live. It will be a tough two days, but Lin will be happy if I can pull it off.

SATURDAY 29 APRIL 2017 06:47

Outside is a terrible white.

We climbed the stairs to the temple, looking for the morning market. We had noodles and jiaozi. I love the steaming vats, the wonky table and chairs.

We grabbed our bags and drove to Lin's mom's place. We had to hang around because her dad was off getting intravenous medicine. We went to her sister's house and that was fine until I spotted a heap of human faeces piled in their garden.

Lin's brother got a car. We collected the parents, the sister, sister in law, and Liu Hao. We drove in a northeasterly direction. We were stopped by the police, who looked in at me, puzzled, but they didn't give us any problems. We drove for two hours, then stopped at a temple where the monks were women. We bought incense, and they burned it and prayed. Lin's mom burned incense in a room with a statue of the

Buddha. A monk criticised her. We stopped for lunch in a strange, empty city. There were apartment blocks, shopping malls, and squares, but all had been empty since being finished five years prior. The whole thing sat in a gravelly river basin, emptied when they'd built a dam. We gave Lin's dad a tweed cap and vest. He showed us the eight layers of clothing he wore at all times, sleeping and waking, never changing. They are another, thicker skin. People were praying at Fox Spirit Cave. There was red firework paper everywhere, drifting into little piles. We walked up toward the dam. At the top we could see the emptied valley beyond. It was threatening rain on the way back to *Lin Kou*. There were no streetlights and no reflective surface on the road.

The rest of the family showed up at the restaurant. I finished early, and hung around with the kids. We walked to the temple at the top of the stairs. I filmed a group of people walking silently in a circle to a Buddhist chant. Davey wanted water, so I took him back to where Lin was getting drunk with the girls. She was sweet and funny.

I am glad to have stuck this out. I am also happy it is almost over. I have been given a new perspective– while we talk about making our Galway house airtight, Lin's parents live in a rickety shack, with gaping holes between cinder blocks and the corrugated iron roof. But family is everything here. They have nothing, and they live in squalor, but they stick together, and look after each other. Davey can feel this, and he would like to be a part of it, and has even spoken of wanting to stay here. He is a treasured member of this family, the very definition of good fortune.

SUNDAY 30 APRIL 2017

We are back at the Swissotel. Davey is laying on the bed; he will fall asleep soon.

Yesterday, at breakfast at the hotel in *Lin Kou* we watched a guy stuff handfuls of boiled eggs into his trouser pockets. I am thinking I'd like to work this trip to *Lin Kou* into the story, to contrast it with my visit to my dad on Denman Island.

Lin read my diary and cried. She said it is your diary and you should say what you think.

MONDAY 1 MAY 2017

We had dinner with Cherry Dou Dou, then I took Davey to the beer garden behind the hotel, where I had a martini.

We'd been shopping on Silk Street earlier, bought jade dragons and a dragon mask. One woman ran after me shouting Money Bags! Lin asked her, what? and it turned out she was selling money bags, not alerting all to the presence of a mark.

I talked to Davey about how my mom died and decided to add something to the story–a time loop in my mom's room on Westview Drive. I made notes on my phone–the empty room, the bed stripped of sheets, the girl washing the body, those two men carrying her down the stairs in a chair.

Back at the room I talked to Davey about truth and knowledge. I asked him how do you know you are not dreaming, that everything is not just a dream? I turned to read my book and after a few minutes Davey said I know this isn't a dream because I can think.

TUESDAY 2 MAY 2017

It is grim and polluted.

Lin dressed to go out for the evening, and I loved her madly as she walked out the door.

Lin got home about half eleven. I knelt at her feet in the bathroom. It has been done, and done again, and this softens me.

WEDNESDAY 3 MAY 2017 05:33

Lin is awake, looking at her phone. Today is very dirty, 331 according to the app. The air is yellow muck. The alarm is set for 5:45, and we leave for the airport at 6:15.

THURSDAY 4 MAY 2017

Yesterday morning in Beijing the pollution was beyond register. I worried our flight would be cancelled because visibility was low. We got out by the skin of our teeth around eleven–a sandstorm kicked in soon after and flights were cancelled. I watched *Captain Fantastic*. There was a crazy *Dongbei* lady in front of us, and she annoyed me, mainly her haircut.

I talked to Chen Xi and she is happy with Tan in Bray with her. She sent a photo of the back doors open to the Sugarloaf.

THURSDAY 11 MAY 2017

I dreamed I had decided to take Davey to Canada to meet my dad. It felt strange that I hadn't done so already. I told Lin to get Davey a visa. Even when I woke up I mused: this will be great, seeing Davey and my dad together. I even thought of jokes, how I would tease my dad that Davey had his lucky ears.

FRIDAY 12 MAY 2017

Chen Xi and Lin are chatting in Chen Xi's kitchen. Chen Xi is frying eggs. I have a cup of tea beside me. Today we will go to Ikea with Chen Xi. It will be a busy day, then Lin and I will go out in Dublin and spend the night in a B&B. I will leave the car here, and we can take the Dart.

SATURDAY 13 MAY 2017

I am looking over the Liffey. Lin is quiet in the other room. Davey is in Bray with Chen Xi. It is a beautiful day. I have a hangover.

Yesterday we walked into town, through Grogans, and then on to Ms Fantasia. There were some serious little criminals in the Spar. We had octopus ink pasta in the busy alleyway near Grogans. Lin had Prosecco and I had red beer. Then we had Brandy Alexanders. We went to the Wiley Fox, where the fetish nights were held. *Nimhneach*. At first I got Lin Mojitos, but she wasn't getting drunk on girl drinks so we switched to Guinness. As we were walking out, Lin found a black wing brooch connected to me. She pinned this good omen to her bag. I spotted a goth club, so we went in. People were dressed like the Sisters of Mercy. My Lucretia came on and I went out for a crazy dance, the first one on the floor.

SUNDAY 14 MAY 2017

Back in Bray we caught up with Chen Xi and Davey, who were walking toward the seafront. Davey jumped up and down when he saw us. I was relieved to see that he and Chen Xi had got along. Chen Xi and Davey went to the playground while Lin and I had eggs Benedict. The cup of tea was especially nice. Chen Xi and Lin walked around Bray Head while Davey and I hiked to the summit.

THURSDAY 19 MAY 2017

Lin and I lay entwined before getting up. We haven't fought in ages, and we are loving and supportive of one another. Life seems to have worked out.

SATURDAY 20 MAY 2017

I collected Chen Xi, brought her through the garden entrance, and showed her the secret place down by the stream. Lin found some *jiucai*, and gathered an armful for our scrambled eggs in the morning.

I served the ladies wine and crab meat, and put on some classical music. I prepared the wedgies while Lin gutted the fish. We gossiped about Aihua. The ladies kept drinking and laughing.

SUNDAY 21 MAY 2017

It was a blustery morning at the hurling pitch. We met Thomas and his dad as soon as we arrived. The coaches lent Davey a helmet and a hurl, and they started in immediately.

It was a great atmosphere. Davey didn't stop running around. It rained heavily the whole time but they kept going. The pitch was just around the corner from our new house. Practice ended with a scrimmage, and Davey threw himself into it. There were minor injuries, but the kids weren't coddled. Later, Chen Xi pointed out that you couldn't do this in China because the parents would sue.

In town, Lin fed swans. She let them eat right out of her hand.

TUESDAY 23 MAY 2017

I took tools into the forest at Oranswell, and cut dead wood into smaller pieces. I wore a nimbus of midges around my head. I worked for a couple of hours before I noticed blisters on my hands, so I shifted to piling the slippery wood in the middle of the clearing.

THURSDAY 25 MAY 2017

We parked on Threadneedle Road, walked to the rocks and sat. I took off my shoes and socks, rolled up my trousers and stood in the lapping water. We lay on the rocks under the blue sky.

FRIDAY 26 MAY 2017

I woke up at two and didn't sleep again until after four. My ears had been ringing since we'd used the wood chipping machine yesterday. I hate machines.

The shredder was the size of a car. He took it to the back of the garden on the cow man's road, and pushed it up against the wall. He showed us how to run it then left. Lin and I ran the wood through the shredder. It was enough to make a man feel small and easily mulched.

SUNDAY 28 MAY 2017

So much bird song in the garden. We found a dead bird that had flown into one of the windows and we put him in the stream in a small bier Davey had devised.

We cut down saplings from around the house and the rose gardens. We pulled these out to the shredder. Lin put tissue paper in her ears and Davey's. Davey sat in the car. Lin turned on the machine and we ran the last of the wood through. We went back into the garden and drank tea from the thermos Lin prepared. It was beautiful and ours.

TUESDAY 30 MAY 2017

Lin with her family online: chatting, laughing, drinking. It was Dragon Boat Day. I went upstairs and lay down. Lin played guzheng.

SATURDAY 3 JUNE 2017

Another terrorist incident last night. Three guys drove a white van into the crowd on London Bridge, then got out and started stabbing.

TUESDAY 6 JUNE 2017

I cleared out a wall of brambles. Then I cut through the rhododendron or laurel or whatever it is, to gain entrance to the little alcove in the northeast corner.

We parked on Threadneedle Road. It rained, but it was a beautiful day of majestic clouds. We sat watching the waves.

SATURDAY 10 JUNE 2017

The house in Oranswell has cost a lot, and we won't have much cushion after it is paid off. We need to make some money.

SUNDAY 11 JUNE 2017

Drops of rain on the window. I feel like I'm trapped in a magic lamp.

THURSDAY 22 JUNE 2017

Four toilets, two showers, three sinks, and a bath.

SATURDAY 24 JUNE 2017

After dinner, we went to the garden. I started to make the spirals coming into the centre of the circle by laying down stones. Lin cut down the plant that was choking the eucalyptus. We need to do the same for the oak tree, cut down the dogwood crowding the ornamental trees, and the grape vines cinching the trellis structure.

TUESDAY 27 JUNE 2017

We cut away at the grape vines wrapped around the trellis structure. Davey collected grape leaves, and put them in the wheelbarrow. We cleared space for the roses. The grape vines grow so quickly, and tie themselves into everything.

FRIDAY 30 JUNE 2017

I located the centre of the apple circle, drew a metre wide circle around it. Red bugles curled over long grass beneath the apple trees.

I got a message from *Nimhneach*. I talked to Lin and we agreed to commit to it.

I was feeling guilty for getting weed, and resolved to be careful with it this time. I want to become a more reasonable person. I want to do yoga, meditation and tai chi in Lin's big Zen room. I want to spend an hour every day in the library teaching Davey something.

I had a toot in the back garden. A half moon hung low, just above the houses across from me. There were two stars in the clear, darkening sky. At the horizon on the other side, just above more houses, there was a band of daylight.

Yesterday Davey said some crazy thing about how my mom had her arms and legs sawn off. I probably said something like this when I was drunk in Beijing. I bent down and told him that I had had a sad life, but that now, he and mommy make me happy.

SATURDAY 1 JULY 2017

Nimhneach

Lin and I left Davey with Chen Xi, and drove to the B&B in Dublin. We walked to Ms Fantasia. Lin tried on a few things, then settled on latex. I got a few bits and bobs. Back at the room, I smoked dope and drank whiskey and beer. Lin changed into her dominatrix catsuit. She got a few catcalls as we walked down the Liffey to the fetish party, but we were mostly unnoticed. The party was wilder than I could have hoped. There were crops and whips, and a dog man snuffling around Lin's ankles. The next morning, Lin had a sore head. She puked out the window on the drive to Bray.

SUNDAY 2 JULY 2017

When we got to Bray, Chen Xi made us tea and breakfast, and gave Lin some Chinese medicine. We drove to Powerscourt, had a walk around the gardens, and laid down on the grass.

THURSDAY 6 JULY 2017

Crossing the canal lock at the *Claddagh*, we saw thousands of jellyfish, a translucent purple swarming. The climate is changing, bringing them up from Spain.

FRIDAY 7 JULY 2017

We dumped ten bags of yellow stones in the centre of the stone circle. We raked them across the central circle, and down the spiral arms to the larger circle.

Davey and I put shiny black and white stones in the centre to make yin and yang.

SUNDAY 9 JULY 2017

We went to the hippy shop, and bought a piece of quartz on a string. We are each going to carry this for a day, then we are going to bury it in the centre of the stone circle. The lady in the shop cleansed it for us by burning sage. We will need to do that smudging trick for our house before we move in. Davey put the crystal around his neck and we went out.

TUESDAY 11 JULY 2017

There is a far off moon in the blue sky. I am wearing the crystal, and we will bury it today. Davey has been conscious of the workings of the crystal. We must imbue it with our wishes.

WEDNESDAY 19 JULY 2017

Lin and Chen Xi mostly drank white wine at dinner. They were happy and laughing. Chen Xi commented on how well Lin and I work together.

SUNDAY 20 AUGUST 2017

I dreamed we had otters on our property, and Ralph and Sam were there. It is possible that Ralph was Davey.

We went to the gym at Clybaun. After a run, I sat in the hot tub in the rain. I was alone, so I closed my eyes and did some meditation. When I breathed in I followed the breath to the top of my head and let light burst from the solar anus.

SATURDAY 26 AUGUST 2017

I got in the car at nine and drove to Bray. Chen Xi spent the first hour or so I was there obsessively cleaning, and I sat in the garden with Chen Fu. I kept admiring his old Chinese face. We had been loyal to each other for years.

I slipped out as soon as I could. The road was empty.

SUNDAY 27 AUGUST 2017

Sometimes a real meanness comes over me. This time I caught myself becoming impatient, and was able to stifle the rage building in my head.

THURSDAY 31 AUGUST 2017

Davey called for Lin, and I sighed as I stood to go upstairs. Lin told me not to get angry with him. I thought this was a weird thing to say, because I didn't have any intention of being angry, though things got nasty between Lin and I very quickly. She said we shouldn't get excited about little things. She said I never read books about childhood development. I said she didn't love me or respect me and she said now we understand each other.

I couldn't bear this, and started swearing. Davey called down don't leave daddy. When he came down for his breakfast he was crying. For the rest of the day I had no strength.

FRIDAY 1 SEPTEMBER 2017

Davey is on our bed chatting to himself. Lin is making breakfast for Chen Fu and Hu Laoshi. It looks like it will be a nice day.

I drove everyone to Oranswell to show them the garden. I'm not sure they were that fussed–only said it would take a lot of work. Hulaoshi refused to go through the tunnel of leaves formed by the trellis structure.

SUNDAY 3 SEPTEMBER 2017

Chen Xi wanted to go home to Bray after breakfast, but Chen Fu wanted to stay longer. The rain stopped as soon as we arrived at Ashford Castle. Chen Fu and Hulaoshi were impressed. We strolled through the gardens, saw people playing with falcons.

When we arrived in town the sun was still out and it was a beautiful evening. I parked at the *Claddagh*, and we walked up Shop Street. We stopped at the Dial bar and went upstairs. I ordered everyone a pint and we watched the All Ireland Hurling Final between Galway and Tipperary. Then, we went up to Eyre Square and watched the rest of the match on the big screen. Galway won and the throng went wild. Chen Fu emerged from the thick of things festooned in Galway tassels.

MONDAY 4 SEPTEMBER 2017

Davey lost his first baby tooth yesterday and received a two euro coin from the tooth fairy. Outside, there are dark grey clouds, and the light is strange.

I had a dream where I was getting ready to move into my dad's big island house after he died, but then found he'd left the house to Scarlet. I had to live in a little shack. I went to the land of the dead and cursed him. I had a hard time getting this out of my head.

I helped Lin get breakfast ready for Hulaoshi and Chen Fu. They said goodbye to Davey, then I took him to school. When we got to the bus station, Chen Fu gave me a look that reminded me of the look my father gave me the last time I saw him. Maybe that was what made last night's dream. I felt empty once they were gone.

Lin and I drove home. I was careful what I said because I didn't want to fight. She had been good to help out with Chen Xi's family, and she proved that she is big hearted. I knew she was thinking her parents would likely never visit us.

WEDNESDAY 6 SEPTEMBER 2017

Davey kept pestering me with questions while I was trying to navigate a skinny road against oncoming traffic. I slapped him on the leg and he started screaming that he hated me. I stopped the car and went around to pull him out. He was in tears; my heart felt like a lump of lava.

I don't know why this has to happen, and why I can't manage it better. He doesn't listen, and kids should listen to their parents, at least a bit. He doesn't feel any obligation to obey me. I don't think that is good.

Later, he called me up, and we lay in bed together.

THURSDAY 7 SEPTEMBER 2017

I had another fight with Davey. I felt the wind blowing around inside my head as I dragged him upstairs screaming and crying. He is spoiled and disobedient, but I should be dealing with his behaviour differently.

I chatted with Chen Xi. I was drunk and messy, and she criticised me. I put photos of her parents with me up on facebook; later I took them down hoping Tan had not seen them yet.

SUNDAY 10 SEPTEMBER 2017

The alarm woke me from a convoluted dream. I think Ralph was in it, or someone like a little brother. There was a dirty toilet. There was Cort in one bed with a girl, and me in another. There was a little guy hitting me with a paddle while I choked him. My dreams have been violent recently. This dream felt like part of a longer sequence.

TUESDAY 12 SEPTEMBER 2017

When I collected Davey, he looked tired. On the way home, he tried to fight with me, but I was patient, and I employed reason. I didn't allow myself to become angry.

THURSDAY 14 SEPTEMBER 2017

I had a weird dream in which I was chatting with a table of muslim women. Their husbands took them out to spank them for talking to me. I realised I had lost Davey. I went to a Chinese shop across the road, and he was playing on a kang with some other Chinese kids. He was mad at me, so I walked away. He followed me.

I wish Davey and I could stop fighting. I worry that he will take advantage of my patience, become even more spoiled. I think of him as having a character like my mom and me, always on the defensive, ready for war, to up the stakes out of insecurity. We are people who say horrible things to each other.

He is a good kid though. When we buried the crystal in the stone circle his wish was that we wouldn't fight anymore.

FRIDAY 15 SEPTEMBER 2017

I met Darby when I got out of the car and we walked the two

boys to the hurling pitch. I said those are two great kids. The future of Ireland, he replied.

WEDNESDAY 20 SEPTEMBER 2017

I had a few hoots, and looked up at the stars. I went way, way up, and thought I was the greatest man in history, with the greatest achievements, and my victories had only begun.

This morning I crashed, and now I am fearful. My inner dialogue veers between "Look what I have done!" and "My god what have I done?"

I walked down to the heron bridge at the end of the road, spinning out magnificent ideas for how to make everything work out perfectly.

TUESDAY 26 SEPTEMBER 2017

I am not dealing well. The dope has made me stupid and forgetful. I am drinking too much. I'm just not clear. It is dangerous and scary. It has been hard waiting for the house to be finished. I fly between confidence and self contempt.

WEDNESDAY 27 SEPTEMBER 2017

Just finished off the last of the dope, and looked at the final bill for the work on the house. The number was what I expected, although I will have to look at it again with a clear mind.

THURSDAY 28 SEPTEMBER 2017

We got the keys to the house tonight, and plan to sleep there tomorrow night.

FRIDAY 29 SEPTEMBER 2017

A mouse just ran and hid beneath the recycle box, but as this is our last day in Fionnula's house, I don't care.

Tom and his guys helped me move furniture. We turned on the refrigerator, and it began to hum.

I collected Davey from Andrew's house. I didn't want to go in, but they insisted. They sat me in a comfy chair. Galway people are kind and we are lucky to have landed here, though that doesn't stop me from feeling awkward in their presence. The house was so clean, the vibe so wholesome. Rosemary gave me a plate of buns at the door.

2

THE HOUSE AT ORANSWELL

SATURDAY 30 SEPTEMBER 2017

First morning in the new house. I am sitting at the big table in the library. I have a cup of coffee beside me. We all slept in one bed.

Yesterday morning I started moving things before breakfast, drove back and forth. We unpacked and tidied up, then I sat with Davey in the two ox blood recliners in the library. After that we lay on yoga matts on the hardwood floor of the Zen room while Lin played guzheng. A cheerless light smirked behind the blustery trees.

Good location. Good house. Good car. A background in Irish history and culture. Chinese. I shouldn't be afraid. And yet I am, and that is why I need to be patient with Davey.

. . .

TUESDAY 3 OCTOBER 2017

Padraig set up the Narnia lamp posts. I unpacked boxes and put books in the bookshelves while Davey did his homework. Lin had an evening class at the university. She is learning to forage.

WEDNESDAY 4 OCTOBER 2017

I dreamed a rabbit hiding under the bed. We were worried that it would starve if it stayed there.

THURSDAY 5 OCTOBER 2017

We heard strange noises and I went downstairs with the knife. Lin brought a hurling stick. But it was just the creaking of the house.

Davey and I discussed him sleeping in his own room, and he said he'd be ready when he was twelve or thirteen. When I said other kids sleep alone, he pointed out that they have brothers and sisters. Later Davey sat with me in the garden while I drank a beer, and then a whiskey. We watched the sun pass above the trees. I went down the tunnel made by the grape vines over the trellis to the centre of the little forest. I looked down into the stream.

. . .

FRIDAY 6 OCTOBER 2017

Lin is tidying the kitchen, humming to herself. Davey is looking at a book in an armchair beside me.

SATURDAY 7 OCTOBER 2017

I see two white horses in the field across from me, and call Davey to have a look.

Books, zinc, bath salts, and essential oils. I drank Chinese tea, and Lin had a bath. I put a candle under the oil burner in the Zen room.

TUESDAY 10 OCTOBER 2017

Storm sound; rush of rain against windows.

FRIDAY 13 OCTOBER 2017

I went to Bray to collect Chen Xi. On the drive back to Galway, she told me about a sort of *Chi Gong* she is doing. You stand, and then spirits dictate your motions, according to the postures that will help you heal. It is a jazz yoga meditation breathing concoction.

When we got home, I began to hoot and drink. Lin showed Chen Xi around, then prepared dinner. I stayed out of the way. I played music. I invented a new drink with soya milk and whiskey. It was Christmassy.

I went for a walk around the property with the flashlight. Someone called out hello, and I said hello. It was the farmer. He said who is it? and I said it's your neighbour. He said, is it David? I said yes, shall I come over to you? I was drunk and blabbering about China is where the money is. I'm not sure if he was holding something dead in that sack or not.

The others went to bed. I kept smoking and drinking. I put photos on Facebook. I took them down in the morning.

SATURDAY 14 OCTOBER 2017

The weather is weird.

I snipped branches around the house. Lin, Chen Xi and Davey gathered hawthorn berries to make syrup. I prepared a cheese board, and poured red wine for the ladies. Chen Xi played checkers with Davey. I cooked steak. After dinner, I drank and hooted while Davey watched *Nexo Knights* upstairs. Chen Xi showed Lin her meditation thing in the Zen room.

A hurricane is coming. I need to move all the branches I cut yesterday, and clean up any other debris around the place.

. . .

SUNDAY 15 OCTOBER 2017

The hurricane will be here in less than an hour. I have never seen a hurricane. I am worried the house will be damaged. I moved anything that could be picked up by the wind and thrown at the house. Chen Xi did her meditation thing in the Zen room. I told Chen Xi and Lin that the hurricane was serious, that buses wouldn't run tomorrow. Chen Xi decided to get a bus home before the hurricane arrived. Lin gave her a bottle of hawthorn syrup to take with her.

MONDAY 16 OCTOBER 2017

We had a nice lunch and I started on the cider at 12. We watched the approach of the eye on the iPad. The hurricane winds were strong, but the trees protected us from the worst of it. When the eye was right over us, there was silence, and it was like the most serene summer's day for half an hour.

THURSDAY 19 OCTOBER 2017

Lin thinks I smoke too much dope. She said it made me into a different person, forgetful and muddled. I know this is true.

After dinner, I smoked a joint, and I became very paranoid. I thought, what have I done buying a big showy house? I moved the camera, swords, guitars, and computers away from the windows. I felt vulnerable, menaced, foolish.

FRIDAY 20 OCTOBER 2017

Yesterday morning when I sent Davey to school I chatted with Ultan. His parents' house at Glenlo Abbey had been robbed the evening before. The gardai said the thieves come from Dublin. Someone drops them off and comes back later to collect them. They are looking for jewellery or cash.

I spent a long time snipping, but when I showed Lin she didn't see much difference. It was raining all day, and I was wet and cold. My hands were scratched by brambles. Lin and Davey were playing, so I read Seamus Heaney. I was frightened and amazed by *The Death of a Naturalist*.

THURSDAY 26 OCTOBER 2017

Lin dreamed that she found a tiny stone. Its skin pulled back to reveal an insect skeleton that seemed to possess a dark power. When she touched it the dark power surged up her finger and turned it black. She threw the stone in the water, and the water turned black. She tried to escape the stone, but it followed her. She found a monk who agreed to help. He held the stone, but it took great effort. Lin understood that he was utilising *Chi Gong*.

It has been a weird week. We all feel lost. The house is nice, but it is hard to change so many habits, to have to learn new ways of doing things. None of us are used to such a big house, to country living.

SATURDAY 28 OCTOBER 2017

Davey slept in his bed alone for the first time in the new house. I got a bit angry at him for squirming around as I was trying to read *The Rabbit Who Wanted to Sleep*. I said I was going to finish and he held onto me and wouldn't let me go. I cuddled him for a time, then went to bed. We talked a while on the walkie talkies, and I went to see him a couple of times. He fell asleep after that. The view from this window is like a postcard.

SUNDAY 29 OCTOBER 2017

I swept leaves with the new broom. A cat came by and I called Lin and Davey out to see him. He is a handsome little guy with good manners. He went right in, and Lin gave him milk.

TUESDAY 31 OCTOBER 2017

I chatted to Fred online. It was depressing. I have been thinking about Aihua recently, regretting that I gave it up. I shouldn't feel that way–we are better off here– but life feels like an endless stream of Sundays.

THURSDAY 2 NOVEMBER 2017

After I mowed the lawn, I went along the eastern edge of the garden cutting the hedges back and pulling things out. Lin worked beside me, pulling ivy from trees, and then she went in and baked bread.

Recently I've felt like she has given up on me. I will write to Chen Xi and tell her Lin has SAD; suggest a visit.

FRIDAY 3 NOVEMBER 2017

I let Davey watch TV while I read *Crock of Gold*, and Lin played guzheng. When we went up to bed, Lin read to Davey, then I stayed with him until he fell asleep. We pretended the bed could fly, and we were way up among the clouds.

It is hard to get used to this life. It is so lonely.

MONDAY 6 NOVEMBER 2017

I am losing weight. Lin says I don't eat much. My trousers are falling off me. Lin said I am very stubborn. I think this was meant as a compliment.

Such heavy rain.

The cat returned to milk warmed in the microwave.

TUESDAY 7 NOVEMBER 2017

I have been up since 5:10. The cat was out last night, and it was very cold, so when I heard him crying I went down to let him in.

I had a big fight with Davey, and I am not happy with how I behaved. I don't know how to help him grow up. I have been talking to him about good behaviour and fairness, but I worry he is, like me, too easily led by his moods. The drugs and booze make me less able to control my mood. I feel bleary, and when I get wrecked in the evenings, I get really wrecked.

I lay down in bed beside Davey, and waited for him to fall asleep. The moon was huge and yellow.

WEDNESDAY 8 NOVEMBER 2017

This is a crazy house.

I read some translations by Ezra Pound. There was one poem in particular that struck me, his version of To-Em-Mei's "The Unmoving Cloud."

. . .

FRIDAY 10 NOVEMBER 2017

We took Davey up to bed, and Lin read to him. I lay beside him for a while. I want the best for him. I wish I could be a better father. I need to be calmer, cooler, smarter.

Yesterday I didn't smoke and only drank nettle tea. I will try to be calm.

When the cat came in he was wet and hungry. I heard trees full of scolding birds.

WEDNESDAY 15 NOVEMBER 2017

Yesterday after I took Davey to school, Lin and I lay together looking out at the autumn leaves.

We went to the parent teacher interview. She said nice things about Davey, that he is smart, that his reading is good. I went out to tidy the stone circle, and Lin made a cake. Life is good these days. I don't deserve such happiness.

On Friday someone is borrowing Lin's guzheng to play at The Secret Garden, a coffee shop in town.

THURSDAY 16 NOVEMBER 2017

I went to pick up Chen Xi in Bray. She made spaghetti sauce with ketchup, and told me Tan didn't want to be my friend. When I sighed OK, whatever, she was angry. On the drive to

Galway, we chatted about Aihua. We wanted to stay away from the topic, but kept coming back to it. We talked about Tan, and about babies.

After dinner, we went into the library and did Davey's homework. I got angry, because I'd told Chen Xi how good he was at reading, but he pretended he couldn't read. We did religion homework, about people who were dead. We talked about my mom and dad, and about Chen Xi's grandparents, then said a prayer for their souls.

FRIDAY 17 NOVEMBER 2017

The girl who was going to play Lin's guzheng appeared, chaperoned by a Chinese guy called Joe. We loaded the guzheng in the back of the car and drove to The Secret Garden. Joe and Barboura set up. There was no booze in the place. I went out with Joe and he sparked a joint. Barboura was excellent. She was knowledgeable, and experienced. She played indigenous Taiwanese music, Norwegian lullabies, and traditional Chinese songs. The members of the small audience were sprawled on pillows, smoking hookahs. The house feels alive with Barboura here.

SUNDAY 19 NOVEMBER 2017

I dreamed that one of my two sons, maybe a younger Deane, broke his leg roller skating down a hill in front of a school. I ran to a Chinese hospital to get help. They wouldn't come and I criticised the Chinese character, so one of them hit me on the head. I thought about retaliating, but knew everyone would attack me if I did. When I got back people were rolling Deane onto a stretcher. Donald Trump was helping out. He was nice, and I said thank you so much, you have changed my opinion of you. He said he was happy to hear that.

I went into the library and played guitar. Barboura came in. I read her the last two pages of *Finnegan's Wake*. It was good to have a chance to talk about such things, but when the conversation started to lag I felt a bit uneasy, so I got up and had a walk around the garden.

I told Chen Xi I hoped she would always consider this house a sanctuary. She looked up the word and was happy with it. She will leave this morning. Back to China for about three months.

It will be strange to be just ourselves again after such a sociable weekend.

TUESDAY 21 NOVEMBER 2017

A dreadful day

The teacher told them everyone has an invisible bucket. When they are happy it is full, and when they are sad it is empty. People could tip your bucket by being mean to you.

I turned off the TV, took away the remote control. Davey followed me, screaming. I dragged him down to the stone room and locked him in. He smashed at the door. I dragged him down the hall and pushed him outside. He kept kicking the door, so I pulled him in and spanked him. He kept yelling, so I did it harder, gritting my teeth. The last spank hurt and he yelled ouch, that's too hard.

I keep reliving this moment, my gritted teeth.

Later Davey asked me why I still had a sad face. I told him I was the worst dad in the world. He hugged me and said he was sorry, and that we could just forget it. I went downstairs to see about the cat. He didn't want to budge. It was rainy and cold. When I tried to put him outside, he hid under the barstool.

SATURDAY 25 NOVEMBER 2017

The cannibal monster is consuming itself. It is dark from four in the afternoon until about eight in the morning.

I worked on the stone circle.

WEDNESDAY 29 NOVEMBER 2017

I worked on the paths around the stone circle. A robin followed me. The cat also followed me. An old guy who works for the fisheries chatted with me at the wall. He told me there are trout spawning in the stream.

THURSDAY 30 NOVEMBER 2017

Davey and I took two flashlights and walked around the stone circle in the dark.

FRIDAY 1 DECEMBER 2017

I cut back branches, heeding Chen Fu's advice that everything should be above head height. When I went inside, Lin and Davey had almost finished setting up the Christmas tree.

SUNDAY 3 DECEMBER 2017

The cat came in from the black wild and ravenous.

I took Davey to see the work I'd done on the path alongside the stream. He wasn't interested. Lin dug. Her cheeks were red, her eyes flashing. Reading facebook in bed, I noticed Scarlet was in Galway, and sent her a message. She said she was only in Galway for the weekend.

MONDAY 4 DECEMBER 2017

On the drive home I honked, and I muttered, fuck this fuck you. I went upstairs to play lego with Davey, but this ended in a fight. Lin and I got into a shouting match. Fuck this and fuck you. I let all the pent up whatever flow out.

Lin tried to put out the cat, but couldn't manage. She felt too guilty about the cold and wet, so I had to go down and put him out. I didn't feel great about it either.

TUESDAY 5 DECEMBER 2017

Davey started arguing with me the moment he woke up, and I ended up dragging him out of the house by the lapels of his school uniform. When we got to school, I sent him out alone, then went out to spy on him. He was standing alone, watching the other kids.

When I got home, I tried to talk to Lin about Davey, and it ended up in a screaming match. She said she had no more faith in me. We left it there, and I chatted to Chen Xi. She wanted help with Tan's visa.

I took more wood from the path along the river. I used the new welding gauntlets, and they were perfect for the job. Lin had a guzheng lesson, and I lay down in bed, exhausted.

I want to go to Charlie Byrne's bookshop and look into

writing groups, poetry workshops, readings–that sort of thing. We are too isolated. It doesn't have to be this way.

WEDNESDAY 6 DECEMBER 2017

After New Year, I will find work. It doesn't need to be anything brilliant, just something to bring in some cash. It has been hard living with this sense of contraction.

Tidying up files on the computer made me feel more confident about our future. I needed a good CV, a cover letter–then I could apply for work with Fluentify or some other online learning system, and approach Atlantic English and NUIG.

I needed a haircut, and my teeth cleaned. I need to do yoga, and to meditate, to only work on the garden for fun. I should not become a slave to the garden.

THURSDAY 7 DECEMBER 2017

I have a bit of dope. I cannot not think about it. The temptation is creeping and persistent.

I knew I should meditate, but instead went out to work on the path alongside the stream. I pulled slippery black wood, wet and heavy, out of the brush. It rained and hailed, but I persisted.

. . .

FRIDAY 8 DECEMBER 2017

It was Lin's mom's birthday. She wore a paper birthday crown.

Things have been better between Davey and I for a few days. It frightens me to think our problems have their source in my moods.

I continued working on the path by the stream, pulling brambles out by the roots. I am approaching the space under the oak tree. It will be amazing when I am done.

Pulling out brambles requires muscle from everywhere. Davey came out while I was working, and played in the snow.

I had a shower and noticed how wiry I had become.

SATURDAY 9 DECEMBER 2017

It was snowing heavily. I had a hoot then worked on the path beside the stream, beneath the oak tree. I was making a magic place. I kept working until I could hardly stand.

MONDAY 11 DECEMBER 2017

My right hip feels strangely cold and numb. Just a few days ago everything was going so well. It's crazy how up and down life is. The circumstances are the same, but the feeling is different.

TUESDAY 12 DECEMBER 2017

I am reading *A General Theory of Oblivion*, but haven't warmed to it yet. The title says it all.

Davey was crying. He was seeing scary images. I lay with him until he slept.

THURSDAY 14 DECEMBER 2017

I ran into Sean the septic tank guy in town. We talked about Dolores O'Riordan, who he was doing a septic tank for. I saw her once in Dublin, in the Norseman.

FRIDAY 15 DECEMBER 2017

The cat came purring through the window. I had been dreaming about tidiness.

I went to the hippy shop and got a Tarot deck. Lin loaded up at the Asia Market.

I pulled out loads of brambles. It will still take a lot of tidying, but at least now I can walk right through. The robin was beside me the whole time.

MONDAY 18 DECEMBER 2017

I am worried about money. I need to be tender in my heart and at peace. Anxiety is good for nothing. I need a power washer and a ladder.

TUESDAY 19 DECEMBER 2017

Last night I dreamed that Lin opened the back door, and the handle was conspicuously loose, rattling in its socket.

Lin said she missed Beijing. Of course I'd been wondering if I had made a mistake in bringing us to Galway, to this bloody big house. It took so much work to just maintain a life we weren't sure we wanted. It was dark and lonely much of the year.

WEDNESDAY 20 DECEMBER 2017 07:06

Lin and Davey come down the stairs in the dark, arguing. My heart is heavy.

I talked to Lin and Davey about how I missed Beijing. Lin shouted at me, saying we shouldn't question ourselves. We went straight to battle. She said we were finished and would get a divorce. She said my idea for a business wouldn't work. I wrestled her wallet and her bag from her hands. She told me I didn't deserve to be loved, that she was going to go back to China. We wrestled over bags in the entry room.

Later we lay on our backs looking up at the roof. The strange numbness in my right leg was worse. It seems I am a man without talent, one who squanders everything.

SATURDAY 23 DECEMBER 2017

I have been feeling weak, like I could stumble. I am having trouble typing. In the evenings, my legs, and recently my arms, are numb and heavy. I downloaded a heart app. My heart rate was 50 bpm. We checked Lin's to see that the app worked, and hers was 70.

SUNDAY 24 DECEMBER 2017

I saw a heron from the kitchen window.

Lin and I had brandy and port, then Darby called. We got very drunk. We drank all the Christmas booze. Apparently Lin made noodles. The next thing I woke up in bed beside Davey, and Lin was down in the stone room with the cat.

MONDAY 25 DECEMBER 2017

When Davey woke up we went down to the Christmas tree to watch him open his presents. After breakfast we played chess.

Lin and I drank mulled wine while Davey played with his new toys. It was a shame not to have anyone to share all this with.

THURSDAY 28 DECEMBER 2017

There was thunder and lightning, and then a wind that seemed as strong as those during the hurricane. They said that parts of Canada were colder than Mars. The wind shook the walls.

I am worried about having to find a job. Everyone asks me what I do, and it is becoming increasingly embarrassing to answer.

SATURDAY 30 DECEMBER 2017

A persistent itch at the back of my neck seems to have sent its tendrils around the front of my chest and shoulders. Last night it was unbearable, and I had to get up. I have been having peculiar health problems, starting with the restless leg.

The wind was strong, and I worried about a branch coming through a window or smashing into the car. I had a dream about the car being ruined, and trying to get the insurance to pay for the damage.

It is coming on New Year's eve. I will try not to worry about the future.

SUNDAY 31 DECEMBER 2017

The itch flares up and burns when I try to sleep.

Lin and I did some self-love themed yoga on youtube. I felt great afterwards. My tarot readings suggested I don't take on too many different projects. The gist of Lin's was that she would find her dreams but she needed to be sure her dreams were what she really wanted.

Davey drew the Two of Cups, which signified childhood innocence. Then he drew the Knight of Cups and The Fool. Would he become an artist, or a hippy wanderer? I contrasted the way the knight looked straight ahead at where he was going, while the fool looked up at the clouds, about to step off a cliff.

We had a walk up and down the promenade. Blackrock was full of seaweed tossed up by the storm. It was good to stretch the legs and fill the lungs. We got a bottle of Prosecco, a bottle of Zenzo and a naggin of Southern Comfort. I tidied away fallen branches. Lin and Davey kicked the football. I had a shower and washed my hair. I changed into my white tai chi outfit. I opened the Prosecco, and we listened to music. Lin told me about the first years after she left home. I just listened. I read *The Fox and the Star* to Davey.

MONDAY 1 JANUARY 2018

When I scratch, the itch moves elsewhere, and my skin feels like wax. It is impossible to think of anything else.

I dreamed about going to a literary conference and not being able to find where to register. The staff purposely sent me in the wrong direction. I'd already missed the first talks.

The holidays are over and it should be time to look for work, but I have this all consuming itch. I took Lin and Davey skating at Salthill. When I got out on the ice, I couldn't do it, not even a little bit. I fell a couple of times, and couldn't move away from the wall. It was humiliating. I have skated many times.

Davey looked at me sympathetically. I don't know if it is a muscle or a balance thing, or both. Davey was good at skating. Lin got better and better. I am getting old. Having said that, there were old guys flying around the rink without a bother.

TUESDAY 2 JANUARY 2018

Storm Eleanor

I am not happy. Davey won't stop talking to me no matter how many times I ask him to.

Lin and I did yoga to a youtube video by the same girl as last time, Adrienne, and then Lin and I did two sun salutations.

The sound of the storm was immense; it felt like it would pull the house apart, but the cat still wanted out. I wonder what he does at night. I will have a look around for damage, though not until the rain stops beating against the window, and the rumble of thunder subsides.

WEDNESDAY 3 JANUARY 2018

The itch has become a constant agony. The skin is sore, and my right arm feels weaker. Pins and needles. I need to make an appointment to see a doctor today.

THURSDAY 4 JANUARY 2018

I dreamed about Ralph. I thought Deane was alive, or maybe it was Deane in the dream and not Ralph. I was in Calgary, at our old home, lonely and bored. I wanted to contact George. Ralph, or Deane, came home. I wanted to have a drink with him. I took him around Aihua. It was sold already, but we said hello to everyone.

I briefly imagined the itch was subsiding, but in the evening it was back with a vengeance. This morning it is lurking beneath the surface, waiting to rise in fury. Lin rubbed cream on my chest.

FRIDAY 5 JANUARY 2018

I dreamed that a gang of derelicts in a little red car crashed into our stone wall out front. When I went out to them they were drunk and laughing, so I went for weapons to run off this drunk little old man, and his gang of laughing old ladies.

SATURDAY 6 JANUARY 2018

Dreams of building a garden feature, undermined by local students. German as well as Chinese would be taught in my school. We were somewhere we would have to stay overnight. The room featured a dead guy and a dog with purple balls. It was poor like rural China. Before this Lin, Davey and I were sleeping in a cosy place in the snow. Before this, something to do with a university.

We went to Salthill and walked down the prom. Lin stopped to let Davey play in the sand. There was an old man walking ahead of me and I tried to keep up with him but couldn't. There is something wrong with me.

I read Ralph's letter. It didn't say much but I was glad he wrote back. I have done so many things that I regret. I wouldn't know where to start with making amends. My life is a swamp of regret. The only thing I can do is try to make a good life for this family. Having children changes people for the better, but I never understood that when I saw it in

Ralph, Dan and Warnock. I would like to think I'm not the person I used to be.

MONDAY 8 JANUARY 2018 06:45

I itched all night and the fucking cows didn't let up for a minute. They are still at it. They don't even stop for breath. It has been so long since I had a good sleep. My head feels like a lump of clay.

TUESDAY 9 JANUARY 2018

The doctor couldn't say why I am having the itch. He gave me a prescription for something I already have.

THURSDAY 11 JANUARY 2018

I had a long and involved dream about a big house. My mom was grouchy with me for the messiness, and for smoking dope. There was a floorboard missing in the kitchen, and when I looked down I saw Li Yue and her family downstairs. Things became messy in a Chinese way. I went out and the government had laid tarmac all around. I went through big gates with a lady who had a pet fox. There were vegetables in the back but I didn't recognise them.

The cows were moo-ing, and I felt we had made a great mistake in buying this house. I thought that no one would buy this house with the cows next to it.

Now my hand is numb. Google suggests nerve damage.

FRIDAY 12 JANUARY 2018

In Charlie Byrne's bookstore I selected a few books and had a chat with Vinny. He told me about the literary scene in Galway. I was glad to make this contact.

SATURDAY 13 JANUARY 2018

Of course I will have a toot. I won't use tin foil anymore. Burning tinfoil might contribute to nerve damage.

I feel floaty. I don't think she knows that I have more dope.

No booze. No sugar. Less meat.

SUNDAY 14 JANUARY 2018

I had a hoot and went for a walk around the garden. My brain flowered with ideas for stories. I was entranced by the shapes of the bushes and the trees. I found a dead rat.

I want to avoid tin foil so I rolled a joint. A joint is too much though, and I came out tripping. Davey noticed, and he was wary. Lin didn't fight me. She said with resignation I won't stop you doing what you want to do. The itch that had been bothering me for days was gone.

I read *Penguin Adventurer* to Davey. When I was done he was scared of the word 'thieves'.

MONDAY 15 JANUARY 2018

The cat's dish clinks against the wall. Dolores O'Riordan died last night; she was only 46.

I kept at the brambles all day, stopping only for hoots and hawthorne gin.

It feels like the wind is lifting the house. I've never heard wind so strong.

While I was grooving with the brambles I thought about including the Secret Rose / Knight Quest / Rosicrucian *craic* into the story. Also, the Yeatsian Antiself. Rashoon Al Hasid. Should he be Masai Boss?

TUESDAY 16 JANUARY 2018

Lin is getting ready to go to Dublin to learn the tea ceremony, and have a guzheng lesson.

Of course I am overdoing the weed. It makes me schizophrenic. I should value calmness and clarity. Marijuana produces disintegration. And yet.

Lin has left. Davey is still asleep. It is all so precarious.

I want to make the Time Traveller the last of a brotherhood that includes Yeats' Knight of the Rose and Kierkegaard's Knight of Faith. They all carry shiny black penguin editions of *Thus Spake Zarathustra*.

WEDNESDAY 17 JANUARY 2018

The Secret Rose may not be what I am looking for. The story feels dated now. It needs to be reduced to its essence.

Davey did his homework in the Zen room. I worried about schizophrenia and my numb right hand. I need to give the dope a break. Lin is emphatic that it changes me.

THURSDAY 18 JANUARY 2018

The Secret Rose and the exaggerated Celticism of the Citizen in opposition to Notes from the Rathmines Underground, the Maasai, the Tontos, and the Chinese wives. The Guzheng that Once Sounded Through the Halls of Tara.

FRIDAY 19 JANUARY 2018

I am colder, deader, dumber than a fish. My diastolic blood pressure is exactly 50. I don't think this can be right. My hand is still numb. It is hard to play guitar, and to type. I always want to rub it.

I'm not sure where I am going with the story. I hoot my way round the garden.

Lin and I had a big fight about me smoking dope. What can I say? I went out and bought two Polish beers.

I cooked dinner. I drank beer, smoked some more dope, and then drank the hawthorne gin. Lin drank hawthorne gin too. She played guzheng music on her phone.

SATURDAY 20 JANUARY 2018

Davey watched TV; I read *Solar Bones*; Lin played guzheng.

My right arm is dead. I need to get rid of these hoots, sort out my health, look for work.

SUNDAY 21 JANUARY 2018

The dope makes me stupid. Maybe this is why my writing has never worked. I have always written when high. I will finish the story straight and see how it goes. It couldn't be any worse than it is.

I need to strip it down, let through only the most condensed and refined material. Be a Diamond Making Machine.

MONDAY 22 JANUARY 2018

Lin is lovely, full of smiles.

The numb hand, weird and dead–Not mine.

What to do with the story?

WEDNESDAY 31 JANUARY 2018

I dreamed about killer whales, trying to keep Davey from going too close to them as they came up onto the shore to eat seals. Lin thought I was being ridiculous.

THURSDAY 1 FEBRUARY 2018

The doctor will arrange an appointment for me in a private clinic. She suggested the numb hand was due to B12 deficiency.

SATURDAY 3 FEBRUARY 2018

My body feels the work I did yesterday. I dreamed last night about Lin leaving me. She seemed serious.

MONDAY 5 FEBRUARY 2018

This morning I realised that I could live another 20 years. We do not have enough money for that.

TUESDAY 6 FEBRUARY 2018

I got an email from Fluentify asking me to make a video introduction. I had a shower and put on a button up shirt.

WEDNESDAY 7 FEBRUARY 2018

I heard a big bang downstairs and Lin and I went down with sword, knife, flashlight, and pepper spray. We found a baking tray had slipped from where it rested against the thing for drying dishes.

Davey came with me to pick up his friend Daniel. I was blabbering, trying to be funny, but I was just weird, and embarrassing for Davey.

When Lin got home she took over, and I snuck down the hall for a hoot. Then, I snuck a few swigs of sherry. I tried to update my Linkedin account. Fear, hopelessness, exclusion.

When it was time for them to do homework the spelling bee turned into a battle between Davey and me. I felt like Davey was trying to get Daniel to go home, and that Daniel wanted to go home, and the whole world and everything in it, every possible permutation of relations between people, was sick and poisonous.

THURSDAY 8 FEBRUARY 2018

I monitored Davey's homework. He made his I as long as his i, and his a as long as his d. I thought he was being a smart ass, so I took him down to the stone room. Cue screams and tears. I told him I would send him to boarding school. Lin thought he really didn't know how long these letters should be. In my defence it wasn't just that he didn't know the comparative length of the letters, it was the way he reacted to my attempt to correct him.

But now it is snowy and beautiful.

I want to feel challenged, not like I am waiting on my final days.

The story needs a different approach. I don't want to feel I am crawling into a corner, sucking my old sores.

SUNDAY 11 FEBRUARY 2018

Davey and I played with the snow on the car. We made slushy snowballs, and hurled them to splat against the wall of the house. While I was dragging wood to the fire, I met Farmer James. Are ye workin' yet?

I hung around with Davey while Lin had a shower and got ready to go out. She was stunning. But she was home at 7:30. I don't think she had a great evening. We went to bed and I began another dark night of the soul.

WEDNESDAY 14 FEBRUARY 2018

Last night I dreamed Deane was still alive, and we were young. In another, I pulled an inch long thorn from my infected finger. I remember showing Lin.

At Galway Clinic, Paddy O'Malley was gruff, no nonsense. I delivered my flow test to the gorgeous Nadine, my cheeks pink with shame. I got up on the table, and it was down with the trousers and in with the finger. I whimpered Jesus. Lin was kind. I felt every moment was precious.

I had been worried about Lin's driver's test. I didn't want her to be hurt, and I was expecting the worst, so it was a surprise when Lee and Vas took a photo of her by the car, holding up her clean sheet. It was a great way to enter the Chinese new year.

SATURDAY 17 FEBRUARY 2018

I went out to the stone circle and had a beer. I got that high feeling, the time machine feeling, everything coming together perfectly and wisely.

WEDNESDAY 21 FEBRUARY 2018

I put on a shirt and tie for the Fluentify interview, which lasted an hour.

I helped Davey with his homework. Then I got him to play guitar. I told him if he started now he could be as good as Jimmy Hendrix by the time he was 20.

THURSDAY 22 FEBRUARY 2018 AT 12:00

I did the Fluentify training. It seems like a popularity contest, which is something I'm not good at.

I collected Davey. Aaron's dad asked, are ye workin' yet? It seems weird that I can't find a job. I could apply to NUIG English Department as a tutor. I could even go to NUIG Human Resources. I will need thick skin to endure such approaches.

FRIDAY 23 FEBRUARY 2018

Online teaching from home won't give me the sense of connection I feel I need. I didn't expect this would become an issue for me. I am going to have to get involved in something, to try to make my life meaningful.

I completed the Fluentify application; now I just have to decide on available slots. I am reluctant to do that with Lin away next week. I have lost all standing since I gave up Aihua.

SATURDAY 24 FEBRUARY 2018

Scarlet and crew arrived at six. I went out for a hoot with Scarlet. She put a huge bag of weed in front of me, but only gave me two buds and a wee nodge of hash. Lin played guzheng, under duress. I brought in the guitars and we all made noise, Brendan hunched over the piano. Davey drew a picture of Scarlet. Davey and Lin went up to bed. Brendan and I remembered evil guys from the bad old days of Omagh.

I had a restless sleep, buffeted by winds of anxiety, writhing in coils of inadequacy. The whole prostate malarky is not good. Why should it all feel so heavy? Meditation, Buddhism. We should move the family toward enlightenment. Modest spending, modest eating. Calmness.

MONDAY 26 FEBRUARY 2018

It is very cold. The Beast from the East draws nigh.

I disrobed in a back room, then followed the nurse through bomb shelter doors. She told me I would be down the tube for forty minutes, then slid me in. I tried to meditate, keep panic at bay. Welcome to the Machine–a demon disco in a sawmill, my breath but a quavering light at its heart. My back was sore but I had to remain perfectly still.

The first thing I saw coming out was Lin in all her splendour.

TUESDAY 27 FEBRUARY 2018

Lin is meant to leave for Paris this morning but there is a weather alert in Dublin, and some flights have been cancelled. She looked stunning in the black coat with fur trim she used to wear in Beijing. At Dunnes I noticed the produce clerks gazing after her. I was humbled by her beauty.

The Arctic is the warmest ever, and it seems the Arctic Vortex, which keeps it cold, has broken down. The cold flows freely.

WEDNESDAY 28 FEBRUARY 2018

Lin is in Paris for a late Valentine's day tryst. Snow is general across all of Ireland, and schools are closed. I will have a walk with Davey later. Cars shouldn't be on the road today. We will bundle up and have an adventure.

Lin's distant music, still falling softly.

. . .

THURSDAY 1 MARCH 2018

We still haven't heard from Lin in Paris.

There is ice on the windows. The snow is deep, and the birds are hungry. I filled the feeders. I can't think about anything with the world shut down like this. I will heat the croissants we have in the fridge and go from there.

FRIDAY 2 MARCH 2018

I carried Davey down from his room so he could sleep with me. Later on we threw snowballs and made a snow fort. I talked to Lin in the *Louvre*.

MONDAY 5 MARCH 2018

There is no work in Galway. Lin and I agreed that I will work on a website, but a part of me is not ready. So many years of bullshit. Must I start up the bullshit machine again?

A student signed up for a class with me on Fluentify. I told Lin yay, six euros in the bank.

I am not interested in gardening anymore. There is nothing here for us. Maybe this is just winter speaking, but I feel like all doors here are closed to me.

TUESDAY 6 MARCH 2018

Davide wanted something other than the lesson I had prepared for him. His pronunciation was weak, and it was difficult to hear him. Eleonora works in forensic medicine. She wanted to chat.

WEDNESDAY 7 MARCH 2018

I feel like King Lear. I gave away my Aihua, and now I have nothing. I don't know what to do with my life. I foresee only the contraction of my resources. I am the lowest of men, good for nothing. On Fluentify, dancing for scraps. People carve out their territory, and hold onto it as they get older. If you give up the territory you have carved out, you have nothing.

FRIDAY 9 MARCH 2018

I am weak and vulnerable. Lin had a dream about a magic head that became a man made of meat, and chased her around.

Chen Xi lost her patience with me when I started my King Lear bit.

SATURDAY 10 MARCH 2018

I opened a bottle of Zenzo for Lin and Chen Xi. They chatted in Chinese while I did my Fluentify session. Chen Xi gave Lin my mom's sapphire ring. My dad had given this to Chen Xi. She had it valued at 20,000.

MONDAY 12 MARCH 2018

The three of us did Chen Xi style meditation in the Zen room. I had a better experience when I was more forceful with my breath. *Chi Gong.*

Lin played guzheng while Chen Xi gave me a head massage with her special stones. It seemed to be about opening the solar anus, and releasing bad chi. Today she will give me a face massage with these same stones.

TUESDAY 13 MARCH 2018

It was very windy . We sat down by the diving board. Lin was taking photos of clouds. Chen Xi commented that Lin was happy here. After my Fluentify session, Lin held onto my hand while Chen Xi gave me a face massage with the sacred stones.

WEDNESDAY 14 MARCH 2018

We all sat in the Zen room watching birds. Chen Xi decided to get the 12:45 bus back to Bray. We dropped Chen Xi off at the bus station. Lin pointed out that I tried too hard, and I think that is fair.

THURSDAY 15 MARCH 2018

Lin was chatting to her family. I thought they were in a tent, because in winter they hang a heavy canvas blanket from the roof of her parent's home.

SATURDAY 17 MARCH 2018

After several sun salutations

Fluentifying is painless–

Lin's bone and lotus soup.

MONDAY 19 MARCH 2018 06:00

I Fluentify at 6:30. I did four sessions yesterday. It takes a chunk out of the day.

Lin went to let the cat out, and found what looked like a little pill or nut on the floor, except it was crawling. I took it in a tissue and flushed it down the toilet. I googled and discovered it was a full tick. Davey had mentioned that he had felt lumps on the cat. Lin had a shower and felt itchy all night.

TUESDAY 20 MARCH 2018

The cat is crying at the window to get in. I put food out for him, but I still feel rotten.

WEDNESDAY 21 MARCH 2018

Lin was whimpering in her sleep, and I woke her. She said she was dreaming we had a fight. She wouldn't give me any details. I held her tight and told her I would love and protect her forever.

The cat sat staring at me through the window while I was Fluentifying–so he is in now.

SATURDAY 24 MARCH 2018

After Fluentify, I took Davey out to practise hitting the *sliotar*, then we walked around the garden. Spring was raising Lin's flowers everywhere–I saw a bee outside the Zen room, and Lin saw more around the heather.

TUESDAY 27 MARCH 2018

I helped Lin get dressed, and dropped her off at the cathedral.

I put Davey to bed, then messaged Lin, and when she didn't answer right away, I unleashed a barrage of increasingly desperate and unhinged messages. She hurried home; I was disappointed in myself for having lacked resolve. She was warm, and would not be provoked.

Feeling weak and empty, I was able to sleep once she was beside me.

In the morning Cinderella mopped the floor, looking tired and run down.

MONDAY 2 APRIL 2018

Morning fog obscures the green that is starting to appear atop the rose trellis. Lin and I are still giving one another the silent treatment.

During the night, though, she stroked my face.

FRIDAY 6 APRIL 2018

Lin, Davey, and the cat are in the other room. The fish is in the Zen room. The finches are in the rose trellis. The magpies are among the nests. There is a big wood pigeon on the power lines in the back. Some poor cows have been let out into the field. I am sitting on a medicinal Chinese heat seat, which emits a smell of grass.

SATURDAY 7 APRIL 2018

The sun came out and everything was beautiful. Davey ran around in the forest while I drank my beer and the rest of a bottle of whiskey sitting on the patio outside the Zen room.

We went into the house and watched magpies making a nest, the pigeons making love. The music of the birds. Later, we saw a bat.

MONDAY 9 APRIL 2018

I went in for my driver's test. The instructor was robotic. We drove around for a while and everything seemed fine, until exiting an estate. I looked left, then looked right, then went forward without looking left again, just as a car came over the hill. I stopped in the lane blocking traffic, and the approaching driver made a horrified face.

WEDNESDAY 11 APRIL 2018

We went to two curtain shops. I left the whole thing to Lin. She seems ominous these days. She told me that she dreamed about fighting with me, so I am concerned that something may be brewing.

I don't see what I am good for.

Lin says we have been in Ireland for two years.

It never stops raining.

THURSDAY 12 APRIL 2018

Lin and Davey say I seem happy. I saw Lin under the stairs this morning, smiling at her vegetables.

MONDAY 16 APRIL 2018

A few hoots make a huge difference in perspective. Paolo told me that Carlo Rivelli got his ideas on time from taking acid. I should prepare a series of topics, an online curriculum including business ethics, the Anthropocene, Irish Literature, Health, Permaculture, Time.

WEDNESDAY 18 APRIL 2018

Yesterday when Rosemary collected Andrew I was out working in the garden and the boys were alone in the house. I could tell as she held my eyes in her penetrating gaze that she knew I was stoned as a coot. I guess as a teacher she comes across that sort of thing.

Out front there are white horses galloping in the field. They are handsome, so different from the poor old cows out back. Rosemary scoffed at the cows looking in at us. She didn't want to see the garden. I will get Lin to hide the hoots for a while.

FRIDAY 20 APRIL 2018

I don't remember going to bed. When I got home, I started drinking, and didn't let up. I drank and smoked in my paradise out among the trees.

MONDAY 23 APRIL 2018

I had a lesson with Alessandro. I want to create something nice with this Articulate, a sort of PowerPoint on steroids. It has a six month free trial. I could call it Things People Should Know.

WEDNESDAY 25 APRIL 2018

I went to the Declan Kiberd talk in the quadrangle. The talk was good, and everything he said about the holy church of Irish literature and culture made sense. I didn't see anyone I recognised. I walked into town and bought *The Order of Time*.

THURSDAY 26 APRIL 2018

I requisitioned the hoots from Lin, opened a Hobgoblin, and got myself twisted. I quickly suffered a bout of paranoia, which began with me feeling exposed in the library, and resulted in my hiding away the swords and guitars. I felt bad for being so fucked up around Davey, and I gave Lin back the dope.

Later I read *Giant Robot* to Davey, then went back to my room to read *The Order of Time*. Rovelli suggests that the future and the past co-exist in a Block Universe. Another way to eternal recurrence. Time is not stream but statue.

SUNDAY 29 APRIL 2018

We made a fire to get rid of all the scraps of branches and dead flowers we had accumulated. The frictions of the past few days melted away into the smoke; we were in harmony. The sky was blue and the air was fresh.

MONDAY 30 APRIL 2018

The cat is in the other room, and the other humans are asleep in their beds. Lin was pissed off with me all day for hooting so much. Even Davey made a comment I didn't quite catch. In the afternoon I told Lin to bring back two Hobgoblins from Dunnes, and she did this very darkly.

SUNDAY 6 MAY 2018

Davey called me in because he had another dream about going into the TV. Over lunch Lin started crying while she was eating, so we had another fight. I am feeling dread about our accounts. I haven't looked at our spendings for so long, I'm afraid of what I will find.

MONDAY 7 MAY 2018

Lin and I had a cuddle and a lay in this morning. The day is grey and drizzly. The coldness of the past month came to a head yesterday morning and we fought.

Davey is off school, for day number five. He is a great little dude but he doesn't give you a minute to think. There is too much time and not enough.

TUESDAY 8 MAY 2018

Davey woke me from a deep sleep of machine-like dreaming, and I still carried a little piece with me when I was awakened.

Lin made Davey a swing. She knocked crumpled dead grape leaves out of the rose trellis, and I pulled dandelions. Davey swung, contentedly. I gathered the dead leaves Lin had pulled from the rose trellis. Then I sat in the garden patio sun, enjoyed a few tins of cider.

TUESDAY 15 MAY 2018

I need to build a website for learning material, and start marketing myself, though this is a challenge when one feels lost, and worthless. I don't know what is the right thing to do, and I don't know what I am capable of doing.

WEDNESDAY 16 MAY 2018

I have no work and I have no idea how to find work. Every time I see parents from Davey's class, they inquire about how many hours I will be working that day. Yesterday morning I screwed around not getting anything done, and then had my session with Antonio, and earned my 7.50.

We went to the garden centre and got red, white, and black currant bushes, and two little apple trees. I dug holes for the currants and the apples and we planted them. The holes were hard to dig through the stones and roots.

I had a quick cider out in the apple circle. Lin was pulling weeds and planting in the kitchen beds. I gave her a kiss and said it was all very beautiful.

THURSDAY 17 MAY 2018

I was grateful for Lin's understanding of the difficulty I would have getting a job, being a bit older, and for her not saying the time I'd spent on the Time Machine story was wasted.

Later I drank my beer on the Zen patio. A bird lay stunned beneath the big window, but managed to rouse itself and fly away. Lin came out and did some gardening. Davey swung in the swing. I put on my baseball cap against the sun.

FRIDAY 18 MAY 2018

I set up the Articulate 360 demo. It is another one of my messy magnum opus projects. I need to bear in mind my purpose. It can't just be to express myself. The real point is we need to earn money.

The writing prompt in the diary app: What was the saddest moment of your life? The final time my mom looked at me. Finding Deane dead. Losing my dad without having made peace. Him dying while my boy was being born. Losing Ralph as a brother.

SATURDAY 19 MAY 2018

I read *A Short History of Nearly Everything*. I waver in committing to my ideas.

SUNDAY 20 MAY 2018

I dreamed. I was in a dirty, bug filled Dublin apartment. Ralph, my dad and I took a speedboat across to Lasqueti Island, following in the wake of a ferry. I was proud that I could point out where the boat should be headed. I was about to ask if I could steer, but Ralph, or maybe Deane, asked if he could steer first.

When we got home, it was still raining. Lin went out and planted things along the rose trellis. I drank in the Zen room. I sent Ralph a message asking him if he ever listened to Jon Hopkins but he didn't answer.

MONDAY 21 MAY 2018

I think I can make something out of the Articulate tutorials. I just need to get down to it, not be too experimental, focus on specific topics.

TUESDAY 22 MAY 2018

Davey went up to watch TV. I read Jane Nelsen's classic *Positive Discipline*. Lin and I would have to work together, as I am too strict and she is too permissive. We need to allow Davey to fail, and give him some responsibilities.

WEDNESDAY 23 MAY 2018

Lin hung the red curtains in the library while I did an Articulate tutorial. Ralph and I chatted about managing our properties.

Lin said I wasn't a man, because I got stressed out about things so easily. We had dry bread for lunch.

I watered plants and drank beer. Davey swung. It was hot, so I put the marijuana plants outside.

THURSDAY 24 MAY 2018

I opened a bottle of wine and poured some into the beef stew I was making for dinner, then drank the rest of the bottle. I criticised Lin for trying to give Davey some ice cream before dinner.

After dinner we walked down the road. Davey and I went to say hello to the horses, and Lin ran back to the house. The feeling became weird. I was saying crazy things to Davey. I lost control of myself, experienced a sort of black out, and then Lin and I were spewing poison at each other back at the house.

So many flaws, such a dirty soul.

Lin is forgiving, but everyone has limits.

I am not a good man.

FRIDAY 25 MAY 2018

Creeping buttercups and midges. I hate things that creep, are insidious. Yesterday as I was pulling up the buttercups Davey said he liked them, so we fought about that.

This morning I felt I deserved a day off from fear and self loathing.

When Davey came down he was beautiful and sweet. I tried not to feel that he might grow up and change into another person who might not love me, who might or might not be happy, might or might not suffer some awful tragedy.

Lin played guzheng. Davey and I messed around in bed. No siblings. We are so isolated. Other people make friends, but we struggle with this.

. . .

SATURDAY 26 MAY 2018

Davey's little wet face in the water, laughing.

On the way home from swimming, I suggested to Lin that I wouldn't come to China, and she was OK with that.

While I worked on the buttercups, Davey chatted about the ghost of the goldfish that died the other day, and how it was helping me. He kept encouraging me to stop. I was getting stiff. I opened a Hobgoblin and drank it in the forest. Lin and Davey came and sat with me. Lin said I should not be afraid to live my life, I should just do what I think is right. We will manage. A flight of swallows broke from the trees, then flooded back into the willow.

I imagined a story about the death of James Joyce, starting with the line, Ah, me holy fucking guts. I told Lin and she seemed happy to hear me enthuse. I googled to look for a book with this topic but couldn't find one. I could write it.

FRIDAY 1 JUNE 2018

Lin and I put on rubber gloves. I held the cat still while she tried to pull the tick out with tweezers, but she only succeeded in smushing its blood sack.

We went to Charlie Byrne's bookstore. I found Ellman's biography of Joyce, and grabbed Beckett's *Three Novels*. Vinny found me a book by Frank McGuinness on the death of Joyce. He opened *Malone Dies* and drew my attention to the first sentence.

I am still reading *Positive Discipline*. Davey shoved me and said what's your problem, and I realised he was probably re-enacting something that happened at school. He and Aaron and Andrew argue about who's dad was best. Aaron said his dad was because he was 38.

Davey played with Lin. I felt jealous of the fun they were having. I turned to *Malone Dies*–the kind of writing I had in mind when I thought about the death of Joyce.

I need to stop drinking. I don't want Davey to think his Dad's a stoner.

SATURDAY 2 JUNE 2018

We walked along the beach at Lahinch, then got Davey into his wetsuit. I stripped to my shorts and went into the water with him. He was laughing and excited by the next big wave. We rented wetsuits and a board for Lin and me. Davey soon got cold in his wetsuit. His teeth were chattering, but he was smiling.

SATURDAY 9 JUNE 2018

I did a bit of work on the project, but quickly started to feel overwhelmed, and to doubt my ability. There is so much to do, and the software is unwieldy. I had a good few hoots while I was working. Then I went up and did some meditation.

Davey and I set up the barbecue. Lin prepared the food and brought it out. Chen Xi called and I showed her what we were cooking. I opened a bottle of Aldi Prosecco. Lin and I pulled out weeds, went for a walk down the road, said hello to the horses, and had a race.

I won't stress about the project over the weekend. I'll try to make it weekday work.

SUNDAY 10 JUNE 2018

I dreamed that a stoat was at the window. We went to get him some food. He looked just like the animal I saw running along the fence near the oak tree yesterday. Turns out the stoat was a cool old man the police were hassling. I tried to stand up for him but a blonde lady cop took him away. I pulled up a chair and chatted with the other cop, about how happy I was with the house.

I am worried that I am wasting time, effort, and money on this project, which is, like everything I do–personal, private and messy. I'm not sure how I can make something that will appeal to other people. I don't want it to amount to nothing.

. . .

MONDAY 11 JUNE 2018

I did some Articulate tutorials, then researched the Midwinter Ceremony, which I remembered from an undergraduate course at the U of C. I am not sure how to organise the information. I thought it would be easier.

Davey sat out back with me while I drank beer and Lin cooked dinner. I got drunker than I wanted to. I made a firm resolution to drink less, and there I was, sloppy again.

Kwakiutl Cannibal Monster. Altered States. Sympathetic magic. Metaphorical tuning forks to the universe. Harmonic resonance. *Hamatsa*.

THURSDAY 14 JUNE 2018

I worked on the project all day. I hooted hard, but I was productive. When I told Lin that I had added quarks, she patted me on the head.

Davey called us down to look at a sore toe, and I made a conscious effort not to criticise. I could see he was surprised by this tack. Apparently I don't need to dominate.

FRIDAY 15 JUNE 2018

Lin made big *baozi* with our own wild vegetables. It was the best meal we'd had since coming to Ireland.

SATURDAY 16 JUNE 2018

I stopped at Dubray's and got *The Tibetan Book of Living and Dying*. I wasn't in the mood to chat at Aaron's party, so I kept my distance.

Davey chewed gummies from his party bag. I read *The Tibetan Book* and *Positive Discipline*. I haven't meditated for two days, haven't done any yoga. I have been hooting hard, and drinking too much. I have lost my resolve to keep myself pure and clear, but I still feel good.

SUNDAY 17 JUNE 2018

The cows are lowing. It is dark and gloomy. I farted around on the project. I put together an animation of two boys pushing the Wild Old Woman into the fire. Lin and Davey seemed to like it.

I did some meditation, then watched a David Attenborough documentary about the *Kwakiutl: The Crooked Beak of Heaven*.

I made dinner, and drank the three beers Davey got me for father's day. Davey kept wanting to eat treats while we were cooking, and I fought with him. I picked him up to carry him down to the stone room before I realised that he felt hurt after getting me the beer. I stayed in the room by myself for a few minutes to cool down, then I hugged him and apologised.

. . .

MONDAY 18 JUNE 2018 AT 12:00

I had a good few hoots working on the project.

Lin and I went to the gym. I did a strong twenty minute run, then went downstairs and hit the bag until I was exhausted.

I played a game of chess with Davey. I read *Positive Discipline*, and *The Book of Living and Dying*.

TUESDAY 19 JUNE 2018 07:16

Davey, Lin and the kitty are in the kitchen. Kelly is in the guest bedroom. It is another rainy morning. It seems like it will never end.

I worked on the project. I got a bit done, but it became convoluted, and I had to take apart what I had done. I cleaned the downstairs toilet thoroughly.

Life is many days.

Last night I got drunk to hide from the guest. I wish I could be more relaxed about things, not so frightened.

FRIDAY 22 JUNE 2018

At Salthill Davey and I went into the water. Davey went in to about his midsection, but I had a proper swim. I felt my body was on fire.

I finished *The Three Body Problem* in the bath, read a bit of *Living and Dying*. I started reading *The Woodcutter's Family*, but kept falling asleep.

I feel that I have been behaving better recently. I have been more easy going, if perpetually ashamed. I felt a few leaks last night, some of the old anxiety, confusion, suspicion, and desperation trickling back into consciousness.

SATURDAY 23 JUNE 2018

Davey, Lin and the cat are in the kitchen. It was foggy this morning, but now it is bright blue. We were woken by the birds chatting outside our window this morning. Davey came down, and we had a family cuddle, then Lin made me coffee.

I didn't manage to get anything done on the project yesterday, and I may not get anything done today either. It is difficult to get anything done when Davey is off school. I need to accept this simple reality.

Lin seemed grouchy, and I found myself slipping back into an old persona. We squabbled, and I drove off to buy beer.

When I got home I was in a fighting mood, so I did some meditation. Later I sat in the back and drank my beer. Lin, Davey, and the cat sat on a blanket on the grass. I spied them from between shimmering leaves. Butterflies were everywhere.

After dinner, I read *Positive Discipline*, then *Living and Dying*.

Lin took Davey to bed, and I read *The Woodcutter's Family*. I kept falling asleep over the same paragraph.

SUNDAY 24 JUNE 2018

I read *Living and Dying* on meditation.

I am looking forward to spending time thinking about the Kwakiutl this morning.

TUESDAY 26 JUNE 2018

Yesterday started well but ended poorly. Davey went to summer camp, Lin and I went to the gym. We had a hot tub and a sauna.

We came home. I swept the sand between the stones outside the Zen room. Then I sprinkled grass seed across the lawn. I understood how old men get such pleasure out of this. It was very hot out, so I went to Dunnes and got four tins of Druid's cider, not intending to drink them all at once. I started under the hawthorn with Lin and Davey, and Davey kept bringing me new ones.

We went for a walk, and I told Davey I would get him a dog when he got back from China. Lin didn't like that I decided this without consulting her. When we got home, Davey tried to pull Lin upstairs. I criticised him, and the whole thing kicked off. It got bigger and bigger, and then it homed in on the French guy.

I told Lin that I hated her, that I would smash her head open. I pushed my fist into her mouth. She kept provoking me, and she wouldn't give an inch. Davey tried to keep the peace, but he couldn't. She was in the stone room. I kept going back down to her to try to fix things, and they got worse and worse.

WEDNESDAY 27 JUNE 2018

After writing my diary I hugged Lin, pulled her down onto my lap and told her I was sorry, that I loved her so much. She told me she was sorry, and that she loved me. We held one another tightly. When Davey came down I made sure he saw us hugging. We praised him for how mature he had been the night before.

THURSDAY 28 JUNE 2018

I feel a wreck. It might not be just lack of sleep. My joints, muscles, head, the whole apparatus feels wrong. I feel like I am a hundred years old. Lin and Davey leave today to spend the night in Dublin before their flight tomorrow morning.

Davey told me he was proud of me when I was principal of Aihua.

FRIDAY 29 JUNE 2018 06:13

I am alone in the house, having had a few hoots. I seem to have a problem with my legs. They ache, especially my buttocks. It has been like this for a couple of days. I took a painkiller. I can't be at ease with all this pain. It is creepy in the house without Lin and Davey.

It was a blue sky morning at Salthill. We took off our shoes, and Lin went for a swim in her underpants. She was so happy, a real Galway girl. Davey climbed up the rocks in his bare feet. I lay down with Davey. Lin came up and we lay together. Lin said kind words to me; let me know she loves me.

I dropped them off at the bus station. I started to feel uncomfortable in my legs. I heated tortellini. I sat outside and had a cider, then watered the garden. I was bitten by a bloody big horse fly. I got a message from Aidon telling me to meet his missus at Centra in Moycullen. I drove to Moycullen, got some water and waited in the car. The missus was a sexy blonde. I was meek and grateful. I got the weed, and drove home.

I keep feeling their presence in the house, then remember they are gone. I tried to do some yoga, but my legs and buttocks have no strength, and I feel as though my muscles are wasting away.

SATURDAY 30 JUNE 2018

I'm having trouble with my legs; there is a sour pain in them. I hope that it's from sleeping with the blanket off and the window open. I had trouble putting on my socks this morning.

Yesterday started with pain. I smoked dope like the billy-oh, and got quite a bit done on the project. Everything flows. I went to Dunne's and got stuff for salad, and more booze. I had a few hoots and cranberry gin in a tin. I did more work on the project. I drank my *Tisingdao* while preparing a salad.

SUNDAY 1 JULY 2018

My legs are still sour and weak. I hobble around with a pain like I've a knife in the side of my skull. Yesterday I'd smoked a lot of dope even before I started work on the project. I worked well through most of the morning. I had toast and tomatoes at 12, then I did more work. I smoked so much I felt creepy, and lost my focus. I staggered around on wooden legs, woolly, aching head.

I must take it easier this morning. Stay away from screens, no dope after morning eye opener. I need to put away my clothes, put on a wash, change the vacuum cleaner bag, wash the floors downstairs and the toilets upstairs. Outside I need to trim the rose trellis, power wash the house and asphalt, mow the lawn.

MONDAY 2 JULY 2018 AT 07:25

When I started work on the project, I focussed on keeping myself calm and mindful. I cleaned up around the house, put away the clothes and did two loads of laundry. I can't remember having lunch, but I probably did. Then I did a ten minute meditation. When I started to feel anxious and confused I reminded myself that these feelings would pass, and that meditation happens between thoughts. Once I started to watch my mind closely, and step back from it a bit, I realised how much I am driven by gusts of panic and anxiety: delusion.

I wrote a letter to Tan asking him to defend Lin and Davey while they were in China.

I did a Fluentify lesson, then I smoked more dope and

resumed work on the project for a while before trimming the rose trellis, which has begun to feel like an entity.

I kept going back to the fight we had the day before they left. I had got Davey to the stage where he had lost hope. At least I can recognise my mistakes now that I am reading these Self Help books. *The Tibetan Book* suggests I need to step back, become aware that the gusts and blasts of feeling that I experience, fear for the future, remorseful pride in the past, have no ontological status–they are extraneous to the True Nature, which resides in the perpetual present.

TUESDAY 3 JULY 2018 AT 07:07

After a bit of work on the project, I did some meditation. I tried to keep in mind all day that meditation occurs in the space between thoughts.

I opened a beer while I prepared a salad, then turned to wine. I got drunk and began to post on facebook. Later I deleted it all. I watered the garden, and clipped leaves on the rose trellis, exposing grapes to the sun.

WEDNESDAY 4 JULY 2018

Warnock wants me to come up to Omagh to help with the hay, but I don't think I can. My legs are so stiff and sore that I could hardly manage sun salutations.

I did a 10 minute meditation. I have been mostly vegetarian since Lin and Davey left. I would like to be a drunken Buddhist monk.

FRIDAY 6 JULY 2018

I am making an animation in which the Yeatsian gyres metamorph into the Yin Yang symbol. I have always wanted to do this.

SATURDAY 7 JULY 2018

It isn't easy for me to be alone. It is raining. I feel so isolated, so left behind, that I wonder if I could even be involved in the world again. I drew gyres and cones, hooted and plotted their movement into Articulate. I wanted to show visually how the Yeatsian Gyres are the Yin Yang in disguise, and how both are embodied again in the movement of the Kwakiutl Cannibal Ritual. It may be a total disaster.

I struggled yesterday with my fear for Davey's safety. Clearly it's not helpful. I tried to control it, but I am having trouble adopting Buddhist ways. It was easier at first. I have difficulty bringing peace into my heart. *The Tibetan Book* asks perhaps too much from me in terms of relinquishing my attachments. And I'm not good with the idea of having a master.

SUNDAY 8 JULY 2018

I'm not sure if it's me or the project that's so scattered. Thinking about the death of my old schoolmate, Vic Alefontis, who was so loved, made me feel exiled from life's rich feast.

TUESDAY 10 JULY 2018

I have lost confidence in myself. I am mediocre, or sub mediocre. I have no confidence in this project. It is bad poetry.

WEDNESDAY 11 JULY 2018

I did a lot of timing and spacing of gyres and yin yangs. It was slow and meticulous.

FRIDAY 13 JULY 2018

I don't remember getting home last night. I drove into town to meet Troy at the skateboard place. Then Scarlet and Caen arrived and we walked into town together for tea and buns. At Salthill, the two boys jumped off the diving board. I stood with my feet in the water. I felt comfortable with Scarlet and her family. We went to Feeney's and got seats out front, drank whiskey and Guinness. I smoked joints with a tobacco/weed mix. We danced in the street, and when the barman at the biker bar took one look at us and said you're not gettin' in here, Scarlet rose up at him and this had me in hysterics. Our behaviour was very bad. I wet my trousers, then must've gone home in a cab. Scarlet wants me to meet them this morning, but I am not able.

SATURDAY 14 JULY 2018

I don't know why the cat is meowing and pushing at me, because I just gave him food and milk. Caen, Troy and Scarlet are in the guest area. It is dark and rainy. I just had a hoot. My coffee is too strong. I woke up brutally hung over, with gaping holes in my memory. I had spent too much money, and was full of remorse.

At 5:30 I went to the cathedral to collect Scarlet, Troy and Caen. They were hungry, but I didn't have anything. They made pasta with passata. They filled me in on the events of the night before. I had done a heartfelt slow dance with a poor old alcoholic guy on crutches. We chatted and Troy played guitar. They had some hoots, and I took a little blim from their bag. I felt bad about that and will confess. Karma and all.

SUNDAY 15 JULY 2018

I confessed to Scarlet that I'd stolen a piece of her hash as soon as she got up. She ended up giving me most of what they had with them.

I had a chat with Lin and Davey. Davey was upset because Zhang You Tii favoured Tuan Tuan. He felt he had no friends. He told Lin that Andrew and Aaron were closer to one another than to him, and that he was on the outside.

WEDNESDAY 18 JULY 2018

I woke up during the night, my mind busy organising and sorting. I wouldn't call it a dream because there was no content, just the sensation of sifting through layers.

THURSDAY 19 JULY 2018

Lin and Davey are upstairs. Davey is about to have a bath. Last night he dreamed about floating comfortably on waves in a sky blue wetsuit.

FRIDAY 20 JULY 2018

When we got home from the bus station, we walked around the garden. We ate our own blueberries and cucumbers. Lin found raspberries. Davey said he loved our garden, and I was happy to hear this.

SUNDAY 22 JULY 2018

Last night I dreamed that I was showing my dad my writing. I had a lot of good bits and I felt confident in them. Across the road, white horses run against the grey.

MONDAY 23 JULY 2018

Lin has had a long face since she got back from China. I wish I knew what it was about. It didn't take long for me to grow tired of the long face, and so we fought. I asked Lin to put Davey to bed and she gave me a look, so I took him down myself.

I find it hard to have Davey home all the time. I have to mind him the full day, answer all his questions, and be his personal slave. And then Lin mooned around, having to suffer living with a man like me.

SUNDAY 29 JULY 2018

Now Davey is afraid to be alone, both upstairs and downstairs. He says he sees scary things. I need to be careful about the kinds of images he is exposed to.

He said he hated me and would kill himself, but I didn't rise to it. We got the car washed. Davey enjoyed the machine coming around the car with its suds and brushes, and I told him if you kill yourself you won't get to see great things like this.

TUESDAY 31 JULY 2018

The cat is in; Greg is in the guest room. It starts a grey day. I had dreamed that someone took the screen of branches from the back of the stone circle, and was dumping them off a dock behind the property.

Davey and I fought. He will not listen to me, no matter what I say or do. I feel embarrassed that this big screaming I hate you fight was heard by Greg down the hall.

Yesterday Davey and I collected Greg at the bus station. Greg was looking well, though he was smoking again. We chatted while Lin cooked beef and tomato stew. Greg brought out some of my old writing he'd been holding onto. We drove to Salthill. The tide was high. We all got splashed by breaking waves. Everyone was soaked from head to toe. When we got home, Davey watched TV, and Greg and I chatted.

WEDNESDAY 1 AUGUST 2018

Greg got up and we had a chat, then he sat and read. It rained heavily all day so there wasn't much we could do. Lin doesn't seem comfortable around Greg. She has been wearing a long face pretty consistently since she got back from China. It seems she doesn't speak English anymore.

Lin dropped Greg and me off in town. We went into the cathedral, and listened to the organ. At Feeney's we got pints and Red Breasts. It was race week, and very rainy, so there was a lot of pent up energy in town. We chatted to the buskers sitting beside us. Greg broached the subject of weed, and one of them might have something for us today.

We chatted with a long haired Galway guy. I thought he was pissed off at me for singing Raglan Road along with the busker, though Greg said he wasn't. Still, I shouldn't bellow out the songs the buskers are singing. We had a few more, and then we had a rib eye at the King's Head. I should have left a tip, because the waitress was very funny. We walked up to the pub the buskers would be at, and saw the whole banjo gang for a drink. The dope wasn't coming soon though, so we went to a place near *Roisin Dubh*.

This morning Davey and I both heard Greg shriek. Apparently he'd dreamed of a demonic child in the corner of his room, having detached itself from the painting I'd done of Icarus, St Brendan, Tang San Zhang and his disciples, back in Beijing. Davey whispered to me, a demon child? I nodded slowly, making my eyes big. In the corner, I added, and we lifted our eyebrows. This was our kind of dreaming.

THURSDAY 2 AUGUST 2018

Greg is flying through *Solar Bones*. There is a heatwave in Europe, but it is dim and sodden here. I got a call from John the banjo player, so Greg and I went into Feeney's. John and Shay were in the back. Shay is the bearded guy from Donegal. We got 50 euro worth from John. Shay is from a *Gaeltacht* in Donegal, Gweedore. He gave me a green gummy candy made with THC, a little bear.

Greg did some reading while I played guitar. Then we walked the circumference of the garden, and smoked a big joint. When we got back, the little green bear was kicking in. I worried that I'd been spiked with LSD. I did some meditation, but was tripping balls, as they say. After dinner, Greg disappeared into his room. I did a bit of poking around the project.

FRIDAY 3 AUGUST 2018

The cat didn't come back yesterday, and there is no sign of him today. It is grim and grey. Yesterday afternoon and evening we had a few welcome hours of sunshine. Lin drove us to Spiddal. We went down to the stones. We drove to a rocky beach. Davey got muddy from rotten seaweed. Greg gathered up garbage.

I played music. Greg sat outside. Lin wandered round the garden. We drank Guinness. I walked through the stone circle. The sun was shining. I tried to help Davey get to sleep but it didn't go well, so I asked him to walk to the crossroads with me. We walked hand in hand.

SATURDAY 4 AUGUST 2018

Davey was scared last night when I told him that the only scary Star Trek was the one with the Grups. He pressed me for details, and then refused to sleep on his own. Greg is in his room. He went to bed early. The cat still hasn't returned. He has been gone for three days. I think we might have lost him.

We drove to Achill. Greg did DJ, played Safesurfer. Much of my favourite music was introduced to me by Greg. We could almost see Croagh Patrick as we passed through Westport. We stopped at a beach and walked over the rocks. Then we drove to a lookout point and climbed up the nearby hills. Greg treated us to lunch. Davey and Greg had fish and chips, and I had scallops and blood pudding. When we got home, I started on the hoots and beers immediately. Greg went outside to read, then into the library, and then to his room. He finished *Solar Bones,* reads continually. Lin didn't like how much I was drinking. Last night I had a dream about setting up a canvas, a white open space where I was going to do whatever I wanted. I had paints in a drawer.

SUNDAY 5 AUGUST 2018

Another dreary day, sheets of rain dragged across the sodden earth. Greg is asleep down the hall; the cat hasn't returned.

Yesterday morning I had been worried about Lin's emotional state. I was probably imagining her dislike of Greg, though also probably not. I do make things awkward by worrying about underlying tensions. I am sensitive to gestures and feelings that aren't even present. I wish it wasn't so, because I like to spend time with friends, when I am not tying myself in knots.

I finished off the dope yesterday morning. I wish I had more. I suggested a walk through the university grounds. Lin stayed home, tired of scurrying around after us. She doesn't follow our conversation anyway. When we got back Greg and I started drinking out back in the wee stretch of sunshine apportioned that day, while Lin gardened.

MONDAY 6 AUGUST 2018

Lin, Greg and Davey are in the kitchen. Lin just got back from sleeping in the car at Salthill. She is limping and ragged. She is doing her best to joke with Davey, who lost a tooth last night. I spent most of last night on my phone. My heart was cinched in pain and regret, and I couldn't find peace. I don't know what will become of us.

Yesterday evening I wandered around the garden and drank. Greg drank with me for a while, and when he turned to his computer. I kept drinking. We ate apple pie that Lin had made from our own apples. It was the best apple pie I had ever eaten. We went out for a walk. When we got home, Lin and I started fighting. She punched me in the face, and I threw her around. I don't want to remember the details. She was kicking me and I was probably kicking her. I took her phone. She was packing, so I threw her makeup out the window. I was angry that she was making this fuss while Greg was here. We went downstairs and packed a bag. I threw it and some of her clothes out the window. She got in the car and drove off. I spoke harshly to Davey, then closed his door with the light off. I sent horrible text messages to Lin, and called her until she turned off her phone.

I will take Greg to the bus station as soon as he finishes his shower. I shouldn't drink; It should be a rule.

TUESDAY 7 AUGUST 2018

Greg's gone and the cat's not coming back. Lin seems to have a broken toe. We will have to take her for an x-ray. She had a dream last night that her mom had died. Davey told me how sad mommy is, how much she cried when she left her parents the last time.

Davey and I lay in bed until Lin returned. I gathered up the things I had thrown out the windows. She came in hobbling and hurt. Greg had heard everything, and wanted me to get him to the bus as soon as possible. He said he sensed that he had disturbed the balance in our family, and should have left earlier. We said a formal goodbye at the bus station. I was sad to see him go, but also relieved.

Lin had a bath. There are bruises on her legs.

WEDNESDAY 8 AUGUST 2018

Lin and Davey are clattering down the stairs. Well, Davey is clattering. Lin is hobbling with what seems to be a marginally less than broken toe. Lin limped around the garden with my grandfather's *shillelagh*, and I prepared a vegetable stew.

When I had finished getting Davey ready for bed last night, he wanted to go and kiss Lin, and the idea that I had done all this work for nothing made me angry. I had lost all the skills I had developed from reading *Positive Discipline* and the *Tibetan Book of Living and Dying*. Meditation is one thing, but it is hard to put these ideas into practice consistently. Davey went to bed and was good enough not to fight with me for being such a dick. Lin was good about it too.

Once during the night I knocked Lin's sore toe. What kind of person am I? I seem unable to improve myself. I should hire a painter. Last night when we came home Davey said our house looked like it was abandoned.

I need dope. If Aidon's ol' lady doesn't call me before Davey comes home I will have to go into town for a snoop.

· · ·

THURSDAY 9 AUGUST 2018

I dreamed that I was building a house next to the Chambers house, but that there was an old Cotter house in the middle, an old rose garden, and a bridge over a stream. Someone was helping me plan the kitchen.

There was a book at the door about Non-Violent Communication.

We went around the garden. We thought we heard kitty and looked for him. We saw apples had started to fall in the back, so we brought some in. Lin made an apple pie.

I have no focus. I am smeared across the day.

FRIDAY 10 AUGUST 2018

Yesterday recalled those parts of *Infinite Jest* about the suicidal feelings that come with waiting all morning for a message from your dealer, or in this case, his wife. I told Lin that I felt as though there was only empty space inside me.

But then I got a message from the dealer's wife, and we agreed to meet in half an hour. I hurried Lin and Davey out of Joyce's and drove them home. I got the groceries into the house, then drove to the Centra at Moycullen. I thanked her in a gentlemanly fashion for taking the time to assist me in this matter.

I cracked a Hobgoblin and had a few hoots. I had the idea that we needed to be more sociable, and maybe I could invite buskers around for dinner. I announced to Lin that we have been doing it all wrong. I said it a few times before she asked me what I was wanting to tell her? I replied in a sage tone that I had better not say anything because one should sleep on great ideas before announcing them. She agreed. Regardless, for no less than an hour I was thoroughly convinced that the way to happiness and fulfilment lay in inviting buskers over to our house to hang around.

We went out to the garden. It was a beautiful late afternoon with huge white clouds crowning the trees. We floated around doing our own things. It was a dreamlike time. I started to strip grape leaves from the rose tube but soon realised it was futile. I tasted a grape; it was sour but not impossible. We went into the stone circle and ate apples from the smaller tree. I found a few white currents and Lin and Davey ate them from my hand. They tasted like nothing else in the world.

I helped Lin get dressed to meet a friend at the Maldroon. Davey and I watched. Afterwards he told me that he felt dizzy and sick from watching too much TV. We went up to his room, and he started in on would I stay ten minutes? I didn't say I would, and he got upset. I said fuck a few times, telling him how frustrating it was to end the day with a big argument about whether I was going to stay ten minutes or eight minutes, and then ten was never enough. Fuck Davey, when I was a kid we just went to bed when it was bedtime, and there was no ten minutes. I was excited and animated and desperate and pleading. He was crying under the blanket. I sat beside him and tried to tell him how I felt and went on and on and then asked him if he agreed, and he said he hadn't been listening. I lay down beside him. I asked him to tell me honestly why he was afraid. He said that a few days ago he had a dream. We were in a fun place. Daddy, mommy and Greg. Everyone went away and you told me not to watch the TV you had left on. He opened one eye and watched it and it was very scary. I was afraid he might have seen some wretched porn video left open on the iPad. I was so sorry for this boy whose happiness could so easily be destroyed by my behaviour.

I kissed Davey goodnight and went back to my room. I waited for Lin to come home. I opened the door, and took her coat. I had a cup of tea ready for her. Everything is so far away.

SATURDAY 11 AUGUST 2018

We thought about places to go and couldn't think of anywhere so we went to Salthill. Lin was grim. Everyone at Salthill seemed grumpy and slitty eyed. Every single look was out of a Spaghetti Western.

Lin played lego with Davey. I had a few hoots and went into the library for The Project. I had become aware that The

Project would be another futile endeavour. Lin says that even if nothing comes of it, I should carry on.

After dinner, I organised a family meeting. I brought out paper and pens and the *Positive Discipline* book, open to the page on Family Meetings. Lin rolled her eyes and said please don't read us the book. I asked Lin why she had been grumpy since she'd returned from China. We tied ourselves in knots. We gave one another no wiggle room at all. The only thing left was to walk out the door but I was too lazy to do so. What would be the use? What is the use of anything? Davey sat quietly listening to neurosis and poison, learning how to tie his heart in knots, and make his inner life a clutter of revulsion and fear. Bravo for me. Well done, father. I got Davey on the TV, and had another go at Lin. We tied ourselves tighter, and Lin disavowed our love. We agreed to stay together for the sake of Davey. I told her I would put Tinder on my phone and she didn't even blink.

She played sad *guzheng* music, the haunting soundtrack to our life in Oranswell, only punctuated by the rollicking squirts, beeps, farts, and chirps of *Larvae* on Netflix upstairs.

SUNDAY 12 AUGUST 2018

I showed Davey a bit of The Project and he wasn't impressed. He asked why the yellow submarine was there. When I finished Vision Quest I looked at it on my Mac, the phone, and the iPad.

At Silver Strand the tide was low, and the sun was out. The Burren was clear, and there were heavy dramatic clouds streaming over its shoulders. The water was still, and it ran off so shallow on the sea's exhale. Davey and I walked together out into the water. Davey lay on his back beside me and we were lifted together by long slow waves. We surfed back in on our bellies.

MONDAY 13 AUGUST 2018

The project's tone needs to be more documentary and less left field visionary. I need to wrap up the Kwakiutl.

We went to Dangan. Davey said you know how you always say mommy is angry at you? Do you ever wonder why mommy is angry at you?

We sat at the top of a grassy bank and watched the river. It was smooth and pure. People were throwing sticks into the water for their dogs.

The Project is no longer fun. It is painful to look at. It is even worse to listen to my own voice.

TUESDAY 14 AUGUST 2018

I had a few hoots and looked at my revisions to The Project. I seem to be unable to write. Before coming down I saw the bruises on Lin's legs. I don't want to think about any of this. Radio silence. Davey is all that keeps us together.

The house is a mess. The outside is a mess. So I started to drink beer. Chen Xi called. She condemned me for smoking marijuana and not being realistic. I told her I was rewriting the words for The Kwakiutl Thing and she told me this merely corroborated her point.

I told Lin about the chat with Chen Xi, and she said that figured, and then she reminded me that I hadn't collected Davey and her from the airport. I only realised then that I had not been imagining things, and that she'd held that against me since she got back from China. Things went up quickly then, loops of recrimination. It seems that this damnable process cannot be escaped.

For the rest of the evening I hooted, drank beer, and exchanged barbs with Lin.

All hope is gone. This house is a prison. Everything is ragged and ugly. What will we do today? What a waste.

WEDNESDAY 15 AUGUST 2018

I am unable to write the simplest thing. Lin took Davey to summer camp, and then we sat down to bicker until we ran out of steam. When she went to the gym I worked on The Kwakiutl Thing, then cleaned all four toilets. I decided to deal with the conflict by being as submissive as possible. I felt peace in this resolve.

When Lin got home she offered me something to eat, but I was on a punishment fast. Lin went to collect Davey, and I did some work on the Kwakiutl. I wasn't getting anything done. I was just staring at the thing. Had I become, or always been stupid? Had I broken my brain? I don't feel like writing when I am not stoned. Lin and Chen Xi are adamant that if I can only write when I am stoned there is something wrong with what I am writing.

THURSDAY 16 AUGUST 2018

The Kwakiutl Thing is incomprehensible, all over the place. Whenever I see a half glimmer of an idea I throw it in.

Lin took Davey into town. I vacuumed, did some laundry, and mopped. Time dragged. I hooted a lot, and felt otherworldly. When I looked at what I had written in the morning, it was utterly incoherent.

SATURDAY 18 AUGUST 2018

After a bit of writing, I vacuumed the library and the Zen room. I am happy to do house work every day. Chen Xi and her mom are coming soon, and I should have the house in order.

TUESDAY 21 AUGUST 2018 07:12

Davey has been chatting away to them in Chinese to Chen Xi and her mom. We gathered apples in the garden. Davey went up on my shoulders to pick some, and then I shook the tree to get the rest.

The river was beautiful. Hulaoshi saw fish, so I decided to cook chowder for dinner. Lin, Chen Xi and Hu Laoshi walked down the road picking berries. The Chinese love anything that is for free. Now Lin is looking for ways to fix runny blackberry jam.

THURSDAY 23 AUGUST 2018

Chen Xi scolded me for too much drinking and dope. She is cranky spending so much time with Hulaoshi. She generally likes to be by herself.

Lin cooked a big dinner with chicken wings and mussels. After dinner I tidied up then went out to meet Aidon. Lin and Chen Xi knew where I was going. When I got back I went up to Davey's room while the ladies chatted downstairs. Davey thought it was unfair that adults got to do whatever they wanted to. I feel more comfortable with Chinese people than western people.

FRIDAY 24 AUGUST 2018

The jiaozi were ready and Lin hadn't returned. I felt pressure from Chen Xi, and called Lin. She yelled at me and hung up. I sent a message saying let's not fight. I asked Lin to come up and talk to me. Trying to talk about not fighting became a fight. I got to the point where I didn't give a fuck and it wasn't nice. Chen Xi and her mom witnessed my nasty face.

Hulaoshi took over cooking dinner. When Lin started to help, I said I would do the noodles. According to Hulaoshi I wrecked them. Lin started crying and Chen Xi went out with her, crying too. I walked with Chen Xi and gave out about Lin, not holding back. When we got home I went out and smoked and drank. I was having so much trouble keeping my mind under control–all its hideous, fantastic hungers and worries–all of the things that meditation is supposed to suppress.

Guests always trouble me.. I worry about who is cooking and cleaning, who feels they are losing face, who is being disrespected, who is not pulling his weight, getting a free ride. Pettiness. They are all up now, and I don't even know how to say hello. Even Davey wasn't friends with me this morning. It's awful Lin and I walking around as if we can't see one another.

Lin and Hulaoshi compete to see who can prepare the most food, and I will clean up the whole mess afterwards.

. . .

SATURDAY 25 AUGUST 2018 09:16

I'm just back from Bray. I left Chen Xi's place at about six this morning. I woke her to close the door behind me. Lin and I are friends again. We fought yesterday but we made up and will try again.

Yesterday Lin and I continued to squabble. I found myself experiencing a sort of mental breakdown. I couldn't accept anything she said.

After lunch, the sun came out. Hulaoshi was laying flat in a beam of sunshine in the Zen room. We joked about how Hulaoshi was like a cat, and found all the places kitty liked. Lin and I made peace somehow, through eye contact or simple interchange. We are in the habit now of criticising everything the other person says.

Chen Xi and I walked to the patio space in front of the Zen room. I picked tomatoes for her. Lin came out and sat on the bench. She advised Chen Xi to take away some sage. I explained the magical and scientific qualities of sage. Chen Xi and I walked down the road. She was excited by the huge blackberries. We turned back at the horses. When we got to Bray. Chen Xi served me two beers and a little tin of whiskey. She made salmon. I sat with Hulaohsi , hooted and drank. Lin sent Hulaoshi a message and she read it out at the table. It was lovely and gracious.

. . .

SUNDAY 26 AUGUST 2018

Yesterday morning I got coffee in Maynooth. I had sausage and black and white pudding in Loughrea. I remembered how the day before, driving with Chen Xi, I began to feel hope and comfort again.

MONDAY 27 AUGUST 2018

Dan arrives in Dublin today. Last night Warnock said he would be coming down. I guess he had been communicating with Dan about his arrival. He is going to bring his daughters so the girls will sleep in the stone room, and Dan and Heidi can sleep in the Chen Xi suite.

It kind of bothered me that Warn hadn't been down to see me in two years and now he was coming down the day Dan arrived. It's no use thinking about things this way though.

I hooted and worked on a drawing of Vancouver Island with the Apple pencil. I drank four tins of Guinness. Lin screamed roughly, dinner is ready! I felt bullied, and Lin and I started a fight, but then we suddenly stopped and got on with it. I got more drunk and stoned, and Davey asked me why I always fight with mommy?

The map of Vancouver Island, The Kwakiutl, The Time Machine, and Where Dean Died are all layers of The Project. I needn't abandon everything. Winter and dark ahead. Time to file, throw out old clothes and receipts.

TUESDAY 28 AUGUST 2018

Dan is outside looking around the garden. I avoided getting too drunk or stoned yesterday, and Lin and I went up to bed at about 8:30. The others stayed up.

Heidi is German, civilised and practical. We started drinking Guinness while I showed them around. When Warnock and his family arrived, we continued drinking Guinness. Lin made a big meal. After dinner, I went out for a walk around the garden with the boys, and we hooted in the garage. The girls and Warnock played guitar, and Danny talked about his treks on the caribou trail.

WEDNESDAY 29 AUGUST 2018

I'm enjoying having all of these people around. Aude and Lin made dinner. Warn told me the ash trees were taking over, and urged me to cut them back. It sounded radical to take out the tallest trees, but he seems to know what he's talking about.

I bailed early on the smoking and drinking. Lin came to me for a cuddle after putting Davey to bed.

THURSDAY 30 AUGUST 2018

Warn and I cut down some rhododendron. He says we need to cut down trees to let in the light.

Warn's girls played guitar, then Warn gave me a bud and his gang departed.

Heidi and Dan gave us gifts. I am wearing hand knitted socks from Heidi now, as are Lin and Davey. I also have a cool little Haida style Raven dope bowl, and a book on Kwakiutl legends.

FRIDAY 31 AUGUST 2018

We were up carousing until late. Heidi made a delicious roulade for dinner, followed by drinking, laughing.

SATURDAY 1 SEPTEMBER 2018

I just smoked a big joint, and feel wobbly. Davey is in the room, studying me. I am having trouble not disintegrating into Pointillism before his eyes.

When we got to Inishmore we chose the same horse and cart team as last time; Andy and Johnny Cash. At Dun Aengus, I lay on my back on the grass getting an Aran Island sun tan. Davey sat on my belly. The others looked around then sat on the grass with us. It was like Hawaii. We watched huge white clouds moving above the stark cliffs, and the black water breaking white along the fierce old rocks. We walked back down the hill and checked in with Andy and Johnny Cash, then had a beer and a beef and Guinness stew

We had to wait until six for the ferry so we got more Guinness and listened to old people speaking Irish. On the ferry Davey sat outside in the back and was amazed looking up at the clean white lines and the breaking black water, the almighty wind in his face.

Lin made tomato and egg noodles. Heidi made mojitos. I took Davey to bed. Lin told me that the night before I made painful noises in my sleep. She urged me to be gentle with myself.

SUNDAY 2 SEPTEMBER 2018

I rolled a joint that was way too strong–I couldn't talk to Dan, so I went upstairs and he went down to his room. When I felt sane again I called them out of their room. We went to Blackrock. It was rainy and grey, but there were people in the water, and going off the tower. Dan dove from the top platform.

We cracked a few Hobgoblins as soon as we got back to the house. I showed Dan my Kwakiutl thing. After dinner, we had a walk and met an old man full of memories under the big pine trees. When we got back, we all sat outside, and watched Dan and Davey kick a ball back and forth. I don't know how Dan was able to keep up the commentary throughout. Lin, Dan, and Heidi had another drink, and I put Davey to bed. He told me that when mommy and I fought it was usually my fault. He said mommy just being quiet didn't mean she wanted to fight.

MONDAY 3 SEPTEMBER 2018

Danny paid for a load of booze at Joyce's. We sat outside drinking beer. Dan played football with Davey.

THURSDAY 6 SEPTEMBER 2018

I am 54 years old today. I got two copies of *21 Lessons for the 21st Century*, at Charlie Byrne's bookshop, one for Dan and one for me. When we got home, I lit a fire. Lin prepared *gongbaojiding* and duck. Afterwards, Dan made hot Kraken toddies, and we had a long chat by the fire. Life is good, Dan always says.

FRIDAY 7 SEPTEMBER 2018

We had breakfast, and then began the long drive to Sligo. We stopped first at the mesolithic tombs. We paid admission and walked around the dolmens and stone circles arranged as calendars. Dan and Heidi wanted to listen to the German and French tour group guides, but I walked on with Davey. We bought coffee from a wagon. The couple making the coffee were hilarious, and I laughed at Danny taking less than a minute to mention that he had spent time in the Arctic.

We followed the GPS to the bottom of Knocknarea, Queen Maeve's Tomb. It was a challenging walk, but Davey skipped along. When we got to the top the view was amazing. We ate fish and chips on the Strandhill promenade, admiring Ben Bulbin and the surfers.

SATURDAY 8 SEPTEMBER 2018

Dan put canvas on the corners of his artwork, *Osiris*, so we can hang it in the library. It is pastel on tar paper, savagely red. I talked to Dan about The Project, and he gave me a digital folder with photos of all his paintings. Davey played football with Dan, and then we sat in the Zen room and listened to music.

Dan and I went out to the stone circle and smoked cigarettes. That's three cigarettes while they have been here. I find it hard to control myself.

SUNDAY 9 SEPTEMBER 2018

We all got up late. Dan told me he had fallen in the creek when he went down to the river to wash some stones and turned right instead of left. I was in ructions, streaming tears of laughter. Dan put up the Osiris painting. It looks good, if a little rough. I'll get used to it. We looked at my old photo album.

We drove through Salthill to the bus station. It was sunny and windy, and the tide was high. I felt like we should all go to the diving board, but the holiday was over and we had to get Dan and Heidi to the bus. As we drove Unspoken, from Four Tet's *Rounds* album came on, and I was misty eyed. I was sad to say goodbye to Danny boy.

We had a melancholy but warm hearted drive home. I went out with a Guinness and drank it in the stone circle. I felt very high, but knew it was time to get back to winter habits, batten down the hatches.

Life is good.

THURSDAY 13 SEPTEMBER 2018

I signed up for a poetry workshop at the Galway Arts Centre. I opened another beer and went out to the stone circle. I felt high, composing poetry in my head–sheets of rain, the refrain. I got Davey to pass me a Guinness out the window, and sat on the back step drinking while the rain poured down.

SUNDAY 16 SEPTEMBER 2018

Maybe the Time Machine story and The Project are neither good, nor even useful. Aidon said he might have something for me tomorrow afternoon. The poetry thing is on Friday, a much needed connection with the world.

MONDAY 17 SEPTEMBER 2018

When I got up yesterday I smoked a reefer made from the leaves off my own plant, and it had me spinning and enthusiastic. I suddenly saw a way forward for the creative work. After dinner, I went out and drank beer in the stone circle. I was hypnotised, staring open eyed at the complexity of vegetation. I had another beer or two, and a couple of gins. Lin came out and walked around the garden with me. We found dark mushroom mountains and a fairy circle. She helped me harvest more leaves from my plant.

I need to stop the remorseless drinking, to become civilised and gentlemanly.

TUESDAY 18 SEPTEMBER 2018

There was a storm overnight; there are still gusts coming down through the chimney. I promised myself I wouldn't, but I had a hoot at the front door.

While we were in the sauna, an old lady came in and poured oil with water from a jam jar onto the burner. She talked about all the moths and woodlice in her house. Her husband, she said, hated the grey guys. They came in all sizes. Moths don't come alone. They had eaten holes in the husbands suits. If you lifted a pillow, there would be moths under. She would use the Dyson to get at the woodlouse and the little spiders up in the corners. But the spiders in the corners could control the woodlice a bit. I don't think Lin understood anything the lady was saying.

Aidon Weed gave me a call at 4:40. I asked Davey to come with me, said I'd buy him a treat. We waited in the car. I spotted Aidon walking all swervy like an English thug in his white tracksuit. He complained about being a family man, talked about how much he could drink. There was something dead and mean in his eyes.

Davey and I drove home. Lin was getting ready to go out. She was ravishing. Davey called her "my fashion girl." We drove Lin to the cathedral. Davey went up to watch TV. I chatted with Warn on messenger. He is opposed to a goldmine in the Sperrins, says there are IRA men up there, they haven't come up against the fighting Irish before.

WEDNESDAY 19 SEPTEMBER 2018

Storm Ali

I decided to take Davey to school despite the storm. As I turned right at the gate a fellow drove by with his window down and said there was a tree across the road that way. It seemed the world was being torn to pieces.

I have been trying so hard in my writing to freeze who I am, as defined by personal history. As for my authentic self, I think the point is that there isn't one. The self is a node of consciousness dragged through time. Having time to waste is essential for getting at Truth. The Time Machine negates hurry; it is pure perambulation. I thought about turning the time machine into a poem, and added a line to the Kwakiutl script.

THURSDAY 20 SEPTEMBER 2018

I got up around four and couldn't get back to sleep. I looked at the script for The Project while having a hoot or ten. Eileen told us there was another storm coming: Bronagh. I dated a young lady named Bronagh in Omagh years ago, and she told me her name meant sadness. *21 Lessons* is good on Algorithms and Big Data, on education, meditation and wasting time.

. . .

FRIDAY 21 SEPTEMBER 2018

It is a good thing to have the opportunity to study, learn, create, meditate, and yet I obsessively worry that I am squandering this time. It seems my creations are not worth the time and effort, and as for study...

I did ten minutes of meditation. I focussed on the feelings in my body, and tried to locate where mind met body, to survey the ground on which feelings are created.

MONDAY 24 SEPTEMBER 2018

Lin chatted to her family on Mid-Autumn Day. They called me in, and from the little screen of Lin's phone there were raucous calls to *ganbei*!

THURSDAY 27 SEPTEMBER 2018

I am losing faith in this project which I have put so much work into. It doesn't know if it wants to be a poem or an expository piece. I didn't think it needed to be one or the other, but it is painful for me to even look at it. And yet I worked on the project for most of the morning, shuffling between the two computers, hooting hard. Faithful faithlessness.

I opened a Tsingdao. Davey asked me why I didn't have a job, and Lin came to my defence.

We are going to get two little black cats. I am entranced by the image of us all sitting by the fire with two little black cats playing on the red rug.

FRIDAY 28 SEPTEMBER 2018

I went to the top of the Arts Centre for the poetry workshop. The teacher was Kevin Higgins. There was only one other guy, from Belfast, and four or five ladies. The level of writing and criticism was good. After the workshop, we went for a cup of tea across the road.

Estranged

Your brain began to bleed
as the clock of Lin's contractions narrowed.
So sudden, or so it seemed
from Maternity at *Yuquanlu*.

They called to say you were gone, dad,
eight hours before my son was born.
I had hoped this little boy
would be our reconciliation.

He had your ears, but you
were nowhere now for me to tease.
We were always certain
that when things died they were dead.

The sad embarrassment of your timing
has left me to a world turned strange,
susceptible to calculations, envisionings,
dissemblings of sentiment.

SUNDAY 30 SEPTEMBER 2018 07:16

Lin is up, and the two black kittens are sprinting and rolling. I think one is behind me now.

WEDNESDAY 3 OCTOBER 2018

White birds over the black water. An old guy had a line with several hooks on it, and no bait. Each time he put in his line he pulled out three or four mackerel. Lin wanted to get a fishing rod, but she didn't want to kill them so we dropped the plan. I have a poetry workshop tomorrow, but I didn't do the homework. I thought I could write a poem entitled Bushy Park, but it didn't work. I couldn't write in Lin's voice. Instead I'll write a poem called No Place.

THURSDAY 4 OCTOBER 2018

I rolled a joint made from the leaves of my plants. It was a nice, mellow high, not too trippy, perfect for working on the poem.

FRIDAY 5 OCTOBER 2018 08:28

The cats are ripping around the place. They are a pain in the ass.

I went to the poetry workshop. It was all ladies and the Belfast guy. We had a nice chat about Yeats to start. Maybe I talked too much. We went through our poems, and everyone was praised profusely, even me.

MONDAY 8 OCTOBER 2018

Had a hoot, and, feeling groovy, I worked on the poem, cutting seven pages down to a sonnet.

No Place

If there was a place called no place
I could consider myself well rooted there;
I'd have a cousin at every corner
and buddies all about me.

But no… The poet's soil was never mine,

nor any other soil:
I have always stood on others' ground,
on someone else's sufferance.

I would tell a tale of there and back
but there was nowhere to return:
My place has been cases and moving vans,
my dreams a diaspora.

No place is mine is what I find:
My neighbours are old ghosts.

TUESDAY 9 OCTOBER 2018

I called Lin in to have a look at the poem, and I think she liked it. We went for a walk at Salthill. It was windy, the tide was out, and the sand whipped our faces. We walked to one end of the prom and back. I slow-clapped Lin when she kicked the wall at the end.

THURSDAY 11 OCTOBER 2018

Storm Callum

At times it seemed the windows would be blown in. I read *The Order of Time* in the bath.

Lin was outside. I cracked a beer and joined her. We brought out the cats. It was a beautiful summer-like afternoon. I was ecstatic to see the cats experiencing the garden, amazed by the gorgeous complexity of everything. I walked the stone circle, drunk and stunned.

FRIDAY 12 OCTOBER 2018

There weren't many at the poetry workshop. Apart from the one dude from Belfast, they were all sweet little old ladies. They liked my poem. They liked every poem. Kevin gave me some helpful suggestions.

Robin and Black Cat

I am waiting out in the rain again,
pockets stuffed with speckled paper.
In the house my wife dreams
she is climbing down a ladder.

Let me be counted one of those
who seek oblivion in dosages survivable,
turning away from this stinking,
bellicose, and baying world.

A robin loiters in the pale light nearby.
I toast him with a lift of tin,
a deep sip of Polish special brew,

and *eureka,* we evade the tedium of truth.

The cat is the crouching spirit of this garden:
slinking soundless, sleek and black,
green eyes gliding over drenched red leaves
fallen from the cherry tree.

The ball point rips at
and the damp paper crumbles
until sudden commotion of soul's cry
and she is upon him, asking everything.

I watch these garden deities dramatise
the poet's lot: my aching heart now understands
no joy should be as wide as mine,
and I shiver as my soul cinches shut in dread.

I turn away and notice her light is on.
I will go in now and shine her boots,
crying out I love you and let this never end,
let there be no mercy.

THURSDAY 25 OCTOBER 2018

I hooted and drank beer. My mind was flying and I was zoning in on the poem.

FRIDAY 26 OCTOBER 2018

I printed up my poem and drove to the Arts Center. There were two newcomers in the class, intelligent women who offered good criticism. All of the poems were good, though I'm not sure about mine. The suggestions for editing were excellent.

Against Dying (Chun Jie in Oranswell)

I step out silent at six am
into the sacred rapture of cataclysmic dawn
the insane revelry of all these birds
celebrates my arrival with seed.
Robins gather round me as I turn the earth.

On such a morning we might forget
this is a dying world.
My little forest breathes out to me
and the stream beside intones
its ancient secrets never ending.

Back inside Lin prepares porridge
sends and receives
greetings to Beijing.
It is their dinner time
and they gather in love.

They fill and wrap dumplings:
symbols of eternity dropped in steaming pots
float to the top.

This little picture of our blessed lives is only that:
no word of god from mountain lugged.
It has all been said already–yes,
but I will speak again against oblivion.

MONDAY 29 OCTOBER 2018

Yesterday morning I wrote a poem. It took a lot out of me. I don't know how to fix things–what needs fixing. I have to consider that poetry and marijuana might not be as helpful a bulwark against the feeling of emptiness that threatens to overcome me. I am not looking after my health. I am not doing any mediation, or any sort of exercise.

FRIDAY 2 NOVEMBER 2018

Lin read my poems, and she said they were good.

The workshop was cancelled. Three ladies I hadn't met before suggested we workshop our poems anyway. I think it went well, and that I was helpful with their poems. They liked my poem, and one of the ladies suggested I should come to the Thursday classes, for more advanced students.

Two Records of a Floating Life

Living what's left

too much with us
meaning
dragged through this moment
from then till then
now the thinnest
increment of time
rushed along
invisible membrane
wave's edge
that is all there is
no then and then
at all
you two
are all that's left of me

Endings are beginnings

Summer was mental:
profusion, infestation

I haven't been
to the stone circle
out back
all these months

Despite the creaks and groans
of flesh and bones,
I need broom,
rake, shovel
to strip winter
back to its cleanest core

Poems come and poems go;
I let them drift away:
grabbing pen and paper
only wrecks them anyway

SATURDAY 3 NOVEMBER 2018

The little cat is up the tree in front of the window, and a council of magpies are haranguing him. I hope it ends well.

I am worried about money again. I need a job, but I just don't know how to get one. Maybe I should ask Fred if they need any help on the online learning material. I should update my Linkedin profile, put up more hours for Fluentify.

SUNDAY 4 NOVEMBER 2018 07:37

I woke yesterday full of hope. We went to Joyce's and got a few things, then I started a fight with Lin, the same old thing, I felt she was distant and disrespectful, that she loathed me.

She didn't try to diffuse the situation, so I got beer. When we got home, Lin went out to play football with Davey. I hooted leaves and started drinking, walked around the garden awe struck by the curlings and cowlings of nature, its proliferation.

I chatted to the guy next door, who was holding two horses while we spoke. I made dinner, and after I finished the beer I opened a bottle of wine. I posted things to facebook which I deleted soon thereafter. I don't remember anything after this–a flash of myself vomiting, waking and wondering why Lin wasn't beside me. Lin told me later that I had locked the door, and came down to find her when I figured this out at 2 am.

I need to do more poetry, but it takes so much out of me. I would love to be able to produce something when I am clear. I want to only drink on weekends. I wonder what Lin and Davey did last night. It could have been such a pleasant evening.

MONDAY 5 NOVEMBER 2018

I read *The Order of Time* while Lin played *guzheng*. Then I watched a lecture about quantum fields, had a hoot of leaves and read poetry in the bath.

TUESDAY 6 NOVEMBER 2018

We went to Salthill. The tide was high, the light stern. We walked along the sand.

I chatted with Chen Xi, who was upset because Tan didn't want her to visit us, even for Davey's birthday, and water had leaked down through the roof from her bath last night.

I read more from the big Irish anthology, and was struck by John Montague and Derek Mahon's work. Laying in bed I conjured a bit of a poem so I went downstairs and wrote it. Afterwards I tossed and turned the rest of the night.

FRIDAY 16 NOVEMBER 2018

Lin is making kimchi, chatting to Chen Xi.

She sent me to the poetry workshop. It was slow to start, and not many came, but the poems were good. Mine went over well I think.

Lin collected Chen Xi. She got beer and Prosecco, so I made Prosecco with sloe berry gin. They got drunk and giggled away in Chinese.

I won't write a new poem this week; instead I will drag out and dust off Our Dragon Prow.

WuKeSong (Five Pine Trees)

He had been riding without a helmet
and his head was smashed to bits.

I looked away, kept the car to the right
to avoid those poor dead fingers
curling open on the tarmac.

There was no stopping, no consolation —
Nothing anyone could do, here
in the immense machine of this city
grinding us all down to bone meal.

TUESDAY 20 NOVEMBER 2018

We took Chen Xi to the bus station. I gave her a hug and Lin saw her to the bus.

WEDNESDAY 21 NOVEMBER 2018

Lin had left me out two buds. I printed up Our Dragon Prow, then started to go through the rest of the box--a lot of poems and other writing. Most of it is dreadful, and should be destroyed. I found the sad burnt folder holding Deane's *Fillardy Goblin*.

. . .

FRIDAY 23 NOVEMBER 2018

Eventually Kevin arrived, and then a full load of students, but I was the only man. The poems were all good.

Our Dragon Prow (for my brother, Deane)

No. I'll never be numb
of dirging you.

This sorrow will not wilt
like the voodoo bouquets
that were once
beautiful like you.

May there be staying
of the sad strong dirge
that brings weeping
for how we once walked glad
together to where
the land became grey sea
that stretched forth
like hunting ground for wolves.

SATURDAY 24 NOVEMBER 2018

I read *Your Brain is a Time Machine*. Lin made tomato and egg noodles for lunch. Then I got her to give me out a couple of buds from the jar. I walked around the stone circle. The cats followed me. I explained automatic writing to Lin and asked her to do some. I did a bit of scrawling myself.

SUNDAY 25 NOVEMBER 2018

Lin dreamed she was growing tomatoes. There was a turtle born in a bird's nest beside a baby bird. I dreamt we had fancy bathtubs and were planning where to put them.

MONDAY 26 NOVEMBER 2018

I messaged Aidon, to see if we might meet this evening. I read Davey the end of *Perseus*, and then I read him *Theseus and the Minotaur*. Lin played *guzheng*, and I read *Your Brain is a Time Machine*.

TUESDAY 27 NOVEMBER 2018

It is pitch black out now, and there is a strong wind. Storm Diana draws nigh. Lin gave me a bud, and I started to work on a poem. I got Lin to translate the bit she had written the other day. Then I did a poem based on what she had written.

WEDNESDAY 28 NOVEMBER 2018

Another dream about tidying the house. The tide was high and the storm was powerful. A crazy old woman swam in the churning sea.

THURSDAY 29 NOVEMBER 2018

I got a little bit of doob from Lin, and I worked on the sea swimming poem. When I showed it to Lin I could see she didn't like how she was portrayed. I worked at being more rigorous in description, less reliant on typification, and she liked it. She made fish for dinner. We sat by the fire. The cats joined us. Lin played *guzheng*. I read *Your Brain is a Time Machine*.

I have three lessons this morning, and the poetry workshop this afternoon. I'll have a drink tonight, and reclaim my jar of weed.

FRIDAY 30 NOVEMBER 2018

I looked at some of the art hung in the Arts Centre before going up to the workshop. Kevin and I had a chat before the other students arrived. My poem went over well. I slipped off when they went for tea afterwards.

At home, there were a few tins of Guinness waiting for me.

Lin gave me a nice big bud, and made stew. She read my poem again and I think she was impressed.

Sea swimming

my husband was afraid
of where i come from
said it was the end of the world
and that we had to give our son
a life away from that white smoke
that black dragon snaking
through the yellow world
south of Siberia
and it was his big idea
brought us here

and i am not someone
who hoped or dreamed of coming here
but I have learned to like it:
we have no such green as this

I am happy here but still
after the boy and man have gone to bed
I treat myself to a costume drama about the Qing

and there was that day before I took our boy
back to Heilongjiang to see my parents

the sea at Blackrock was still and clear
like nothing in this world and I couldn't resist
the shock of the cold water made me laugh
when I went in for the first time, just me
and from down there so low
at the level of the sea
my face reflected amongst
cloud up behind me
magic white flowers round my head
eye to eye with Clare and Galway
spinning round me I felt
my own body become a bright pin twisting
into that pure and burning water
twisting into all this beauty
into all this good fortune
becoming a part of here
and I wanted to sing or shout
I am of Ireland and there at the shore
my husband and my boy were laughing
among everything around
in circles inside circles
bright sea stones yes all the world
laughing with us

SATURDAY 1 DECEMBER 2018

Lin didn't want to give me back the whole jar, but I have it now. I wrote what I thought was a good poem, a little one, but Lin wasn't fussed, so I went back to the drawing board.

I lit a fire. Davey and I went out with Davey to chop wood. I made a dramatic karate chop sound each time I swung the axe.

I chopped up the veg and put it in the oven with the lamb that Lin had prepared. I made drinks with mead, sloe gin, prosecco, and tonic water.

After dinner Davey and I went up to watch TV. Lin sat by the remains of the fire and watched a costume drama about the Qing.

SUNDAY 2 DECEMBER 2018

I spent the morning trying to write but nothing came out. Afterwards I raked the path beneath the rose trellis, while Lin prepared a fire. Lin and Davey went inside but the cats stayed out with me. I took off my jumper and worked in my t-shirt.

I want to type up Deane's goblin story, write two more poems, and finish the Kwakiutl thing before the solstice.

. . .

MONDAY 3 DECEMBER 2018

I tried to meditate but it was impossible to achieve stillness.

FRIDAY 7 DECEMBER 2018

It is stormy outside and dark. The wind is heaving through the trees in front of the window.

When I finished with Antonio, I edited the new poem and read it to Lin. She dropped me off in town. I perambulated a while before going up to the poetry workshop.

Not many people attended. When I read my poem, I didn't get the response I expected. I don't know why they didn't seem impressed. Kevin had given some good suggestions, but then the criticism bogged down in debates over repetition. I suppose I am being overly sensitive.

What should I do with this poem? It's not like I ever believed that writing poetry would lead to fame and fortune. I will just have to persevere with the utmost of sincerity, the magic ingredient.

I left quickly after class. A taxi driver from Connemara lectured me on the preparation of boxty: grate the potatoes and twist them in a cheesecloth to drain off the starch. I opened a beer, and began to hoot ferociously. I opened the gin and got wrecked. Lin made a nice big fire. She played chess with Davey and they had a tight battle. I don't remember much after that.

Paper

Yet, despite these persuasive arguments in favour of eternalism, we must acknowledge that the laws of physics fail to account for what would seem to be one of the most robust and unequivocal observations human beings have ever made: that the present is special and that time does flow.

1. MY MOTHER

After you'd died
I dreamed you visited
and we joked and laughed
until I realised
you needed to go.

Where are you now?
Where is the light of your eyes,
the grace of your laughter?
Can the black beetle creeping
over your beloved face
be all there is?

I cannot say goodbye
though it has been

on my lips
for a thousand years.

Could we but rush back
along the track of light,
twisting past all of gravity's troughs
you would be here beside me.

2. MY BROTHER

Your scorched journal
has followed me around the world,
through all my moves
and many lives.

A blue binder,
cursive ballpoint legible though
the paper's edge is seared.
It is something that died beside you.
Full of future
you'd bought a van,
drove from the prairies
through the Rockies
to the spruce forests
of the Island.

I found this fantasy novel
tucked between

the blackened sleeping bag
and your scorched thighs
that windy seaside morning
over thirty years ago.

I will get typing now.

SATURDAY 8 DECEMBER 2018

Lin made seaweed and egg drop soup with oven-heated rolls. Chen Xi called to tell us that Chen Fu had lung cancer. He is going to have the same operation Chen Xi had. He is still smoking, and I can understand that.

I went to meet Aidon. I got frozen fish and Polish beers in Centra. When I got home, there was a nice fire going. I hooted and drank beer. I didn't mean to, but I drank all four, and then started on the sloe gin. I took a photo of my little dudes playing chess in front of the fire, and put it up on facebook. It got a lot of likes, even one from Michael McGarry of Swan.

Lin, shiny Asian, went to The Galway Munch. I felt anxious for her to get home. Jealousy, fear, the exhilarating thrill of my god what have I done? She returned at about 12:30, and took a while to settle down. I made her a cup of tea. She asked me not to make her do this again. We went to bed. She wore the blue Who-ville-jammies Chen Xi got her.

SUNDAY 9 DECEMBER 2018

I tried to write a poem, got a bit done on my dad's story about the kid who made the flying machine out of junk. We relaxed by the fire. The girl cat was being reasonable, but the boy kept going up on the counters.

WEDNESDAY 12 DECEMBER 2018

I hooted and tried to work on the poem and on the Cannibal Monster thing. Nothing. The Cannibal Monster is a total mess; the poem is insipid.

THURSDAY 13 DECEMBER 2018

When Lin got home, I showed her my poem, and talked about how to fix it. We had a walk by the river. It was dark and grim; there is little sunlight these days. When we got home, Lin and Davey put up the Christmas tree. I went down to the stone room to work on the poem. As I drank and smoked the poem began to come together. I shifted to wine and then sloe gin. I got a poem. Lin made baozi. I read my poem to Lin and Davey.

FRIDAY 14 DECEMBER 2018 08:12

A bit crushed

Lin and Davey are in the other room eating porridge. It is still dark outside. I had a last look at the poem and printed it up. I arrived at class early, sat alone with Kevin until the feminist lady came in. She was writing a book, *On Men*.

After I presented my poem there was silence. One lady asked if it had really happened and I said of course not. Kevin said we need to ask if this works as a poem? What does anyone think? No one said anything. He said then in a cheerleader voice, well I think it does. He offered some good suggestions. The feminist lady looked at me and said of Kevin, he's great isn't he. Later, there was a discussion about the sorts of male behaviour that make women uncomfortable. I took the elbow of the little lady beside me to demonstrate a point, and she nearly crawled out of her skin. They went for tea but I just slipped away with a meek see you all next year.

The boy cat kept getting on the counter. Then he came in and piddled on the red carpet while we sat on it. I would like to get rid of them. I am not happy with these cats.

Departure

When I was four or five my dad led
our family across oceans, through frozen forests
driving days across yellow plains

I was beside my father in the car;
The moon kept pace beside his head

Along that prairie highway he gave a story
from Glenties before he was born

Of a boy who lugged iron scraps from the dump,
piled it up in his back garden those short, dark days

Neighbours jeering and pressing faces between slats
snorting, munching, slavering–who would not have
sought escape?

Sitting on a scarlet chesterfield atop his heap
he gripped a lever between his legs with both hands

The yobs gawped and the heap hardly rattled
as it lifted, whirred an instant, poised
Before shooting off into cloud

SATURDAY 15 DECEMBER 2018 08:25

It is black outside, and pouring rain. My lungs are sore from that fake weed Aidon sold me. I had tossed and turned through the night with a sense that everything had gone wrong. Yesterday I hadn't managed to do anything. I looked at the wreckage of the Kwakiutl thing. There is no point of entry. Why am I compelled by impossibilities?

I joked to Lin that we needed to get out of the house for some sunshine.

TUESDAY 18 DECEMBER 2018

I had a long and vivid dream about Aihua. It was a complete upgrade: there were climbing walls, theme areas, hundreds of teachers, and Mark Gallup in a bigfoot costume.

I played chess with Davey, and we sat by the fire. I closed all Fluentify slots until solstice so I can finish the Kwakiutl thing.

THURSDAY 20 DECEMBER 2018

The symbolism of completing my work on the Kwakiutl today. I sent Davey into school and when I got back, Lin went to town. I stayed and was hard on myself. I smoked a lot of dope and didn't eat anything. I wrote until it was time to collect Davey. I went out into the stone circle to drink a beer and smoke a cigarette. A mere blip. I had finished writing the thing, though Magic, the final chapter, still needed to be typed.

Chen Xi said Chen Fu is in the hospital to have surgery to take out a bit of a lung. Is this why I bought cigarettes yesterday? I hear Lin making breakfast, and the cats around her meowing. My son is still asleep. Now the days will lengthen.

SATURDAY 22 DECEMBER 2018

After the holiday I want to ready the place for airbnb. I will keep writing, get this Kwakiutl thing up on a website.

I need to get off drink and drugs. The cloudiness of my mind has been holding me back. I should have been able to do something, but have always failed at things I should have been able to succeed at.

SUNDAY 23 DECEMBER 2018

I am not looking after myself–I always need to be wrecked around Christmas. I suppose that is why I went so mental on facebook yesterday. I posted something about We are the children of the Apocalypse. Brett Smith, Scarlet, and Tony commented. Tony made fun of the article. I deleted it, then reposted it.

I snuck a CBD/sloe gin and tonic. Then I had a little bottle of Guinness. After that I switched to hot rum toddies. I posted and reposted and made weird comments. I played some Dead Can Dance and remembered bad times in Calgary. My dad diving for the shotgun.

Long night of the facebook soul. More drink, hoots, squid for dinner. I grooved on the guitar a while before going back to posting, deleting, posting again. It is daytime now, but it is very grey. My head hurts, my muscles feel that they are wilting, degenerating. The hoots will be done soon. I need to do meditation, go to the gym. I know I have said this before, many times.

MONDAY 24 DECEMBER 2018 06:46

I played Risk with Davey on the red rug in front of the fire. Lin prepared a leg of lamb, roast potatoes, and cabbage. I snuck around hooting and it felt awful. The wee pipe I am using is gunky with tar. The weed I am smoking gets me weird and out of control.

Darby called, and he and Rose stopped by. Davey stayed with Rose, and I gave Darby a CBD sloe gin. Darby was funny and he got a bit drunk. I had a drag of his e-cig. He told me he likes to smoke dope and I will get it from him next time. When he left he gave me some cigarettes. Later I snuck into the garage and had one.

THURSDAY 25 DECEMBER 2018

Only I am up. I snuck out for one of the cigarettes Darby gave me. I started writing this diary when I quit cigarettes, and now they seem to be exerting a hold over me again. Scarlet called. I talked about booze. I didn't feel comfortable so I chatted about my CBD sloe gin, which was of no interest to them. We drove to Salthill and saw the Christmas swimmers. It was standing room only.

Once dinner was in the oven I went out for another beer and the last of the cigarettes. Farmer James gave me a bottle of potcheen. We started drinking Bailey's. I played the Pogues. I mixed the potcheen with the Bailey's, and it had me weeping and laughing at the same time.

WEDNESDAY 26 DECEMBER 2018

I lay in bed this morning, dreaming of yellow trees and having dark thoughts. Yesterday I felt utterly hopeless, thinking about how I didn't do anything, didn't have any friends or connections with people, and wasn't good at anything. And yet, despite being superfluous, I was prepared coffee by Lin. The day was mild and the windows fogged.

It was a lovely afternoon so we stayed in the garden. Lin said this is a beautiful place. I was surprised because I thought we were past saying that. The cats were tearing around. Passing neighbours said hello over the stone wall.

Even if the money were to last, I face the prospect of dying as a guy who had no job, who was part of nothing, who left his loves naked to the winds because he was not good at anything. I need to take action. Drink and drugs may power the time machine, but they make me into a shameful heap. Over Christmas the potcheen made me teary and maudlin. When I talked to Scarlet, all I could chat about was getting drunk and the marijuana in the sloe gin. Lin and Davey see me behaving in ways that no one else would tolerate. So many bridges burnt. Why do I make myself so unpleasant? I realise it would be almost impossible for me to get a job working for anyone being as I am; I am pretty much unemployable. I need to try to work on my own terms.

THURSDAY 27 DECEMBER 2018

We walked up and down the prom. I got a West Indies Porter, then I snuck back in for a pack of cigarettes. I need to stop this immediately or I am fucked. Cigarettes have great power over me.

Last night I dreamed about being late for Fluentify and then turning up in person to meet a crazy guy with a giant beard. I think Lin and Davey, or Deane, were with me. We discovered we were in Belarus, and then we were arrested, and taken to prison.

. . .

FRIDAY 28 DECEMBER 2018

Yesterday was spent sneaking out for cigarettes; at first they made me dizzy, later they made me bored. I rolled up the last of the hoots and walked around the place. I jotted down notes for poetry. I threw the remains of the packet in the stream.

I could organise and advertise Corporate and Executive Services for Chinese Business People Travelling to Ireland. Failing that, I can go to the employment bureau.

SUNDAY 30 DECEMBER 2018

Yesterday morning Lin came to the window in my old black coat, said she couldn't find Bagheera. I found him dead on the road. I brought out two shovels, and Lin helped me get him into a box. I put the box in the wheelbarrow.

When I told Davey he laughed at first, then was sorry. I said it's normal to not believe when you hear someone is dead. I buried Bagheera in the back by the farmer's wall. I dug the hole a bit deeper because I didn't want to squeeze him in. There were big stones and crossing roots. I sent Lin and Davey away but Davey hung around for the internment. I tried not to look at the little cat, but I had a glance. He was so beautiful, such sleek black fur. I said you are beautiful, and poured the compost over him. I didn't look down. I cried, and repeated you are beautiful. I shovelled the rest of the dirt and scraped stones over the hole. I didn't press down.

I went to Lin and Davey at the forest end of the rose trellis. I told them he was beautiful, and it was sad, and I cried some more. We went into the house. I regretted that I had not been kinder to him. We talked about how funny he was.I suggested tea at McCambridges. Lin said that they didn't have the big apple pie she liked, so we went to Coco's and I got Lin the last apple pie. The apple pie was served warm with cream. I finished what Lin and Davey left. The big voiced Alabama busker played Aqualung, and I thought I saw him crying while he sang.

I went to the shop to get milk and cigarettes. I had one immediately, felt pleasantly dizzy. When I got home, we went out to drop off gifts for Darby's girls. Darby pressed a bit of weed into my palm.

I rolled a joint, opened a beer and went out to the stone circle. It was getting dark. When I came back I chatted with Davey. I told him that I didn't not believe in magic, and then I said how Bageera would be communicating with the crystal we buried under the stone circle. We talked about continental drift, how the continents are flecks pushed around the top of a boiling ball, how mountain ranges are pushed up by continents pressing against one another. I showed him how mountains were pushed up with my fingers, as my father had once done. We talked about how wishes work. I told him about Midas, I told him how Genies often turn your wishes against you, if your wishes are selfish or trivial. He said he would wish to make Bageera alive. I told him you shouldn't do that. I told him the only mistake Jesus made was when he raised Lazarus from the dead. I was remembering William Defoe. Davey asked me how Jesus raised Lazarus from the dead, and I told him he hugged Lazarus and said I love you, you are beautiful. When Lazarus woke up though, he said no, what have you done, I was dead, I was where I was supposed to be. You shouldn't have brought me back here, it's not right.

I went out and smoked another joint. I remembered a dream years ago where my mom came back and we both knew it wasn't right. When I came in Lin was serving fish and chips. I said I'm sorry you have to carry so much weight for the family. She said I don't, you do. I left it at that. Over dinner Davey and I talked about the speed of light. I asked him how long it took light to get from the sun to the earth and he said eight minutes. He said he remembered me telling him before.

I was feeling wrecked. My back was sore. I confessed to Lin that I was falling, but assured her I would get back up soon. She said I can't afford to fall too many times. She began to cry and said she didn't want to be left alone like the girl cat sitting at her feet, loving and clingy.

I had a second beer but resolved against a third. Lin took Davey to bed. When she came back, she delivered a kiss and I went down and rubbed his back. I read Rilke.

Tomorrow I will reset myself. I need to tidy the garage. clean the house, look into a website, make sure we paid taxes, keep enough USD on hand, put up shelves, get sports shoes and start running, clear branches, finish the Cannibal Monster, type Deane's goblin story.

MONDAY 31 DECEMBER 2018

Last day of bad habits

I snuck a few joints with my coffee out in the stone circle. Davey came out and we swept it clear of leaves. Then he put together a cardboard marker for Bageera's grave. We went inside and Lin built a fire. I drank my two Polish beers while I made mashed potatoes and savoury mince. I walked around the house, admiring what we had done.

SATURDAY 5 JANUARY 2019

Yesterday I got up early and went out and fed the cat. I stayed outside for a while. It was good being out in the quiet night. I took my Guinness out to the stone circle, and then went around removing twigs and weeds from the gravel path.

There seem to be no emergencies on the horizon. I have been so uncertain about what I should be doing. Should I be working on the Cannibal Monster? Should I be writing poetry? Should I be working on the novel? Should I be focusing on Fluentify? Should I be looking for a different job? I guess I should be doing all of these things, but it is such a dissipation of energy, and when I expend so much effort and none of these things come through, it makes me feel superfluous.

If I smoke any more, I will need to say I am smoking again. I can't let that happen. I need to look after my health so I can protect my family.

MONDAY 7 JANUARY 2019

I dreamed I was living with a Trinity girlfriend, and her dad and I were arguing. Catherine was unhappy that we weren't getting along. I said we were like brother and sister, that we had little spats but we got along. I went out for a walk, and couldn't find where we lived again, because we had moved to a Chinese community. I was trying to call to find out where we lived, and the liquid was draining out of my phone. A lady drove by and slowed down and I said hello and she said wow about how messy my hair was I guessed, and then she drove on. I looked in a window to see how my hair looked. I kept trying to get my phone to work. I could see the liquid draining out. I decided I would have to get a new one.

Lin and I went to the gym. I put some new music in my playlist and it was helpful. My new shoes were great. My knee didn't hurt at all. I ran 5k, and so did Lin. I did some weights. I am definitely getting weaker.

When I went to get Davey I felt empty, exhausted by the thought of the rest of the day. I got a pack of cigarettes and smoked one. I made a cup of tea, went out to the stone circle, and had another two cigarettes.

After dinner, I was still empty. I didn't do anything, just sat with Davey. I felt impatient because he was loud and silly. I guess that's just how kids act.

When I finished reading *Ithaca* I looked at the acknowledgements and there were so many people who supported him.

WEDNESDAY 9 JANUARY 2019

I made a new folder for my poems, and set up a document for Deane's *Fillardy Goblin*.

On the bridge, I chatted with a wino named Henry, who said I looked distinguished.

Lin and I had a cup of tea and apple pie at Coco's. The people were warm and eccentric. We stopped at the Asia market on the way out of town.

FRIDAY 11 JANUARY 2019

When I went to collect Davey, I bought a pack of cigarettes. I am smoking heavily. I can't control it, plain and simple. Ceaseless trickles of want trigger complete compliance.

I went out with my Polish beer, walked around looking at things. I wandered and tidied. I watched Lin through the kitchen window as evening gathered. I called her over and told her I love her. I am always afraid that this happy life will be taken from me. I am enjoying the perfect life, the perfect place, the perfect family. It is too good to be true; who am I to have this happiness? And so, I am not happy with my happiness.

I read Beckett, *Death of Malone*, *The Moon and Sixpence*, John Banneville's *The Sea*.

Since I have had no weed I have not made the slightest creative effort. The only thing I have done for art's sake is move poems from the desktop into the poems folder.

WEDNESDAY 16 JANUARY 2019

I am up early this morning because I have a lesson at 8:30. I have been out to feed the cat and sneak a cigarette. The sky is full of stars.

Lin did the money management, and I started typing up *Fillardy Goblin*, the story of a bonfire party.

Davey was unhappy because his teacher was always yelling. He said he didn't like school now, and I felt this was a pity. The teacher told him to stand against the wall. I went back to the judo and watched for a while. When they started competing, it was too much pressure so I went out and had another cigarette at the side of the river. The river was heaving and gleaming darkly. I looked to see bobbing beneath the surface the young guy who disappeared a week ago, the guy Greg and I had a drink with at Feeney's. Quiver of minnows.

I read *The Sea*, and then I turned to my phone. I slept okay, but woke at twelve thinking it was morning. My lungs were stiff from smoking. My body is not up for smoking anymore. I had a hoot of Davey's inhaler.

THURSDAY 17 JANUARY 2019

I dreamed a teacher told me to sit facing the wall but I refused. Then I went for a coffee. I walked through heavy traffic. A bus passed right beside me. I sat drinking coffee near two people I knew from long ago.

Yesterday morning I left a cigarette on the table with my keys, and Lin saw it. Davey asked me if I was smoking again. He was tender to me, and gave me a hug. When Lin criticised me harshly he told her not to be so mean to me.

. . .

FRIDAY 18 JANUARY 2019 04:41

I feel awful. I keep feeling the urge to smoke, and feel myself slipping. I didn't think about it for three years or more.

SATURDAY 19 JANUARY 2019

I have nothing in me

I started up the chainsaw, then put it back in the garage. I am terrified of it.

I got another beer and went out again. I sent Darby a message asking for more weed. I was a bit drunk and I sent Colin a message asking him to set me up a website with domain name theblockuniverse.

MONDAY 21 JANUARY 2019

I did a bit of *Fillardy Goblin*. I might make it into a self referential thing, with footnotes providing a running interpretation, and commentary on the culture we grew up in. I decided to take an old poem to poetry class.

When Lin and Davey got back, I went out and drank my beer in the stone circle. It was lashing cold rain.

TUESDAY 22 JANUARY 2019

I typed up some of my old poems, written in Calgary in 1984. I realised they weren't very good. I thought about revising them, but was okay with the realisation that these poems weren't good. They are soft and vague–have nothing solid in them.

This diary should allow me to look more closely at myself, to give me a stronger moral sense. The poems I wrote in my 20s weren't any good, and Deane's *Filladry Goblin* is not good. I have reams and reams of writing that isn't any good. *The Time Machine* is not good. I think some of the poems that I have written recently are good, but they took so much out of me.

WEDNESDAY 23 JANUARY 2019

Lin heated up the savoury mince from the night before, and put some leaves in a bowl. I lay down on the sofa. I found a Comfortably Numb lesson by that guy Marty on youtube, and tried to learn it, but it was beyond me. Lin was in the Zen room playing guzheng. I tried to play along with her, but truth be told I am crap at guitar.

Lin went to get Davey, and I finished my hoots and went to the stone circle with my West Indies Porter. It was raining, but I felt inspired. I recorded what I thought was a good poem on my phone. I felt enthusiastic about this, and thought that I would fix it up and bring it in today, but now I don't think so.

FRIDAY 25 JANUARY 2019 02:45

I feel wretched. I can't sleep. I am so empty, so heavy. So many things I need to do: write a poem, set up the website. Something with the Kwakiutl. Revise The Time Machine. Finish typing up Deane's story, as well as my old poems. Play guitar better, keep up the garden.Find a job, update profile on Fluentify. Eat better, meditate, yoga.

TUESDAY 29 JANUARY 2019

I got the poem together and I was happy with it. I felt that I could bring it to the workshop. Today, I'm not sure. I want to write something sweet and simple, to align myself with the bees, but I am writing like one of the spiders. I can't seem to achieve quiet and this is maybe because of phones and facebook. My poem feels like an essay broken into lines. As well, it is morally wrong on many levels.

THURSDAY 31 JANUARY 2019

I took Davey to school, and when I got back, I told Lin I had been smoking. She was upset, and she cried. I convinced her that I would quit. I could feel the harm that it was doing me.

I mooned around the house and slipped out to the garden to think about the poem.

I went up to the poetry workshop. The poems were good, and Kevin didn't call on me until last. The poem was well received and there were some good suggestions. I got a cab home, and Lin had a fire going. I read them *The Hobbit*. Lin fell asleep by the fire while I was reading.

I will use meditation and yoga to help me quit. I need to keep my mind clear. If I am not smoking there is nothing for me to be worried about.

The Last Give of Ground

I landed in Beijing,
cushioned by its grime and abundance.
With my hairy forearms, big nose and white skin
I became a mighty Xiao Zhang in suit and tie
bestowing smiles on students and staff
as I passed them in my corridors.

I wanted this me to be me but now
I am the clunking monster who feeds the birds.

Not until my boy was born did I notice
the sidewalks were rank with choleric gobs
coughed up from choking lungs.

Despite what I told the foreign teachers
as their wee pink faces gave way to grey
the cotton-wool air that sank into the city was not fog at all.
After I wheeled my baby out in his blue buggy
his nostrils were clogged with black snot.

We drove out of Dublin in a rented beamer,
running fast from the end of the world.
Now Lin goes out and gathers herbs.
We pull apples and berries from our bushes and trees.

I stoop to pick leaves from my path,
glance wryly at the weeds I'd dreamed would delight me,
and wonder what use a 50 year old stoner can be.

I've got bundles of bad novels and reams of bad poems.
I sought to gather sweetness and light
but I am only a spider churning out old tears,
crouching here on the last give of ground.

FRIDAY 1 FEBRUARY 2019

Yesterday morning was very cold. I did nothing. There were so many things I could and should have done, but I did nothing. I could have cleaned up the house. I could have done something with Articulate, and tried to put it on the website. I could have done something in the garden. I could have done meditation or yoga. I could have written a poem. I did none of these things.

We attended the movement of the body of Johny Creaven, the judo coach, to the church, as well as the funeral mass. The kids lined the road when the hearse and mourners passed.

I read Davey and Lin a few pages of *The Hobbit*. We arrived in Rivendell. Davey made sure I sat in the middle so mummy could see the pictures too.

SUNDAY 3 FEBRUARY 2019

We sat by the fire, and I read *The Hobbit*. We were taken prisoner by goblins.

I felt a bit restless, like I was going to have a crisis. I worked on Comfortably Numb, and All Along the Watchtower. Last night I had a dream that I was listening to the Comfortably Numb solo and it was so beautiful I was crying. I typed up some *Fillardy Goblin*, then had a game of chess with Davey.

After we brushed our teeth, I asked Lin if she still loved me. Davey said, Daddy, you don't have to ask her if she loves you. I called him Mister Wisdom.

MONDAY 4 FEBRUARY 2019

It was Chinese New Year, so Lin was sending and receiving messages. Though Davey was home sick he was bouncing around.

Lin went to Dunnes to get things to make dumplings. I did a bit more work on the poem, then I walked around the garden with Davey. I lifted fallen branches and threw them in the pile. I pulled weeds out of the stone circle.

We chatted with Lin's family in Heilongjiang. Lin opened her beer and I opened mine then I went out to the stone circle for one more run through the poem. We opened a bottle of wine and had the *jiaozi*. After dinner I said I was going outside, and Lin began to cry and say you don't need to do that. She knew I was going out for a cigarette.

I went out anyway. When I came back in, Lin was drunk and not feeling well. I got her up to bed, and got Davey to brush his teeth.

TUESDAY 5 FEBRUARY 2019

Lin made cucumber soup and pancakes. I worked on my poem. I was not confident in it when I woke up, and then I was confident in it, but now I am not confident in it again.

I did yoga, meditation, then went out to work on the poem.

My phone is damaged, and I'm not sure how long it will last. There is rainbow oil leaking from it. I hope it isn't toxic.

I was wheezing and I took the last blast of Davey's inhaler. There is really nothing in it now.

MONDAY 11 FEBRUARY 2019

Lin and I went to the gym. I ran 5k but it was difficult. I did weights, but I seem to be getting weaker. I had some ideas for the poem on the treadmill and I remembered these in the sauna. I decided to call the poem Soil, and write about how I have no soil. This cluttered the whole thing, with nothing really jiving.

When we got home, I went to the garden to work on the poem. Lin went to get Davey, and while she was out I gave up on the poem. It was a mess.

Davey went up to watch TV, and I read *King Lear*. While I was reading, Davey came downstairs and gave me a hug and told me he loves me. He went back up and I read on.

TUESDAY 12 FEBRUARY 2019

I got up and the kitty and I went out. She was wild; there seemed to be night animals around. She kissed a big frog. I went to the stone circle and worked on the poem. Maybe it will do. I might use footnotes as in *Notes from a Coma*.

THURSDAY 14 FEBRUARY 2019 AT 12:00

I just stepped outside and smoked a joint. My heart feels like it will jump out of my chest. It is like a feeling of extreme terror, but not.

I was thinking about Deane's story, and an introduction to it, and putting it in theblockuniverse, then putting in my poems, and The Time Machine.

I did an hour and a half of Fluentify. I got dressed and grabbed the poems and went out with Lin. She dropped me just behind the cathedral and I walked to the Arts Centre. My poem was well received. When the class finished I hurried out. I stood by the canal and read the poem once more. Then I got a cab.

When I got home the house was warm and alive. Davey was a jumping bean, a hurricane of delight. His enthusiasm and his energy were hilarious, and Lin and I beamed at him as he yammered on at a mile a minute.

Lin cooked a healthy Chinese dinner. We ate well and I thought about how big and strong my little boy was becoming. I looked at my beautiful wife, and marvelled at what a great mother she was.

We lay down, with me in the middle, and I read *The Hobbit*. Bilbo and co are trapped in the trees with wolves beneath them. The King of the Eagles of the Misty Mountains has spotted the commotion.

Soil

I list my secrets and blood
weeps from the words.

Red Hand.

The North's hatreds scattered us:
so we wandered lost and died
in foreign lands.

Appalled I pull away
no local I cradle dusty ganglion
broken nerve ends
phantom limbs, hot or icy tears

Why would I try to write them back?
They are gone and there is no amends.

The light of yesterday
its rage pain fear
love even laughter sometimes
extinguished.

The past grinds my face
into this unending moment.
I have no time machine.

FRIDAY 15 FEBRUARY 2019

Yesterday morning I smoked a big doobie as soon as I got up. I felt strong after the good reception of the poem the day before. Lin kindly offered to take Davey to school. I made notes for a poem that might work, and kept hooting.

Lin went to get Davey, and I went out to the stone circle with my gin and my West Indies Porter. I finished the pot. When I went back in, I played guitar, and then made drinks with the sloe gin and the hawthorn cordial. Lin made a pizza base and I topped it with anchovies, capers, and olives.

After dinner I opened a bottle of wine. We drank a glass and left the rest. Then I went up and played Don't Starve on the PS4 with Davey. We didn't get very far before we died of hunger and sadness.

I fell asleep. I had more joyful dreams. In one we were hurling and we were so strong we broke the hurls.

FRIDAY 22 FEBRUARY 2019 07:57

The kitty is at the window licking her lips after a bowl of milk, looking for another mole.

I did some meditation. It really showed me how muddled I am. I tried to think of a poem but nothing came to me.

Lin and I sat by the fire. When she got up to make dinner, I went out to the stone circle, and thought about how difficult it is to write poetry. I remembered–Irish poets learn your trade, sing whatever is well made, scorn the sort now growing up all out of shape from toe to top, and this went round and round in my head.

WEDNESDAY 6 MARCH 2019

The clouds and I glow gold.

I looked through old bits of writing but couldn't find anything to turn into a poem. Lin was doing a big clean up. She vacuumed and cleaned the toilets. I had a look at the Li Bai poem she translated for me and decided to use it.

Lin gave me a bit of the weed. I went out to the garden, had a hoot, and came up with a poem. When Lin got home I showed her the poem when she was hardly in the door. I blabbered until she got tired of listening. I can't tell if the poem is good or not from Lin's reaction.

Lin's guzheng fed into my meditation. Clouds over treetops and golden light. I completed a half hour of meditation, then did yoga. Davey sang a little song in Irish and I told him he sounded like Gandalf or Elrond.

THURSDAY 7 MARCH 2019

Lin went outside to garden while I meditated.

I finished editing Drinking Alone and printed up fourteen copies.

I walked up and down the street a couple of times before I went up to the poetry workshop. There were a lot of people up there already. They were all very pleasant, but I managed to feel as though some of them didn't like me; this inability to feel confident that I can be liked by others is my greatest mental problem. The poems were all excellent, and I felt that it was hard to stand my ground at this level.

I did my poem toward the end. It was well received. Of course all of the poems were well received; but still, if the poem was a complete disaster they let you know it. I slipped out quickly, got a cab.

Drinking Alone (after Li Bai)

I brought a bottle
of Writer's Tears
into the forest

Giggling, spouting poetry,
I woke the prudish moon.

Lifting her sidelong gaze
she asked me
why I drank alone.

I laughed until I cried
so she cast a shadow for me
but he would not say a word.

I did all the talking.

I told them poetry
is not paperwork,
and implied
that if I died
none would still see
those ones not here.

I think I saw
my shadow weep
to know that then
no one
would hold him up.

The moon retreated
behind the trees,
and he left me too.

SATURDAY 9 MARCH 2019

I went to the stone circle and drank beer. When I went back in, I asked Lin to give me a few hoots. We had lamb stew in the slow cooker. I told Davey there was a poem in my head slowly cooking.

I went out to the little woods and smoked. I drank rum toddies and had the notepad with me. I started a poem, Family.

At dinner I blabbered and Davey said you're just drunk daddy, and Lin looked down.

Afterwards we went out with Davey on his bike, the three of us wearing safety jackets. When we got home, Lin played guzheng.

When the power went out again we went into the Zen room, lit candles and gathered torches and phones. I did some yoga. Davey became quiet. When the lights came on again we almost felt it was a pity.

WEDNESDAY 13 MARCH 2019 AT 12:10

Lin and Davey are asleep. The cat is sneaking around. I will have to herd her back to her zone; I may need to lure her with food. I have been up for about an hour. I read the poem through twice. I slept for a couple of hours. I am feeling wretched. The wind is pulling at the house.

When I got back from the school run, I started to work on the poem. I worked on the poem all morning. I have sort of finished it. I had hoped it would feel more malleable at this stage, but it feels stiff. Lin went to get Davey. While she was gone I turned off the poetry machine and relaxed. I lay down for a few minutes and then I got up.

I will try not to do too much on the poem tomorrow morning.

THURSDAY 14 MARCH 2019

Last night I heard Davey calling and went down to him. He'd dreamed I had a magic fire sword that filled my belly with fire and burned the house down. Of course they know I am smoking, although no one says anything.

Lin drove me to the Cathedral, and I walked to the Art's Center. I was one of the first ones up there. Everyone was friendly. The poems were good. Mine came toward the end. The guy from Alaska started to clap when I finished and everyone joined in.

When I got home, Davey was funny and beautiful. As soon as I walked in the door he was telling me about his day with unbridled enthusiasm. Lin was cooking a Chinese dinner. I went down to the stone room and looked at my poem.

Family (for Davey)

I
Sleep well my little boy while I build this
for you, to tell you from where and why,
now that we're almost settled in our house,
there has been no family to visit us.

Rain lashes the windows, and the wind
does its best to tear this house apart
but it cannot; we are well grounded here.

II
Our Adam was named in *The Orkneyinga Saga*.
The battle lost in the west of Scotland,
Ottar retreated with his mob to county Cork
where the Cotters became more Irish than the …

Sir James Cotter fought with the Irish
at the battle of the Boyne. His son,
Sir James the Younger, was made a baron
for renouncing faith and father.

III
I once had a tattered little photo
from which glowered a gruff man
in black coat and stiff white collar.

He was a schoolmaster from Cork
who moved north to Glenties, in Donegal,
the first of us Cotters from Ulster.

IV
The schoolmaster's son was Jimmy Cotter,
my grandfather, manager of the Ulster Bank
in Glenties, then in Omagh, Tyrone.

I spent a day with him in 1969
and I remember every detail.
He walked me through his forest garden
and lifted leaves to show strawberries beneath.
Introduced me to Icarus.

V

Jimmy married Noelle, youngest daughter
of David Sydney Clements,
Justice of the Peace for Omagh,
with some hazy relation to Lord Leitrim.

He had five sons killed in the First World War.
His house looking up at the court
was bombed in 1970, and sat
derelict for more than twenty years.

VI

My father was named after Davey Clements.
In Glenties he was sent to the shed for religion.
Living in Omagh he recalled with glee
watching the Luftwaffe bomb Belfast from a hill.

I was born in Mwadui, Tanganyika.
He did his PhD at Queens after that
and then it was off to the oil fields of Alberta
Via Flin Flon, Manitoba.

VII

Deane and I would sit on our mom's bed
in Calgary. Lilacs at the window
cast shadows on her bedroom wall.
Then she glowed like Monroe, but torn

from her roots she withered and died
on the bald prairies. Evenings became
accusations and tearings at my quiet father.
She died upstairs on morphine.

VIII

I made life hard for my little brother.
He worked six months in the oil patch,
bought a van and moved to the west coast
to be a writer.
One windy morning we woke
to find his burnt corpse inside the van.
I still have his scorched papers beside me.

IX

I returned to the country my mother died mourning
but found nothing here to hold me.
My father remarried and retired to an island.

I visited them once
and left vowing not to speak again.
He died eight hours before you were born.

X

I often wonder what he would have thought
of you, your mom, our Galway house.

I can see him in your face, your ears.
When you came I changed. I could not
raise you in Beijing. You are learning
Irish now, and can speak Chinese.
You are good at school, and at making friends.
May you grow up to be the best of us.

XI

Your mother came to me at two am
one Christmas eve, stayed the night,
said nothing.

She was from the moon. I was from Crom.
She'd travelled from Black Dragon River
to find work in Beijing and found my school.

Our languages were different worlds.
What could we have found to talk about?

XII

Storm Gareth rattles the windows
and my wife sleeps on. Our house is sound.

You wonder why I hurt myself but trust

that I am trying something beautiful.

You make me want to live, you
are my reprieve.
Silent your songs
of exile from the other room haunting
fingers weaving time on your 古筝.

WEDNESDAY 20 MARCH 2019

Lin and I were in the Zen room measuring where the green sofa would fit, when we saw a fox come down the rose tube toward us. He walked up to the stairs down to the stone yard, and then on around the house. We felt blessed. After dinner we saw pheasants at the bottom of the garden.

SATURDAY 23 MARCH 2019

I held the ladder for Lin while she cleaned out the gutters around the house. It was a relief to get it done. Davey came running to say he had seen the fox go into the back.

MONDAY 25 MARCH 2019

After I finished working on the poem I went out to the rose tube and used the pitchfork to drag dead leaves down from the web of grape branches above. Lin and I lifted what I'd pulled down and put it on the compost pile below the septic tank.

Lin saw the fox by the food we'd left in the stone circle. He ran off when he noticed her filming. Magpies finished his food.

TUESDAY 26 MARCH 2019

I went to the stone circle to look at the poem. It needs to be totally reworked but there isn't time. It feels insincere.

I flattened the gravel in the rose tube. I felt weak from not eating and it was difficult work. I went back in and lay down in bed. Lin came and lay on top of me to apologise for waking the monster in me. I took a while to cheer up, but she was patient.

I will have another look at the poem, though I think it is destined for the junk pile.

WEDNESDAY 27 MARCH 2019 12:41

I am up, wheezing badly. I can hardly catch a breath. It makes me claustrophobic. I must quit smoking.

I felt hopeless about the poem, Breach. I thought that it would be shameful to present it at class. I took coffee out to the stone circle, went through it a few times, and made a bunch of changes. Now it is good—not perfect, but at least good enough to read at the poetry workshop. I felt good about overcoming these difficulties.

The delivery guys were friendly and funny. We took the green sofa and stools through the Zen room door. I could tell Lin was pleased with the green sofa. I grabbed a West Indies Porter, and went to the stone circle to do some more work on the poem.

Derek Mahon's *Against the Clock* speaks to me. I got the poem done yesterday without marijuana, so that shows it can be done. I feel this poem and the last one have opened up a new vista for me, a more formally realised poem. What I have been passing off as poems until now have been notes. I think a poem needs structure.

There is much to be positive about: the garden, health and fitness, writing.

THURSDAY 28 MARCH 2019

Yesterday morning I went out to the stone circle and did a last revision on my poem.

Kevin didn't call on me until second from the end, and most people had left by then. The poem went over well enough. Someone said it was polished. It's hard to gauge the reaction when all of the poems are so excellent. I like the people in the poetry class. They are sincere.

Breach

Among other worlds I am broken open,
exposed to the cleansing racket of birds,
there a fox like a gift on the garden path,
a beetle moving slowly beyond measure,
weeds through the tarmac, slower still,
and I am but a piece of all this dying.

Back inside, shabby coat on skeleton,
I meet the shining joy of my young family,
their gentle lives infinities outside of me.
A terror that is love rushes in and I pray
let there be no more ruin, provide
reprieve from all dyings and departures.

We sit by the fire and my son writes a story
then says he sees letters floating everywhere.
For how long will I be here to guide this boy?
I reach for words, and still more words,
to staunch this breach, forestall collapse,
every poem completed cries out for another.

FRIDAY 29 MARCH 2019 12:55

Woke up wheezing. There needs to be an end of it. I must persevere, one minute at a time. There is no pleasure in satisfying an addiction.

I sent a message to Chen Xi and we exchanged a few short messages. It seems she is now under Tan's control.

SATURDAY 30 MARCH 2019

Everything felt ugly and wrong. I drove to the little shop by Davey's school and got cigarettes. I had one immediately.

I drove home then and had another two before going in. When I went in I had a chat with Lin and apologised. I called Davey in and I explained it to him also. I said I would quit at 2 that day, but it didn't work out that way, as I spent the whole day running around. They were both understanding and supportive. I went out to the stone circle and smoked.

SUNDAY 31 MARCH 2019 AT 23:52

Up again with the wheeze.

Davey and I went to hurling. Dermott joked that they'd chosen me to play centre forward in the adult game. The kids were playing and Dermott gave Davey a green vest to play on the Moycullen side. I thought fuck you and I wanted to ask him for a fight. I gave him a little shove when I got a chance. Ultan said hello to me and I blanked him. I also have no good feelings for fucking Declan. My feeling was fuck the lot of you. I know I am wrong and that I shouldn't feel this way.

After hurling, Dermott, Declan, Rosemary, and Aaron's parents were palling around. I put Davey's helmet in the car. When I came back, he was nearly crying because he didn't know where I was. His classmates were playing soccer but he didn't want to play because he doesn't like soccer.

When we got home, Lin and Davey went to Dangan for a bike ride. I drank and smoked in the stone circle. I read *The Master and Margherita*, and fell asleep. 11:40, and up like a jumping bean.

My connections to the world are growing thinner and thinner. I don't seem to be able to make friends or become a part of anything.

MONDAY 8 APRIL 2019

I opened my beer and started to make chilli. I went out and drank my gin. When Darby arrived we chatted and he gave me some weed.

After dinner, I rolled a doob and went out to the stone circle. My creativity blossomed; I felt alive.

I came in and played guitar and Davey said it was good. Life seemed so amazing, so full of potential.

Lin and I went up and watched *Our Planet* with Davey. It was unbelievable.

I read Derek Mahon. I was blown away by this dialogue with Yeats.

When Lin came back she brought a kiss from Davey. I went down and rubbed his skinny back.

TUESDAY 9 APRIL 2019

I felt my heart drop when I saw Declan and Rosemary coming down the road. At first Declan pretended he didn't see me, but then he looked up at me with a sneer and said great day for gardening. I felt bad to give him an opening by looking so grubby; I remembered him sneering at Davey at hurling. As we walked away, Davey reached into my pocket and dropped a pack of cigarettes at my feet. I reached down and put it back in my pocket. I felt like shit. Lin wasn't super happy with me either, but she didn't blame me.

After dinner I went out to the stone circle for a hoot.

SUNDAY 21 APRIL 2019

When Lin woke up we cuddled, then Davey came down and we all laughed and joked in the bed. I am glad that we have got most of what we wanted to do around the house done. Lin wants a bench for when we hang around in the garden, watching badminton or what have you.

MONDAY 29 APRIL 2019 6:04

Darby stopped by and gave me a couple of buds.

Lin and I ate broccoli soup and toast, then I went out and had a hoot. I jotted down ideas for poems. I felt so alive. I was in awe of everything growing, enraptured by the varieties of green, the inward glow. I tidied up theblockuniverse so that it looks well on full screen, tablet, and mobile. Lin collected Davey, and I continued to stoke the the fire in my head.

When they got back, Davey could tell I was elsewhere. I played Comfortably Numb. I continued to slip out to the stone circle. I did two sun salutations.

I sat in the red armchair in the library looking out the window. I felt empty and full of bliss, emptied by bliss. I was just soaking in beauty.

I read Derek Mahon's *Against the Clock*; it is a battlecry, a mission statement for the time of life I am entering.

TUESDAY 30 APRIL 2019 07:27

I finished what Darby gave me the other day. The sky was full of stars, and there was a white bank of cloud to the southwest.

I exchanged text messages with Greg. He hasn't mentioned The Block Universe except to ask why the name. I will write something good explaining the name. I will put this under the title, and move the Dean Buonomomo quote elsewhere. I added a few words in a note last night. Membrane.

I did a couple of sun salutations while Lin and Davey were out scootering. I felt stiff yesterday, like I was made of wood.

I went up and watched Full House with Davey. Then we got ready for bed. He took off his tai chi outfit and lay down beside me. His skinny little boy body breaks my heart and floods me with love.

THURSDAY 2 MAY 2019 AT 07:15

I should probably work on the poetry. I was very grand with Greg about writing until the pen slipped out of my trembling fingers, but I'm not actually writing now, am I?

Cigarettes. Booze. Dope. Why does writing have to be tied to these things?

Greg only read Estranged of all the poems I sent. I am embarrassed by it now. I no longer like Estranged or No Place.

FRIDAY 10 MAY 2019

I arrived at Chen XI's place at about 10:30. She and Tan were having breakfast. We drove to Galway. It was nice to chat with Tan, if not easy. They seemed to like the house. Lin got a lot of compliments. Tan said she appeared to have developed harmony, but this morning he revised this to say she has developed confidence. I think both are true.

Tan and I went and got Davey. Davey was shy and excited to see Tan, and they became good buddies again right away. We went home and Tan and Davey kicked the football and hit the hurl. Tan and I went to watch Davey's hurling blitz against Barna. One of the dads said Davey is a real little battler. There was a terrible downpour and we were soaked to the skin, but they kept playing.

We hung around in the Zen room chatting until about 9:30. Everyone was comfortable and at ease.

SATURDAY 11 MAY 2019

Chen Xi wanted to go to the cliffs of Moher, so there we went. I drove the coastal road. I haven't seen the cliffs on a sunny day before. We sat on the grass at the edge of the cliff. Tan did some meditation in lotus posture.

After dinner, Chen Xi and Tan went out with Davey for a walk down the road. Lin and I went into town.

We met the guys at The Munch but it was crap. We peeked into a few bars, and then we went to The Front Door. We ordered gins. They cost 20, but we ended up leaving them on the table. The pub was mental. It was like the crazy bars in the Workers Stadium in the old days of Beijing. Young people were dancing madly, ladies dolled up with boobs hanging out. Lin hated it. I danced a bit and tried to like it, but it was not for us.

The street was raging with testosterone. Some guy was being dragged out of The King's Head with a smashed up eye. A guy grabbed my collar and asked his buddy, was it him? The band was playing Jumping Jack Flash. Some guy caught my eye and started giving me funny faces. I grabbed Lin by the hand and pulled us out.

We met a group of lovely Thai girls. The first girl asked Lin where she was from and invited her to her birthday dance at Hello. I gave her the Thai greeting and she gave it back.

It was tempting, but Lin was cold, and we had already given up, so we got a cab home. The stars were out so we walked around the house. We understood how fortunate we were. We went into the stone circle and looked at the stars. We were thinking about Davey and wanting to kiss him.

Davey is beside me now chatting away at a mile a minute. I will go out again for a bit of quiet time, and then I will tidy up and prepare breakfast. I don't have anything to do today except host Tan and Chen Xi. I will leave decisions to them. I won't stress out about when they want to go.

SUNDAY 12 MAY 2019

Lin made a big feed of noodles with tomatoes and eggs; over breakfast Tan and Chen Xi advised us on how to run our airbnb.

I got Tan to sit in the Zen room. The white roses were coming out on the trellis.

MONDAY 13 MAY 2019

We snacked outside: wine, chicken wings, crackers and cheese. I took Tan out to the stone circle and we chatted there for a while.

WEDNESDAY 15 MAY 2019

Lin played Irish music while she made a breakfast of black pudding, white pudding, and avocado. We chatted around the table. Davey hugged Tan and Chen Xi, and then I drove him to school. At the bus station, I thanked Tan for his lead role in the selling of Aihua. Tan declared us brothers forever. We all hugged.

It was a warm and beautiful day, so I didn't want to just sit around the house. We drove to town and parked at the Claddagh. Lin and Davey fed the swans. They were so graceful, and the gulls so obnoxious. I tried to explain grace to Davey.

Lin watered plants, and I went out to the stone circle to drink my beer. Lin got some spinach from the greenhouse and made soup. She prepared cold beef, Chinese style. I helped Davey research wrens.

I'd love to quit smoking today. My slavery to cigarettes has reached Beijing levels. I am just moving from one cigarette to the next.

SUNDAY 19 MAY 2019

I worked on a poem about why I need to smoke to write poetry and to make clear that if I need to smoke I will have to quit writing. It seemed like a good idea at the time, and, of course, I smoked quite a bit.

Lin and I had a drink out front of the Zen room to mark the anniversary of our wedding, and I told her getting married to her was the best thing ever happened to me. We kept the conversation light, and chatted about how well our lives had turned out.

TUESDAY 21 MAY 2019

It was a fabulous day. I drank cider, smoked dope and wrote in the stone circle.

I want This Ridiculous Albatros to be a swan song.

WEDNESDAY 22 MAY 2019 06:53

Lin is being very quiet downstairs. It rained through the night, and it is drizzly this morning. The horses in the field across from me are wet and shining.

We went to Silver Strand and had a walk on the beach. Davey gathered sea shells and Lin chatted to old ladies gathering seaweed for their gardens.

I woke at about twelve and my lungs and my shoulder were sore. When I went back to bed I heard some animal, maybe a baby fox, in trouble.

THURSDAY 23 MAY 2019

I wore my ninja sports outfit rather than a jacket and shirt to the poetry workshop. Lin dropped me off and I walked around a little bit and then went up. I chatted with a few of the nice ladies. More and more people showed up. We went through the poems slowly. I was toward the end. The poem was well received. One of them suggested I read the poem at the Beyond the Edge Open Mic, but I don't think I could bring myself to do that.

I left the workshop and went into town. I had a pint of Guinness at Feeney's and listened to some buskers. They played Horslips, Trouble with a Capital T.

. . .

This Ridiculous Albatross

1.
Stop awhile, for I have wandered far
and now all that is left me is
the telling of this old story,
adrift on this immaculate, still sea.

A quiet life of contemplation, of sipping Chinese tea,
performing yoga, meditating. I dream
beneath big windows of positivity, proaction,
and safety.

I drift from room to room
compressed into dead end
by this tedious content.
Always these ragged feathers.

Know you that I killed the bird
that caused the breezes to blow.
For this my lungs cry out to be seared
my mind to be blown.

2.
So goes another day of drinking and smoking, another
day to let my good wife sigh as I pass,
an old ghost lost in time.

Out of my face, sentiment a riot disguised
by placid moon, quiet stream,
little things eclipsed by dream

but then the plummeting from intensities
that numbing lethargy, this interminable presence.

But still, always, I
ascend once more this funky time machine
write another poem that no one wants.

FRIDAY 24 MAY 2019

I got a booking from airbnb. A guy and his wife will be here from Brittany June 10 to 12.

SATURDAY 25 MAY 2019

I went to the little shop for coffee and tea. It was a nice morning, though I fell again on the way back. It has been raining and will continue.

We had another booking from a Spanish lady and her partner.

I went out to the stone circle and had a joint and a beer and a cigarette, then I threw the remaining cigarettes in the stream. Davey and Lin were playing football. I tried to play with them but my knee and shoulder are bad.

SUNDAY 26 MAY 2019 06:18

It is strange, rainy, bright one moment, dark the next, with a special luminosity emanating from the ground.

After dinner we walked around outside. We went to the stone circle and looked at all the berries coming in. Lin and Davey kicked the ball. I sat watching, then went inside.

THURSDAY 30 MAY 2019 06:02

The cat was disturbed to find I didn't have soft food. I gave her milk, but she still looked at me with blazing eyes. It is pouring. It has been raining steadily for three or four days. The lawn has gone wild.

Lin took me to the Chinese doctor. He got me down to my underpants and poked at me. He thinks the knee and shoulder are related, and there is a problem in my balance. He poked and pushed and it started to feel better. Then he gave me acupuncture. After sticking in the needles, he left me for half an hour with the needles in.

I worked for a while on my own things, fruitlessly. I tidied up the guest area. I vacuumed and then shone shiny areas for a few hours.

Lin made lunch and I ate with her and did more cleaning. I felt great to be cleaning up. My mind was empty, and my body was moving.

SATURDAY 1 JUNE 2019

I got up late today and thought there might have been coffee ready, or some breakfast, but they were in the Zen room and the kitchen was untidy. I made my coffee and put away the dishes and when I went to do my diary I noticed there was way too much food in the fish tank. When I mentioned this Lin started screaming at me.

I went out to the stone circle with my cider, threw the rest of a pack of cigarettes in the stream.

I have no idea what is wrong with Lin. I hope this doesn't become a big thing.

FRIDAY 7 JUNE 2019

Lin is in the kitchen chatting to her father. The cat has been fed and is out. The fish are in a clean tank.

I cleaned up the downstairs shower room, the toilet and the tiles, the shower glass, but I didn't complete the job--it was too much.

We sat at the diving board, joking and laughing. Davey learned how to make fart noises with his armpit. The water was still and blue.

SUNDAY 9 JUNE 2019

There is a bird spinning round on the feeder, and a horse moving slowly in the field.

Airbnb guests are coming, so I cleaned up the two toilets and tidied coats and things. It was a tough old slog. I went out and had my Hobgoblins. The stone circle was mind-blowing. Every time I go out it is wilder. I drank my beer and sat enraptured by the sight of the birds and bees filling the space, and the green flooding everything. I was enchanted, and drunk. I thought about something I read about the climate catastrophe, how everyone should make an ark, and I realised this is what we have been doing here. Davey called me in for dinner; tofu and bean sprouts.

MONDAY 10 JUNE 2019 06:21

Lin and Davey are asleep upstairs, Claude and Odile in the guest room.

Yesterday afternoon Lin and I had a drink in the stone circle. Lin went off to cut elder flowers, and when she came back to show me the flowers, she caught me smoking.

Claude and Odile didn't have much English. When they arrived I made coffee and we chatted in the Zen room. They seemed happy enough. They went to town for dinner, and will go to the Cliffs of Moher today.

. . .

TUESDAY 11 JUNE 2019

Lin and I went for a walk at Salthill. We felt positive about how the airbnb was going, and about how we could make money doing this. It was a morning of dramatic clouds.

Davey had trouble sleeping, so I went down to him. In his room you could hear the guests talking, and he said he could hear the cows also. I lay down with him until he fell asleep.

SATURDAY 15 JUNE 2019 AT 06:56

We have a lot of guests lined up. There were new bookings yesterday, and there were two new bookings last night. It is hectic, but at least there is money coming in.

SUNDAY 16 JUNE 2019

I saw a dead pigeon in the driveway; Kitty was covered with feathers. I went out with a shovel and fork to move the body just as Davey and Lin got home.

It was a rainy day, and the guests stayed in their room. They showed me photos of their family and their house.

When I woke up, we found we had more guests arriving today. We're feeling a bit of pressure now.

MONDAY 17 JUNE 2019

We hung around until Agnes and Jochen left, then tidied up the room for the next guests. They arrived at 4:30, a young American couple, Elizabeth Moon and Travis. They were like Aihua teachers. They brought in their bags and then went out for dinner.

I did a session with Fabiana, a laughing Italian lady. I had a look at Davey's report card, and it was really good.

It is a beautiful morning. There is a blue sky above the hills across from me, and the horses move slowly across the hillside.

While it is nice to be earning money, I need to find a way to work poetry and exercise into my life again.

TUESDAY 18 JUNE 2019

Lin dreamed she was standing beside the sea, and Davey was walking toward it. It began to hail stones; big splashes in the sea. She tried calling Davey back from the sea. This dream is about more than just me smoking, and getting hash from Darby last night.

I grabbed a Polish beer, took gloves, shears, and the wheelbarrow out to the stone circle. I sat down and drank the beer, smoked three cigarettes. I was in heaven. I started to tear out the vegetation flowing into the stone circle, the stone benches and the surrounding path. I emptied a barrow load by the compost, continued. Lin came out with her pink gin and sunglasses.

WEDNESDAY 19 JUNE 2019

Yesterday I smoked through the morning. It made me feel clouded and unclear. I answered Airbnb messages and completed Fluentify feedback.

Lin went shopping. I went out to the stone circle, and started working around the paths. I cleared space for the apple trees and the currant bushes. Then I went down the back path along the stream. Lin wasn't happy with me being muddle headed. She went to get Davey. I went out to the stone circle for another hoot and to finish the Polish beer.

After dinner, Lin took Davey to hurling. I sat out front with tea and a cigarette. The guests arrived, and I could tell they were a little taken aback by the shabbiness of the mossy drive, but when they went inside they were happy.

THURSDAY 20 JUNE 2019

We have four guests.

Yesterday was hectic. I did my diary, and then I replied to airbnb bookings. I took Davey to school, and when I got back, I prepared for a nine o'clock session with Mattia.

Franziska and Patrick came out just before I went in. Lin saw to their breakfast while I did my session with Mattia, and then I came out and had a short chat with Franziska and Patrick before they left. Lin tidied up the room, and then went for groceries. I had a session with Elisabetta.

Lin got back, and Ligia and another girl arrived with her. We gave them tea in the Zen room. Ligia's friend had a sore head, so I gave her an aspirin. They went down to their room to rest.

I went to the stone circle and had a cider, then played hurling with Davey. It was fantastic; everything was beautiful. Lin gathered strawberries and shared them with us.

FRIDAY 21 JUNE 2019 05:27

I tossed and turned in bed, suffering an agony of constriction. This woke Lin, so I went down and made her tea. I made coffee for myself and smoked two joints outside.

I had a good conversation with Franziska and Patrick about children's literature and mythology, time and time travel, Ireland and Germany. Lin took Franziska to the Zen room for the Chinese tea ceremony.

I tidied up a bit, and then the other two girls came out. I helped them get going with breakfast, and had a hoot. Then I showed them the big map on the wall, locating the Cliffs of Moher and the Burren for them.

SATURDAY 22 JUNE 2019

I got up early to set up the guests' breakfast. I looked at videos on how to clean toilets–all those tiny hairs! Lin was impatient with me but I kept my cool.

I went to Dunne's for cleaning products. When I got back, the guests were gone. Lin said they had taken two apples for the road.

Guests called and said they were coming. I turned on the lights and waited outside for them. They got lost, but arrived eventually, then turned around and went out to get dinner.

MONDAY 24 JUNE 2019 08:05

Lin and I have been up since six preparing breakfast for four guests. She is annoyed with me because of why I am coughing.

Kitty was criticising us through the window. When I was out in the stone circle she kept pushing herself onto my lap.

I did a big cleanup, and set off the robot vacuum. I cleaned the stone room bathroom, then I went up and did our room, and a few loads of laundry.

I cleaned Davey's room and his toilet. I went out to the stone circle with a tin of cider. I heard Lin talking to Davey about an umbrella, so I said let's get one. We hopped in the car and drove to B&Q.

The sun was beating down. I was flying. I was thinking of a poem about cleaning.

THURSDAY 27 JUNE 2019 07:30

It is grey out, and there is a weird low undulating sky moving slowly over us like a giant sheet.

I got up early and set up the breakfast space. I fed the cat and the fish. Jochen and Agnes got up, then Cathy and Joe, and I chatted with them too. When they left I went to their rooms and gathered the bedding.

I set the robot vacuum running, and Lin and Davey played football outside. It was a beautiful morning. Lin said she didn't feel a need to go on holiday because this is the most beautiful place in the world. We parked at the cathedral and walked through town. It was buzzing. We met Darby in the Latin Quarter. He was sunny and clean. Lin made *mala xiang guo* which we ate under our new blue umbrella.

FRIDAY 28 JUNE 2019 07:21

I have been up since before six preparing things for the guests' breakfast and tidying up. Davey is calling Lin from upstairs. I fed the cat but not the fish. I've already smoked two doobies and two cigarettes. I did come up with an idea for a poem or at least an introduction.

When Lin and Davey went out to see a movie I began to clean in earnest: two bathrooms, dishes, counters, outside tables, compost and bins. When they got home I was wrecked. I went out to the stone circle with the intention of having a last cigarette. I saw a missed call so I called back and it was a cab driver who said he'd been driving an American couple to our place, but couldn't find us so sent them to Glenloe Abbey. I went in and messaged Lynda and Dick. I said goodbye to the girl at the desk at Glenloe Abbey and got in the car. I checked my phone for anything from the Americans and saw a You are Missing a Session notification from Fluentify.

When I got home there was a red car in the drive. I went in and Lin said nothing about them until I asked. I ascertained that they were not Lynda and Dick. I wrote to Massimo Milano or whoever he was offering profuse apologies. I went back out and there was a mother and daughter. They explained to me about the little sister being delayed on a flight to South America, and I explained to them about my missed Americans. They told us they'd had a hard time finding us. Lynda called from Moycullen and I tried again to explain where we were.

When they finally arrived, Lin made Lynda and Dick Chinese tea and sat them in the Zen room. Dick has a yacht and travels up as far as Nanaimo to wash his clothes. We talked about Dan and the Arctic.

Lin criticised me for all my sighing. I drove to the little shop to get cigarettes, and had one outside.

Davey said he will hate me forever.

SUNDAY 30 JUNE 2019

We had a visit from one of the few Chinese families in the area. They had two boys, the eldest, David, was about Davey's age. Towards the end of their visit, David and Davey started to stretch little Daniel by his arms and legs. Daniel kicked and thumped. David thumped Davey on the shoulder. Davey retaliated, but being an only child he hadn't learned how to thump. David grabbed Davey by the throat in a Cotter clutch and pressed him into the oxblood chair. I stood up, but stopped. Dad separated them, though they continued thumping and kicking. When they left, Davey called out the door bye bye loser, making an L with finger and thumb at forehead, kicking out his legs one by one.

I went into the toilet and found a puddle across the floor as far as the bin. I criticised Davey and he made a deep noise of exasperation as he passed me. I gave him a whack on the bottom. I was shocked by his reaction: Never do that again! His face was red and tears erupted. I have seen that strength of reaction in Lin before.

When Lin arrived on the scene, Davey kept repeating, he whacked me. I explained why I had done it. I felt I was wrong, and felt sorry, but I needed to explain why I had done it. I was quiet then, and Davey brushed his teeth. When he came back I put him on my knee and told him I was sorry. He gave me a hug.

TUESDAY 2 JULY 2019

I snuck out to the stone circle for a cigarette. As I returned through the rose tube she was sitting there straight ahead cross legged in the Zen room. As I neared she narrowed her eyes and made a gun at me with her fingers. I looked down and went in.

I woke up coughing at 12:40. I read my phone, then I got a cup of tea and sat looking out at the stars. I went back to bed and slept until about five. I got up and smoked a couple of reefers outside with coffee before setting the breakfast table.

WEDNESDAY 3 JULY 2019 AT 12:00

I sat with Davey and had a pint of Guinness out front of Freenies' while he had an ice cream. He looked worried, so I asked him what was wrong, but he was far away, only saying that he was tired.

Yesterday morning the American couple came out first. They kept asking me about what work Lin and I do. Carter is a football and wrestling coach, maybe just retired. He had a naughty grin. They left as Rose and Pat came through. I let them eat and then we chatted. They live in Ballsbridge / Sandymount. They are highly educated, but I never learned what they do. They wished us the best on our new venture.

THURSDAY 4 JULY 2019

At about nine Davey told me the guests had arrived. I went out in my white tai chi outfit. The guy was out back of the house, and when I went forward the girl closed her door.

I brought them in and they treated me like a shopkeeper. I shouldn't be too sensitive about this; they are probably quite nice.

FRIDAY 5 JULY 2019 05:54

Lin and Davey are asleep in their respective beds. The French father and daughter are in bed after an evening in the city. All is prepared for breakfast for the guests. I have had three reefers. It is a grey morning; the sun is only just up.

The guests from Mumbai emerged in a great clatter. I inquired as to the pronunciation of the gent's name, and he told me I could call him Mr Patel. I saw the wife asking if there were any eggs and Lin getting them out. When I went back in they were still eating. When they finished eating we took photos with them and for them, then Lin and I started cleaning up. They hung out in their room until nearly noon.

After a few more photos we managed to get them out so we could tidy. In the bathroom, there was urine on the seat and on the floor. There was a heap of face powder scattered around the toilet. The gent had been trimming his beard at the sink.

I began to detail all of this to Lin, and she gestured to indicate that they were still outside taking photos.

I slipped out for a cigarette. As I finished my cigarette I noticed them outside the Zen room. I took them back to the stone circle and took more photos for them. They asked me how much the house was worth, what I do.

SATURDAY 6 JULY 2019

When we got ready for bed I found Davey's bed was wet. I told him he should have asked us to change the sheets, and he said he thought it would dry. I explained that if it dried it would still smell. I had trouble finding replacement blankets, and I was using a lot of fucks.

Davey was patient with me while I had my freak out. When the freakout was over and he was in bed, he started reading. He had said he didn't want me to stay with him. Why would I want this big grouchy guy sitting here, he asked. I kissed him and told him I love him and he hugged me and said he loved me. I checked on him later and he was asleep.

Lin arrived home and she looked so beautiful. I have been dead to everything recently, there has been no spark in my heart, but she was so beautiful.

Davey came down at about six and lay between us. The morning light was ghostly.

SUNDAY 7 JULY 2019

The cat waited by the door, and when I opened it she squeezed herself in. She pulled at her scratch toy and hid under the bar chair staring at me with empty green eyes. I lifted her and she came along quietly to the garage where I fed her. Poor wee lady.

Setting up the table for the guests has become a Zen routine. Everything is made to shine. I snuck out for two reefers and then two cigarettes. I spent some minutes panicking and following Davey around so he wouldn't make a mess. I lured him into the library and eventually he gave up on doing the loser dance at me and started reading Greek myths.

Lin went out to Dunnes. Davey and I lay down and messed around on the bed. He read to me and then I read to him. I tried to give him the brother experience of wrestling and messing around. I tried to engage him as much as possible, and listen to his chatter. Today he is going to a Young Einstein summer camp.

Lin started to make hummus. I snuck out to the stone circle to drink beer and hoot and smoke. I felt near collapse, like I could just drop down in a seizure at any moment. What's worse, it felt like there was nothing left inside of me. I tried to decide where I should sit for the best view, and was nearing beauty burnout, the capsule hitting atmosphere.

TUESDAY 9 JULY 2019

I hurt my shoulder opening the door to go out for a cigarette. It was a blinding, icy pain. Some creature had been digging in the wet lawn.

We went to Dangan for a walk. I felt very weak, as though my muscles were disintegrating.

I don't feel any urge to write. I think I need to push through the cigarette thing and find what is on the other side.

FRIDAY 12 JULY 2019 AT 07:15

Lin got ready to go out. She looked amazing. We drove her into town and dropped her off at Massuman. When Davey was asleep, I had a shower then cleaned the toilet in our room. I read, and went out again and again to smoke. Lin sent a message telling me to go to bed. When Lin got home she was funny and beautiful. She'd had a lot of fun.

. . .

SATURDAY 13 JULY 2019

It is a beautiful day–the sky is blue, and there are birds everywhere.

I slipped out for coffee and cigarettes. When I came back in I lay down. Lin was nice with me. We have been getting on great recently.

I don't have any cigarettes, and I'd love to keep it that way. I'm not sure if I will manage, but I will try.

TUESDAY 16 JULY 2019 06:58

Lin and I went to Salthill. My legs are weaker than they were, and it was difficult to walk the length of the Prom.

Davey keeps wanting me to play the shooter fight game with his lego, and I know I should, but I just couldn't bring myself to do it–the idea filled me with dread.

To quit smoking I must treat withdrawal as a positive challenge, focus on the feeling of my body regaining its health. It is the next cigarette that I need to avoid. My lizard brain will clamour for a cigarette, but I won't allow myself to be tricked back into the slavery of addiction.

WEDNESDAY 17 JULY 2019 07:21

I have been up since around 5:50. I have set up breakfast for the guests. I have snuck out a few times for cigarettes, two each time. I am rancid.

When I woke at four there was a beautiful moon illuminating the cloud above the forest at our feet.

I think if I could just get one full day of non smoking under my belt I could make a go of it. I am so weak. My self respect is in tatters.

FRIDAY 19 JULY 2019 07:37

I had a minor crisis setting the breakfast place for the guests. I have had four cigarettes already.

Davey and I took Lin to the Mandalin Hotel. It was raining heavily, the gutters outside the kitchen window seemed to be plugged. I took aspirin and put a bag of frozen peas between my legs against my prostate. It helped a bit. I read *Dune* and kept sneaking out for cigarettes all day and evening.

When Lin got home I made her a cup of tea and she drank it upstairs. She looked beautiful beyond belief. I told her how much I loved her a hundred times.

SATURDAY 20 JULY 2019

Yesterday morning I felt weary of getting breakfast ready for four guests. After the guests had left, I cleaned up the rooms. Davey asked me to play lego again, but I went to the stone circle to drink and smoke while Lin played chess with him.

Another dreary day. More guests and a sore prostate.

SUNDAY 21 JULY 2019

I got up and prepared the space for two guests. When Lin and Davey came down I went back to bed. I floated in bliss. When the guests came out Lin dealt with them. I felt I should hurry down and chat to them, but I couldn't get up.

We went for a walk at Salthill. My legs were so weak, my right foot was flopping as we got about half way.

After lunch, I went upstairs and lay down. I was exhausted and I drifted in and out of consciousness. Lin had a bath. Davey sat beside me drawing a complex electric gun. I got him to read to me a bit. It was lashing rain. They played chess. I did yoga, but even one sun salutation was beyond me.

Late in the evening we heard the Americans downstairs moving around the kitchen. I went down and found them drinking cider in the Zen room. I snuck out to the garage for a smoke. The rain was pouring and the wind was rattling trees against the northern wall of the garage.

FRIDAY 26 JULY 2019

Yesterday when I got up, I took my vitamins and then stretched and did yoga in the Zen room.

When we went to Dunne's, Lin kept tabs on me so I couldn't buy cigarettes. Davey did the watching you gesture, pointing at his eyes with two fingers.

MONDAY 29 JULY 2019

I stood out in the rain in the rising light. I am no better today than I ever was.

Yesterday I got up super early and had breakfast set like a hero. Christof and the little woman got up and I chatted with them. He is gruff and huge. She is timid, but likely formidable.

I just heard Davey gallop down to Lin. It is 6:17. I am resolved to another coffee and hoot now. I have one cigarette left. Then what?

TUESDAY 30 JULY 2019 AT 05:42

Lin and Davey are upstairs. Lin was down with me around five. She had a cup of tea and watched me set up the breakfast area. She was impressed with my Zen precision.

Under big boiling clouds I went out for a reefer. Lin let me know that she was on to me.

We went for a walk down the road. I chatted with Davey about the border with the north, Brexit and the EU, and about how Vikings met Skraelings in America.

THURSDAY 1 AUGUST 2019

Lin was talking in her sleep, saying why you have to? She doesn't know what she was thinking about. I asked if it was smoking, or the whole cuckold hobby thing, and Rhino? She didn't think so.

I drank a beer and had a hoot. Then I washed the Zen room windows inside and out. Lin planted new flowers. I gathered white currants in the stone circle. They were ready, and there were tons of them. I brought them in and we gobbled them. I explained that I had always remembered these from the walk in my grandfather's garden.

FRIDAY 2 AUGUST 2019

I set the table; had a hoot. I kicked myself for what a wreck I am, for indulging this never ending party.

I got up at five something with a woolly head. We have all been having weird dreams.

I had another hoot and was blotto. I went up with Davey and watched TV. I couldn't register anything, just kept falling asleep. Occasionally Davey would flick me awake.

SUNDAY 4 AUGUST 2019

I found leaves and twigs–and even a slug– in the girls' room. Had they been performing naked witchcraft in the stone circle? Lin was annoyed by the makeup powder covering everything. The shower floor was covered in mud that didn't look native.

The English guests arrived. I saw the young fellow looking at the frayed elbows of my cardigan. And then I am remembering things from way back. Wrongs done against me, the humiliations of which I am composed.

MONDAY 5 AUGUST 2019

Buckets of rain poured down on the roof of the garage, where the cat huddled in its little box. She has been in there for three or four days. When the rain takes a break, she sits on the kitchen windowsill.

When the guests awoke, they were surly and false–though it could have been me, as I'd had four or five reefers by then.

FRIDAY 9 AUGUST 2019

The guests had gone out and Lin and I went into town. We left the car to be washed and cleaned inside. We walked into town and did some shopping. I helped Lin look for perfume and underpants. I am very nervous about Monday.

SATURDAY 10 AUGUST 2019

Lin moves between the kitchen and the Zen room, tidying her Chinese tea things. There are four guests asleep down the hall.

After dinner I had a glass of wine outside, and then I sat with Lin and Davey in the Zen room. Davey was jumping over cushions, and Lin put her arm over me and stroked my head. Davey came over and we all sat together happily on the sofa. I took a photo of us in the big mirror.

It is a strange time. We are both nervous about tomorrow.

SUNDAY 11 AUGUST 2019 06:50

Farmer James has the most melancholy cows. I have been smoking at Beijing levels for the past few days.

The next three days will be very difficult. I will persevere, then start my life over.

MONDAY 12 AUGUST 2019

Lin dressed casual and cool. I knelt in front of her. She went to Shannon to collect Rhino.

Once she was gone I made the stone room and toilet immaculate. I left chocolates on the pillows.

I collected Davey, and he was OK with his yoga camp. We went to Joyce's and got a few things for dinner. When we got home, Davey played with his new Pokemon cards, and I went out and had my beers. It took quite a while to get Davey to bed.

Once he was asleep, I dressed and went down. I knocked on the stone room door meekly, brought them wine and snacks, and knelt in a corner while they chatted and drank. She was perfect and she wasn't mine. When they sent me to bed, I suffered dreadfully.

WEDNESDAY 14 AUGUST 2019 07:53

In the kitchen Davey shows Lin his Pokémon cards. We have no guests.

I have hurt myself performing this psychic alchemy of brimstone and treacle. It made me feel things I had forgotten. I am ok now. Lin is being very kind to me.

Davey and I sat around outside. I drank four Polish beers and smoked. We watched a caterpillar move in segments. Davey went in and played War Robots, and I felt hopeless.

THURSDAY 15 AUGUST 2019 06:55

Lin made a lovely breakfast with bagels, avocado and salmon. We took Davey to camp, and then went to Salthill for a walk. It was too windy and wet, and we turned back after a few hundred metres. We sat in the car and had a beautiful, heartbreaking conversation.

SUNDAY 18 AUGUST 2019

When we got to Chen Xi's place Lin and Chen Xi got drunk, chattering and laughing in Chinese.

MONDAY 20 AUGUST 2019

Chen Xi on her way to Tibet, we drove north through Belfast. We continued North toward the Giant's Causeway. I was disgusted by all the Union Jacks. Davey and I were poisoned in Ballymena by the rancid fish and chips served up in that horrible little town. We drove on to the Giant's Causeway. When I stopped for water, some young guys must have seen our licence plates and they drove by slowly giving me the red hand out the window, in case I didn't know where I was. We paid and walked to the causeway. Lin and I bickered up the hill to a higher vantage. Back at the car, Lin booked a B&B. We drove to the rope bridge. We saw Scotland, and dolphins.

The room in Portrush was excellent. Davey watched TV from the sofa bed, and Lin showered. I drank beer on the balcony, which looked out over the town centre. I was the King of Portrush, lording over all the holiday goers on their rides and ferris wheels from the balcony.

My mother liked Portrush, and my father liked Port Nu. I guess my mom was a bit of a party girl.

WEDNESDAY 21 AUGUST 2019

We had a full Ulster Fry, then a walk on the beach. I'm glad we didn't go to Donegal. As it was, we drove six hours.

I was glad to see the end of Union Jacks.

FRIDAY 23 AUGUST 2019

I mooned about the internet wasteland of perversion, violence, the burning Amazon, and the end of days.

I must quit smoking. The pain in my shoulder is getting worse.

THURSDAY 29 AUGUST 2019 07:33

Lin makes breakfast for Davey while he changes into his school uniform. There are two Mexicans and two South Carolinans down the hall. I woke at 1:30 and set the breakfast space.

When I finished, I continued to lay sleepless. I must have slept a bit, because I had a dream about horses crowding their faces into Davey and me. They had big moon eyes. A local Galway guy sneered at me for calling a Griffin a Griffith. It is pouring rain, utterly miserable. It is going to be a long winter.

FRIDAY 30 AUGUST 2019

Lin and I talked about the heart, and it became very dark; it was like we were caught in quicksand. The most sensitive part of me emerged, and I felt very hurt by the truth.

We thought we might solve the problem with a bottle of wine, but that only made things worse. I packed a suitcase and said I was going to Barcelona, but Lin laughed at me. Instead I smoked two packs of cigarettes, and could not sleep for a second night.

SATURDAY 31 AUGUST 2019

I woke in agony, then moped around. I resolved to go on strike, to withhold words of love and adoration, to desist kissing and cuddling her until she realised she could not thrive without my worship.

I said things to Lin to hurt myself. Words of self pity, mingled with words of self reproach.

Darby arrived and gave me a few buds. I had a smoke, and wrote a poem.

At dinner I had an animated discussion with Davey about all things and everything. Lin and I opened a bottle of wine, and sat outside. Davey chattered away; Lin was quiet.

SUNDAY 1 SEPTEMBER 2019

We filled the big wooden bowl with apples. I made apple stew. Lin made apple pies with filo pastry. I got a big bottle of cider. We listened to music. I smoked up a bit of poetry, and then read *A History of Philosophy*, by A.C. Grayling, in the bath.

Davey is having breakfast across the library table from me now. Lin is in the kitchen. She is a creature of silence.

MONDAY 9 SEPTEMBER 2019

I smoked outside, then set the table at two am. Lin went downstairs to chat with Rhino.

SATURDAY 14 SEPTEMBER 2019 07:26

Collapse

Davey is in the library with me. I have just shown the Dutch guests images of a shrew. Kitty was in their room last night. The other guests are down the hall. They are beautiful, friendly Germans.

Darby stopped by and gave me a giant bud. At dinner I talked to Davey about Bishop Berkeley. Ideas were flying through my head. When I cuddled Lin it was otherworldly.

But when I went into the toilet I felt a sudden, violent pain, and fell forward into the toilet. I got myself up and sat at the end of the bed. Lin gave me gulps of water.

SUNDAY 15 SEPTEMBER 2019

Canadian mom and daughter sleep down the hall. I feel so weak. I am losing weight. My legs are so skinny. It rains, so I read philosophy. Psychedelic images impede efforts to sleep, so I got up and set the table.

MONDAY 16 SEPTEMBER 2019

Lin's mom was being interrogated by the police for selling the rat poison that was used to kill some local cows.

WEDNESDAY 18 SEPTEMBER 2019

When we got home I went to the stone circle and hooted and drank two beers in quick succession. I tried to write a poem, but produced only rubbish.

I felt wretched, hung over, jangling and dry. I looked in the mirror and I looked like I felt. We drove to hurling. I stayed in the car. Other adults looked happy and fit. I snuck away for cigarettes.

THURSDAY 19 SEPTEMBER 2019 05:46

The cat seems to spend the night in the stone circle. I worry that she is protecting the fallen apples from waves of rats. She appears mournful when she meets me these midnights and mornings. The fish is in many ways the favoured one. It is easy to feed him, and he grows fatter, and greedier.

Our Airbnb reviews glow. We have done a good job. Lin took Davey to school and I spent time with our guests at the map.

We drove to Silver Strand, walked over the beach in bare feet and shorts and into the water. It was shallow for a long way out but icy. We all managed to get fully under. I stayed under for a while.

We drove home and Lin opened a bottle of Zenzo while I prepared fish and chips.

FRIDAY 20 SEPTEMBER 2019 08:09

I don't know what to write. I have no hope.

Kitty warms up one of the guest chairs.

The days are shorter, bright and cold. Pure. So why am I bent on destroying myself?

THURSDAY 3 OCTOBER 2019

Davey and I had two sides of the same dream. I dreamed I lost him at my high school reunion; I looked everywhere. Davey dreamed he was lost at an amusement park. When we got up, there was a pheasant on the lawn.

We went to Blackrock and watched big waves breaking on the pier. We got treats and beer and wine for a hurricane party. When we got home, we unpacked the groceries and put all of the garden furniture in the garage. I opened the wine for Lin and drank my beers. Lin ate peanuts with her wine.

I fell asleep beside Lin. When I woke at three she was watching TV. I went down and had tea and cigarettes.

We let Davey into bed with us. He squirmed so much that we were going to send him back to his bed, though I relented, and ended up cuddling the little guy like a hot water bottle.

FRIDAY 4 OCTOBER 2019

When Warnock, Aude, Troy, Wren and Nina arrived Warnock and I snuck out and smoked joints and drank beer while Lin made spaghetti for the others.

Davey peeked through the Zen room door at Warn and me. We were sitting at the table outside the Zen room. Davey brought us cushions.

Troy came out, and then Davey brought out guitars. Wren, Warnock, and Troy passed around the guitars and played. Warnock and I sang Where is my Mind. Davey was taking everything in. When I suggested we go to bed, Davey said no, this is what it's all about.

WEDNESDAY 16 OCTOBER 2019 07:23

I have no desire for any woman but Lin. The moon illuminates the rose tube, powdered white and ghostly.

THURSDAY 17 OCTOBER 2019

The world is sodden. It is like living underwater.

I cleaned up the two rooms. It is a small and frustrating job.

I dream kaleidoscopically.

SUNDAY 20 OCTOBER 2019

At 2:45 I set up the breakfast space. When I went back up to bed I dreamt vividly. Davey, Lin and I entered a hotel room where a big native American guy at the door asked if there was anyone here with us. Then I was outside. A Chinese monk pointed at a spot on the tarmac and then disappeared. I remembered this was the place where the lawn mower and power washer kept cutting out, and realised this spot was cursed. I got into the back of my bus and someone else was driving. There was construction along the road and he kept banging the bus off things. I explained to someone about the Chinese monk.

TUESDAY 22 OCTOBER 2019

When he came out of the house he asked are you having a sneaky cigarette daddy? and I had to admit I was. On the drive, he told me he didn't want me to get sick. He said he knew what I meant when I described Tom Yorke's voice as skinny.

I went out and drank beers and smoked in the thin rain, wrote a bit of a poem.

WEDNESDAY 23 OCTOBER 2019

I provoked a fight with Lin. Davey was ready to cry and he told me not to start a fight with mommy. I drew back.

We went out for a walk. Davey rode his bike, and I gestured angrily at the cars whizzing past to slow down. There was a dead hedgehog on the road.

I was feeling sorry for myself, so I started up again the spat with Lin. Afterwards I went down and smoked, set the table for the morning.

THURSDAY 24 OCTOBER 2019

Climbing the stairs to the poetry workshop, an old guy in front of me spoke a line from All Along the Watchtower. I said the next line, and we continued alternating lines up the stairs.

My crappy little poem was well received. I commented a good deal during the workshop and my comments were also well received. I seem to have been accepted into the fold.

Who am I?

Going a hundred
only a twitch
to veer into the path
of an oncoming truck.

I don't trust
these smoker's hands
their idle curiosity
their distance, their indifference;
a pair of cats.

I write this standing out
in the thin rain,
the paper folded in four
and dampening.

Whose fingers are these?

SATURDAY 26 OCTOBER 2019

When we arrived in Rome it was evening, and there were lights everywhere. Our rooms were around the corner from the Trevi Fountain.

SUNDAY 27 OCTOBER 2019

We woke up in Rome. I got coffee downstairs. It was the nicest coffee I have ever had. I tried to learn Italian from the barista.

Alessandro got in touch, and we went to the Spanish Steps to meet him and Daniella. We walked around the city and they showed us the sights. We walked and walked and Davey was tired. We stopped for pasta. They took us through a square to Borghese Park and said goodbye. We looked over the city as the sun went down.

MONDAY 28 OCTOBER 2019

A cab let us off in front of the Vatican. Davey was receptive, though he sometimes looked tired and bored. He pointed out the massacre of the innocents to me, and I was proud of this. We walked back across the river, winding our way through back roads. We had spaghetti carbonara for lunch. After a rest, I snuck out on my own to bum a cigarette and have a beer. Davey came out to me. I got into my city mode, chatted to everyone, was funny and cheeky. Davey loved this, and we had a lot of fun.

TUESDAY 29 OCTOBER 2019

We walked through the Coliseum, then the forum. The tour guide showed us where Julius Caesar was cremated, and the steps from which Mark Antony gave his famous speech. Lin and Davey went up to the room, and I came down and got a beer and bummed a cigarette. Lin called and said Davey wanted to come down to me, so I threw the cigarette away. He looked so funny running down the crowded pedestrian street toward me. I got a strong cocktail from the five euro cart. Davey and I joked around, chatting with black guys, making friends. We sat down at the fountain with my arm around his shoulder.

WEDNESDAY 30 OCTOBER 2019

We walked through a park to the Galleria Borghese. The fountains and gazebos made me think of Keats and Shelley. We had coffee and chatted with people. Birds came to our table and ate crumbs from our buns. The trees were full of parrots. The galleria was full of Greek and Roman gods. I explained how it was all Ovid's *Metamorphosis*.

We got a couple of pina coladas at the five euro cart, and sat at the fountain, but we were told we weren't allowed to drink there, though I thought it was because Davey was using the laser he'd got from a Bangladeshi vendor.

We went up to the place around the corner and had a few pints. Lin and Davey caught me smoking, so I placated Lin by telling her I had found her a nice shirt. When Lin was off buying her shirt, Davey told me he needed eight euro. He said it so earnestly I just gave it to him. He went off and haggled the price on a gladiator t-shirt.

THURSDAY 31 OCTOBER 2019

When we woke up, Davey told me his dreams. He'd been reading in a whale's belly, and then in a shark's. Clearly the whale was Rome, and the shark was the nightlife around the fountain. He had been studying this too.

FRIDAY 1 NOVEMBER 2019

We packed and tidied the apartment, took our bags down and had coffee. Davey had a tiramisu. I said *arrivederci* to my friend the barrister, and we went to the subway station. When we got off, we found ourselves in a place like Mentougou. It was more difficult to bum a cigarette at the airport, but I managed by disregarding a few long faces. We landed in

Dublin, disembarked and got through customs in one piece. It was yet more difficult to bum a cigarette. We got the bus to Galway. I had a guy beside me dying of influenza, and not covering his mouth as he hacked. It was pouring in Galway.

SATURDAY 2 NOVEMBER 2019

We got the kitty in the car. At first Davey thought the kitty's ceaseless horrified meowling was cute, but soon he started shouting at her. The kitty did a dreadful poop, and Davey was gagging. We rolled down the windows despite the submarine weather. There was, of course, a traffic jam.

When we got home, I disappeared to the stone circle for a cigarette and Lin unboxed kitty, removed the poop and cleaned her with a towel, which was then thrown out.

When I came back, kitty was in the house as though she had never been away.

THURSDAY 7 NOVEMBER 2019

When I got back from dropping off Davey, I had a few hoots and looked at my poem. It was nice to be sitting outside and not smoking.

I went up to the workshop. There were so many people we had to search for more chairs. My poem went over well.

I got a cab home. The driver was from the Aran Islands and he talked the whole time. I went out for my tin of Devil's Brew and my last wee hoot from the bong.

Two Records of a Floating Life

Living what's left

too much with us
this moment
from then till then
the thinnest
increment
invisible membrane
wave's edge
no then at all

Endings are beginnings

Summer was mental
profusion, infestation.

I haven't been to the stone circle
out back in months.

Despite the creaks and groans
of flesh and bones,

I need broom, rake, shovel
to strip winter back
to its cleanest core.

Poems come and poems go
I let them drift away,
grabbing pen and paper
only wrecks them anyway.

FRIDAY 8 NOVEMBER 2019

I have been sleeping well since I quit smoking. Everything is better since I quit smoking.

We walked past Blackrock. My new right shoe was a problem. I became floppy footed toward the end of the walk.

TUESDAY 12 NOVEMBER 2019 07:30

I did a bit of work on my poem. I thought it was good, and then I thought it was crap, and now I am leaning towards good again.

Lin played guzheng. Davey did his homework. I read something hurtful on Lin's phone, but she reassured me gently later on.

THURSDAY 14 NOVEMBER 2019

Lin and I went to town to look for props for next week's drama, then I left Lin to do her own thing. I had a double espresso at Cocos and listened to the banjo player. I drove home and tidied up, had a few nuts and berries for lunch.

I drove to the cathedral and parked where Lin usually dropped me. She took the car and I walked off toward the city. I stood for a while looking into the river.

There were not many at the workshop. I felt comfortably humble. Kevin said I really should try to get some of my poetry published.

I hope this feeling will continue.

Blinking Out / Bouncing Back
(*for my secrets*)

How to be Stoic
when all this love
is pouring out of me?

Here writing blindly
I am of the devil's party.

I cautiously descend
following ritual guard rails

gothic & gnarled devised
over decades, through
the murk, disappear.

Oh to be again
that lowest of men!

What did I see there
where there was nothing?
Forevermore
this sliding meniscus
and nothing else.

What are words for
when you are alone?
Why and from where
do they keep coming?
To whom do they belong?

SUNDAY 17 NOVEMBER 2019

I wrote to our little Whatsapp group. Lin calls him Rhino; I call him Mr Fiore.

We lit candles on the cake, sang happy birthday. I went out to the stone circle and drank my two beers. I needed to calm my mind.

MONDAY 18 NOVEMBER 2019

I went out for a few hoots, and then tidied up the guest area.

When Lin got back, I gave her a massage. I was helping her get dressed when she got a message saying the visit would be delayed. I could see how disappointed she was when she momentarily thought the visit might not happen.

I lay beside Lin feeling dark in my heart, and prepared to get up. She coaxed me back to bed and we cuddled. It was nice to see her sweet again. In the morning I showered her face with kisses. I told her I wanted her to be sweet with me again after all of this was over. She said of course and I was happy.

TUESDAY 19 NOVEMBER 2019 06:59

There are two guests down the hall. Lin is one of them.

She dropped me off near Dunnes on her way to Shannon. I walked to Mr Price, to Dunnes, and then to Bushy park. My right leg flops and drags when I walk a long distance.

I met Declan and Rosemary and felt very small. Davey and I watched TV. At eight, I got him to bed.

I came down and set the table for their breakfast. I waited up. I was called down for a moment and then sent to bed. It was hard to get to sleep.

WEDNESDAY 20 NOVEMBER 2019

This is so difficult. I have no words. I cannot be human.

THURSDAY 21 NOVEMBER 2019

Oblivion

I have myself under control. This meek stoicism offers a sort of comfort.

I waitered the table. He demonstrated that he was smarter than me. Lin laughed. They are an enviable couple, the very picture of romance. Perfumes and colognes. Exquisite twistings of the knife.

FRIDAY 22 NOVEMBER 2019 AT 15:51

This is my capitulation. I have suffered greatly for poetry. Mercy!

SATURDAY 23 NOVEMBER 2019 07:45

Davey is beside me playing iPad. Lin is upstairs changing her face.

I stayed at home and tidied the guest rooms, smoked the last of my cigarettes.

We went out for a walk at Salthill. The tide was high and the water was still. We went to the top of the diving board and Davey threw in a stone.

In bed, I told Lin how much I love her. It felt luxurious to be so humble.

WEDNESDAY 27 NOVEMBER 2019

Lin was on the phone all morning with her sister, who has an advanced cancer in her hip. Lin might need to go back to China for a while.

Lin went to get Davey from school, and took him to piano class. I went out and drank four beers and tidied up this week's poem. I sat in the stone circle with the green cushion under my bum. It was difficult but I think I got the poem into a presentable condition.

THURSDAY 28 NOVEMBER 2019

Lin went to the gym, and I went to the garden to work on the poem. It was difficult, and I felt very tired.

At the workshop the level of the poetry was high. I was eager to read mine. The initial reaction to my poem was enthusiastic, but then a few points were picked up on, and teased out, as is often the case.

. . .

It isn't even the past

I.
I watch my little boy
playing happily in the light,
my wife beside him,
kicking back the football
with a laugh.

Both of them alive,
a puzzle I am here to decipher
a reward for I don't know what.

I feel my cloud of ghosts
twine and settle on my mood,
their sad grey faces,
naked backs bruised
gather across the trench,
step forward and drink
deeply of my now.

II.
Firstly the beloved adversary
her emaciate walking corpse.

Then the little brother,
forever a young man
enclosed in soot, thighs scorched,

a dried runic trickle of blood
from one nostril.

Finally the father's gentle eyes
the quiet accusation
of the long farewell.

III.
Time stuns with its numbers.
Mom was thirty nine
like clockwork wound down
died at forty four.

I was eighteen.
Three years later Deane was nineteen
when that fire closed him round.

For thirty years beloved father,
whether you loved me or not
your spirit hovered over me
until eight hours
before Davey was born.

I tremble, project guilt.
How is it right that I,
the most selfish of men,
should enjoy such happiness?

IV.
I show Lin and Davey
photos of you
but seeing nothing
they turn away.

My memories are all
that keep you from
never having been.

I blow at the embers of your lives,
pilot a time machine
back through our history,
fracturing this past
into thousands of futures
where versions of you can live,
and we can all find happiness.

Remorse and regret drive me
to build a block universe,
and hold out for forgiveness.

Time's arrow outpaces memory;
you are erased in that dolphin torn,
gong tormented sea.

The ball rolls toward my feet.
I look up, kick it

back to Davey.

SUNDAY 1 DECEMBER 2019

My knee hurts, and I am run down. Yesterday I smoked two packs of cigarettes. When we got home, I went out to the stone circle and drank and smoked and looked at the poem I have been working on. Lin massaged my knee with tiger balm, then put a heating plaster on it.

TUESDAY 3 DECEMBER 2019 07:21

I tossed and turned, dreamt that Lin was in the room, and that I was outside the window, pretending to be a ghost. I could shriek. I ran my face along the angle between the wall and the floor. When I couldn't see Lin I started to scream, and woke up.

After my session with Antonio, I went out to the stone circle with a beer and the green cushions and worked on a poem, This Saturday. I am happy with it, though it is simple and soppy.

THURSDAY 5 DECEMBER 2019

I had a flat white at the usual place. The lady who seems to fancy me stopped for a chat, and we went up to the class together. The poems were all good, I felt intimidated, so when it was my turn, I read very poorly. Still, the poem was well received.

After the class, we went to Monroe's. I ordered a beer and then got stuck at the end of the table. I chatted to the people around me, who advised me to publish my poetry.

This Saturday

The last day of November
and winter has settled;
we bring in turf briquettes,
sprawl in front of the fire.

My darling son never forget
your bright and happy days.

My wife when you are old and grey
know that you have been
everything to me

And this poem
a reminder of our Saturday,

sealed away forever.

WEDNESDAY 11 DECEMBER 2019

I got up at 3:30, had a cup of tea and a couple cigarettes.

Lin talked to me about going to China next week, and I didn't argue. It reminded me of the dream I'd had the night before, and darkness cinched my heart.

I'd been feeling good about quitting, but now I was feeling sorry for myself. I had two cigarettes at the shop. I thought of how strange I'd not made even one friend in Ireland.

When I got back, I had a cup of tea and more cigarettes outside, then started to clean the stone room toilet. I was ignoring Lin but she came in and we agreed that she would book the earliest appointment with a doctor for her sister, and would go then.

SATURDAY 14 DECEMBER 2019 08:18

Davey is under a blanket with a cool wet face cloth on his forehead. I heard something about a bug doing the rounds at his school. Lin and I tossed and turned, then I thought I heard kitty meowing in the heavy sleet, so I called her from the windows downstairs but she didn't come. I set the table for the guests.

There was a Christmas buzz in town. I went into Dungeons and Donuts, and bought a big Warhammer starter set. It was expensive, but I felt happy that I bought it.

I went out and had my Polish beer. When I went back in I opened up the Zenzo. Lin has started to outpace me once the wine is opened. I sliced chicken into strips, put it into flour and fried it piece by piece. Then I made teriyaki sauce. Lin was a bit drunk, and she was sweet and frisky.

THURSDAY 19 DECEMBER 2019

Davey didn't go to school. We both felt awful. Davey had his favourite salty duck eggs in Chinese porridge for breakfast, while I went to the shop for cigarettes.

When I got back Lin was chatting to her family. Her dad was very talkative. Lin pointed out how dirty his fingers were from a hard working life. I stood behind her, held her shoulders and kissed her head.

Then I went back to bed. Lin went to the supermarket. I was drifting in a fever bliss. Davey came and lay beside me. We were both out for the count.

WEDNESDAY 25 DECEMBER 2019 10:30

We followed Davey down, and have been assembling and painting fantasy miniature figurines since dawn. I assembled a couple of Golden Warriors, and then Lin assembled the entire Skeleton Army. Now Lin and Davey are looking for birds through binoculars.

I prepared lamb, potatoes and Yorkshire pudding; Lin boiled cabbage. Davey painted Skeletons; I painted Golden Warriors. Davey liked the lamb; he was gobbling little pieces as I cut it. Afterwards, we watched two episodes of Dr Who. No one got in touch with us.

SUNDAY 29 DECEMBER 2019

Strange days and nights; strange dreams return. Being off the cigarettes has made everything jagged.

Lin and Davey were painting figures. I felt a bit of a panic so I drove to the little shop and got a pack, got my weed from where Lin had hidden it.

When Lin announced that she had booked her flight to China for the 6th, the day after Davey went back to school, I thought of how scary it would be for Davey if I died in my sleep. Her sister has hurt her leg and can't make it to Beijing to meet the doctor that Lin arranged for them to meet there.

Lin and I have not been good. I can't help but feel that she sees me as negatively as I do. She says when I smoke dope I am like a ghost. Chen Xi used to say something similar, that after I'd smoked my body seemed empty of soul.

I wrote a few lines of poetry, looked at a note in my phone that contained some stuff that floated to me unbidden over Christmas. When Lin came back she and I chatted. I was still who I was, and she knew I had been sneaking hoots. She smiled at me sadly.

I did a bit of yoga. If I get into the habit of yoga and walking and drinking green tea I should be in a stronger position to quit smoking.

When I needed a cigarette, I went for a walk with my phone in my pocket, gathering data for well being. Hope is a tent that billows in the wind and drops.

TUESDAY 31 DECEMBER 2019

Yesterday was pretty good. I snuck out for doobies, and had a cigarette whenever I walked down to the horse gate, did 14,000 steps. I no longer sit on cold surfaces. I did five or more sun salutations, and rolled my shoulders. I had a bath, washed my face, brushed my teeth, put on moisturiser and trimmed the hair in my nostrils.

Lin painted figurines. Davey played piano. How many times in recent days has he asked me the difference between immortal and eternal?

Two joints this morning. Two cups of coffee. I can feel my heart jumping in its cage.

. . .

TUESDAY 7 JANUARY 2020

I took Davey to school and when I got home I assembled a few notes into four poems. I am not sure how good they will seem this morning.

I don't know what else I need to do before I collect Davey at 2:30. Lin should be in China by now. It is after lunch for her.

SATURDAY 11 JANUARY 2020

I dreamt two guys were beating me up around the kitchen table. Davey said I jumped in my sleep.

I didn't have much to give Davey for breakfast. We are out of bread and almost out of milk. I heated some beans, and peeled him an orange.

We went up and watched Rick and Morty, ate cherries and grapes. It is difficult for Davey and I to spend the whole day in the house, just us two.

WEDNESDAY 15 JANUARY 2020

I had a dream about Fan Cheng. I wanted to do some boxing. I crossed the bridge at Gucheng, negotiated a maze of blocked ways. I got to the end and Fan Cheng started to help me with a ladder, but when I said he was lazy he took the ladder away.

When I got up I called Lin and she showed me how to make Chinese porridge for Davey. We listened to Pretty Hate Machine on the way to school.

Lin was sad to leave her family. I tried to comfort her and she said I was good to her. After dinner, Davey and I walked around the house several times. It was fun in a boring way. We finished Rick and Morty, and then I took him to his room and lay down with him for a while. I managed to make him laugh so hard he got hiccups. I have to try to be less funny.

I will quit smoking at 2 o'clock.

THURSDAY 16 JANUARY 2020

When I started to paint the Iron Golem figurines the movement of my hands took me back to being a teenager. I felt ashamed to be doing this at my age.

I chatted to Lin before I went to get Davey. Throughout the day I promised myself I would quit smoking at two. At two, I decided to quit at four.

I got Davey and we drove home. I didn't want him to see that I had spent the day painting figurines. I keep looking ahead to a better me, a better way of living, but I am stuck in a loop of endless postponement. I had planned to do work around the garden while Lin was gone, but it was so rainy. Today is sunny, but I will smoke and maybe go to Dungeons and

Donuts and buy more paint. I can't imagine how I could have a job or do anything worthwhile.

FRIDAY 17 JANUARY 2020

I painted Iron Golems. Lin was cold and distant. Of course she is with the French guy, and I know it is my own fault for organising this drama. She will get on the plane sometime today.

Davey won't eat anything I give him. The garden looks ragged. I just need to get through today. Tomorrow Lin will be back.

SATURDAY 18 JANUARY 2020 05:22

I got up planning on giving a cold response to an expected morning greeting from Lin. But there was no message, so I sent her a nasty one. Davey and I went to Salthill for a walk. I got a reply from Lin on the way, and we started to fight. Davey walked slowly behind me. By the time we started back my right leg was a piece of wood.

I let Davey play on the iPad and went out for a beer. It didn't feel good. I hadn't had a drink since Christmas. Lin and I had a proper fight on wechat. I heated up the leftover chilli but Davey only ate a few bites.I drank a little bottle of rum and the fight got pretty bad. Davey heard everything.

It feels like everything is ruined.

SUNDAY 19 JANUARY 2020 7:09

I woke up hungover and remorseful. Lin had missed her connecting flight in Frankfurt and needed to stay there another ten hours.

Davey and I drove to the Centra and got sausage, hash browns, and black and white pudding. We did ten walks around the house, and then went up and watched Rick and Morty.

When she got home we brought her in the front door, I felt shy. I made her a cup of tea and heated her some spaghetti carbonara. After she had a shower she came to bed and we cuddled. She told me about her time in Beijing with the French guy and I felt jealous but happy too. It felt good to be so resolutely put in my place.

WEDNESDAY 22 JANUARY 2020

I managed to run a leisurely four km before my right leg got sloppy. In the sauna, Lin talked about how the French guy told her there was a serious virus in the south of China, and it was going to become a big deal.

. . .

THURSDAY 23 JANUARY 2020 07:20

Two days / no cigarettes

Lin trimmed my beard, and I got a haircut in town. It is Chinese New Year's eve so Lin got some jiaozi wrappers at the Asian Market..

Maybe I will manage to quit smoking this time, though I'm thinking that maybe I quit just a bit too soon–that I should have had just one last smoke.

SUNDAY 26 JANUARY 2020

I dreamt I was in a Dublin apartment with Chen Xi and Tan. I decided not to go up north, but to stay in the apartment to smoke weed and write. Catherine Giltrap said she would stay in the apartment also. I mistook the Chinese *ayi* at the door for a chicken. There was spilled chicken and mushroom soup. The *ayi* spoke disparagingly of Chen Xi. She might have been Ashley, one of our first Aihua sales people. It was a rainy night, and there was thunder and lighting this morning.

After dinner I tidied up, and squabbled with Lin. Davey adjudicated and everything turned out OK. Lin was pretty reasonable too. We did ten laps around the house. Lin took Davey down to his room. I read *Thus Spake Zarathustra*.

. . .

TUESDAY 28 JANUARY 2020

I sent Chen Xi a message when I got up, wanting to know about the Coronavirus in China.

I tidied up then did some yoga. I dug out the fennel, and snipped the straggly lemon leaf thingy. I snipped a few branches from the apple tree, the ones that hung down into the middle of the stone circle. I went back in and did more yoga, a few push ups and some kettle bell squats.

Davey brushed his teeth and they both gave me a kiss before Lin took him down to his room. I read an excellent death poem by Philip Larkin, and then the Nietzsche introduction. I hadn't heard about Lou Salome before. There was a photo of her with a whip in a cart pulled by Nietzsche and another guy.

WEDNESDAY 29 JANUARY 2020

We drove to the Cathedral and walked into town. Lin was worried that people would start to look at Chinese people differently now that there was Coronavirus. I felt like a fool buying the Derelict Ruins and Cypher Lords–tucking them into my coat as though they were porn. It is hard for me to control myself.

Chen Xi is quarantined in Hainan, playing Mahjong with her parents. Tan is trying to get back to Hainan from Anhui.

I did Davey's homework with him, then he played piano. He is getting better at the Bare Necessities. I read more of the introduction to *Thus Spake Zarathustra*. I am comforted by the concept of eternal recurrence.

THURSDAY 30 JANUARY 2020

Lin went to the gym, and I spray painted the walls of the Derelict Ruins white. I did a bit of yoga, then I painted over the Ruins with black contrast paint, and dry brushed over this with white. I felt bad about not going to the poetry workshop,, but reading Nietzsche on overcoming the self made me feel some hope.

Getting ready for bed, I joked with Davey about people who are mad for football and he laughed until he started hiccuping. Lin was annoyed by my elitist tone, but called me handsome for the second time that day. It took me a while to get to sleep. Lin made sad sounds throughout the night. She got up at 5:30. She is teaching herself how to play The Sound of Silence on piano.

I have been thinking about a D&D campaign for Lin and Davey. They would be fallen Stormcast who need to discover their true identities. Lin would go the healing route, and Davey would develop lighting powers.

FRIDAY 31 JANUARY 2020 05:40

Lin and Davey are asleep upstairs, and the kitty is in. She was in a dreadful state when I opened the window. I don't think she is sleeping in her bed in the garage–she seems to be spending the night on the windowsill.

The Italian pizza guy gave Lin a free bun. When we were lining up I mentioned that Lin was blushing, and she said she felt hot. The ladies behind the counter looked at her as though she had Coronavirus, which made her turn redder.

I painted and Lin played Scarborough Fair. I know she was depressed about her sister, who can't get treatment for the tumour in her leg while there is Coronavirus, but is in a lot of pain.

We went for a walk to the crossroads. It was fresh, windy and cold. Cars whizzed past with no concern for our lives.

I got my kisses and then Lin took Davey down to his room. I had an idea for a poem about the boy who died in a storm drain in Edworthy Park when he fell, bumped his head, and drowned in shallow water. I remember him standing on the swings with a snotty nose singing Everything is Beautiful.

SUNDAY 2 FEBRUARY 2020

I sent a few messages to Fred suggesting a course of action for Aihua. My messages were unsolicited and unwelcome.

When Lin got home, she was pissed off because she could tell right away I had been hooting.

Davey and I played Warcry. I was the Crow Boys, and I swooped down for Death from Above. Davey did a Whirlwind of Death and a Human Battering Ram.

MONDAY 3 FEBRUARY 2020 05:42

I am just in from smoking a reefer. Davey is up now; I hear him in our room. I have just rolled up another reefer. I will get Lin to put away the hoots. She is upset, though not actively fighting with me. It is a difficult psychology. I know I am much happier when I don't smoke, but after a while the world seems flat, persistent.

I looked at the stuff I wrote after Christmas and it is rubbish. I have been thinking about writing without smoking, and I think it is possible. When I got home, Lin went up to bed. I went out for a hoot and painted the Cypher Lords. I got a terrible pain in my neck, and one numb asscheek, so I did some yoga. I am getting to be quite bendy. Lin came down to me quietly and gave me a sincere hug.

TUESDAY 4 FEBRUARY 2020 07:02

I feel like a wretch. I just smoked a reefer and it floored me. I had to hold onto the wall to get into the house. I sank down onto the sofa in the entry room. My head is still spinning. It appears I have serious health problems.

Yesterday morning I made great resolutions. My gimpy leg felt OK, and I felt strong though the walk back to the car was like walking on stilts. I had to stop at benches to sit down.

THURSDAY 6 FEBRUARY 2020

The sky is clear. During the night the moon made the grass look like snow.

Lin made me some porridge before we went to the gym. I ran four km. My gammy leg made me shuffle around holding onto equipment for support. I sat in the passenger seat so Lin could drive. I've started to suspect that the problem with my leg is related to the prostate. I will have the operation if it gives me some extra years.

I went to the Parents' Association meeting. There was a guy there, Tom, who expressed himself very well. I didn't say a word. I felt shy, or far away. I am so far from being a professional person now, the kind of person who could hope to succeed in a job interview.

FRIDAY 7 FEBRUARY 2020 08:18

We went to the pharmacy to get masks, but they were sold out. Lin gave me a little blim of the weed she was hiding. I rolled a joint and went out to the stone circle. When I came back I blabbered, and she said when you smoke you always talk like this. I went into the Zen room and wrote a decent little poem called Prophecy.

SATURDAY 8 FEBRUARY 2020 AT 12:00

Yesterday I woke up feeling like a hole that needed filling. Lin left me a bit of weed on the table.

I think the poem I wrote this week, Prophecy, is enough to get me back to the poetry workshop. I can't give up, although I have given up for today.

MONDAY 10 FEBRUARY 2020

I read Nietzsche in the bath while Lin sat painting her nails. We watched heavy snowflakes drifting down like feathers.

TUESDAY 11 FEBRUARY 2020

I printed up Prophecy then worked on Our Christmas and That Dark Interval. I may put them together as a sequence. Prophecy deals with painful memories. Deane's death is an unbearable black hole in my soul. The death of my mom is another. The three poems move from devastation to consolation.

WEDNESDAY 12 FEBRUARY 2020

The moon is big in the sky.

I took Davey to school, and when I got back, Lin gave me a little piece of dope. I printed up the sequence on Why it has to be this Way. I read the poem through to Lin, and she seemed to get that it was a good poem, but she said don't hurt yourself too much.

THURSDAY 13 FEBRUARY 2020

Lin cleaned up around the house. I felt bad to see her cleaning up while I was wandering about lonely as a cloud, but I left her to it.

At the workshop I chatted to the lovely older ladies about Coronavirus. The poetry was very good; my poem went over well. Everyone was advising everyone to publish here or there. When the workshop was over I hurried out, walked down to the Spar, got a Polish 9% and a pack of smokes. I saw two guys from the workshop, and it was strange to hear someone say hello David.

Why it has to be this way

Prophecy

He came home again vomiting,
clattering between the toilet
and his room.

Our dad upstairs
in our dead mom's bed
heard nothing.

I went into Deane's dark room
to beat him up
to thump and roar
for his own good or mine.

I stepped to the bed
with fists clenched.
His sleeping face, sideways:
sad, dead, and pure.

I put down my fists
and went back to my room
stricken, and I have never
shaken this solitude.

That Dark Interval

I need more words
but they do not come.
It always need to be a big production:
only destitute,
on the border of oblivion
may my burning fingers
grasp at this torrent of loss.

All other days are waiting,
wasted, vain.

I have no belief in beyond
but have known in life
this dark interval,
how it cuts a path toward where words
would be true.

It doesn't matter how much I have
damaged self in seeking
if I can find a way of speaking only truth
for forty words or so,
twelve or fifteen even…

Our Christmas, remember
I still carry my father's
many disappointments in me,
nurse them down rainy roads,
heed their whispers, see
his disappointed face
abashed by my greed.

I've spent a life trying, on and
off, to write this shame away;
Now we teeter on the fulcrum
of happiness.

Our Christmas, remember,
we stayed in, we three
the way it should be
assembling figurines,
painting them, together,
new memories
to cover the dead.

FRIDAY 14 FEBRUARY 2020

We intended to do a big cleanup but went into town instead. Lin wore her long coat and high boots and looked like a fantasy queen. At Dungeons and Donuts I got Lady Olynda and some paint. It cost 75, which was more than I expected, but Lin didn't blink. She just said firmly that she would paint Lady Olynda.

SATURDAY 15 FEBRUARY 2020

Yesterday was stormy. As soon as he got up, Davey continued painting his Knight Azaros. He rushed it, but did a good job for an eight year old. Lin was engrossed in painting Lady Olynda, so I took Davey to Joyce's for pizza. We listened to Hurt, by NIN and then by Johnny Cash. Davey said that dark is sad, lonely, and calm, but not evil.

MONDAY 17 FEBRUARY 2020

Lin left to collect Mr Fiore, and I tidied the house despite feeling weak on my feet. My head was spinning and my limbs were watery. They arrived at 1:30. I said hello then went to get Davey. When we got home, Davey did his homework then played on the iPad. I don't know how I will keep going all morning.

TUESDAY 18 FEBRUARY 2020

I got up before five. Lin came out of the stone room and I made her a cup of tea. She suggested I dress properly to serve breakfast.

I waited on the table meekly while they breakfasted. They went back to their room and I tidied.

I crept and knelt, amazed by what I saw. I accepted who I was. I felt all the love in the world. Bliss of the ghost.

I collected Davy and we had dinner then watched TV. I got him to bed.

I felt strange and lonely. I read Nietzsche. Lin and Mr Fiorre were out on the town. She sent a message telling me not to wait up. I couldn't sleep.

WEDNESDAY 19 FEBRUARY 2020 07:45

The writing prompt at the top of the page today is have you ever had a dream or fantasy that came true?

When I got home from taking Davey to school, I got dressed and served breakfast. Lin giggled when I answered Mr Fiore's questions meekly.

I knelt in the corner of the room and saw it all. It broke my heart, but felt so right. I had suspected that the sexy couple thing had only been an act, but I was stripped of this delusion. I came out alone, wind rushing through my heart. Nothing was mine.

I went to get Davey. I complained to one of the parents about the weight of the endless rain on our hearts. Davey and I watched *Henry Dangerous* and ate Pringles.

THURSDAY 20 FEBRUARY 2020

Lin is not home.

I dropped Davey off and stood by the table attentively while the sexy couple ate.

After school I let Davey play iPad and went out to the shed for a beer. As I walked back I saw Lin through the bathroom window of the white room. She called me over and I chatted to her for a few minutes through the window. I asked her if she was in love again and she said she wasn't, though I think she is. I asked her if I was disgusting to her.

Davey and I went upstairs and watched *Kid Dangerous* then got ready for bed. I read some poetry and then I looked at my phone. I received photos from the Salthill Hotel. Lin looked exquisite; he was very dashing.

It is hard to know why people feel the way they feel. I know nothing. I am tired of being me. Be careful what you wish for in youth because you just might find it in middle age.

FRIDAY 21 FEBRUARY 2020 07:02

My resistance failed and I began sending sulky messages to Lin. She became frustrated, and things got dark. I sent messages to the Whatsapp group, and Mr Fiore advised me not to be puerile. Italians use the best English.

I took Davey to bed and stayed with him a while. I went to bed and fell asleep reading. I woke to see Lin at the door. She got into bed beside me, and cuddled me. I was sorry for upsetting her. I was relieved to have her back.

I don't understand myself and I have trouble accommodating my contrary impulses. Lin suffers because of this.

SATURDAY 22 FEBRUARY 2020 AT 07:25

Yesterday morning Lin made noodles for breakfast. Afterwards we lay down and had a talk, smoothed out all the wrinkles. I believe she will love me forever.

She made stew for dinner, and we drank a bottle of champagne. She sent messages to Mr Fiore, and got me to help her with the wording. I felt adoration for the person she has become since her lover left– alive, confident and sexy.

I hope Lin can keep the fire that is in her now. She needs to get out of the house more, have more contact with people outside of the family.

SUNDAY 23 FEBRUARY 2020

The bit of morning sunshine didn't last long. Lin's sister's situation is dire. The tumour in her leg is causing pain and growing, but no hospital facilities are available.

. . .

MONDAY 24 FEBRUARY 2020

The local clinic told Lin that under the circumstances they should remove the leg at the hip. China's economy is collapsing. The news is all about sickness, market collapses, and people buying gold.

WEDNESDAY 26 FEBRUARY 2020

I sat down in the Zen room to write, and got a bit of a poem about my first day at kindergarten. Maybe it is too narrative, but I will stick with it.

I called airbnb to cancel all our bookings. They are going ahead with the amputation of Lin's sister's leg. Coronavirus has made it that there is nothing we can do.

I went out and pulled weeds from the gravel by the front door, then from along the shed.

THURSDAY 27 FEBRUARY 2020 07:10

I composed an emotional letter to the Airbnb guests, written as a poem. Lin suggested changes. I'm glad she did. She asked me if I'd gotten more dope. I said I had. She said nothing.

I went out for a hoot. When I came back I looked at my poem.

Markets are crashing. The ramifications of the virus will be huge. If it comes here, we will play D&D, and I will write poetry, dredge my past for enough material to tie the sequences together.

FRIDAY 28 FEBRUARY 2020 AT 04:55

I did a couple lessons, talked with Mattia and Alessandro about Coronavirus.

Lin thinks about her sister while I plan a D&D adventure. I need a Dungeon Master's Guide, graph paper for maps, boots for the Ghost, a boat across the river big enough for only one, and a key for the magician's house.

We are going to self quarantine this weekend, and keep Davey out of school. There's another named storm heading in.

Extended youth in the timeless Realm of Sigmar. The Knights of the Secret Rose, inviolable.

SATURDAY 29 FEBRUARY 2020 07:46

I snuck out for a joint with my first coffee in the cold rain. Lin begged me not to let myself become so raggedy, so I went up and had a shower.

Storm Jorge kept us in the house all day. Lin painted red wings on the Furies. Davey played on the iPad, and I read Joseph Campbell, *Masks of God*.

Lin chatted to her family, and read about Coronavirus on her phone. I went out into the storm, then lay on the sofa.

SUNDAY 1 MARCH 2020

Lin went to the Asia market and Davey and I went to Dungeons and Donuts. I bought *The Player's Handbook* and *The Monster Manual* as well as *The Dungeon Master's Guide*, spending much more than I had expected. We were wearing masks and a college girl laughed and did a fake cough.

MONDAY 2 MARCH 2020

It is a difficult time for Antonio in Milan, which has a Yellow Severity Warning for Coronavirus.

Lin is suffering. She can't get back to be with them. She would need to quarantine, and she couldn't be confident she could get back to Davey and me.

TUESDAY 3 MARCH 2020 07:06

Davey plays on the iPad on the sofa beside me while Lin is in the other room worrying about her sister.

I worked on my poem. I made some changes then changed them back. I can write more poems like this if it proves to work. This could be the way forward for me.

Antonio asked me why my family has no friends. I was taken aback by his words, but when I talked to Lin, she said that this was the price we had to pay for leaving Beijing. When I was talking with Antonio, I kept thinking about how heavy it feels when I am with other people.

Chicken curry and a bottle of champagne. We chatted and laughed. After dinner, Davey and I went into the library and played D&D.

WEDNESDAY 4 MARCH 2020

Lin broke down crying after the surgeon refused the money she sent. The surgery will be done in the local clinic.

We went to Aldi and did a big shop. I made sure we got tinnies against the end of the world. We went to Salthill and walked to the diving board. It was a beautiful day and spirits were high. I chatted to a guy on the top of the tower, asked him if Prince William would be going for a swim when he visits Blackrock. Lin and I sat in a quiet place and watched waves unfurling at the shore. I meditated. I found it hard to walk over the rocks. My balance was completely gone.

Lin showed me a picture of the room her sister is in and I tried not to take it in. Life has been hard for this beautiful and spirited person, and now will be even harder. Her parents will drive for two hours on a motorised tricycle to get to the clinic. It is cold there.

Facebook says there are four new Coronavirus cases in North Clare, just across the bay.

THURSDAY 5 MARCH 2020 07:09

Lin slept in the stone room because her sister was to have had her surgery at midnight our time, but it was postponed until midnight tonight. She messaged most of the night, and kitty stayed with her.

I saw Prince William briefly in the window beside me as his motorcade passed. I told Lin it is wrong for him to be here not because he is British, but because it isn't right for one person to have so much privilege. Shop Street was full of huge policemen. At Dominic Street I had a coffee. I saw some of the poetry people there but didn't join them; instead I sat out front smoking.

There were liquorice all-sorts at the workshop; I went somewhere in the middle. Afterwards I turned down an invitation for a cup of tea and instead got a Polish beer at the Spar, jumped in a cab. First thing back I had a great piss in the bush and got some doobie from Lin. I rolled up a joint and went out to the stone circle with my beer.

Lin sat at her chair caring for her skin, and then she went down.
I turned off the light and tried to sleep. I kept thinking of what
Lin's sister was facing. Such horrible and unnecessary suffering.

The worlds we inherit

First Day

From Mwadui Shenyanga to Belfast by boat,
Flin Flon by plane, and then through the prairies
to southwest Calgary by car.

My mother cried as we walked through
our new home; I thought at first
the tears were from happiness.

She took me to kindergarten the day we arrived.
I watched the children scream and riot
and when I looked back she was gone.
I went to follow but the teacher shouted *door guards*
and the bigger boys wrestled me down.

Troy Praunchuck was supposed to walk me home.
The sky was purple and drenched in sorrow;
Packed snow crunched under my feet.
I followed Troy to a shop across the road

but when I looked around he'd run away.

I cried and my fingers burned from the wet cold;
I wandered crescents and avenues, alien
feathers drifting down through streetlite
hoar frosted branches.

Little Linda stood in the light of her door,
called out *why are you crying?*

When my dad got me home
my mother kissed my fingertips
a hundred times.

It began with banging

We left Mwadui because my mother heard
about beheadings in the Congo and didn't
trust the Masai who took my father hunting.

Bang bang. Elephant, cheetah,
leopard, warthog, gazelle.
On the ship around the horn of Africa
he shot clay pigeons from the deck
and Muriel Hemingway told my mother
I would grow up to be a strong man
because I cried so hard.

In Belfast the boy across the road
burst my head open with a broom.
I looked up at my mom through the blood
as she screamed at my father.

In Flin Flon a babysitter, Marina, molested me,
said my parents were never coming home.

In Westgate Elementary kids tortured other kids
while teachers sipped coffee inside the endless
days of winter. Robert Hall got it worst,
but I knew it could have just as easily been me.

Fight after school

I saw them hunting Deane down;
I went over as they rubbed snow in his face.

Conrad was from Mexico;
we'd held hands one morning.

I pinned Deane down with knees on shoulders
demanded he call himself fag
until my dad came out and asked me
If that was what someone called me?

Danny Miller had Conrad in a headlock
and I told Danny to fight me instead.

When he had me in a headlock
the ring of voices knotted around us
shrieked *pound 'is face in*.

Alex Karmis smashed Barry Yee's
amazing toothpick battleship
and I jumped up and grabbed him.

He punched me in the head
until the disabled teacher
hobbled over and parted us.
Karmis said *after school, Cotter.*

I ran home through alleyways.
When Deane said that night
you're chicken of Karmis
I beat him in a rage.

In the morning he showed our parents.
the bruises on his back.

Everything was lost the day
she told us she had five years.

FRIDAY 6 MARCH 2020

Lin stayed in the stone room last night and all morning, texting her family as her sister underwent surgery. She looks about to collapse.

The Italians are worried about Coronavirus. I'd never seen Antonio down before. The girl from just outside the red zone was worried for her parents.

We opened a bottle of wine, and I prepared dinner and tried to distract her with small talk. As Davey and I got ready for bed Lin's people started contacting her, so I took him down to his room.

SATURDAY 7 MARCH 2020 06:39

I got up at four, and went to the all night petrol station for cigarettes. I drank coffee and hooted and worked on a poem about Lin's sister.

I got Lin to just give me the whole jar of buds so I wouldn't have to keep bugging her.

Davey and I got ready for bed. Lin was on the phone to her brother in law. He said the light was gone from her soul.

MONDAY 9 MARCH 2020

Lin doesn't want to look at my poem. We're keeping Davey home. I worry about him falling behind, but won't go against Lin on this.

TUESDAY 10 MARCH 2020 07:09

Day 4 of isolation

Davey has been playing iPad too much. We need to look into homeschooling.

I woke up early, worked on the poem. I sent messages to Chen Xi, Chen Fu, and Tan. I asked them for a line in Chinese to describe the sense that there is always a wall between people, that we can't share another's pain.

After dinner, Davey and I played Dungeons and Dragons. We had an argument over whether or not Iron Golems can swim. He was pissed off, but we got over it. I made sure he found some treasure.

These will be hard times. Tan has been quarantined for forty days.

THURSDAY 12 MARCH 2020

Notice of school closure

Yesterday we were all prickly in the morning. Lin was stressed out about her sister, who is experiencing phantom pain from the missing leg.

She made noodles for dinner, then we walked around the house 25 times, and felt a bit happier.

Schools will be closed in Ireland starting today. Scarlet called, concerned about coronavirus.

SUNDAY 15 MARCH 2020

I dreamed people broke into our house. I ran toward them but something held me back. I was making a grunting noise as I tried to get to them. Lin rubbed my back to wake me up.

We read our phones about Coronavirus. Things could become very bad here in Ireland. It sounds like we will remain in isolation for a long time.

MONDAY 16 MARCH 2020 05:43

Lin is awake, looking at her phone.

We got to Aldi before eight and were surprised to see a line of people waiting to get in. Lin went in with a mask and rain coat. When we got home she left the groceries in the garage and had a shower.

I painted more orcs. I have no energy, and I don't feel like doing exercise, or anything else. I have been smoking more than a pack a day.

I had a session with Antonio. His business is crashing; he has a million euros worth of goods in a warehouse that he can't distribute. He will have a problem paying the mortgage on his office and factory, which are guaranteed by his home. I didn't know what to say to him.

Lin cooked Chinese dinner. She has red blotches on her face. We walked ten laps around the house exchanging the pink weights.

I am not happy with how I am doing the orcs. They are too luminous. I am careful in my plans, but in my execution I just thrust the paint brush forward. A lot is lost between head and hand.

THURSDAY 19 MARCH 2020 AT 07:38

I did a poor job painting orc eyes. I have no talent, as Cindy said years ago. Lin took over the orcs.

FRIDAY 20 MARCH 2020 AT 07:04

Lin was thin with me for doing so much Fluentify. We organised worksheets to keep Davey busy in the morning, but he just foothers around. We haven't made plans for how to manage ourselves during this time.

Davey loved the first half of *Fellowship of the Ring*. Lin was in a blue jumper and ponytail.

SUNDAY 22 MARCH 2020

I dreamed Lin and I were in a coffee shop, talking to a police lady. I went to buy a book but couldn't because I had ten traffic tickets. The book store guy asked me if I'd like him to call the police to come and talk to me. A police woman was jumping on the bonnet of a fire truck.

It is a mild morning. Lin has gone out to get food from the shed while I read Nietzsche in the bath. We finished *The Two Towers*. I love Davey's imitation of golem.

TUESDAY 24 MARCH 2020 AT 07:02

I woke around three and read my phone until Coronavirus was coming out of my ears. I had stayed off cigarettes for two days and then I slipped out yesterday morning and got a pack.

I did a bit of yoga, painted goblins and then started on Fluentify. Lin was haggard from dealing with Davey, and doing a big clean up of the house.

I feel like butter spread too thin over toast.

THURSDAY 26 MARCH 2020

Lin managed Davey while I Fluentified, and her spirit was more positive. I got Davey to draw a wraith, a man of Gondor, and a rider of Rohan.

I did ten squats with the kettlebell, and ten push ups. My muscles are deteriorating. Simple things like jumping jacks are beyond me. Lin and Davey played tag.

SATURDAY 29 MARCH 2020

My knee is very bad. I went to the little shop and got a pack of Silk Cut, and a pack of Drum tobacco. I was very careful, and when I got home I had a shower. We ran around our garden ten times before my knee gave in.

I put bird seed in the feeders and then we did some work on the wall. I dragged out wood and Lin piled it up. Davey loaded the wheelbarrow at the stone circle. We saw people walking by but avoided chatting to them.

I made spaghetti carbonara, and Lin fried up black and white pudding to make an intercontinental carbonara. It was a bit dry, but when we added Chinese chilli oil it was just right.

We went up and finished *The Desolation of Smaug*, then started *The Battle of Five Armies*. I couldn't bend my knee, so I lay it on a pillow, and applied heat.

Davey's new teacher spent most of her letter telling us not to worry about homework.

MONDAY 30 MARCH 2020

Lin dreamed she was at the beach with Davey and a tsunami wave was rolling toward them. Lin fell into a hole with spiky things in it. A weak, skinny guy came to help, but he had trouble getting her out.

WEDNESDAY 1 APRIL 2020 08:15

Scarlet's going mental over 5G causing coronavirus, and the government planning to chip everyone with the vaccine. She's not havin' any o' tha'.

Lin is resolved to get a six pack. Davey wants one too.

THURSDAY 2 APRIL 2020 07:51

Lin did a run; I hope this makes her feel better. Davey and I had a row about whether or not it is a good idea to eat shortbread for dinner.

The Italians are depressed. They cannot hug and kiss one another. I am tired of talking about coronavirus.

SUNDAY 5 APRIL 2020

Lin and Davey did some exercise and I started painting the Goblin Boingers.

I went out to meet Darby. I tried to keep my distance, and got him to whisper. It was strange and grim. He wanted a cigarette so I gave him three. I had to step up to him to do this. I worried that I took risks. I think I will die if I get Coronavirus.

WEDNESDAY 8 APRIL 2020

Davey is playing Stairway to Heaven on the piano, and I have abandoned myself to getting drunk and stoned after Fluentifying all day.

THURSDAY 9 APRIL 2020

What to talk about with Paolo? I sent him Blake's picture of Newton calculating. Also a quote: May God keep us from single vision and Newton's sleep.

We are becoming more quiet. It is working well for us, the mystic stillness of quarantine.

FRIDAY 10 APRIL 2020 05:46

Five feedback forms finished, four more to do. Freaked out about the destruction of my body after the third joint.

Lin was unhappy with me, Davey desperately bored. I walked a few times around the garden. It is spring, and things are awakening.

TUESDAY 14 APRIL 2020 07:58

Lin plays piano while Davey daydreams. He does more of that these days. I sit with two robins and the cat in the mist of morning.

After my last class, we opened a bottle of Prosecco, and I made dinner. I sat in the stone circle and hooted and then joined Lin and Davey in the chairs outside the Zen room. We opened another bottle of wine. I hooted more. We were feeling great. Lin was DJing. She played Led Zeppelin, NIN, and Supertramp. I talked to them about Apollo and Dionysus. Lin seemed impressed.

I have ten sessions today. Trump has withdrawn funding for the WHO, and it appears world economic collapse is imminent.

FRIDAY 17 APRIL 2020

Davey dreamed of a floating head and a kid trying to escape a fire giant in a time machine he didn't know how to drive. They called his mom, who had super powers.

When they saw the fire giant destroying the city, they went into the time machine. The floating head wasn't really floating; its body was invisible, and its head was not. There was a basketball court in the time machine. They managed to escape, and the kid's mom defeated the giant.

We finished *The Lord of the Rings,* and Davey played The Shire on piano.

When we got ready for bed Lin complained that I always sleep in the middle, and she gets sucked into my gravity well.

SATURDAY 18 APRIL 2020 AT 12:00

Lin made aubergines for lunch. After Davey did a Chinese lesson we played Dungeons and Dragons.

Davey and Lin are getting very good on the piano.

I opened a bottle of Prosecco, drank it out in front of the Zen room. I do love Prosecco and a hoot.

SUNDAY 19 APRIL 2020

Lin doesn't seem to have noticed that I have not cuddled her since she complained about the gravity well.

We did a few sprints around the lawn. I did one sun salutation.

Lin made stew in the slow cooker. Chen Xi called, concerned about the growing negativity between China and the West. I will have to follow up–I think I know what she is feeling, and how to reassure her. Darby called and told me in detail his daily schedule, as though it were the finest product of scientific rigour.

I opened a bottle of Zenzo. Lin was grumpy because I had been hooting all day. When I finished the Zenzo I was taken on a walk, dragging my leg behind me.

TUESDAY 21 APRIL 2020

Muscle mass is diminishing and my knee is absolutely bolloxed. I need to see someone.

Lin continues cranky and forlorn, Davey almost impossible to manage. I Fluentify. I'm starting to think I should use my diary time to write something else.

WEDNESDAY 22 APRIL 2020 AT 12:00

We talked about getting a dog. We looked at ads. I did lessons. We had lunch. The days whirl by. They start and then they finish.

THURSDAY 23 APRIL 2020

Davey and I drove to Moycullen listening to Zombie and Bohemian Rhapsody. It felt great to be on the road.

After watching the end of Captain Fantastic, I went out for a hoot. Lin and Davey came out, and we walked around and around the stone circle.

When we went in, the dog lady called. We will collect him from Limerick on Saturday. We hope the police will not turn us back; we really want to get this dog.

FRIDAY 24 APRIL 2020

Shahin urged me not to hesitate, to just drive down and be damned with the police. I told the dog lady I could talk my way past the police.

Davey couldn't stop asking what were the chances that we will get the dog. The lady hadn't called and we had given up.

While we were watching *The Hobbit*, Dierdre messaged Lin to say she couldn't travel over the weekend, but would hold the pup, and make the transfer on Monday.

SATURDAY 25 APRIL 2020

We did a half hour workout video. It was difficult for me. I read in China that people get weaker before they die. I worried about leaving Davey to grow up without my guidance.

I am out of reefer. When I got it I imagined I could manage it, and maybe even quit smoking cigarettes while I had it. Such delusion.

MONDAY 27 APRIL 2020 06:33

On my way to Adare to get the dog I was stopped by the police at a roundabout coming into Limerick. I tried to reason with the guy, and told him how much Davey needed the dog, but he was implacable. He directed me to turn around at the roundabout, but I went straight and he jumped in his car and blazed the siren and lights. He was very pissed off. Apparently I was the eighth person in Ireland to get a ticket for this newly-created offence.

I called the dog lady, and she said she would try to make it to Bunratty Castle. I chain smoked while waiting. The dog got out of the car trailing a string of drool a yard long. I got him into the back of our car without taking necessary protections against coronavirus. I sent a quick photo to Lin, and then set off.

Ares whined and I talked. I stopped at the Newcastle garage for cider. Davey and Lin came running to the car when I pulled in. We got him out and he blinked and groaned. He wouldn't let me out of his sight. We put on his lead and he pulled Davey around the place. He is huge. Kitty hissed at him, and then snuck up to our room.

We got up early to let the dog out. He is beautiful but very smelly, and not trained at all. Kitty is bummed out. I have a lot of Fluentify this morning. I was so rattled yesterday that I didn't register the amount of the fine. I need to take my insurance to the Salthill Garda station.

She and Davey look happy running around the yard with the dog. I think we have done the right thing.

TUESDAY 28 APRIL 2020 07:51

Ares shat on the red carpet in the library. I put his nose in it and dragged him out by the scruff. Davey said I was mean, but I felt I had to do it. I put him in the garage for a while. Lin is teaching him to give a paw. She has been watching videos on how to train dogs. We walked him around and around the loop

Facebook suggests that the fine will be 2500. I try not to think about it. It was stupid; I no longer feel that I was justified. I can't be sure for two weeks that I haven't brought the virus home with the dog.

Ares did a giant dump in the zen room. I gave him a hard time, and dragged him into the garage. Davey was pissed off that I beat Ares.

WEDNESDAY 29 APRIL 2020 AT 07:30

Lin does yoga, and Ares gnaws on his own flesh at Davey's feet. He seems to have mange. Kitty is sleeping beside me on her pillow at the library window. The fish is flashing. I need to feed her soon.

Ares did another full size poop in the zen room. I put his nose in it and beat his ass while Davey shouted don't be so cruel.

Later there was trouble. Lin had told him to go to his room, and he had refused. I got heavy and sent him up to his room. He screamed that he hated me, that I wasn't his father.

Lin made a lovely lunch. Afterwards, I let Davey go out with Ares instead of staying upstairs. I saw him marching grimly by the window with the dog at his heel, muttering to the dog about how mean and cruel I was. I was happy to see them bonding like this, uniting against the oppression of the Dad.

After dinner I went out to the stone circle with a tin of cider. It was a beautiful evening. Lin and Davey came out later. We kicked the soccer ball and Ares ran after it.

Davey kissed me, Lin kissed me, and then she took him down to his room. When Lin returned, she delivered a kiss. I went down to Davey, gave him a kiss, rubbed his back, and told him I loved him. I went back to bed and cuddled my tender girl.

THURSDAY 30 APRIL 2020

It is a glorious morning, though my right leg is wrong; sometimes it twitches and spasms, most times it feels heavy and dead.

I started a fight with Lin over her not cuddling me. We fought hard until I declared that I would no longer eat. She laughed and turned to cuddle me.

FRIDAY 1 MAY 2020 AT 07:06

Lin does yoga while Ares scratches himself. Davey clatters down the stairs. Kitty wanted in but Ares chased her away. We appreciate her cool character now that Ares is here. I woke up with a grungy mouth and lungs. It is a beautiful morning, and I have already had six cigarettes.

Yesterday Ares pissed in the kitchen first thing. I tied him up but he kept choking himself and it seemed too cruel so I let him off right away.

We had a perfect evening just wandering around chatting while Ares galloped. We left him in the entryway and finished *The Hobbit*.

SATURDAY 2 MAY 2020

Quit Smoking for one hour

Davey and I set up Warcry, then went to the Centra in Moycullen. Out front of Centra people milled around not keeping distance–no masks or gloves in sight. I felt it weird that I got the fine, when it was clear that I took much more care than other people. I got a small bottle of wine for Lin, a cider and a pack of cigarettes for myself.

Ares was bullying Davey, so I tried to explain to Davey how to deal with him. I told him that he couldn't be afraid of the dog, or the dog would know. Ares was closest to Lin yesterday, because she has been training him with treats. Things will find their level.

SUNDAY 3 MAY 2020 AT 12:00

Yesterday morning I took Ares out with my coffee. I have gotten to smoking three cigarettes with my first coffee.

Davey and I played Warcry. After Warcry, I went out and drank my beer and smoked. It felt very nice. Lin prepared dinner. We went out and drank a bottle of Prosecco and watched the big dog cavort on the lawn. We walked around the garden. Butterflies and flowers.

I was showered with kisses as we got ready for bed. Lin took Davey down to his room; when she came back she delivered a kiss. I went down and gave Davey a kiss, rubbed his back, and told him I loved him.

Then back to Lin, so tender and perfect.

MONDAY 4 MAY 2020

I woke at three, my back in agony after showing Davey how to wrangle the lawnmower around corners. It was very difficult for him to pull it around for the turns, but he persisted.

Lin spread the grass clippings around the stone circle in a moment of unbearable beauty.

WEDNESDAY 6 MAY 2020

I've neither cigarettes nor hoots left. It is a soft, rain sodden morning.

Yesterday was Lin's birthday. Ares is in love with her.

I am losing weight. I have twinges and surges up and down my gammy leg.

THURSDAY 7 MAY 2020 08:38

Davey is playing Get Lucky, Lin is looking at his Chinese homework, and the dog is running around wrecking the place. I woke at two, feeling glum about the dying feeling in my leg, and that was it. I went down and drank tea and smoked cigarettes.

FRIDAY 8 MAY 2020

Davey met his classmates on Zoom. He was excited and he showed off his dog and his house. Lin didn't like this, but I felt it wasn't a big deal–he is just a little guy.

After tidying the dishes, I made a gin and tonic, and sat outside the Zen room. I smoked while Davey sat beside me. I have become shameless. Davey said I smoke like Gandalf. I didn't want to hear this.

We drove into town. Lin got alcohol-based disinfectant from the Asia market. We drove through the city. It was Friday evening but there was no one about. There were people in the water at Salthill, and in groups along the beach.

SATURDAY 9 MAY 2020 08:24

Kitty is on her perch. Ares growls and barks, but she doesn't budge– just stares down at him with blazing eyes.

TUESDAY 12 MAY 2020

I felt myself becoming nasty, so I broke down and got a pack of cigarettes. Lin and Davey didn't stay upset long. I did some yoga with Lin, and she tried to help me with my leg.

I bought and downloaded a game for the PS4; Davey and I will have a go at it today.

I tried to sleep, but my legs felt sour, and my bony knees ground against one another. I took a painkiller, and put a heat patch on my knee.

WEDNESDAY 13 MAY 2020

I walked around the garden while Lin exercised in front of the Zen room. She was healthy and beautiful, flesh glowing, a gleam of sweat on her brow.

I drank a beer while Lin and Davey played in the garden with Ares.

Davey and I played Divinity. We'd only planned on playing for 20 minutes, but continued for over an hour. When we got ready for bed, I told Davey that he is my best friend. It is nice that we share a love of D&D and fantasy.

I am worried about the increase in racism towards Chinese people, the bullying of China by America, and this virus that will not go away.

THURSDAY 14 MAY 2020

I went with Davey to Moycullen for booze. I saw black toes on the back of a cigarette pack: Smoking Causes Clogged Arteries. I googled this, and found that the problem I have with my leg is almost certainly smoking related. I am such an idiot.

Ares is disgusting. He eats his own shit. He swallows socks and gnaws at shoes.

SATURDAY 16 MAY 2020

It isn't even a question, there is no choice in the matter. I must not smoke.

SUNDAY 17 MAY 2020

We did yoga, and I drank Chinese tea. We did a 20 minute walk in the rain. Davey was keen to use his fitbit.

My leg hasn't gotten any better, but I am hoping it will, that I may have back a body that is fluent and subtle.

MONDAY 18 MAY 2020 AT 12:00

I had a hard time sleeping with the mooing of the demented cows.

WEDNESDAY 20 MAY 2020

We went to Silver Strand and walked with Ares. The tide was low and there were a lot of people but we made the best of it. We need to be careful; Galway is getting more Coronavirus cases recently.

Ares was a bit rough with Lin. He jumped up on her and wouldn't stop. He is much stronger than when we first got him.

My knee feels much better. Taking time off from Fluentify has allowed me to enjoy this life without smoking.

THURSDAY 21 MAY 2020

We put Ares in the back of the car and drove to Silver Strand. The tide was out, and Ares behaved well. We took off the lead, and he stayed near. The Burren was crisp in the distance.

When we got home I did some shadow boxing in the Zen room. It was the first time I had sweated in a year. I did some push ups, some squats and some planks, a sun salutation. It all felt fantastic. My knee was definitely better. When Lin went for a run I took Davey into the Zen room and got him to hit the pads to New Dawn Fades and the Pixies. Then we walked, competing for the title of Steppy Jim. I got 24 thousand steps.

SATURDAY 23 MAY 2020

I'm sleeping well, and my leg seems less sore. I don't expect I will ever be able to do a deep squat again, but I am able to run, and I was able to move a bit when I was shadow boxing yesterday.

Sometimes I get a terrible rush of need. Worms in my head whisper seditiously of sneaking a single cigarette, and I worry that all this positivity will begin to ring hollow.

I felt icy pins and needles in my back, sort of like a panic attack.

. . .

SUNDAY 24 MAY 2020

Meltdown

Yesterday morning I was impatient to get started on our boxing exercises, but Davey hummed and hawed and I lost my temper. I threatened no iPad, but he refused to go to his room, so I dragged him up. He screamed that I was hurting him, and things turned ugly. On my way out the door for cigarettes, Lin thumped me, and told me she hated me. I drove to the Bushy Park shop and got a pack. I smoked one and threw out the rest.

When Davey told me lunch was ready I ignored him. When I went down all of the dishes were still on the table and Ares was up with paws on the table eating from my plate.

I went to Centra and got another pack of cigarettes and a Birra Moretti, then went out to the stone circle. Ares followed. He wouldn't stay with me so I tied him to a tree. When he squealed in desperation I set him free. When I came in for a refill, Lin dumped the rest of the Prosecco down the sink. I opened one of our good bottles of wine.

I went to the stone circle, drank and smoked. I sent messages to Rosemary, Willow, and Troy, saying we'd had a meltdown. Willow sent me back a thumbs up. Either she is a rotten person or she doesn't know what thumbs up means. Rosemary called and I chatted with her a bit. I cried. She said you poor thing and tried to console me.

Lin made dinner, but I didn't eat any. She got in the car to run away and I pinned her down on the driver's seat in the Cotter clutch. She kicked me twice in my good leg, so then I was limping both ways. I ran out of cigarettes and tried to drive to the shop but was too drunk. I turned back. Davey ordered me not to drive. I said horrible things to him. I nearly kicked down the door of the white room where Lin was hiding. Pure mayhem.

I got more cigarettes and drank more wine. I chatted with Antonio, and told him too much about my failings. I smoked in the kitchen, and we fought some more. Things were getting very nasty, and then I just turned it off, and we made up. Suddenly we were friends, and she was kind to me. We went upstairs and lay down. Davey came to us and we all joked and laughed. I took pain killers.

I squirm in abject remorse to think of all this, the morning after. I took Ares out for a cup of tea and three cigarettes in the stone circle. I threw away the rest of the pack, but almost immediately felt the creeping need for another.

Lin and I talked about how to avoid fighting. We are both very stubborn.

TUESDAY 26 MAY 2020

Lin and I did yoga in the Zen room. After lunch, we drove to Silver Strand. The tide was out so we were able to walk along the cliff to the sandy spit around its back. We had the beach to ourselves. Lin and Davey took off their shoes, and waded in; Ares went bounding through the shallow water like a dolphin.

SATURDAY 30 MAY 2020

Painkillers for my knee before bed. My toes felt hot. Lin rubbed my feet, and was lovely to me when I woke. I will call a doctor tomorrow.

TUESDAY 2 JUNE 2020

Eighteen days off cigarettes, not counting the meltdown. I dreamed plaster and bits of ceiling and wall were crumbling. I lit incense, put on the meditation music, and did yoga.

SUNDAY 7 JUNE 2020 07:55

I thought I heard kitty fighting a cow last night, and the fish was bonkers this morning.

The day started off well, but when Lin and Davey started to fight over whether he could pour his own cereal, I intervened. I sent him to his room but he wouldn't go. I began to rage, and then pulled back and drove to Moycullen. I felt my day was ruined, and maybe my tomorrow too.

When I got back, I tried to make peace, but it was a bumpy road. We walked to Tonabroky; I was hobbling the whole way.

Seeing Davey come in this morning, I felt so sorry for this skinny body, and I remembered Deane.

I want to smoke and drink. My diary is a waste of time, and I seem to have given up on poetry.

TUESDAY 9 JUNE 2020

I dreamt about arguing with Davey. We have been arguing a lot. He has a new, defiant look.

I saw a video of myself playing with Ares last night, and I moved like an old man.

SATURDAY 13 JUNE 2020

The tide was high; we stumbled through rotten seaweed in the rain. Ares pulled the muddy rotting corpse of a spurdog from the muck and carried it about. Things got better beyond the reeking mudflats–there were big rocks, and then a lovely little beach with clear water.

On the way back to the car I stumbled on a rock and fell down. Lin helped me up out of the muck.

. . .

FRIDAY 19 JUNE 2020 AT 05:03

I woke up darkly glad to sit alone in the dark woods and let a slow cigarette open my soul. I have fallen again.

Things go around and around. My knee, my leg, is maybe worse than it was. I will begin again at day one, and keep a strict count this time. Yesterday morning we drove through Moycullen to the beach near Inver. Ares and Davey scrambled over the rocks. The tide pools were nowhere so rich as when I was a boy. There were no purple anemones for one thing. I didn't mention this, because I didn't want to let Davey know that his world was less than mine.

When we got to our beach there were people camped there. They had driven a camper up onto the grass and left garbage around. At the Joyce's in Inverness everyone spoke Irish.

SUNDAY 21 JUNE 2020

Lin and I prepared *xiujuyu*. I sliced the fish very thin, and Lin did the rest. We drank a bottle of Prosecco while Davey played piano. After dinner, we walked around the garden. Ares got rough with me when we were playing. He can be a little scary when he's riled.

I feel like an ashtray that worries about money. Worry worry worry.

. . .

MONDAY 22 JUNE 2020

I got up before seven and went out for coffee and a smoke. I can't understand myself; it feels like a different person is managing me. I need to see a doctor.

I ordered Rocksmith to learn guitar on the PS4. I am going to order the canonical Camus: *The Plague, The Outsider, The Rebel, The Myth of Sisyphus*.

TUESDAY 23 JUNE 2020

When I went out for coffee I saw Ares had left a heap of diarrhoea in the entryway. I stepped over it, prepared to clean it up on my way back, but Lin insisted she should do it. I watched, gagging.

We left Davey in his room while we cleaned up. He threatened to jump out the window. I feel exhausted. There is too much to manage, my ass is sore from sitting at the computer, and my heart is tense.

WEDNESDAY 24 JUNE 2020

We parked at Threadneedle Road. The beach was full. We couldn't let Ares off the lead, because he kept examining tiny children. Andrew and Davey walked around in consultation like wise old men. When Declan arrived we played at tossing balls.

SATURDAY 27 JUNE 2020 08:14

I got up, smelt something awful and found Ares had done a massive, gooey shit by the door. I prepared a coffee and stepped over the shit into the rain. I drank my coffee and steeled myself for the task. I used a doggy glove to remove the semi solid bits, then got a kitchen roll and smeared up the reeking filth, filling a shopping bag. I got bathroom spray and squirted everything.

When I went out for more coffee I ignored Ares. When he looked at me I looked the other way. I went back in and smeared more shit up with kitchen paper while he moaned in the window from out in the rain. I went up to Lin and Davey and told them about the drama. Even after I washed my face and brushed my teeth the smell of shit lingers.

After lunch, we drove to Salthill and had a walk in the wind and rain. Ares approached small children and sniffed them. He is weird about little girls. A skinny, whippety thing attacked him. I thought this was good for him.

When we got home Davey and I plugged the Strat into Rocksmith. Davey learns quickly; his timing is good. I get flustered easily and lose the plot, even on something simple like

Paint it Black. Davey says he is good at music but not at sports.

Life is full of things. Messages, worries and concerns. A feeling of windy empty hunger, a lethargic panic, resentment toward Ralph, Sam, and the relations up north, Scarlet's Benny. Loneliness, being left out of the world, having not a friend. Davey's Tarot reading.

Rocksmith today. Divinity. Rain. Yoga maybe, maybe not. Hard to walk in this horrible rain. Hard to cope.

SUNDAY 28 JUNE 2020

After dinner we played Rocksmith. I was drunk and didn't play well. Davey called me out for being drunk. Very quickly we were all shouting at each other. I was a drunken bully, and Davey was stubborn and churlish.

We went outside and the whole thing dissipated. I wrestled Davey, and Ares jumped on me to protect him. We tried again, and he did the same. He is a good boy, if he could stop shitting in the house.

MONDAY 29 JUNE 2020 07:24

I had to clean up a small squirt of diarrhoea in the entryway. It was disheartening regardless.

The body is full of pain–back, leg–it is all bad and getting worse.

On the way home I stopped at a shop for milk and the other thing. This crashed my morale completely. I am sneaking around again.

TUESDAY 30 JUNE 2020

We walked in a field. Ares was too rambunctious, jumping up on Lin. I threw him down very hard, and hurt him. He was humble after this, and I felt guilty. Later I read *To the Lighthouse* in the bath.

THURSDAY 2 JULY 2020 06:54

Lin and Davey sleep upstairs. Poor, wet Ares is at the bottom of the stairs, waiting for Lin to come down. I have changed my attitude, and decided to let him into my heart. I have been slow to do this, but yesterday I decided to accept him as a family member. He is a humble soul.

SATURDAY 4 JULY 2020 07:34

Lin is upstairs singing; Ares had been looking for something to swallow, but then settled at the bottom of the stairs to listen.

I went to Dunne's for the first time since the pandemic began. There was a lineup before opening, but it was no problem. I wore a mask, and stayed away from others.

SUNDAY 5 JULY 2020

I got up at just before four and caught the dawn chorus. The moon was low, full, and orange. I went back to sleep, and was full of dreams.

Silver Strand was busy and windy. It was hard to find a place to park. Davey kicked up a fuss that he was going to die of Coronavirus, and that he needed a hazmat suit. He went back to the car on his own and waited there. It was too windy for us to enjoy ourselves.

MONDAY 6 JULY 2020

Feels like when I am doing a lot of Fluentify I cling to cigarettes to keep from slipping into the void. And my fingers smell like cigarettes.

TUESDAY 7 JULY 2020

Poor old kitty at the window crying in exile. She dropped a worm from her ass in the Zen room yesterday, and now she is not allowed in the house.

I made soup and fish fingers for lunch. While we ate I described the ways in which I was similar to Mr Ramsey in *To the Lighthouse*.

I have a headache every night. I have a lump in my neck. I have trouble pulling on socks, and numbness in my back and kidneys. I also have little bites all over my body, and it feels like I am crawling with insects. I should see a doctor.

THURSDAY 9 JULY 2020 05:46

Davey did a Chinese lesson; I read *Steppenwolf: for Madmen only*.

It was busy at Salthill. Lin threw the ball for Ares, but when she threw it in the water he couldn't figure out how to get to it, so I had to take off my shoes to retrieve it. The water was searingly cold, and the process of getting my socks and shoes back on arduous.

Scarlet came to Galway to collect a boat that Benny bought so they could take to the sea in the event of apocalypse. They brought a bottle of wine and we sat in the garden. Davey saw the cigarettes in my pocket, and Scarlet gave me a bud. Lin was exasperated with me, but didn't get nasty, though she did blurt out *wo bu guan*, and that stung.

FRIDAY 10 JULY 2020 06:33

Two joints and a coffee, sitting in silence with good boy Ares. My knee is visibly bloothered. Other places are bad too. I have a dreadful night time headache. Kitty is at the window, outraged by the injustice of the housing arrangements, by the injustice of the skies. I will let her in, worms and all.

SATURDAY 11 JULY 2020

Despite having solemnly quit this morning, I felt I couldn't appreciate the sunshine without beer and a cigarette.

Davey and I drove to Moycullen. I got a Moretti, a cooler for Lin, and a Lilt for Davey. When we got back, I went out to the stone circle.

A packet over the hedge, another into the stream. I feel that Davey has lost respect for me; I know he smells them on me.

MONDAY 13 JULY 2020

We bought a tent, an inflatable mattress, and a boogie board at Outback Jack's.

I had gin and tonic in the stone circle while Lin and Davey set up the tent, a cross between a tent and a bouncy castle. Davey was excited to be inside it, though it appears I have developed a loathing of tents–I almost fainted when I first went in.

WEDNESDAY 15 JULY 2020

I got up at four and went out for coffee and cigarettes. Then I went back to bed, and dreamt we were in Chen Xi's apartment in Portugal, a messy place full of people, and we didn't really know which part was hers. We went into a room with no furniture. Lin went out and I had a fight with Davey, who ran off with some other kids. I saw him through the door knock over a bin full of paper. I looked at bags of old food Chen Xi had left laying around. There were many empty boxes of chocolate. I ate a bite of a sage-chocolate confection but it was awful. Chen Xi had received a bong as a gift, and I considered taking it. Beds were removed from our room and brought back. I went for a walk and found they did giant *yangrouchuan'r*. Beds kept being changed and removed. Someone told us we needed to bring beds up from the basement. I began to worry about where Davey was.

THURSDAY 16 JULY 2020

I continue to observe this grim duty, my evil watch.

Davey says he is having wild, psychedelic dreams. I didn't get to watch Davey at hurling, as I was recruited to hold the dildo-topped training pole while the kids whacked wildly at the ball just beyond my backward pedalling shins. Colm and I were about to slip away when Darby gave us a nerf football and told us to play keep-away with the kids. Whenever we dropped it we had to stoop in among them to pull it up. I couldn't bend down, but the kids were low and quick. I felt demoralised, and began to struggle, straight arming the kids rushing at me. They had helmets on, and I floored a few of them. Fionn was winded a couple of times, and the kids began to keep their distance. Afterwards I agonised over my behaviour.

Later still, Lin was pissed off when I came back from meeting Darby for weed.

SATURDAY 18 JULY 2020

We stopped at Outback Jacks for sleeping bags and a little stove.

We got to Glenties and I looked at the river they threw my dad's ashes into, thought about how Glenties was his place.

There was a crowd at Scarlet's: Ruby, and two of her kids; Caen and his girlfriend. We passed Benny and Bill on the road. People I did and didn't know appeared throughout our visit. We set up the tent and went to the beach with Troy, Caen, and grumpy Osien, Ruby's son. It was otherworldly. We walked along the shore under the arch of spindrift. On the way back to Scarlet's place I saw Jo-Anne Finlay in her car. She was still beautiful. I started to hoot and drink hard with Benny. There was a football game and Davey joined. A fire was lit, and the teenagers played music. Davey sat with them and did a bit of drumming. Lin sat beside Scarlet at the fire. The ladies had blankets over their laps. I brought Port for Scarlet and Lin, and had a bit myself. I offered Benny gin, and he gave me beers and mushrooms. Scarlet declared an end to festivities by throwing a bucket of water over the fire. We slept in the tent. In the morning we boiled water and looked at seals through binoculars. We took down the tent and sat on Scarlet's outside sofas, drinking coffee, Ares plumped in the middle.

We drove to Portnoo, Naram beach–my dad's holy place. We got out and walked along the beach. Lin stood ecstatic in all that beauty. It was a long drive home. Davey said it was such a different world at Scarlet's place. Our home is quiet, peaceful, lonely.

THURSDAY 6 AUGUST 2020

Yesterday is lost in the sands of time. All I remember is remorse.

FRIDAY 7 AUGUST 2020

I opened a beer and cut the lamb shoulder to make *yangrouchuan'r*. I got Davey to help me light the fire. I drank freely and smoked freely. Lin prepared the skewers. We were happy. I wore my sunglasses and Lin's hat. I felt beautifully debauched. I decided to read *Under the Volcano* next. When we finished the meat I helped Davey roast mini marshmallows. He put on Linkin Park, and we danced and played with crazy Ares, wriggling and jumping.

Covid numbers are way up in Ireland; America is falling apart.

SATURDAY 8 AUGUST 2020

We grabbed the hurls and went to Dangan, idyllic under the blue sky and wispy clouds. Ares was sunbathing unbothered by the click of the slither. Afterwards we walked down to the river.

MONDAY 10 AUGUST 2020 08:40

As I picked up the robot vacuum my right leg crumpled under me and Lin had to help me up. Davey saw the leg crumple a few times and asked me if I was alright. I don't know what is causing it. I have five days off Fluentify so I will try to quit tomorrow morning.

I was uncomfortable on the sofa watching Smallville. My hips were sour; I stood behind the sofa and tried to stretch them but the pain was too much, so I took a couple of painkillers, and had a hot shower. The relief didn't last.

THURSDAY 20 AUGUST 2020

When the donkeys came over to look at Ares he got low and wriggled forward, yapping.

Lin made soup. Davey played piano. I was chilling out on the red chair in the library when I heard Lin and Davey arguing. I told Davey to go to his room, and it turned into pushing and dragging. Ares rose up and started barking. He was heated and wanting to get into it so Lin closed him in the library. I battled Davey up the stairs. He pretended I had broken his leg. Ares was berzerk in the library.

I went to Centra and got West Indies Porter for Lin and me. When I got home, I drank one outside before going up to Davey, who pleaded dramatically, please don't hurt me, cowering in the corner with a plastic sword.

As we ate the lovely dinner Lin prepared, we praised Ares. Not many dogs actually protect, but he is one who will. He is better than a gun.

SATURDAY 22 AUGUST 2020

Darby was going to walk to the crossroads with his kids and dogs. Davey and I went out to meet them at the thatched cottage after the yellow cowshed from which the strange man peers. Darby slipped something into my pocket. We talked about Covid. Their little dog seemed to think Ares was a cow.

As Warny says, there's nothing like an ould reefer.

Magic seeps away is the problem, and can only be called back through this ritual.

I played guitar. I was feeling it. Then I wrote a poem. I tried to show it to Lin but she was in no mood. It was only four weird lines. I will take the best out of The Time Machine, polish it carefully, intermingle it with poetry to make a book.

SATURDAY 29 AUGUST 2020

I poured a whiskey and went out to the stone circle. I refilled my whiskey several times and smoked almost a pack.

I bullied Ares and paid Davey a Euro to take a sip of whiskey. We had a row, and I fought him to his room. He was scared of me, cowering behind a door. How dare they criticise me for being drunk?

I feel bad about getting drunk in front of him, and it doesn't help that he is so forgiving. I am a drunken asshole. I am fed up with making excuses. I have no job. I have no place in society. My health is bad, and I am weak. I can't stop smoking. I sleep and I wake. What more can I do?

. . .

SUNDAY 30 AUGUST 2020

Sick of myself

Dangan was crowded. Davey was freaking out about Coronavirus. Lin and I chatted about whether we were too cautious. There were kids doing exercise, and I felt this would have been good for Davey. It is hard to know what is right.

After lunch I poured a whiskey and opened a beer, sat in front of the Zen room and chain-smoked. I sent messages to loads of people, exchanged a few words with Greg and Ralph.

Lin and Davey fought, and then Lin and I shouted at one another. She said she was tired of me. I told her to keep her distance, that I was tired of me too.

TUESDAY 1 SEPTEMBER 2020 07:44

Davey is in his school uniform,

Antonio says my hair is invidious.

Tomorrow I see the doctor.

WEDNESDAY 2 SEPTEMBER 2020

On the way to Davey's first day of school since Covid we listened to Supertramp's anthem to mass education.

I had a bath, then did meditation and yoga. The meditation went well. I focussed on my bodily sensations, then became a mountain. My right leg is noticeably smaller than the left.

THURSDAY 3 SEPTEMBER 2020

The doctor pushed and pulled my leg, all the while saying well done. I thought I was doing well at these things, until I realised she was speaking to me the way one speaks to a child.

MONDAY 7 SEPTEMBER 2020 04:17

I woke about 3:30. I went out through the thin, feathery rain to the garage for a cigarette and found kitty there. I stroked Ares' lovely head and told him he was the best boy ever as I passed.

I bought cigarettes on the way back from driving Davey to school, though I hadn't planned to. I didn't smoke much yesterday, maybe seven.

When I got back I tidied up then phoned the doctor. My PSA level is high, at 10, and I have been referred again to Doctor

O'Malley. This doesn't seem to have anything to do with my leg.

We did tai chi, the eight positions, and then the bit where you slap your body.

I got a lot of birthday wishes on facebook.

TUESDAY 8 SEPTEMBER 2020

I got some nice replies to my replies to the birthday messages; I communicated with people I haven't seen since primary school.

Lin and I did tai chi, the eight postures, and then the old lady pat yourself routine. I did ten minutes of meditation. I felt flexible, not like someone dying.

I went and got Davey. I was wearing sweat pants with holes in them and I felt shabby when I talked to Declan in his suit and tie. Ares has eaten all Davey's socks.

The e-cigarette gives me a dry throat and sore head.

THURSDAY 17 SEPTEMBER 2020

I did 20 minutes of meditation, using the tape Eoin sent me. I repeated Lam.

I chatted to Nicola. Declan came over, all bluster and no mask. I felt scruffy.

I went out to Moycullen and got four ciders. When I got home, I went out to the stone circle and drank one. It was so nice I had another.

Davey was upset because he had been scammed on Roblox and lost everything in his inventory. I wasn't sure of the connection, but Lin and Davey were pissed off at me, so I went out for another cider. Over dinner they continued to be mean to me, so after dinner I drank the last of the ciders.

I drove us to Dangan. We fought in the car. I gave Lin the keys, got out and started to walk home. They drove by and slowed down to let me in. I told them to fuck off. Someone honked at them, and I gave him the finger.

I smoked as I walked. My leg began to give in. I pissed myself. On our road, my knee collapsed backwards and I fell down. I was like something out of Beckett. I couldn't stand so I crawled the final 200 yards.

When I got home Lin was mowing the lawn. Ares barked as I crawled past him, warding me off. I pulled myself onto a chair beside the door and roared at Lin. I asked Davey to come to Omagh with me in the morning. When he said he didn't want to I told him to fuck off. I got a glass of wine.

FRIDAY 18 SEPTEMBER 2020 05:55

Yesterday began in grim fashion. I was in pain; I had not slept the night before, and had smoked way too much. I went to Moycullen, and ignored Lin and Davey when I returned. Lin took Davey to school.

I went up for a bath. Lin came up, said she was sorry, and gave me a kiss.

I went down and had a piece of toast. I paid our home insurance, and verified that our health insurance was valid. Then I went back to bed. I was very tired.

SATURDAY 19 SEPTEMBER 2020

I mowed the lawn; Davey raked leaves, and Lin trimmed overgrown bushes. I went out for Guinness and cigarettes. When I got home, Davey had taken over mowing, so I snuck around smoking before retreating to the kitchen to prepare a giant quiche. Davey played guitar. I drank four Guinness, Lin two.

Tomorrow I need to do something about my leg. Scarlet is bringing me some weed, which I intend to use to get some writing done.

MONDAY 21 SEPTEMBER 2020

We walked Ares in the fog at Dangan. Scarlet suggested we should give him the snip. Back at the house we sat outside the Zen room and spoke about things realistically. They convinced me to do something about my leg.

TUESDAY 22 SEPTEMBER 2020 05:11

Yesterday morning I got up and began hooting, and continued throughout the day. I could tell that Lin had given up on me again, though she made no accusations.

I have got to quit smoking. I see myself huddled over, face etched in pain, sucking on a dirty cigarette. I didn't sleep well last night. My chest was a seething pit of tar, my mouth a sponge used to clean toilets. There can be no more excuses.

WEDNESDAY 23 SEPTEMBER 2020

I didn't smoke for most of the day. I had no interest in meditation, yoga, or tai chi. I didn't want to play guitar. My knee was sore, and I felt weak.

After a lunch of salad and toast I was empty and entropic, a hundred years of futile gesture my prospect.

On the way to pick up Davey I bought a pack of cigarettes. I had one behind the shop. My leg was awful. I limped back to the car under Rosemary's gaze.

Davey wouldn't get off the iPad. He hadn't done his homework yet, but I didn't shout at him. Things were already strained between us. I had to write to Leah's mom to tell her Davey couldn't come to her party because of the virus. It sucks that the kids cannot mix. I sighed and mumbled profanities, and Davey criticised me for using bad language.

FRIDAY 25 SEPTEMBER 2020 06:48

I had planned to wake early, slip the reins of restraint, and revel in my poetry. I had pawned Davey off on the iPad when in the middle of my second reefer I realised that I had an appointment with the Chinese doctor at nine. My pulse thundered and rattled.

We went for a walk at Dangan. I give Lin no reason to be happy. She sees me still smoking, still drinking, without resolve. I make matters worse by blithely inquiring as to why she is displeased.

My right leg was a dead thing dragged behind me.

When we got home, I decided my scraggy hair was the problem. Lin said I did nothing healthy for myself. I said I couldn't live to do yoga and meditation, that I needed to write, but when I looked at the time machine story it felt like such a mess. My sense of self worth has collapsed. I feel like something that has crawled into a hole to die.

SATURDAY 26 SEPTEMBER 2020

The Chinese doctor seems a strange and muddled man. I was stripped down to my underpants, wretchedly aware of Lin looking at my pitiable condition. I had trouble describing the pain in my leg. He got me on the table and massaged me. He probed into places that felt pain, and there were a lot of them. He wanted to do acupuncture and couldn't comprehend why I would refuse. I told him that I was suffering from a special sensitivity. He rubbed me with oil–checked my head and held me at the eyebrows. I was uncomfortable lying there, especially when, despite my protests, he spread a dirty old blanket over me and told me to close my eyes and have a sleep.

Later I hooted and looked at my poetry. Some of it is strong I think. I would like to publish some poems. I decided to print up my scraps, work on some of the wild and dark phrases in there.

SUNDAY 27 SEPTEMBER 2020

Yesterday morning I got very high and made resolutions. Now Davey is beside me, reading *Wimpy Kid*. Ares is at the foot of the stairs, waiting on Lin, who is singing. Kitty has settled on her perch, and she watches us with scorn. My brain is boiling. I have ideas coming.

FRIDAY 2 OCTOBER 2020

I woke around five and admired the moonlight flooding the room. I cuddled Lin and she mewled sleepily.

After dinner, we drove to the Claddagh and walked down the pier to watch the fishing. Ares brought smiles to people's faces. The tide was high, the water smooth and deep.

SATURDAY 3 OCTOBER 2020 07:25

They put the line in the water and pulled out mackerel. The clouds above were majestic. I stayed with Ares. Lin was laughing, shining.

The cigarettes I smoked this morning were retrieved from the bin where they had sat on top of a bag of dog shit since yesterday. I need to brush my teeth, and then go and get more cigarettes.

TUESDAY 6 OCTOBER 2020

When I met with Darby we probably didn't observe our distance as well as we should have. He could tell I was down, and told me to remember all I had achieved. I don't think so.

It is hard to envision a positive future. I have gone too far my own way to be integrated back into the world of work. I worry that one day I will let Lin and Davey down.

WEDNESDAY 7 OCTOBER 2020

I put tomatoes in pita bread while Lin chatted with her family. They seemed happy, and Lin's mom laughed every time she saw me.

THURSDAY 8 OCTOBER 2020

The long arm

I woke full of worry and darkness. I found three summonses at the door. I can't find my licence and one summon says I will go to jail if I show up at court without it. The second summons is for failing to produce my insurance, but I'm certain I did this at the Salthill Garda station the day after. I wrote it down in my diary.

When we drove to the Salthill Garda station to look for a record of my submission of insurance the guard found nothing. He said if that's your story, you should write to the guard who made the summons. I felt crushed to hear him say if that's your story. It is difficult to be assumed to be a liar.

I sulked in the stone circle drinking beer. Lin shouted at me for being so down. She called me a coward. Davey said I was the worst person in the world. I'm not sure where that came from. I drove to Moycullen and got two tins of mixed whiskey. I talked to Darby outside Centra. He said he would give me something today. Now everything hinges on this. After a tin of whiskey in the stone circle I tried to have dinner with Lin and Davey but it turned into a fight and I went out for another whiskey.

FRIDAY 9 OCTOBER 2020

Darby called and said I could come over to pick up. Later I thought about poetry, and whispered a sexy story to Lin which made her giggle.

SUNDAY 11 OCTOBER 2020 07:38

I tried to fight Ares into the house, and he leapt in the air like a spring lamb, with the happiest face imaginable.

Lin and Davey drove off. I had a coffee, a hoot, and a cigarette. My mind had ideas for the time machine but they disappeared after the third reefer, and I no longer have the heart to hunt for them.

After a Guinness I was perched precariously in the anterooms of horror and bliss. I prepared carbonara and drank white wine. Darby called. He said, look at you, on the drink at three in the afternoon.

Lin pleaded with me not to get drunk. She was soft with me, and said it was scary. I promised not to be scary. She threw out some wine, poured the rest into a glass for herself, but I drank it anyway.

SATURDAY 17 OCTOBER 2020

Davey played Don't Fear the Reaper and Stairway to Heaven on the piano. After his Chinese lesson we went for a walk at Dangan, dodging other people, cutting across fields. It felt like I was walking on a wooden leg.

At hurling Lin and I nodded at Rosemary and Nicola then sat in the car looking at our phones.

SUNDAY 18 OCTOBER 2020

I snuck a few cigarettes in the trees outside the Galway Clinic before I went in. They asked me Covid questions and then I went up for the MRI. They slid me down a sarcophagus tube. The machine seemed to be saying Bad Bad Bad. Then it began to bellow CUNT CUNT CUNT. I counted my breath to ten and started at one again, drawing air up my chest over my head, out down my spine. I was afraid if I slipped I would be dismantled in the universe of Heironyous Bosch. I was humbly withdrawn from the tube, and meek in reply to the Polish nurse.

MONDAY 19 OCTOBER 2020 08:44

We kept Davey home as there was a case of Coronavirus at his school.

It poured all day. I finished off my hoots, then moped around. I felt very weak after the MRI; Google said that you can.

I did my lesson then tinkered at the time machine. I could hear Lin and her sister laughing together, talking mainly about her husband and how she worried about him doing all the work at the farm on his own. He had given her a short haircut when she got out of the hospital, and he was spoiling her and loving her. I was amazed to hear her laughing so soon after losing her leg.

When Lin and I got back from shopping at Dunnes, she received a message saying her brother in law was dead. He had crashed his motor trike into a bus. Lin listened to her sister sobbing. She couldn't stop. Davey and I watched TV, then Lin cried in the bed beside me. She received a call from her sister's son. Liu Hao said he didn't know what to do, his mom couldn't stop crying. Lin didn't come back up to bed.

Ireland entered lockdown tonight. Galway is rife with Covid.

MONDAY 26 OCTOBER 2020

I can hardly remember yesterday. All days seem the same as always.

THURSDAY 29 OCTOBER 2020

Storm Epsilon, cold and dark. I resolved to be pure, but it didn't work. I hooted and worked on organising my poems into a book. When I finally printed it up, Davey and Lin seemed proud of me. I sent it to Greg.

TUESDAY 3 NOVEMBER 2020

I went to Galway Clinic and made my way to the emergency department, where I waited in a chair until they opened. I was taken to a curtained cubicle. The guy who took my blood hit a nerve, sending a strange signal down my arm. The doctor was an eastern European. He tested my strength and sensation, then sent me for an X ray and an MRI on my knee. A girl put another needle in my arm. There was a spray of blood. I went for a CT scan. A bald black lady put dye in my arm. I waited with the needle in my arm. The doctor had no idea what was wrong with my leg. They took the needle out. I paid 600. I'm having a hard time thinking I can ever write anything worthwhile.

. . .

TUESDAY 10 NOVEMBER 2020 AT 07:28

Raise the wind and the rain

That one tomorrow

I will no longer know

Something something something again

I cleaned up a poop, completed five feedbacks, smoked two joints, two cigarettes, and drank two cups of coffee.

I kept my distance from Lin when she was on the phone with her sister's primordial despair. I tried to arrange an MRI for my back, but was shunted around and put on hold.

Dinner was tofu and pak choi, followed by Lin's pumpkin pie. I tried to read *The Rebel*, but kept missing the point.

WEDNESDAY 11 NOVEMBER 2020

I called Galway Clinic, and was again told to wait for a callback. I sat in the car with the windows fogging, reading *The Rebel*.

I didn't dare to look at the video of Lin's sister on the ground crying in the police station, pleading for compensation. The bus driver has higher up friends than they do, so they have to dig deep.

. . .

SUNDAY 15 NOVEMBER 2020

Greg sent me a google doc of the poems, but when I looked I was disappointed to see that he had only taken a peek at the first stanza of the first poem.

The poetry has lost its lift of late. All I have left is the endless river of cigarettes and joints, the disintegration of my health, the horror of mortality.

There were a lot of people at Dangan. We had to stand in the muck as runners passed in knots, leaving no room on the path.

I got a message from Darby and went out to meet him. Ares sniffed Darby and whined as we made the exchange.

FRIDAY 20 NOVEMBER 2020

The traffic was bad on the way to see Dr O'Malley. I signed in and read *The Rebel* while I waited. When I went in he said you've not got prostate cancer, and stuck his finger deep into my ass and pushed around. I hissed Jesus, and slapped my leg repeatedly to indicate submission. He said good, and withdrew. I apologised, and said thank you.

SATURDAY 28 NOVEMBER 2020

I asked Greg to read my poetry, and he said he would, but also suggested that I write something about my time in China. I woke at one seething, and tossed and turned until two something, then went down for a cup of tea.

TUESDAY 1 DECEMBER 2020

The GP said there was arthritis in the spine and knee, but needed to see the MRI of the lower back to know for sure whether it was the cause of my woes. Either way I need physiotherapy.

Lin brought quiche and lotus roots out to Troy and I. Ares was snooping around trying to hump Troy's legs.

Later I found an exquisite sentence in Knausgaard.

WEDNESDAY 2 DECEMBER 2020

Maybe a prose piece on my experience in China could open a door for my poetry and the Time Machine. I drank the rest of the cooking wine.

FRIDAY 4 DECEMBER 2020

At the hospital, I went down the tube thinking how easy it would be to freak out down there. Again, BAD BAD BAD, and then, CUNT CUNT CUNT; as if I didn't know that already. Driving home, I got honked at by a truck on a roundabout.

FRIDAY 11 DECEMBER 2020

Lin and Davey set up the Christmas tree, and Lin also strung lights in the stone room.

Davey and I battled until he told me he hated me, and then I chased him up to his room, roaring. The rage made me feel light headed.

I went to the shop for cigarettes.

When I got back I noticed that the fridge was empty, and the gutters needed cleaning, the paths cleared of moss and weeds.

I went down to Davey, and gave him a kiss.

MONDAY 14 DECEMBER 2020 05:59

Lin said you can't do that and whined in her sleep so I woke her. She had been dreaming about weird airbnb guests who made their own spaghetti and had no mouths. I dreamed that Davey died, felt like all hope was gone from the universe. Davey dreamed he'd won a prize for being a good student, but kitty had eaten his prize. I beat kitty, and then we were painting mini figs on a boat on the river.

I decided that I do want to write the China book.

WEDNESDAY 16 DECEMBER 2020

The GP called to say the MRI showed arthritis in my lower spine, and a bit of disk bulging, but didn't adequately explain all my symptoms. She suggested I see a spinal surgeon, but I said I should go to a physiotherapist first. My legs are frighteningly thin. I feel like Winston at the mirror in room 101.

All day I was haunted by my dream of Davey dying. I want to quit Fluentify to write about China.

SUNDAY 20 DECEMBER 2020

I opened a bottle of wine and went out for a first glass. Davey played piano while I sliced cucumbers and spring onions for Lin's Chinese roast duck. After Davey finished piano I played a 70s smooth rock mix. Everything felt good.

TUESDAY 22 DECEMBER 2020 AT 07:49

I had a bath and got ready for physiotherapy. I am down to 77kg.

Town was crowded with rugby/hurling dudes not wearing masks. When I told the physiotherapist my symptoms she told me it sounded more like cancer than a musculoskeletal thing, and that she wouldn't deal with my case until after I had seen the urologist again.

I met Kevin Higgins on the street. He asked if I was writing poetry, and told me they would get me back to it in the new year.

THURSDAY 24 DECEMBER 2020

Davey has opened his gifts. It is black, wet and cold out, but we are happy. I will make a fire this morning.

I prepared beef stew. I made a stock, sealed the beef on a high heat, then left it on low.

Lin dressed up nicely, and we drank brandy and port while Davey played piano. When I went back to the room I was too tired to read. I cuddled Lin and we went to sleep.

FRIDAY 25 DECEMBER 2020

After a walk at Dangan I assembled the Ogroid Myrmidon while Lin and Davey played cards. I wore the pyjamas Lin got me, sprayed lilac on our duvet and Davey's. Lin took Davey down to his room and I read a bit of *A Man in Love*. When she came back she pulled my shirt down over my kidneys.

SATURDAY 26 DECEMBER 2020 08:33

I tossed and turned all night thinking about the China book, and what a messy person I have been in my life. I am afraid this book might hurt my family.

I opened a bottle of Zenzo; it was dreadful, undrinkable. Storm Bella announced herself.

SUNDAY 27 DECEMBER 2020

We hung around the fire most of the day. Lin finished the Ogroid and Davey and I set up trees and bushes on the board.

Greg and I chatted about quitting smoking and how much I should reveal in my book on China. It was inspiring.

TUESDAY 29 DECEMBER 2020 08:49

I woke up with a sour pain in my shoulder, and when I squeezed it it felt like the shoulder of a different person. I came downstairs despondent. I am afraid of dying, and frustrated that no one can figure out what is killing me. Lin and Davey need me.

Writing a novel about China will be difficult, but I think I can do it.

SUNDAY 3 JANUARY 2021 07:46

I woke with a sour hip, from the cold and/or poor circulation I think. I went out for a cigarette at about 2:40; it was very cold, and the sky was full of stars. When I came back in I wrote 500 words of the China story. It took a while to get back to sleep.

5000 new cases of Covid yesterday. We went for a walk at Dangan. It was bright and frosty, and we kept to the middle of the pitches. I walked a bit better and it felt like being able to fly. Lin was busy messaging back and forth with her family in China.

MONDAY 4 JANUARY 2021 08:52

I shouldn't let Davey play so much on the iPad, but what else can he do under lockdown? The virus numbers were around

6000 again last night. It is likely Davey won't be going back to school for a while.

I drove to the all night shop and bought cigarettes. As I was preparing to have one, a dodgy guy came and asked me for a euro, please, I just wanna bag a Taytos. He seemed like the sort of desperado who would become a threat to our safety in the coming hunger, as society disintegrates.

The doctor called just as I was getting out of the car at Dangan. She wants me to come in for a blood test on Friday, and go ahead with the biopsy. She also wants to do a brain scan. I realised that maybe a brain scan would catch something like Aunt Rosemary's MS.

The talk with the doctor took the wind out of my sails. I had an hour or so of sleep and so many dreams. My mind is moving on the China story. I am starting to figure it out.

TUESDAY 5 JANUARY 2021 08:18

Couldn't sleep, so I came down and got another 500 words on the story written. When I went back up I I continued unable to sleep. My visualisation of the time-flying bed didn't get the three of us to Lapland.

WEDNESDAY 6 JANUARY 2021

Again I got up early and worked on the China story, then went back to bed. Lin and I are on day five of our 30 day yoga program with Adrienne.

THURSDAY 7 JANUARY 2021 07:04

Fitful sleep. My brain felt like a stone shaking in a box. I needed to turn off my brain for a brief reprieve.

I went down to the stone room and wrote 800 words. I was happy to feel that I could write this story, invoking the muse of memory.

Darby called and offered me some dope. I don't want to let this break my resolve.

FRIDAY 8 JANUARY 2021 08:30

To fall and fly again

I showed Davey how many entries I have in my diary, going back to our time in China. I've been up since four working on the story. It is good, but I need to be careful to write only when not smoking. It has to be that way.

Yesterday Darby gave me some hoots. I let this slip into the story, and I think it momentarily became something else because of this but I think this is the right something else and I can persevere with not smoking to write this thing. I gave Lin the hoots this morning, and I will try to persist with a healthy life.

The story seems to be punctuated with strange outbursts of violence.

SATURDAY 9 JANUARY 2021 09:02

I am smoking again. I just wrote 1000 words.

Yesterday morning I got up at four and hooted and wrote. When I finished writing I gave Lin my hoots and told her to keep them from me.

Getting ready for bed I had a big argument with Davey, with screaming, banging doors, and a slap on the head. I drove to Moycullen in the black and bought more cigarettes. I smoked one outside the Centra, and another when I got home. I smoked this morning to get the story going. My chest feels vile. I don't know what to do.

SUNDAY 10 JANUARY 2021

I have decided that quitting is more important than writing, though I still have a bag of weed. I got up this morning at 6:50, smoked the last of my cigarettes, and wrote about 700 words.

. . .

MONDAY 11 JANUARY 2021 08:48

I got up before seven and wrote 700 words.

Later I went up for a snooze. Davey and Lin were squabbling over the home schooling so I came down and shouted at them, then drove to the shop for cigarettes.

TUESDAY 12 JANUARY 2021 08:34

Chen Xi and I are back in Dublin.

I finished the cigarettes and I feel panicky, even doing something as innocuous as watching Lin and Davey bounce the ball with Ares.

I will read Peter Hessler's *Country Driving* to get a feeling for writing about China.

SATURDAY 16 JANUARY 2021

1516 words. I am up to Mr Xu.

SUNDAY 17 JANUARY 2021

Lin gave me out a little bud, and I got a lot of writing done. Davey is reading *The Lion the Witch and the Wardrobe*.

. . .

TUESDAY 19 JANUARY 2021

I got a big sized bud from Lin, and completed Xu, about 1500 words. I was happy with the writing, and shocked by how wild the story of Aihua is.

WEDNESDAY 20 JANUARY 2021 11:47

I drove to The Bonne to see the neurologist. I was to wait in the car until called. An hour after the scheduled time, I went to the doors to say I would come back another time, as I had to teach a lesson at 1:30. Dr Habib Rahman came out and got me. He said my muscles were degenerating, that I probably had a degenerative nerve and muscle disease that might or might not be curable.

THURSDAY 21 JANUARY 2021

Got up early and brought the manuscript up to the tense confrontation with the Alabamans, Daniel and Paul. Afterwards, I lay down exhausted. When I got up I fought giant wolf spiders with Davey.

FRIDAY 22 JANUARY 2021

The story has been coming along quickly. I just finished SARS.

I am worried about my wasting muscles. Now the bad leg seems the least of my problems.

In the evening we played D&D. We're trying to help Lin figure it out. She is very unlucky with the heavy metal dice. I am hoping the elven dice will roll better for her.

SATURDAY 23 JANUARY 2021 07:15

There is snow on the ground; I got up early and did some writing. We went for a walk at Dangan. It was frosty. On the way home I got cigarettes, a bottle of wine and milk. Later we played D&D, and went out for a look at the falling snow.

SUNDAY 24 JANUARY 2021

Lin gave me some hoots, and I got quite a bit of writing done about the development of the school, but it was difficult to place everything in order.

I had a bath and when I came down Lin trimmed my beard. We went for a walk down the road and I hobbled just behind them. When we got back, Lin and I did yoga. It is hard for me to do anything, even to clean up around the house.

When I told Davey I was too tired to play D&D, he was upset, but I talked him down. Quarantine has shrunk his world terribly. He has been moving through the Narnia books quickly, and is onto *Prince Caspian*. When I went down to Davey to return the kiss he'd had Lin deliver he said best daddy ever, as he does these days.

MONDAY 25 JANUARY 2021

I woke at one and tossed and turned until 2:45, then I came down, drank coffee and started writing. I finished the Molly part, and will return to Canada for the first visit when I resume.

We walked at Dangan, then went shopping at Aldi. Lin gave me some hoots and I did some writing. I was exhausted when I finished, and lay down on the sofa before my lessons.

I didn't do any exercise. I am desperate to move on with the story.

TUESDAY 26 JANUARY 2021 08:23

I got up around five to work on the story. I think the end is in sight, and then I will live well and edit.

WEDNESDAY 27 JANUARY 2021

I wake at twelve every night, and toss and turn until I come down for youtube and tea. When I go back up, I continue to toss and turn until I come back down at five or so to write.

I am leaving too much on Lin's shoulders. I need to finish this story and then take time to edit. I will read it through twice before I consider showing it to anyone.

SATURDAY 30 JANUARY 2021

I got up at four and wrote up to the near simultaneous birth of Davey and death of Dad. Later on I drank Guinness and wine and hooted intermittently during a four hour D&D session.

SUNDAY 31 JANUARY 2021 08:37

I slept until four, then got up and started working on the story. My brain is buzzing. I expect to be done the first draft in two days.

It rained all day. I felt lost and torn until we played D&D. It went well and we were happy.

MONDAY 1 FEBRUARY 2021

I got up at three to write. I have only one sit down left to complete the story.

TUESDAY 2 FEBRUARY 2021

I got up at three and finished the book by seven. I felt a great relief to have wrapped it up. I will have to edit now, but I am confident.

WEDNESDAY 3 FEBRUARY 2021

Yesterday after I finished the first draft of the Aihua book, I slept for most of the day. This morning I got up at five and started proofreading.

FRIDAY 5 FEBRUARY 2021 07:45

I called Chen Xi, said hello to Chen Fu and Hulaoshi.

SATURDAY 6 FEBRUARY 2021

I found myself an hour early at the MRI place and sat down to work on the map for our D&D adventure. The scan took an hour, and was very difficult. My back ached, and my hands were numb. I didn't think I would last.

When I got home, we played D&D. Later, when I went down to give Davey a kiss he was reading *The Silver Chair*.

I read *Long Peace Street* and then *Country Driving*. My leg was twitchy and hyper sensitive, so I went down and took two paracetamol for the second day running.

SUNDAY 7 FEBRUARY 2021

My hip is sour and uncomfortable and I feel very weak. I read through my story, and I am not happy with it. I think I may have fucked up again. I have smoked a lot today, but I hope to quit when I finish this pack.

Yesterday morning we went for a walk at Dangan. I started off walking well but toward the end it was exhausting to be swinging on the strength of one leg. When we got home, we played D&D, and had great fun. I had a tin of Guinness and then I finished the bottle of wine.

I was given kisses, and then Lin took Davey to his room. I didn't feel great so I took two pain killers. I hate the feeling of the jumpy leg.

MONDAY 8 FEBRUARY 2021

It is not easy to quit smoking. I have lost confidence in the China story. My limp is getting worse, and my muscles continue to deteriorate. Sometimes I can't help but feel that all this pain is in retribution for some grave moral failing.

Davey did homework and Lin tidied up. I had a snooze. I floated half asleep in a groggy bliss.

3

PARTY'S OVER

FRIDAY 12 FEBRUARY 2021

Dr Rahman told me I had MS. He tried to show me the lesions on my spine and brain, but I didn't want to see. I told him I couldn't tell Lin and Davey, and then I started crying. I apologised and he said I was a true person.

I took Lin down to the stone room and told her. I sobbed and she held me while I shook. When we came out Davey needed to know what we'd been talking about, but I didn't want to tell him.

My brain is full of lesions. There are lesions in my spinal cord. The coatings of my nerves are being eaten at by something in my blood. I need to spend the week after next in the hospital.

I hate my writing when I am not high. When I am high, I love it. My China story is a catalogue of violence. It is just a raw list of events. It is like being pulled dizzily through a series of doors. And it is impossible to justify my behaviour.

SATURDAY 13 FEBRUARY 2021

Scarlet called and we had a long chat. She was supportive, and I was grateful. Lin came down very early, about five. She'd read some articles about MS.

I have been smoking savagely for the past couple days.

MONDAY 15 FEBRUARY 2021

Yesterday morning's walk was difficult. My MS seems to have bounced up since the diagnosis. It is painful to sit, because I have no ass muscles.

I tried to call the police in Limerick but couldn't get through, so I guess I will need to go to court on Friday. I will talk to Scarlet and Darby about a lawyer.

TUESDAY 16 FEBRUARY 2021

Scarlet advised me to get turmeric and probiotic. I walked with Lin in the stone circle. I hadn't been out there in a long time. Ares galloped around like a pup. Lin gave me a little bud, and I had a few hoots.

WEDNESDAY 17 FEBRUARY 2021

Chen Xi called. It was good to hear her voice.

When I held Lin in bed she cried. I said don't feel sorry for me. She said she was crying because I love her so much. The story is so messy.

THURSDAY 18 FEBRUARY 2021 07:16

I go into the hospital on Tuesday, and have a Covid test tomorrow. Scarlet sent a photo of the two of us when we were little.

SATURDAY 20 FEBRUARY 2021

I can't sleep these days. I am full of fear. I don't know what is going to happen to me. I am overwhelmed by weakness. It has gotten worse since I saw the doctor.

After lunch, I chatted with Scarlet, then Lin and I did yoga. I got hoots from Lin and smoked a few joints with a small tin of mixed whisky. We opened a couple of tins of Guinness and played D&D. They stopped the goblin ceremony, and got the Holy Avenger from the room with the Orbs of Seven Hells.

Darby called while we were playing. He had googled MS, and he passed on a lot of scary information. I didn't want to hear these things.

SUNDAY 21 FEBRUARY 2021

I read about MS online. It seems I am pretty much fucked.

Ares is out in the garden gnawing a large bone; Lin is unpacking the shopping, and Davey is reading *The Monster Manual*.

My life has been eclipsed by weakness. I worry about becoming a burden, that I can't protect them anymore.

MONDAY 22 FEBRUARY 2021

I cancelled all my upcoming Fluentify sessions, and chatted with Willow.

I was overwhelmed by sorrow and fear. I realised it was possible I would wind up bed-ridden, and I felt I couldn't bear this. I imagined saying goodbye to Lin and Davey before taking my life, and realised I also couldn't do this. I had trouble not crying whenever I spoke to Lin.

I didn't want the day to end. There was so much love and I was so afraid of what was to come.

TUESDAY 23 FEBRUARY 2021

Such a lovely yesterday with Davey and Lin, my darlings. And now the sadness of the morning, the image of a needle going into my poor back.

WEDNESDAY 24 FEBRUARY 2021

Cried with the first nurses, who had come for my blood. Reading *The Last Battle* and *Boyhood Island*, listening to Dungeon Dudes and making plans.

THURSDAY 25 FEBRUARY 2021

Didn't sleep a wink, another long night of the soul. Davey brought me *Magician's Nephew*. They didn't stay long. I cried when I talked to the MS nurse.

FRIDAY 26 FEBRUARY 2021

Sleeping tablet made for a perfect sleep. The lumbar puncture was a hard two hours on my back followed by a steroid drip. I dealt with it by focusing on my breath, imagining myself to be in Narnia, in the fresh air at the beginning of the world. I had a nice talk with the MS nurse. She had left me some brochures about anxiety, financial and social. This got me worried that treatment would be expensive, but she said it wouldn't. Also that I would become a dribbling idiot. She suggested I mightn't.

SATURDAY 27 FEBRUARY 2021

Sleeping pills didn't work so well. I tried to sneak out for a cig at four but the nurse wouldn't let me. Just as well.

Another steroid infusion. Felt tender afterwards. Davey and Lin visited. I received messages from Lin's sister, and had nice chats with the Chaplain and a Phillipine lady.

There are four guys in my room. Guy right beside me watches TV. All nice enough though. I felt a bit paranoid about one nurse but eventually thanked her.

SUNDAY 28 FEBRUARY 2021

Up at five. At 6:20 I am waiting for the door to open at seven so I can have a smoke.

Someone died on our floor last night. I saw the coffin and hearse out there when I was smoking. How futile the last rights must sound at that moment. I would just like to hold

Lin and Davey's hands and tell them I love them, that I will await them in Narnia.

My arm was butchered in the search for a vein. Finally the doctor had to come to do it.

Lin and Davey collected me, and when I got home I smoked a lot of dope, and drank two Guinness. I wrote a poem and made a world map for D&D.

MONDAY 1 MARCH 2021

We did a tea ceremony in the Zen room, to help me quit smoking. I read out my intentions, and they washed my hands.

TUESDAY 2 MARCH 2021

On our walk at Dangan I had to lean heavily on my shillelagh. Ares played with a white dog and the two of them knocked me flat on my back.

Lin took the bandages off my arms and underneath was a horror show. When Lin and I did some yoga I noticed my muscles just hung there. It is quite frightening. I want to escape into D&D.

WEDNESDAY 3 MARCH 2021 08:06

I am happy though I didn't sleep well last night. I got up at one something, and bought a black dragon, then this morning I bought the PHB for DnDBeyond. I feel compelled to buy stuff, but at the same time feel I deserve to. I need my hobby during this time.

THURSDAY 4 MARCH 2021 07:36

Beautiful life

I slept well, and the morning is mild with a subdued light. Lin and I talked about Zen on our walk, and then we did yoga. At the end, when I pressed the third eye, I saw a flash of colour.

SATURDAY 6 MARCH 2021 AT 12:00

We drove through Salthill. People looked to be living normal lives. It felt like we were the only ones under quarantine.

The Ettin and Orcs battled outside the Hag's cell. Jimmy Twigfeather was killed, but Davey protested with tears in his eyes, so I accepted Dawn Hunter's prompt laying on of hands, followed by the Guardian's healing spell. Later Lin and I had a chat about my poor broken body.

. . .

SUNDAY 7 MARCH 2021

I fell up the stairs and spilled the tea I was bringing Lin all over the middle landing and wall. Lin and Davey help me clean up.

Lin was tired so I took Davey down to his room. He was worried about going back to school because if he got Covid it would be dangerous for me.

I want to bring the green sofa out into the main room and make us a cosy living area.

MONDAY 8 MARCH 2021

Now that I can see the garden I want to tidy it. I let things slip this winter. Yesterday morning I had a cup of coffee and I enjoyed it without feeling I needed a cigarette.

In B&Q a maskless guy ignored the staff when they told him to wear one, and he got thick when I went over to ask him about this. As I walked away he started c'mere ya fekin' cunt but I just walked on. I used to eat guys like this for breakfast.

When we got home, I moved the table in the library up against the wall, and then moved the sofas to opposite corners. After I brought down the desk from the stone room Lin helped me tidy up. It was great to feel some enthusiasm to change.

I have the windows open now and there is a breeze coming through the room. I can hear the birds very clearly. I will tidy the garden over the coming weeks. This should be a place where I can look out at something beautiful.

Tasha's Cauldron of Everything arrived, and Davey looked happy leafing through this in our new living room set up, on the green sofa. Antonio told me his colleague with MS once went blind for 20 minutes.

WEDNESDAY 10 MARCH 2021

I have the two windows open, a cup of coffee, and my feet in the *AiJiu* heat device.

Lin's sister said she wanted to see me. She and Lin cried. Her father told me to be careful of my health.

I emptied out the shelves in the entryway, then moved them into the library and the miniatures onto these shelves, and put the nice carpet from Beijing down. We are lucky to have this house and one another.

THURSDAY 11 MARCH 2021 07:46

The windows are open and the cool air slips into the room. There is one bird singing.

We went for a walk at Dangan. I walked pretty well. We drove home through Salthill. It was windy; the sea white crested.

I called Chen Xi. She was having a body treatment while we spoke. She hangs around every day at her wellness centre. I think this suits her. She told me that English schools in Beijing have been shut down for re-evaluation.

I could see Lin was concerned about me zooming around in Mr Tidy Up mode. I had a lot of energy that I haven't felt in a while. I was also feeling a bit on edge.

Davey had an online art lesson, and he drew a dragon. I tidied up the library, moving figures from one shelf to another, then rearranging book shelves. I saw kitty clawing at the nice silk carpet and chased her out. She is now banished from the library, as is Ares.

We went for another walk at Dangan. I was enjoying a natural, healthy stride. It felt good to be able to walk somewhat normally.

We went home and I prepared leek and potato soup. Davey played piano while I was cooking: Dreams, Get Lucky and Don't Fear the Reaper. Lin made a loaf of bread.

SATURDAY 13 MARCH 2021 07:25

I have the windows open a crack and am listening to birds, feeling the cold slink along my body.

I bought the DM guide for Beyond D&D and Dungeon Tiles. I am keeping myself buoyant with these purchases.

Lin and I did a yoga routine called shakti with lion mouth poses, and some good twists. We should add mindfulness / wellbeing to the mix. A yoga mat and cushion arrived. We will need to keep them safe from kitty.

Davey and I went to Centra, and I got a bottle of wine, four Guinness, and snacks. We played D&D.

Spring is coming. I should put out bird seed. It is nice to listen to them singing, watch them hopping. Life is opening up again.

SUNDAY 14 MARCH 2021 06:36

I managed the difficult positions of the meditation yoga we did today. I liked the meditation and the breathing and am becoming attuned to this–I feel I could go on a yoga voyage.

MONDAY 15 MARCH 2021 07:10

Two weeks off cigarettes; Troy got in touch and said he had

some herb for me. I washed my hair. It is floppy now, but Lin and Davey say it is godlike.

TUESDAY 16 MARCH 2021

I was tempted to roll a joint with half a cigarette that I found, but I resisted, and just hooted a tiny bud off a pair of tweezers. It didn't do much for me. I went into the library and completed yesterday's feedback, then looked at the D&D maps, and ordered books on Zen Buddhism.

Lin and I went out and cut at the rose tube. It is very messy, a shaggy caterpillar full of spiders and hanging slugs. Lin tidied her raised beds, and I brushed Ares.

We did some yoga, a session for the heart. I tidied up, vacuumed, ran some drain fluid down the upstairs sink, then felt very tired. I lay down on the sofa to await the mailman, who brought a load of goodies.

I picked up the herb from Troy, who said he had another essay he'd like me to look at. When we got home and had a walk along the road to the horse gate, I let Lin and Davey know that I was ready to fight if they gave me any guff, and things calmed down.

FRIDAY 19 MARCH 2021

A resurgence of pain

The back pain and the sour legs could be the result of a kidney infection. Up early I hooted and got a lot of work done on the world building: Voodoo, Yeatsian mythology, The Kwakiutl Cannibal Monster, Populations, Calendar, Mechanism for Economy. When I got back from taking Davey to school, Lin was grumpy with me for hooting. She suggested my sore back might be from that.

I went up and lay down. I drifted, not sleeping, but enjoying the kind of numb bliss that I have enjoyed since I have been sick.

The Zen book is about meditation, the breathing and sitting that I already sort of understand. It is the stuff in Headspace. Counting the breath.

Later, in the garden, I picked dead twigs from the rose tube. I stopped and stared at the whole feature intently in timeless wonder.

SATURDAY 20 MARCH 2021

Yesterday morning Lin was grouchy again about my hooting and inhabiting dreams. I built the D&D World throughout the day. Lin painted the Ares figure, and I printed up what I'd done to show to Davey, who made some good suggestions. Davey played piano while Lin painted the Remorhaz. I played 70s music, found a tin of Guinness and went out to the stone circle for a few hoots. I knew Lin was worried that I was smoking.

I watched Lin painting, and Davey playing with the figures on a flip mat. I ordered some more flip mats and a Gargantuan Red Dragon. This should be the last of the D&D things.

Is tomorrow 3 weeks? Today is day 20. How many days to build a habit? 22 was it? I am feeling pretty good about not smoking.

SUNDAY 21 MARCH 2021

Davey and I pulled dead branches out of the rose tube. I had to manhandle Ares down to the bathroom for Lin to wash. I went up and lay down and drifted in the bliss of oblivion.

I got Davey to help me set up the D&D, drank a small gin and had a few hoots. We continued with Lost Mines.

Adele messaged to ask if I had followed up on publishing my poetry, told me that I have a talent for words. I will write back to tell her I have MS, and am focussing only on D&D.

I feel broken, weak and always in pain, sorry for Lin having to lay beside a sad old skeleton.

. . .

THURSDAY 25 MARCH 2021

It is a strange morning. There is a weird, soft light, and it is very still. I will get another cup of coffee, then open the windows and listen to birds. This is Davey's last day at school before the Easter holidays.

I read the Zen book. We are parts of processes rather than things. I would like to think that I'm trying to trace these processes in my writing.

I need to keep a Zen peace in my heart. I am almost four weeks off cigarettes. I'm feeling better, though know it would be easy to crumble.

FRIDAY 26 MARCH 2021

A Hungry Feeling Came O'er me Stealing

Lin and I went for a walk on the hill at the bottom of the road. We talked about the meditation books: *Zen Mind, Beginner Mind*, and *Practical Zen*. And yet I felt needy, like I wanted to smoke.

SATURDAY 27 MARCH 2021

I watch the bony trees sway through a window spattered with rain drops.

I felt needy all day. I looked around for a hoot. I dreamed the night before that I'd found one. I considered a vape, but figured it would only prolong the need.

We walked to the hill at the bottom of the road. When we got back to the bee hives, we met Pat and his white Belgian Shepherd. We let them play, and Ares ran right through Lin's legs, knocking her down. She bumped her head when she fell, and was covered in mud .

Pat said there were no bees in the hives, so Lin and I leaned against them. But then we noticed Ares being stung, and I looked down and saw bees crawling out of the hive. They were all around our heads. We ran and I felt them in my hair. I pulled off my jacket, and got one out of my jumper.

SUNDAY 28 MARCH 2021

Muck, moss and rain

Yesterday it rained all day. After diary and breakfast, I was panicky so I hurried around sighing and tidying things up; I washed the bathroom floors then got Davey to help me rub the living room floor with wet wipes.

MONDAY 29 MARCH 2021 AT 07:38

Today is four weeks off cigarettes. I feel ropey in the hip and kidneys.

Lin made noodles using the chicken stock; Davey did a drawing lesson; I read that there are two aspects of Zen, something you need to seek for, and something that is always already with you, the jewel sewn in your cloak.

TUESDAY 30 MARCH 2021

Chen Xi replied perfunctorily to the message I sent her this morning.

Lin and Davey started to fight over breakfast. I jumped in and it became a big battle. I gave him a slap on the leg, and sent him up to his room. Then Lin and I had a big fight, and of course I went to the shop and bought cigarettes. I had a couple in the stone circle and then threw them in the stream. I had a chat with Lin about why I am feeling so stressed out recently, but I don't understand it myself.

I opened a bottle of white wine and made a vegetable soup. Lin painted the gargantuan red dragon. She put my hair in a ponytail then joined me for a glass of wine.

I should spend more time with Davey. He is lonely, and needs attention. I am sometimes harsh with him. But I also must avoid being driven by guilt, which almost always leads to oscillation between extremes. Balance, Equanimity, are what I need.

WEDNESDAY 31 MARCH 2021

The documents the MS nurse gave me suggest that marijuana is good for the pain. I got in touch with Troy and asked him to help me find something. I ordered a coffee table book on the history of D&D artwork. Let's say this phase I am going through, buying whatever I want, is part of the mourning period people go through when they discover they have MS. I am keeping it at arm's length with this fantasy world, and by spoiling myself, getting everything I would have wanted as a kid.

I floated in exhausted bliss, a sensation I have only allowed myself since the diagnosis.

Lin and I had a glass of white wine. I opened another bottle to compare.

THURSDAY 1 APRIL 2021

The morning lights the gorse-covered hill to the west. I contemplate what happiness might be possible with a broken body. I feel poetry this morning.

FRIDAY 2 APRIL 2021

Ceaseless pain is beginning to best me. It is black out and all I can see is my reflection in the glass.

I was sad about my broken body, and how making love could never be joyful again.

We will let Davey take us on a D&D adventure. I don't know if he will go back to school or not the week after next. We are so isolated. I feel like I am floating in space.

SATURDAY 3 APRIL 2021 06:26

Ares is puking out front of the window. I wonder is he so dumb because of the voice we give him when we talk for him in our comic dialogues? These animals can't seem to behave in a civilised fashion.

Lin took over the lawnmower. I drove to the gas station in Moycullen and got some petrol and a pack of cigarettes. I had one there, and then a couple when I got home. I threw them over the hedge this morning. Lin and I sat in front of the Zen room and drank Guinness. I went out to the stone circle. There are blossoms in one cherry tree. I hobbled back to Lin and sat beside her. We thought about the blueberries and the strawberries that will come with the summer.

Lin talked about violence against Asians in America. We talked about Davey learning judo. I will start to hold the pads for him again, and teach him to punch. We opened a couple more Guinness. Davey took us on a D&D adventure. We were involved in a bar room brawl, and my Thandon String-beam played slapstick with Grease and Wizard Hand.

Life is good if you tilt your head and look out of one eye.

SUNDAY 4 APRIL 2021

Lin worked with the power washer while I started getting rid of dead grape vines in the rose tube, until I realised I needed eye protection.

Lin's dad called, his face bruised where Lin's mom had beat him, and there were black, scabby bite marks on his hands and forearms. It seems this is a regular thing.

I went to Centra, bought a pack of cigarettes, had a couple, then threw the pack away. I got four Guinness and a bottle of wine, some crisps and some peanuts. We got way too much treasure on Davey's adventure.

MONDAY 5 APRIL 2021

The vape broke my resolve. I must climb this mountain again. I am going out one more time, then I will throw them over the hedge.

Lin trimmed my beard and made it like a wizard. When Lin and Davey went for a bike ride, I snuck out to Centra and found what I had left under the stones. I had two and then brought the rest home.

TUESDAY 6 APRIL 2021

Lin and I did the second yoga routine in Adrien's series. I watched two beautiful birds at the top of the rose trellis.

The mailman delivered D&D art books, a few figures and forest battle maps, as well as a couple of Zen books, including *Each Moment is the Universe*.

When Davey's lesson finished Lin was pissed off about his sighing, and I was pissed off that they were both pissed off. We went for a walk down the road. I managed to cheer them up by threatening to get cigarettes if they continued to be grumpy. When we got back, Lin painted the dragon, and I did a bit on the map for the town. Davey looked at D&D books. He is proud of his vocabulary.

WEDNESDAY 7 APRIL 2021

The cloud cover is moody and beautiful. I can hear birds. At Dangan I started off stiff, shuffling, baby steps, but as I walked I loosened and started to feel better.

After lunch I shouted at Davey for dumping rice on the floor when he gave some to Ares. I was fucking this and fucking that. I went upstairs, lay down and read the PHB. The day stretched emptily.

I told Lin I would go to Centra for lasagne and a bottle of

wine. I was also thinking about having a cigarette. She said she would cook and I let it go.

I did an ointment egg dripping over the body meditation, guided by a hypnotic UK voice.

After dinner we had a walk down the road. I had violent thoughts toward the cars who passed us too quickly, though in my diminished state I could never follow up on these.

I have been pulling on the vape this morning. I felt as though I needed something.

I should get the snippers Scarlet mentioned, work at the rose trellis when I feel like this. And I should keep writing–the new Zen book might give The Time Machine a kick start, and if I could integrate this with the China story, I would have one story to rule them all.

Then and only then let my epitaph be writ.

THURSDAY 8 APRIL 2021

I woke with awful pain in my lower back. I nearly died pulling on my socks. At Dangan Lin and Davey kept having to stop and wait as I crouched with hands on knees gritting my teeth. I drove to Centra for pain killers and got a pack of cigarettes. I had a bath and read *At Swim Two Birds*. When I got out of the bath, I was so weak I couldn't get dressed. I cried telling Lin how poorly I felt.

She made cabbage soup.

I am reluctant to contact the doctor today. When I do I will step onto the Treadmill of Institutionalised Pain and Degradation again. What a horrible way to end The Story of My Life.

FRIDAY 9 APRIL 2021

The sky is pure blue and my body is in bits. It was a trial to put on my socks. I have so many discreet pains. There is the lower back, the right intimate groin, the knee, something hidden on the inside of my left upper arm. I must try to remain positive. It was not so many days ago that I felt better than I had in a long time.

I snuck out to smoke, leaving everything to Lin. She made scrambled eggs on her homemade bread.

They went for a walk without me. Before she left, she kissed me and smelled cigarettes. When she was gone, I had a few then threw the rest over the hedge.

Davey played guitar, and Lin and I did a single sun salutation. I went upstairs and drifted in bliss of immobility. They went out to do garden work. Afterwards, Davey lay down beside me and I joked with him and pulled him close. His face was bright and shining.

Trees still and upright into the blue sky; a stark magpie, perfect and precise.

SATURDAY 10 APRIL 2021

MS makes typing difficult.

We went for a walk round the hill at the bottom of the road. Davey and Ares were ahead in the sunlight. We drove through Salthill. We could see the Burren clearly and there were people in the water.

Lin and I had two tins of Guinness before I opened the bottle of wine. I played Song To the Siren. She is getting tired of my sad songs.

I am afraid of losing Lin's trust over the lying my smoking seems to require. I was so uncomfortable that I didn't think I'd be able to sleep. My knobby knees ground against one another and my legs twitched spasmodically. So I took a sleeping pill.

MONDAY 12 APRIL 2021

Davey's first day back at school starts on a cold, beautiful morning.

Over dinner we talked about string theory, quantum theory, and dark matter. I explained e = mc squared, how Einstein's famous equation established the fundamental equivalency of energy and matter, showed him Brian Greene's *Elegant Universe,* and Bill Bryson's *Short History of Nearly Everything,* before pushing *A Brief History of Time* into his hands.

WEDNESDAY 14 APRIL 2021 06:48

I see gorse glowing golden above the hills . Blackbirds hopped around until I let kitty out.

Lin drove to the neurologist. I was feeling dark and we didn't say much. Dr Rahman said so this is the queen. I said yes, this is the queen. Lin put her hand on my leg to calm me. The doctor told me I will be on medicine for the rest of my life. He showed me a list of drugs, all with dreadful side effects, including suicidal tendencies. He suggested Avonex. I would need to inject myself a couple of times a day. Whichever drug I choose will block my immune system, so Dr Rahman said he'd contact my GP to get me priority on the vaccine list as a vulnerable person.

When Lin went to get Davey I smoked a couple of cigarettes. I could almost feel them eating at the coating of my nerves, and I threw them over the hedge.

The fucking farmer was grinding at his machines, and I thought about going over and stabbing him or throwing a molotov cocktail into his barn. Instead I'll get a bird feeder and that little snipping tool Scarlet suggested.

THURSDAY 15 APRIL 2021

Lin went out to cement the cracks between the slabs outside the Zen room. I tried to help her but after a few minutes I was wobbly. When I went back into the house my ass and legs were burning.

So I started dinner. I opened a bottle of wine and had a glass. It tasted awful at first but after a few sips it was better. When Lin came in she had a glass of wine or three, and made salad using shredded mango and mango chutney. After dinner I felt a bit rough. I don't know if it was from the wine or the vape or the activity or just my illness in general. I was cranky with Davey, hurrying him to brush his teeth, apologising as I went.

Lin took Davey down to his room. When she got back, I wriggled up against her. The cherry trees blossom pink at our feet.

FRIDAY 16 APRIL 2021

Overwhelmed by weakness and pain. I had a bad leg before I went to the hospital, and now my whole middle body has seized up.

I read about losing my memory and my ability to learn, that function lost before treatment cannot be reclaimed. Davey told me not to think of the worst case, that I was the best daddy ever, but I felt hopeless.

I can't go back up to sleep yet because I smell like cigarettes. Kitty meows at the window but I won't let her in.

SATURDAY 17 APRIL 2021 06:53

I woke up early and upset myself reading about the loss of bodily autonomy that comes with MS; I worry about this less than I do the unravelling of the self.

Lin was cooking and I put on Suspicious Minds, Johnny Come Home, Small Town Boy, How Soon is Now. I was in a flow, crying and laughing, and I wanted to get drunk. Lin and I danced. Kitty ran away then Ares did too. We played Lincoln Park and Davey joined in. Lin was wrecked, pukey and skinny. We ate our dinner, *malaxiangguo* muck, then Lin collapsed on the sofa.

No surprise then that none of us slept well last night, and that Davey came down with the flashlight to tell us about his zombie invasion dream in which I was making scary faces and eating raw meat out of the sink, or that he ended up crawling into bed between Lin and I.

SUNDAY 18 APRIL 2021

I need to get on top of things, manage myself better. My resolutions are beginning to unravel. I read in the Zen book about a long, straight railway track, and the importance of consistency. This is my problem: I veer one way and then the other.

I haven't heard back from Chen Xi; it would be a pity to lose yet another person. Is my attempt to write my life merely clinging to delusion?

Willow messaged me to say that things don't change with death. Davey thinks the miniatures are a waste of money. He is already wiser than I am.

MONDAY 19 APRIL 2021

I got up at three, came down, hooted, and was immediately flooded with ideas for World Building. I went back to bed, tossed and turned, suffered dark thoughts. I drifted in and out of a poem about violence and fear.

Chen Xi said our friendship is money in the bank.

TUESDAY 20 APRIL 2021

Lin put out two bird feeders. The cherry blossoms are in full bloom. My blood squirted on the doctor's wrist when she jabbed me.

WEDNESDAY 21 APRIL 2021 04:42

Lin went out to the garden to work on cement, and I poked around at World Building. I thought it would be a great idea to roll up a reefer of pure weed. I smoked this and Lin was not happy with me, droopy faced at the table, way too high.

I went to Centra and bought a cider and two Guinness. When I got home I drank and pulled at the vape.

THURSDAY 22 APRIL 2021 06:04

Behind pink blossoms the sky is blue and with pink clouds.

FRIDAY 23 APRIL 2021 03:19

The two middle toes on my left foot are numb. I saw myself in the mirror, a frightening skeleton.

I hooted and channelled feelings of creativity and vitality into my work on the World. My practice seems fundamentally opposed to clarity. I hooted some more and tidied up the World, then opened a tin of Guinness and painted orange robes on the monks.

I was drifting with ghosts, and Lin was not happy.

When Lin and Davey got home I was drenched in self loathing. Davey could tell I was stoned out of my face. I followed Lin out back and pulled dead leaves from the rose tube. She said I looked sleepy. We had a walk up the road. Davey led Ares. When cars whizzed past I worried Ares would pull him out in front.

Need to get back to Zen mind. Checking in on the breath, calling yourself back when something pulls you.

TUESDAY 27 APRIL 2021 07:04

Windows open, blue sky above cherry blossoms waving like flags of happiness. Last night the moonlight was silver and pink. I cuddled Lin, and kissed her face.

We did some meditation. I sat for the first while, and then I stood. I was still and empty. The cherry blossoms.

THURSDAY 29 APRIL 2021

I had to stop for a rest on our walk on the hill at the bottom of the road. Everything is a challenge: pulling on socks, climbing stairs, bending over to lift something from the ground. So many awful things in store for me: blindness, incontinence. The slurring of speech will ruin my chances of becoming a professional DM.

I cried and apologised to Lin for it all.

FRIDAY 30 APRIL 2021

I am like one of those push up toys, that when you press the base the figure sags, drunken and ungainly.

SUNDAY 2 MAY 2021

The sea was a mirror. We climbed a hill and sat on rocks looking out at the Burren and the Aran Islands. I drank the rest of the bottle of wine, and had little control of my body.

MONDAY 3 MAY 2021

We went for a walk at Dangan. Davey and Lin hit the sliotar. I became very tired, and could hardly make it back to the car; it felt like I was wading through treacle.

TUESDAY 4 MAY 2021

We were getting ready to do yoga when Scarlet called. She is against Big Pharma and advised looking into other options. She wants me to call her Norwegian friend who had stem cell replacement therapy and is now fully recovered, ASAP.

I power washed the moss, tired quickly, came in and lay down. Lin continued with the power washing until she went to get Davey.

After dinner Scarlet's Norwegian friend called. He advised Stem Cell Replacement Treatment in Russia or India. He said it feels like crucifixion but you wake up a new man. He eats no sugar, not even fruit.

I fell asleep beside Lin, touching the palms of her bare feet with mine.

THURSDAY 6 MAY 2021 06:49

When Chen Xi told Lin she was going to sell her house in Bray I reacted angrily, taking this as the end of our friendship, making me feel hopeless and unsupported. Lin reminded me that Chen Xi loved her home in Bray, and I changed my attitude, felt sad for her.

FRIDAY 7 MAY 2021

I had a few hoots and worked on the D&D campaign. I incorporated Bugbears, Hags, and Ballywugs. I hooted in the stone circle.

Chen Xi said she would be in Ireland next Sunday. I cried about the end of our friendship, but she was kind and sincere.

SATURDAY 8 MAY 2021

On our walk at Dangan I felt self conscious about the hair blown across my face, was worried that Davey was ashamed of his disabled dad.

I lay down exhausted, read a bit of *Each Moment* about silence and magnanimity. I put down the book, and lay back. When Lin came in I turned away. I had no reason to be displeased with her, but I felt betrayed by the entire universe–fuck everyone, fuck everything.

Yesterday Davey asked me why I write my diary, and I told him it was a writer exercise, like writer push ups. He reminded me that I don't write anymore. Is the D&D campaign a worthy focus for my creative energy?

MONDAY 10 MAY 2021

The MS nurse advised me to go on Gilenya rather than Tecfidera. She said Stem Cell Replacement Therapy was not an option for me.

TUESDAY 11 MAY 2021 06:10

Lin has done a lot of work in the garden and it shows. She trimmed my beard and then I washed my hair. It is fluffy now; she said I look like a god.

Happy flowers in the blue pot by the front door.

WEDNESDAY 12 MAY 2021 06:13

Our magpie picks around the base of the rose tube at the finches' leftovers.

We did a ten minute sun salutation, during which I tried to gauge the progression of my weakness. I nearly fainted, but also found moments of extreme clarity as I sunk down to the pivot of nothingness, floated almost all on the now, with only a trace of 'is this enlightenment?' diluting the purity of my entry into the conjunction of time and space in unending presence.

After the yoga, I had to lay on the green sofa, and I spent much of the remainder of the day there. Lin gave me some hoots before taking Davey to hurling. I lost myself in World Anvil, painted contrast on muscles.

When I saw them drive in I was as happy as Ares, who ran over to the car and jumped up and down, crying. Davey was glowing, red cheeks and blazing eyes.

THURSDAY 13 MAY 2021 06:25

We opened a bottle of white wine, and it went down smoothly, so we opened another. Lin wept over my condition, her plight. I swung myself around the kitchen like Quasimodo. She slept on the green sofa.

The magpie doesn't seem to notice me.

FRIDAY 14 MAY 2021

I nearly fainted doing a ten minute sun salutation; enfeebled by MS, it seemed harder than climbing Croagh Patrick.

Worldanvil: four Omphalos. Lallon is a level 18 Warlock for Aslan. Dresh is a level 18 Warlock for a Shadow Demon. Another Omphalos is guarded by Cathbad and the Owl Queen. Stone Circle itself has been seized by Shadow with the help of Peggy Pigtooth.

I slumbered half awake until Davey galloped down with his big smile and got into bed between us. I brought up tea for Lin, spilling a bit with every step.

SATURDAY 15 MAY 2021

We played a short game. Dawn Hunter arrived in the Village and was recognised as the son of Lallon. He and the Guardian are in the church now. I opened a Guinness while we were playing, and then finished another four out in the stone circle, hooting in pure bliss.

Davey called me a junkie.

SUNDAY 16 MAY 2021

I went out for a smoke in the middle of the night. When I came in I sat beside Ares. There was something beside him I thought was a poop. I lifted it with toilet paper and it hissed. I put the little bat out the window.

WEDNESDAY 19 MAY 2021

Arrived at Ennis, I checked in, then waited out front of the courthouse. The lady checking names at the door introduced me to a solicitor, who represented me without charge.

When they called me in with the final group I waited in a line outside the courtroom door. The little girl with tattooed-on eyebrows standing beside me didn't wear a mask. When I looked at her sidelong she cracked her knuckles.

When it was my turn, the lawyer told my story, though not as well as I had written it, but the judge was sympathetic, and only made me pay a hundred to the poor box. They won't take a card, so I'll have to come back before next Wednesday.

MONDAY 24 MAY 2021

Yesterday I had a slug on my head. I guess I got it in the Rose Tube. Washing my face, I ran my hand over my head and felt something sticky. There in the sink was a good sized slug.

Lin and I listened to Crime of the Century on the drive back to Ennis. The clouds were high in the sky. While we waited for a receipt a garda arrived. I said beautiful clouds. He looked up to confirm and said yes. After I got my receipt I really needed to piss so I went against the back of the building. I shouldn't have given Lin the thumbs up while I did this.

Chen Xi called and said she was coming on Thursday, and would stay until Sunday.

TUESDAY 25 MAY 2021

Chen Xi was crying and roaring. We tried to find out where and how she should get a Covid test. We looked into how she could renew her learner's licence. She told me she was divorcing Tan. When I tried to talk to her out of this, she got angry.

FRIDAY 28 MAY 2021

When Chen Xi hugged me I could tell she was shocked by how much weight I had lost. After our walk at Dangan I was going to help Chen Xi look through a contract, and when it was time to do this, she effortlessly sat me up from a lying posture to show me her computer screen.

. . .

SATURDAY 29 MAY 2021

We sat outside the Zen room, drinking and chatting. I got so drunk and high Chen Xi had to help me back into the house.

SUNDAY 30 MAY 2021

Chen Xi and Lin sat in front of the Zen room, had a drink and a giggle. It was the hottest day of the year. I sat with them awhile and then snuck out to the stone circle.

FRIDAY 4 JUNE 2021 07:03

It is grey and cloudy, very still, as though everything were just hanging in place.

SUNDAY 6 JUNE 2021

Davey finished a drawing lesson, and began declaiming his ennui. I argued with him over lunch. He has no siblings, no neighbourhood kids, and I am not fit to play with him, so I feel bad, but don't see what I can do. Lin and I try to get along, but I am so grumpy because of my discomfort that it is hard to maintain equanimity.

So I lay on the sofa in despair, revolted by the degradation of my legs–now only skin, jelly and wires. I kept thinking about the anger and hatred that festered between me and my mother during her protracted dying. I told Lin I was worried that my pain and loss will destroy the love in our family.

FRIDAY 11 JUNE 2021

Chen Xi cried when she told me Tan agreed to the divorce. She seemed small and alone.

TUESDAY 15 JUNE 2021 05:27

I have been up since four. I just had two strong reefers that set the world atremble. The MS is rampant. My heart is clutched in terror, but at the same time I am exuberant as the wind in the treetops, above the serene garden meadow.

Lin and Davey wanted to determine the range of the walkie talkies, so she carried one when she took Ares for a walk, and the buzzing and the beeping was shredding my patience; I was seething inside and even though I knew that Lin was right, that Davey should be allowed to play at this, when he came into the library beeping and buzzing my mood went into free fall.

He put the walkie talkie beside me and said can I leave this here? I said no Davey. He persisted and I grew frustrated and backhanded him across the chest harder than I had intended. He looked at me with shock and anger, just as Lin walked into the room. He began to repeat *that* man hit me! Lin glared at me, and I explained what had happened, but it was pointless to say anything. Lin told us both to be quiet. I shouted at her once, and then went out for a cigarette.

I insisted on taking Davey to school. I put on the new Favourites Mix, and the first song was UNKLE, An Eye for an Eye. I turned it up loud and drove fast. When we got to school, he turned his back to me, but as he closed the door he looked at me for an instant and I looked back at him with love. I remembered the love and sadness I felt when our eyes met the last time I saw my father as he left me at the airport.

I felt no interest in anything. Before me yawned a day on my back on the green sofa scrolling through facebook.

We walked into Barna woods, and I bent over sobbing, told Lin I couldn't go on. The thought of my muscles wasted away to cables floating in gel and the image of Davey meeting my eyes as he left the car, the love and trust and dependence in those eyes.

When we got home I phoned the neurologist's secretary and texted Troy to score me some weed. Lin and I took another walk along the river at Dangan. When it began to rain I stepped under some trees beside an old man and said may we share this shelter with you, Sir. He was a kind old man and he looked and spoke like a college lecturer. As we walked away Lin asked is that what your father was like?

I was exhausted but the thought of laying on the green sofa horrified me so I went up and lay in bed. As I got undressed

Scarlet called. She had talked to someone very wise who had advised that I should arrange to do the Stem Cell Replacement. I didn't want to hear this. I lay down and drifted in emptiness. I got a message from Troy with the phone number of a guy who I arranged to meet at Kinlay House in Eyre Square. I hurried through town, conscious of my bizarre appearance. I had washed my hair and it was like a badly thatched roof.

I got the weed and hurried back to the car, and drove home full of dread and jubilation.

I heard a ruckus in the kitchen, and realised Ares had snarled at Davey. I grabbed him by the scruff and whacked him as hard as I could on the hock. I was prepared to do more but he turned and snarled at me. I realised I couldn't hit him again. Lin took over and I backed away from his ominous head.

Ares was outside looking in from the rain. We talked about what happened. He had been eating Kitty's food and Kitty was whacking him. Davey yelled at him, trying to chase him away. Lin screamed at Davey and grabbed Davey to pull him away. Ares snarled at Davey, and I came running out to beat him.

I hurried through my dinner, and asked Davey to clean up though I knew Lin would end up doing it. I rolled a joint and went out. I spoke softly to Ares but he ignored me. I drew an analogy between my violence to Davey in the morning and what had happened with Ares. We create a tone and an environment. Ares is a gentle dog and he behaved in this way because he was scared. We have the power to create an environment in which he wouldn't snarl.

I went in and explained this to Lin and to Davey. Davey interrogated my assertions closely. He was intrigued by the distinction between causation and analogy.

I put on my glasses and read *Masks of God*. I was drawn into it deeply. I remembered taking a journey into Gnosticism, Christ the serpent, the first time I read these books. I connected it to the first chapters on Satan in Albert Camus' *The Rebel*, and William Blake on Christ coming back with a sword to tear down old laws. I remembered being at a tree planting camp on a lake as a young man, espousing the theory that Christ was Satan Prometheus who thought for one second I will not serve and was cast down from heaven as a comet to become man and tear down old laws, replacing them with the inexpressible law of heart and of love.

I slept. I woke. I woke the last time at four. I looked at my phone and got up and started writing this at 5:30 something. It is 7:29. I have smoked at least five reefers. I hear Lin running the blender. I will smoke this last one out in the stone circle, where I used to think of poetry.

WEDNESDAY 16 JUNE 2021

Low pitch murmur of all pervading dread / patches of blue between slow drifting clouds. I asked Lin if she wanted to read yesterday's diary entry. but she didn't. This crumbling brain is not me; it is a place I inhabit.

THURSDAY 17 JUNE 2021

It is a still and pleasant morning; there is no wind, not even up high.

Lin and I went to Dr Rahman's Office. He said that my brain would only deteriorate by .06 per cent per year. That seemed OK. I asked him about marijuana and he listed impressive benefits. I was glad Lin was able to hear this.

I lay down on the green sofa and read *Masks of God*, from which my academic stance was taken. It led into my work on Joyce and Masochism, the Gnostic Dionysian sex ritual, the collapse of oxymoronic binaries in truth.

FRIDAY 18 JUNE 2021

Scarlet urged us to come up to Donegal for the weekend. We stopped at Port Noo. The roar of surf, arch of spindrift in the evening light. Sea of memories.

Scarlet offered us dinner. I drank with Benny, Wren, and Troy. Long after Scarlet had gone up to bed she came down roaring at Benny to turn down the music. We laughed and listened to a few last songs, then Lin, Davey and I went back to the wee cabin.

SATURDAY 19 JUNE 2021

Scarlet called us down to do a sun salutation on the grass, in front of the sea and Mount Errigal. Scarlet made breakfast, with her own sourdough, and boiled eggs from her own hens.

Lin, Davey, and Scarlet went out on the paddleboards. Lin went under after Ares grabbed her paddle board back by the string and started pulling it towards shore. Scarlet chased Davey and pushed him in. Ares was at the edge of his depth whining for them to come back.

Late afternoon and a band of young people in their early twenties, Hannah, Caen, Ossian, Rubin, Telluala. Davey drifted at their periphery.

Scarlet got me to sit next to her at the fire, and shared her bottle of warmed port with me. Warnock's three-legged dog, Ziggy, had been tormenting Ares all evening, following him around, humping him anywhere he could get leverage. Suddenly there was snarling as Ares went for Ziggy.

Scarlet jumped up, shouted no, and grabbed Ziggy. Ares bit the back of her thigh and she dropped the whippet and said I've been bit bad. She'd suffered puncture wounds, was white and out of it. We kept drinking and laughing while we decided should she go to the hospital or what.

SUNDAY 20 JUNE 2021

I had a strained chat with Benny and Warn; Ares stayed in the car.

They told a story about Richard, the sailor sleeping out in his boat coming home to find the guy from Omagh he'd let stay there bent over the sofa as though he were praying. He asked what are ye at and tried to waken him, then realised he was dead. We laughed till we cried.

Benny took Scarlet to hospital, and we drove to Dooey and walked the endless beach. I recalled how Scarlet had said to me we love the sound of seagulls because we used to go on beach holidays when we were kids. Lin and I walked along the exquisite sheets of water unfurling at our bare feet.

MONDAY 28 JUNE 2021

I hesitated, then messaged Ferdia. I parked at the back of the train station and met him at the blue door at the end of the alley.

I saw Lin and Davey standing in the backlight at the pink gate, and my heart felt as if it would burst from my mouth.

THURSDAY 1 JULY 2021

Scarlet continued to argue for the Stem Cell Replacement. We laughed about drugs that might make the month of crucifixion bearable. The Gilenya therapy sounds devastating–a whole new type of invalid life. I have started devising lines of poetry in anticipation of the pain of chemotherapy.

Lin came in to ask Scarlet about her apple crumble. Crumbly Bumbly she calls it.

FRIDAY 2 JULY 2021

I drank Guinness and hooted and achieved a weird, hovering mindfulness.

Lin wandered the garden then she and Davey played badminton. Ares claimed the strawberry patch. He was in it shovelling and rooting, munching wetly. Davey is speaking now for Ares, declaring Happy Wednesday, and Lin says he is a silly guy.

How could I be more happy? How could I live a more beautiful life?

. . .

SATURDAY 3 JULY 2021 07:39

I couldn't sleep last night because of the pain in my left kidney, and it is hard for me to sit now. Lin had to put my socks on for me. Handfuls of Panadol don't help.

Lin massaged my back and knees with tiger balm. Davey said my newly trimmed beard makes me look like a rebel. At first I didn't believe him when he told me that a black hole is smaller than an atom.

SUNDAY 4 JULY 2021 05:55

The poetry of days on my back, empty of all but pain.

MONDAY 5 JULY 2021

The doctor got me on the table and moved my leg this way and that; I sobbed from humiliation and despair. Lin squeezed my hand. I looked up at her, blinded by tears, said I'm sorry, so sorry my love.

She prescribed me Panadol and sent me on my way. The Long Term Illness Card doesn't cover GP visits.

WEDNESDAY 7 JULY 2021

Davey and I resumed our discussion from the day before, whether or not the song Hurt is a suicide note? I told him that I had decided that it was an affirmation of life, drawing on something I'd read in *Masks of God* the day before, about how impure art ascribes the suffering of the world to socio political causes, whereas pure art recognises suffering as intrinsic to the human condition, and celebrates this. Lin didn't like what I was saying.

When Chen Xi said goodbye, she was crying and said she loves me. I didn't reply but later sent a message saying of course I love you too. She sent a message saying regular people wouldn't understand our love because it is very high.

I prepared soupy stew and when Lin got home we opened the big IPAs. Lin began to weep and I tried to cheer her up by speaking for Ares.

SATURDAY 10 JULY 2021

Yesterday morning I looked at my poem: Sing Now Marsyas, and at the China story. Why am I such a bad writer?

I was exhausted by the time we got home from our walk to the crossroads, and had to sit gasping for breath on the pink chair by the front door.

My feet and hands were burning, my hips sour and seething. I took a sleeping pill but there was no comfort or relief. I told Lin she didn't love me, that I was only a burden, but she was slow to rise to my provocations. She snapped, shouted in Chinese, and wept when I told her I had not seen her smile or laugh in weeks. I smoked to punish her. Davey came down and begged me not to fight with mommy.

SUNDAY 11 JULY 2021 07:19

Ares' nose is a compass always pointing at Lin.

I read through the China story. It wasn't as bad as I'd expected. A mirror facing into a mirror.

MONDAY 12 JULY 2021

Ralph called and we spoke for about fifteen minutes. It felt like a Fluentify lesson.

FRIDAY 16 JULY 2021

We opened beer and sat under the hawthorn tree. I started a 70s easy listening playlist, and Lin and I stood together dancing slowly. Davey laughed when I pulled up my trousers to show him the style of an old Chinese leader, Deng Xiao Ping. Lin told me when she first met me she thought I was silly because I was too open and honest, and people would take advantage of me.

SATURDAY 17 JULY 2021 07:07

Feathered clouds above the trees look as if painted with flicks of a deft brush.

The beach was busy. We went down to the water with Ares on the lead. I was conscious of my wasted body. Ares whined and tried to pull us out of the water. I sank down to my neck slowly, swam a bit on my back, found a deep place and treaded water.

I felt so good I suggested we go right away for a walk at Dangan. The soft air soothed my body. It was such a relief to walk without pain. Lin suggested we spend winters in a warmer place.

TUESDAY 20 JULY 2021 05:55

We went to Silver Strand without Ares. There were hermit crabs around our feet. I didn't tell Lin and Davey that I saw jellyfish. I lowered myself to my neck, treaded water. We swam around in the fog, then hung off Davey's boogie board. Lin and Davey agreed it was like a dream. We three facing each other, the whole world spinning round us.

I sent Ferdia a message and he replied promptly saying he had something. Lin sat in the car while I went over to the blue door. When we got home I had a hoot and saw stars, little traces of coiling photons, curlicues of absolute brightness.

Chen Xi was at her bossy best, and dismissive of my story. She suggested it was only reportage and not beautiful emotion like a quote she had from her London Lady English Lessons: the moon, the sun, and you, etc.

Davey dreamed he and his friends were in a boat. They fell out of the boat and made it to a rocky, boggy island with Portaloos. They were in Africa. A kid said look, there's a penis. They got to Wexford. There were mountains. One of the coaches flirted with a lady, accompanied by the Ring Theme.

FRIDAY 23 JULY 2021

Lin got a Covid Jab, and Davey and I went to Dungeons and Donuts and got Magic the Gathering cards. We sat on the grass in Eyre Square. Near us was a raving clan, with crates of beer. One strutted around the field with his arms out like Conor McGregor. Another guy kept roaring at a disabled woman: you're a Monster, a Monster. There was the guy with the burned face, tuft of hair like an alien from Star Trek. Davey urged me not to interact with them. We opened the Magic cards, spread them out on the grass. I made a Deck of Angels.

SATURDAY 24 JULY 2021 07:26

Chen Xi huffs and puffs in the Zen room. She is thin, and her skin glows. I hear Lin singing on her way down. They speak in Chinese. I don't try to understand, but I hear Chen Xi call Lin sister.

I will smoke another reefer then work on the China story. I am thinking of just slipping the Time Machine into it.

SUNDAY 25 JULY 2021 06:38

Chen Xi does her English studies at the big table while Lin stretches.

I started the barbecue, and Lin cooked steak. Thunder rumbled and it started to pour icy rain from on high. When I got in, I was soaked to the skin. I grabbed rain coats for Lin and Chen Xi, but they came in laughing with cushions over their heads.

When the rain stopped we walked down the road toward heavenly ladders that had burst from ruptured clouds.

WEDNESDAY 28 JULY 2021

I am breaking the China story into chapters. Lin cut me off from the beer, so I went up and watched TV with Davey. I could hear Lin and Chen Xi laughing and drinking outside.

THURSDAY 29 JULY 2021 05:52

After Lin came up to bed, I heard Chen Xi weeping and went down, but she wouldn't tell me what she was crying about. I told her it was the gin, as they had finished half a bottle between them. I continued to press, and she sobbed that she had hurt Tan, that he was a good man, but she just didn't love him.

SUNDAY 1 AUGUST 2021

We walked the bog path, Chen Xi's favourite. She was playing ABBA, The Winner Takes it All, which was strange and annoying. At the start of the next song I asked her to turn it off and she complied without resistance or resentment.

We walked up the rocky hill, sat looking at the Burren, the cliffs, the Aran Islands.

THURSDAY 5 AUGUST 2021

Bernie got me wired up like a car for repair. I cried when I took the Gilenya.

I sat for six hours attached to the machine. I read *Masks*, had a chicken sandwich and green soup. Bernie likes to talk. She loves Bernese Mountain Dogs, and attends a writers' workshop in Dublin.

I wanted to go down for a cigarette, but needed to wait for Dr Rahman. Bernie didn't want me to let me outside with all her equipment attached to me, but I convinced Cliona to let me go out back, and I smoked two cigarettes with the cables still stuck to me. Dr Rahman was as friendly as a restaurant owner. He asked after Lin and Davey and said I would start to feel better now.

I had a few hoots in quick order, then a glass of gin and more hoots. I told Lin I would stop drinking, and I would cut back on the tobacco.

Lin drives Chen Xi back to Bray this morning; I will take my second Gilenya.

MONDAY 9 AUGUST 2021

It rained heavily yesterday. I feel stiff, and have little control of my right leg. I am constantly on the brink of exhaustion.

I finished another read through of the story, then began to resolve the forty yellow highlighted sections I had slated for revision.

At Dangan I kept having to stop and bend over with my hands on my knees. Lin mowed the lawn. I snipped at the fringe of the rose tube. Davey and I went out to the stone circle and ate white currants.

TUESDAY 10 AUGUST 2021

There are three variables: mobility, pain, exhaustion.

I made a lot of progress on the story, tidying up messes. What will I do once done?

WEDNESDAY 11 AUGUST 2021

At Dangan I drifted and stumbled along the path, supported by Davey, as though I were a child learning to ride a bike.

I worry that the story is rubbish. I can't imagine what it would be like for someone else to read. I don't know why I care, but I want the story to be read. It would be like redemption.

FRIDAY 13 AUGUST 2021 05:11

I talked to Davey about my lifetime of writing and how I needed to get something published.

It is black out now but not raining. I sit here writing, wait for the Dawn Chorus, for it all to come to life. I want to be finished.

SUNDAY 15 AUGUST 2021 05:31

I look at the black window. The silence hums. I look to the story.

MONDAY 16 AUGUST 2021

I felt an absence of affection on our walk at Dangan; when I stopped and bent over Lin didn't rub my back. I stopped myself from bringing this up.

When we went to bed, my legs were burning and frolicking of their own accord. Lin stroked my face. I was careful to say nothing, and stay still as though a bird were nearing me.

TUESDAY 24 AUGUST 2021 05:21

From the position of the moon, I was sure it must be one or two. When I checked my phone it was 4:50. I was happy to see this number; it was a perfect time to get up. It is black but not raining, and the moon is almost full.

I worked long and hard on the story. When Chen Xi and Lin arrived the car was full of stuff, and they brought it all in.

WEDNESDAY 25 AUGUST 2021

I did some editing on the story, and started another read through. I felt In Dublin got a bit confused, jumped about too much. If it is unclear to me, what will it be like for a reader?

At Susan's office, Chen Xi went into a high dudgeon after Seamus called to say the movers had left her grey chair behind. She passed the phone to me to deal with the movers while I sat across the table from Susan. I called Tan, and translated for Susan. He signed the form agreeing to the sale of the house in Bray. I wanted to chat but he hung up as soon as the signing was done.

Chen Xi was now freaking out about getting Covid tests before her flight. I could do nothing but lay down on the sofa.

When we were getting ready for bed. Chen Xi hadn't got back from her walk and it was getting dark, so I went out looking for her in the car, worried she was lost on a dark road with no phone. I met her on the road and drove her home.

. . .

THURSDAY 26 AUGUST 2021 06:51

The response I received from Susan De Mars to the letter I had written to her asking about a writing workshop pissed me off. My brief fantasy that I could expedite getting this book published went up in smoke. I lay on the sofa listening to Chen Xi and Lin drinking and laughing.

SUNDAY 5 SEPTEMBER 2021

Chen Xi came out of her room quite worried this morning, after hearing us fight. She fits in well.

TUESDAY 7 SEPTEMBER 2021

I exercised to Chinese meditation music. The ladies made dumplings for my birthday. Lin dressed me up in my new shirt and did my hair like a Dao master. We drank beer, then Drambui. The ladies took photos of me.

SATURDAY 11 SEPTEMBER 2021

Yesterday I went through the last of the sections of the story that I had highlighted for revision.

I got my hair in a ponytail, put on a new shirt, and took Davey to Andrew's birthday party. I met Declan at the door and he invited me in but I declined. As I got in the car I saw Nicola and Rosemary arriving but just drove on. I am allowing myself the luxury of not caring what people think of me.

MONDAY 13 SEPTEMBER 2021

I messaged Greg. I need to do something with this story.

Lin made a simple Chinese dinner. Chen Xi talked about Tan. He is an awkward man, but I am one to talk. When we went up to watch TV I felt sorry for leaving Chen Xi on her own, but I supposed she was good at that.

TUESDAY 14 SEPTEMBER 2021

Still in a black mood about the story—what should be done with it.

Troy called and told me his first essay was on what is art? I realised this was the question that had been breaking my heart since I finished the story.

When Chen Xi got up she commented on the beautiful smell of the stew. I drank Guinness and Lin and Chen Xi opened a bottle of wine. I hooted and discussed what is art? with Davey.

This question has both a horizontal and a vertical axis. On the horizontal axis we ask is philosophy art? Is a diary? Sourdough? Stew? On the vertical we ask what is good, better, best, and bad? What are the criteria? Can it be at all objective?

After dinner, cheesecake, and a couple hoots, I added another axis: pure and impure, static and kinetic, that brought together Shopenhauer's timeless moment and Zen practice, escape from the world of karma and need. Self liberation.

WEDNESDAY 15 SEPTEMBER 2021

I took Chen Xi to AIB to get money transfer forms, and exchanged messages with Greg and Markus, who are both reading my story.

THURSDAY 16 SEPTEMBER 2021

Greg messaged to say he liked the first two chapters.

SUNDAY 19 SEPTEMBER 2021 06:27

The house feels emptier without Chen Xi here.

. . .

MONDAY 20 SEPTEMBER 2021

I am lost with no story to work on. I ate breakfast, swallowed my pills, felt absence.

TUESDAY 21 SEPTEMBER 2021

After I hooted I started thinking about how stupid I was to still be smoking cigarettes, so I took the broken machine for a walk. My soul weighed me down, and it was hard to keep walking. I stopped many times, sagging down, resting hands on knees, visualising the operation for prostate cancer.

WEDNESDAY 22 SEPTEMBER 2021

None of those who have read the story have gotten back to me. Chen Xi has begun a four week quarantine in Tianjin.

THURSDAY 23 SEPTEMBER 2021

Finlay would not say the story was good. I tried to push him, and even told him about the MS, in a blatant attempt to elicit sympathy, but he refused to satisfy my need for affirmation. No word from Greg or Markus either. It seems I have failed again.

Lin put together the basketball hoop outside the garage

doors. When Lin went in to cook dinner, Davey and I played basketball. He said he would never say he was bored again.

SUNDAY 26 SEPTEMBER 2021

I woke up a few times during the night, obsessing about the story, not sure why it doesn't work. Is it the lack of dialogue? I don't think it is hard to read. Am I really good for nothing? Should I call it *A Man without Talent*? Should it start and end with me now?

I saw a message from Greg, who said he had been too busy to finish reading the story, suggesting the story loses momentum in the middle.

MONDAY 27 SEPTEMBER 2021 04:17

Troy came through with the hash. Greg said he too was too caught up in the question of what is worthwhile in art, and unwilling to hazard an opinion on the story. Markus still hasn't written back.

TUESDAY 28 SEPTEMBER 2021

Lin drove me to meet Ferdia. His weed was much better than the hash, and I was soon feeling more positively about the story. Maybe it needs some maps: two stories overlain–as one moves forward, the other moves back.

WEDNESDAY 29 SEPTEMBER 2021 07:15

It is still mostly dark out, with a dull light above the hills. I am asking myself whether it is possible that Markus didn't reply because the story shows that I am a shitty guy. I think the attack on Paddy is problematic. It would not be the right to leave it out, but I need to show more recognition that it was wrong. I want it to be a story of redemption, but is this no more than vanity?

I opened the bottle of wine, cut onions, leaks, carrots, and courgettes for soup. Lin made sourdough and cooked a few pieces of fresh fish.

After dinner Lin spoke to her mother, who seethed with resentment built up over decades, that she took out by battering her now-ancient husband.

THURSDAY 30 SEPTEMBER 2021

Davey and Lin fought at bedtime. I went down to console Davey, but he was pissed off and said he probably wouldn't speak to mommy until he got home from school. I told Lin and we laughed. Davey called down, I can hear everything.

I am smoking way too much. There is no excuse. I am such an idiot. Fucking writing.

SATURDAY 2 OCTOBER 2021 06:51

The window is a wall of black, my shoulder is sore, and my other MS symptoms are through the roof.

I received my third vaccine amongst my people–immuno-compromised, and mostly limping.

Chen Xi had a panic attack in quarantine. She smashed the window with a stool because she couldn't breath, and then they took her outside for a walk.

THURSDAY 7 OCTOBER 2021 06:14

Lin left me a bud before taking off on a run. I worked on the story for almost six hours, pulling apart and reassembling Aihua Classic and Beijing Underground. I see now what the problem is: I need a narrative structure, a logical sequence of events. Round and round the sun we go.

FRIDAY 22 OCTOBER 2021

My body felt much better today; I don't know why. I did a long walk without trouble, felt like skipping and dancing at the end. Lin didn't want me to get my hopes up, but I was just happy that I could still have a day like this.

Lin was unusually talkative, telling me about her family and growing up, and I just listened. She said this house is our home now.

We parked at the bus station and I passed a beautiful girl on the stairs up to Ferdia's place. I got my weed and left; the city was buzzing, people everywhere.

SATURDAY 13 NOVEMBER 2021

I upset myself working on the story; there is so much to do, and I just don't know if I am capable. I did a bit of yoga, focussed on breathing.

SUNDAY 14 NOVEMBER 2021

Ares snarled and snapped at Davey, so I put him out in the rain and turned off the lights.

THURSDAY 25 NOVEMBER 2021 05:30

I felt relieved to finish writing about Deane's death. It was the last piece I needed to be done. I felt on top of the world, confident in my story.

MONDAY 29 NOVEMBER 2021

I felt very weak on our walk. I got Lin to stop at the little shop so I could buy cigarettes. As I was about to go in I started to cry from the relentless pain. Lin went in for me.

I went to meet Troy. He is a good kid. He gave me the weed. I think it was from Scarlet. It was in a jar and it was shaggy.

We had falafels. My knees and shoulders were sore, and I began to cry again. Blinking through tears, I said don't get me wrong, I am happy.

When we finished *Lord of the Rings* for the umpteenth time I went down first, because I don't like seeing all the hobbits crying.

TUESDAY 30 NOVEMBER 2021

I drove Davey to school. We listened to Placebo, Meds.

When I got home I phoned Holly. Things are hard for her. When I told her how hard my life had become I couldn't stop laughing.

TUESDAY 7 DECEMBER 2021

I sent the story to Dan and Tony, and researched manuscript appraisal services. Maybe it is not such a good idea. I will write to Adele, and maybe Kelly Pitman. Maybe Greg.

THURSDAY 9 DECEMBER 2021 AT 07:13

I am a wreck. I took two sleeping tabs and a painkiller after I found a lump on my abdomen, just above and to the left of my penis. I had been feeling uncomfortable sitting down, and when I got up and felt the protrusion I broke into a cold sweat. We thought about going to emergency.

The rain was crazy, and yet the sky full of stars. Lin looked out and said wow.

SATURDAY 11 DECEMBER 2021

Davey and I made Lin an omelette when she got home. I hoped this little thing would make her happy. There is so much on her shoulders now. I was going to have a walk, but then decided against it, thinking it would make my guts squirt out.

Lin and Davey set up the Christmas tree.

SUNDAY 12 DECEMBER 2021

Troy asked me about Heidegger's famous take on Van Gogh's peasant shoes. I had a lot of ideas and I talked to Lin about it. I asked her to think about her own mother's shoes, and what was unique about these artefacts, formed by her feet and the pressure of her walking, how they depicted the struggles of the humblest life.

I lay on the green sofa painting orcs, my guts squirting out of me. Lin sat beside me painting the Magic Temple.

TUESDAY 14 DECEMBER 2021

The surgeon's secretary told us he wasn't in yet, and we waited 50 minutes for this grouchy Arab guy who wasn't a doctor, and who typed with two fingers, and had the hands of an auto mechanic. He told me I should keep tucking my guts back in when they fell out, and gave me a ticket for an MRI.

I got a bit of weed from Troy, who has never had a girlfriend.

FRIDAY 17 DECEMBER 2021 06:21

Greg agreed to proofread the story. It is hard work, and he has expertise.

The MRI lady called. Rahman wants another brain scan on the 7th. I am lining up the biopsy and hernia operation.

Davey returned home pale and drained-looking, his eyes shadowed.

SATURDAY 18 DECEMBER 2021 06:53

In the afternoon, Nicola let us know that Aaron had Covid, and there was a letter from the school saying two kids in their class had Covid as well.

Davey went up to his room, and the plan was for him to stay there. Lin took him up dinner and we ate with him on messenger. Now I feel I might be sick.

SUNDAY 19 DECEMBER 2021 05:52

Davey tested positive for Covid, Lin and I negative: sufferings and emergencies; hold onto the here, the now.

MONDAY 20 DECEMBER 2021 06:57

Davey and I both feel fine, except for the hernia which popped out as soon as I got up. I lay on the green sofa while Davey and Lin went for a walk, fed apples to a Shetland pony. Greg sent a link to a google doc he had created for editing the story, having gone through the first chapter.

WEDNESDAY 22 DECEMBER 2021

It was nice to see Lin's parents looking happy on the phone. She told them about a dream she had that she lost me in the jungle.

We opened a bottle of wine. I quickly got drunk, and told Lin don't give up looking for me, because I will always be looking after you. Lin held me and we cried.

THURSDAY 23 DECEMBER 2021 05:19

I have felt sore since I took to the couch to mind the hernia. Davey tested negative, so we can bring him down for Christmas.

FRIDAY 24 DECEMBER 2021

More of Greg's revisions. Now Davey is negative, and Lin positive. I sort of wanted to be positive too. I still lay up in bed, pure sloth and despair. Darby delivered sweets and a bit of weed.

SATURDAY 25 DECEMBER 2021 06:31

Davey opened his presents. He was happy, but it was difficult with all of us in masks, trying to maintain distance. Scarlet advised me to just get COVID, be done with it. Maybe she's right, unless she's wrong.

I assembled a Darkoath Savage, and Davey some scatter terrain. Lin and I had a drink, and were happy and jolly. I tossed Davey's hair, which I had missed doing.

SATURDAY 1 JANUARY 2022 AT 07:06

At Silver Strand Davey was laughing and lying back into the wind with arms spread.

Lin had a shower and dressed up nicely. Davey and I played D&D, then Lin and I drank a bottle of wine. I was so big and strong in a video Lin watched of Davey and me playing in Beijing.

MONDAY 3 JANUARY 2022

When I took off my trousers it was awful to see how thin my legs had become. I wanted to weep for them.

WEDNESDAY 12 JANUARY 2022

I smoked my electronic cigarette, then went through Greg's revisions. The GP advised me to see someone about my mental health.

SATURDAY 29 JANUARY 2022

I have to go down the MRI tube for an hour and a half this morning, but I am not afraid, for I have the Shield of Xanax.

TUESDAY 1 FEBRUARY 2022 AT 07:19

Greg alluded to my low moral fibre in his notes on the story. I was surprised to realise that I had not even considered the moral dimension. I had always felt this to be almost negated by the phenomenological project of absolute sincerity, the brutal truth of Blakean impulse.

WEDNESDAY 9 FEBRUARY 2022

Lin held my arm as I shuffled beside her. Dr Rahman said the MS may have stabilised; he got me on the table and tucked my hernia back in.

I mostly hooted the rest of the day. I am not able to push the hernia back in easily, and when I do, it just pops out again.

WEDNESDAY 16 FEBRUARY 2022 06:41

I tidied up the last notes in the story, and added a couple as a sort of goodbye to Greg. Storm Dudley kept us inside.

THURSDAY 17 FEBRUARY 2022

Greg and I discussed the word Sentimentality in the margins of my story. It rained heavily between Storms Dudley and Eunice.

. . .

SUNDAY 20 FEBRUARY 2022 05:53

Now it's Franklin. There is a noise like the squeaking of a runner on a basketball court that I think is one of the alarms warning us it is running out of batteries.

THURSDAY 24 FEBRUARY 2022

Stefano cancelled his lesson because of the Russian invasion. His work involved providing advice and support to Italians doing business in Ukraine, Belarus, and Russia, so he was a bit preoccupied.

SATURDAY 26 FEBRUARY 2022

I am trying to produce a Package for Publishers, as all the best sources suggest, so I wrote a Chapter by Chapter Synopsis.

I had breakfast and my pills, then took Davey to Wildlands for Sidd's birthday party. We entered the facility and stood near Dermot and Adam's dad. Adam's dad didn't even look at me. I know that my hair and my general appearance are off-putting. I tried to stand straight and puff out my chest, but I couldn't get away quickly enough.

Reading *Beyond Good and Evil* for the umpteenth time I'd been put off by Nietzsche's arrogance, which I'd found so appealing as a young man, but after these recent incidents I was newly struck by the need to distance oneself from other people, making me feel like a co-conspirator of a sort.

When we went to collect Davey Declan and Dermot greeted me and then turned back to their huddle. When we got home I drank a bottle of wine, hooted, and hid behind a haze.

FRIDAY 4 MARCH 2022

I spent the morning trying to keep my fear at bay. Lin came into the hospital with me, but I sent her away. After two hours Ali Zaki arrived, arrogant and abrupt.

After another hour's wait, I was taken to a room, and told to change into a gown. People came in at intervals to take blood, etc. I didn't feel comfortable to sit, so I stayed standing. Eventually I gave up on my delicate reluctance to assume, and lay down on the bed to read of people being gutted left and right in the *City of Bohane*, which didn't do my spirits any good.

Down to surgery and onto the table. A guy asked me why I smoked so much marijuana, and pushed a needle in me. I started to explain and then I was looking up at someone standing over me. I asked if it was over, and it was. I didn't remember how I got up to the room, where I was plugged into fentanyl and ketamine.

When I got up to piss, I noticed my balls were the size and the colour of a coconut. The night doctor, a beautiful black woman, seemed horrified by the state of my balls, and went off to do some research. She came back, apologised for being freaked out, and told me it was normal.

In the morning Ali Zaki had a look. He grunted that it should go away. I went down for a cigarette. When I came back Ali shouted at me in the hall for going down. The fentanyl was wearing off, and I was sore and upset.

SATURDAY 5 MARCH 2022

I ate a bowl of porridge and some watery scrambled eggs while waiting to be discharged. I finished *Bohene* and started on *Purity*.

I smoked a couple of joints, lay on the sofa, then went up and got into bed. I ate laying down. Lin and Davey looked after me. I read *Purity* then managed to sleep.

SUNDAY 6 MARCH 2022

I spent the day in bed, reading messages from Sherry Markham describing the gruesome death of her son in Cochrane, Alberta. This and the war in Ukraine made the world seem very dark.

I asked Sherry for her address so I could inspect the scene of the horror on google maps.

. . .

WEDNESDAY 9 MARCH 2022

My cock is a little black nubbin, dangling dead. Lin tried to calm me. She chatted with a Chinese doctor, who said this could happen, that I should just move carefully and not too much.

FRIDAY 11 MARCH 2022 07:30

When Lin took Davey to school, I went back up to bed, very swollen. Ali Zaki was on holiday, so I called the Bonne, and waited on the phone, but got no help. I called the GP and made an appointment for 3:45.

She cringed at the sight of my coconut balls and shrivelled black cock, and told me to go to Emergency at NUIG immediately. I sagged in despair. She said sorry, this is not my area of expertise.

We went home and got ready. I knew the Emergency would be *City of Bohene* on Friday night. I hooted and decided against. I decided to ignore the discomfort and see what happened.

I looked at my phone for a long time. I took off my underpants and lay nude. I felt like I'd just been kicked in the balls.

SUNDAY 13 MARCH 2022

I went into Emergency. They didn't let Lin come in, and there was a lady with Covid right in front of me. I couldn't sit, so I paced about, and my constant sighing made the other patients uncomfortable. After a few hours I was led to a hallway full of people in plastic chairs. I couldn't bear the idea of waiting all night.

MONDAY 14 MARCH 2022 07:08

Davey has COVID; I stayed in bed with my skeleton's leg.

WEDNESDAY 16 MARCH 2022 07:38

Davey is isolated in his room. I drink the coffee Lin made me after smoking two reefers.

I switch between the red sofa, watching videos about the tension in Russia, and bed, reading *Freedom*.

THURSDAY 17 MARCH 2022

I watched Vice News coverage of Ukraine's attack on Russia-occupied Donetsk: a mother and daughter dead at the edge of a crater, a skinny guy despairing over the bodies. I went up to read *Freedom*.

. . .

SATURDAY 19 MARCH 2022

Seeing only a few smokes left, I am filled with fear. I want to quit but I am already making back up plans. I know that it is impossible for me to restrict myself to a reasonably small number per day. I believe that to succeed I need to take positive pleasure from not smoking.

SUNDAY 20 MARCH 2022 06:22

I dreamed of big machines, chimneys, and furnaces. I have no tobacco, and couldn't even find any butts, so I opened *A Man Without Talent*.

MONDAY 21 MARCH 2022 07:08

Again the sensation of being among machines. Maybe I have too many pillows around me. We went for a walk at Dangan. I walked carefully. It was nice to be out of the house.

TUESDAY 22 MARCH 2022

My resolve is crumbling.

WEDNESDAY 23 MARCH 2022 07:26

After a broken, jolty sleep I had breakfast, and then took Davey to school, waited until the little shop opened, and bought a pack of cigarettes.

We went for a walk at Dangan's, then got diesel. Lin commented on how expensive it was now. When we got home I laid down and finished *Freedom*. The end was so beautiful that I whimpered with little gasps.

FRIDAY 25 MARCH 2022

I lay back on the crinkling blue paper and slipped down my trousers. Ali Zaki looked down at the swelling. I held my hand right over his, and when he moved too close or hurt me I gripped his hand. He said the blood had filled these areas, and he hoped it would withdraw of its own accord.

A technician hooked me up to a needle and I could feel the dye coursing through my body. When she took me out of the tube I said I would love to get the needle out. She took me to the other room, slipped it out, then pressed the hole and chatted. She was from Donegal. Wants to go to India to learn yoga in an ashram then return to teach. She talked about mindfulness and suggested I write. Lin took my arm and led me to the car.

. . .

FRIDAY 8 APRIL 2022 07:46

The sun lights the frost on the fields to the east. Lin remarked how sunny it was in the Zen room, so I went in and did a guided meditation. Lin washed the car and Davey played basketball.

SATURDAY 9 APRIL 2022

We went to the Westside Tool Rental Place for a hedge trimmer. The machine was heavy and difficult to use. Lin did most of the work, but I did a bit. I felt good for having used my body.

SUNDAY 10 APRIL 2022

Lin went shopping, and Davey and I went out to the rose trellis. I cut at it with the hedge trimmer, and took out the front segment completely. How many years of knotted grape vines? Now a carapace, mutilated.

I stretched in the Zen room. It felt good to move my body a bit. I listened to *Ulysses*, Hades, then a Stop Smoking Hypnosis.

TUESDAY 19 APRIL 2022 08:22

I felt wretched, hopeless. A future of grinding pain, like a big hand squeezing my balls.

FRIDAY 22 APRIL 2022 07:26

Chen Xi's flight was cancelled because of COVID.

SATURDAY 23 APRIL 2022 07:53

Lin collected Chen Xi from the bus station at four am. I heard them downstairs, so I went down for a cup of tea and a reefer. It was nice to see Chen Xi. She had jet legs and was very chatty.

MONDAY 25 APRIL 2022

Beijing is going into lockdown. Scarlet called Chen Xi a Houdini of the Skies.

TUESDAY 26 APRIL 2022 07:15

We walked around the garden in the mild air. Chen Xi said she wouldn't be in the west again for three years or so. We played basketball with Davey, laughing and happy. Ares tried to get up on Chen Xi, but she kept him at bay with a rake.

FRIDAY 29 APRIL 2022 07:52

We got up before five and went out with Chen Xi's bags. I gave her a hug, and told her if she ever needed she was welcome, that this could always be her safe place. Lin drove her to Shannon. She was flying to London.

SATURDAY 14 MAY 2022

Davey and I sang happy birthday as we carried the cake to Lin. She was blushing and happy. She said she could see the love in our eyes. We had a family hug, with Ares trying to get in the middle.

Lin made broccoli. Her face became red. She'd worked in the heat all day. Also the Guinness. We sat outside. I felt bad for bringing so much booze into our home.

MONDAY 16 MAY 2022

A fortune teller told Lin's sister she will have a short life, but that people who love her could pay for a little bit extra.

TUESDAY 24 MAY 2022

I did a bit of stretching before I took Davey to school. The stretching is reducing pain in my shoulder, hip and knee.

Lin and I went for a walk. I felt good and walked well, not perfect by any means, but better. Clouds stood around like statues.

Lin went to the garden centre for roses. I listened to *Ulysses*, then did some yoga. I disappeared in meditation, then vacuumed.

WEDNESDAY 25 MAY 2022 07:03

I ran out of weed yesterday, and it has left a bit of a hole. Everything was going like clockwork. The healing, the floaty Zen.

After dinner, Lin went out to her roses, and Davey kicked the ball.

FRIDAY 27 MAY 2022 06:54

Davey learned Sweet Child O Mine at his guitar lesson. I opened a bottle of wine. We ate and then Lin went out to mow the lawn. I played Davey Sweet Child O Mine from *Captain Fantastic*, and couldn't stop sobbing. Davey put his hand on my shoulder. I hooted and finished the bottle of wine. I went out and did a bit of mowing in tight to the rose trellis. We heard Ares barking and who should come round the corner but Darby in his good suit, trying to keep Ares off him.

. . .

SUNDAY 29 MAY 2022 06:36

After lunch, Davey and I played D&D. The Vampires fought the Owl Queen to gain access to the hub. The Owl Queen told Duvall that the Dark Brother was like the breath going out and the body sinking down, while the bright twin was the breath coming in, and the body rising up, as in meditation.

Lin and I drank wine outside the Zen room, under the umbrella. *Ulysses* and yoga is my balance. Someday finish the story.

FRIDAY 3 JUNE 2022

I did a long yoga session with incense and a 174 Hz binaural healing loop. I listened to *Ulysses*, repeated this cycle, then tidied up in Zen mode.

When Lin got home from the International Morning at Davey's school, she was tired but happy. She had spoken to people, including Agnes, the crossing lady, who took a particular interest in her, and discussed reincarnation and Buddhist beliefs.

When I collected Davey, he thanked me for paying for his guitar lessons.

After a bottle of wine drunkenness makes me stumble, and Lin gets rambunctious. Davey came down and criticised Lin for being drunk. I shouldn't let her drink like that.

SATURDAY 4 JUNE 2022 08:06

I bought Darby a bottle of Redbreast for his birthday, and Lin dropped me off at Darbys place. I drank beer with some guys in his garden. I was shivering, but I refused to accept a blanket from Darby's wife.

THURSDAY 9 JUNE 2022

Lin drove me to hospital for the biopsy. I hobbled along the wall and had a cigarette on the way to the reception. I was called into the day ward and given a bed and a gown. I waited a couple of hours, reading *Morning Star*.

In the space I was taken into, the medical staff were hanging around like it was a pub. A guy jabbed a needle into me, and I felt cold surging up my arm. They put an oxygen mask over my mouth and told me to breathe. I tried to catch the moment I disappeared. Then I was awake and I asked a guy if it was over. They wheeled me back to my cubicle where I had to wait until I passed urine. Lin and Davey waited in the car.

. . .

FRIDAY 10 JUNE 2022

I spent most of the day in bed reading *Morning Star*, trying to drink as much water as possible. There were gobs of blood that looked like meat in my urine. I took paracetamol, felt like a zombie. When Lin returned she delivered a kiss. I kissed her with all the love in my heart.

I am able to sit gingerly this morning.

SATURDAY 11 JUNE 2022

The barber was a cheeky dude from east Europe who referred to me as daddy. Davey was happy with the new haircut. He switched Lin's Ringo Starr cut for that of a smart young soccer player. Davey noodles on his guitar throughout the day, mostly Sweet Home Alabama.

I hooted and took a bit of cocaine. I must be allergic, as my nose is pure torture now.

THURSDAY 16 JUNE 2022

I had a quick hoot before I went to the GP on Cappagh Road. At my insistence she prescribed three days of Xanax for getting off cigarettes. She suggested I see a psychiatrist, and asked me about myself, my family, my life. I was grateful for her time.

Later we opened a bottle of wine, I took some cocaine the way Darby suggested, rubbing it against my gums. I got very high, and I think this made Davey feel uncomfortable.

SATURDAY 18 JUNE 2022

When Lin and Davey came in from the garden, she joined me on the wine. She was speaking to doctors about her sister, so I took Davey up and got him into bed.

My balls were very sore. I took three painkillers, but the pain remained. I read Knausgaard on Angels.

I had a lot of strange dreams, but my mind doesn't allow me to remember them, though in one that I did Davey had grown up to be a strong, handsome man.

MONDAY 20 JUNE 2022 07:06

It was a beautiful morning, so we did some cocaine, and went for a walk. Lin wasn't sure what she should be feeling, but she was smiling beside the smooth slipping waters of the Corrib.

When we got home, she chatted with her mom, and I did yoga. We did more cocaine, then went out and gave Ares his first wash in a year. We sat out in the garden looking at Lin's beautiful roses.

. . .

TUESDAY 21 JUNE 2022 07:24

I didn't smoke yesterday. Lin and I went for a walk at Dangan, then I took a Xanax, and did some yoga. I listened to *Ulysses*, then read more of Knausgaard on Angels. The Xanax served its purpose; I was too wasted to think about needing to smoke.

WEDNESDAY 22 JUNE 2022

I vacuumed, then Lin and I went for a walk at Dangan. I walked very well, much better than before. I took a Xanax, and did some stretching. I played healing meditation music, then listened to *Ulysses*. Then I went upstairs and lay down, read *A Time for Every Purpose*, and slept deeply.

THURSDAY 23 JUNE 2022

It's my fourth day off cigarettes. The Xanax plan has worked. The crap is starting to come out, and I don't feel like smoking. Soon Davey will be off school soon though, and it will be a challenge having him around the house every day.

We went for a walk at Dangan. I walk a bit better every day it seems. When we got home, I took a Xanax, and did my stretching. In the shower, I noticed my balls are still swollen and purple.

Davey and I fought. I slapped him on the arm, and Ares tried to nip him.

SUNDAY 26 JUNE 2022 07:28

As I emerge from this cocoon of pain and despair I have more energy and more clarity. Davey has only three days of school left. It will be tough, but we will manage.

MONDAY 27 JUNE 2022

We rubbed cocaine in our gums and went for a walk at Dangan. When we got home, we meditated to healing music, which I continued to play outside while Lin cut grape branches from the tube to make way for roses. I moved the fallen branches. I felt strong and healthy. We had a cup of tea. I could smell the roses.

TUESDAY 28 JUNE 2022

Scarlet said that yoga should be enjoyment, and that making it about discipline might become onerous.

There was a break in the rain, and we went out to the garden. Davey kicked the football and Lin worked on the grape vines. I took wheelbarrow loads away and dumped them under the big pine.

I feel that my being so positive about everything has, perhaps, created the impression that I am further along than I am. I noticed this morning that my legs still look skinny as ever, and last night the jumpy leg and burning feet were bad. I worry about a crash, but so far I am still not smoking, and I am walking a lot better after all of the yoga and stretching.

WEDNESDAY 29 JUNE 2022

It seems a gentle day. Two white horses stand in the field across from me, there are flowers everywhere.

Lin talked to a doctor about her sister. I wheelbarrowed grape leaves and vines away from the tube. Lin and Davey lay on the grass. I lay with my head on Davey's belly, looking up at the clouds.

I feel a bit lacklustre; it is hard work being positive all the time. I hope we will manage OK with Davey off school. We couldn't find any camps or activities for him, and we can't travel because Lin needs a visa to go anywhere.

SATURDAY 2 JULY 2022

Lin and I rubbed cocaine in our gums, then went out to continue dismantling the grape tendrils over the rose trellis. I surprised myself with my strength and endurance, and how much we got done. I worried that I would suffer neck or back pains today, but I am fine and we have only one small segment left.

I held Lin tight, and we stayed that way while the morning sun shone through us.

I am almost afraid to say it, but I seem to be recovering. It is more than I would have hoped for.

SUNDAY 3 JULY 2022 06:47

We had a cup of tea, then went out to work on the rose tube. We worked hard until we had finished.

I went in and had a hoot, and put on a shepherd's pie, while Lin and Davey stayed outside; Lin inspected the open trellis, and Davey played football.

It seems miraculous to feel this much better.

MONDAY 4 JULY 2022

We thought Lin might have Covid so I slept facing the other way. I have started dreaming again; strange, distorted, hard-to-remember dreams. I guess all the marijuana was keeping them down. They are long and convoluted, seemingly senseless, hard to hold onto.

I listened to *Ulysses*. Davey played guitar then read. Lin did something in the green house. Davey and I followed her out, and I tightened the bolts on his soccer goal. I swept the path of the rose tube, and Lin tried to make the pink roses arch over the trellis.

SUNDAY 10 JULY 2022

Lin mopped and I vacuumed. We let Davey play PS4, then Lin and I did some cocaine. Lin went out to her roses, and I meditated. Incredible truths heaved wordless behind and between my eyes, empty, enraptured. If you seek it you lose it because you already have it.

MONDAY 11 JULY 2022

We drove Davey to his cooking class, and I went in with him. He was shy, hoping I wouldn't embarrass him. I thought what a good looking wee fellow he was with such beautiful eyes.

TUESDAY 12 JULY 2022

I walked through town at a good clip, up to Moloney's to collect the acoustic. I didn't play it because I wanted Davey to feel the first zing of the bright new strings. I had a hoot and did a big Zen yoga, going deep with the meditation.

Davey had made sushi and a sort of apple pie at Cooking Camp. . He appreciated the glimmer of the new strings. We walked around Lin's gardenwhile Davey kicked the football. We looked at the new roses, and found many red currants out back.

I decided to start looking at the story again after the meeting with the Urologist, next Tuesday.

WEDNESDAY 13 JULY 2022

I was very Zen on our walk at Dangan. I am able to use my breath to get into the meditation place, a deep breath can make me feel like I did with the cocaine.

We tidied up around the house, then I did a long Om meditation. I nestled down into the instant of now, surfed the slipping peak of eternal presence.

I read, then snoozed. I called Davey off PS4 and he lay joking with me awhile. We went for a walk to the horse gate but it started to rain and we turned back. Lin was outside working in the garden. Davey beat me at chess. We prepared nachos. I listened to *Ulysses* while Lin had a shower and Davey read the *Wizard of Earthsea* Quartet. I slept well. There was a big moon, a silver disk at the level of the trees peering in at us.

THURSDAY 14 JULY 2022

In the Secret Garden, I ordered two flat whites, and took a seat in the little garden in the back. Lin ordered a bun. Scarlet arrived and had a flat white. Troy turned up toward the end. He was going to the Pixies that evening. They made Galway during the festival sound like a magical place.

SATURDAY 16 JULY 2022 07:38

27 days off cigarettes and drink.

I walked well at Dangan, and we chatted with people who stopped to admire Ares. When we got home, I did yoga while Lin ran errands: fish food, diesel, coffee, dog medicine. I did more exercise then had a bath. My body did not appear as much of a horror show as it did a few months ago.

I got a bit of weed from Troy. Lin's brother texted her to complain that she would not come home to help the family during the time of her sister's dying. Lin's sister told her that their mother had beaten their father again, this time quite badly.

MONDAY 18 JULY 2022

Lin changed an orange rose for a white rose outside the stairwell window. I did a good Om session, then played a game of chess with Davey. I started strong, but he defended well, and it came out a draw.

Meeting O'Malley for a verdict on the prostate today.

TUESDAY 19 JULY 2022

I dreamed that Lin didn't love me anymore. Antonio mocked how the MS made me more childish.

I sat for a while in the Galway Clinic before Nadeen sent me in to see Paddy, who told me right away I don't have cancer. On the way out I bantered with Nadeen about her holiday in Spain, then called Lin to give her the good news.

FRIDAY 22 JULY 2022

I suggested to Lin we take the last of the cocaine, but before we did I asked her if she would need to deal with family problems, and she said she would try to not talk to them. It was sunny and Davey was still asleep. We rubbed the cocaine into our gums, then looked out at the garden from the Zen room. We stepped out as if into another world. I started disassembling the thorn bushes behind Davey's goal. Lin dragged the branches away.

Davey didn't get up until 11:30. He organised breakfast for himself, and Lin and I snuck the very last of the cocaine, and went for a walk. The weather was brilliant; Dangan idyllic. The river was so clear. We thought about how different it was to Beijing. A couple swam across the river. I walked so naturally it felt like flying. We walked the whole way past the student accommodation down to the pier, and sat in silence while the water slid beneath reflections of the sky. Everything felt just right, such peace and bliss.

SUNDAY 24 JULY 2022 07:16

Troy's roommate had Covid, so he handed me the stuff through the window. I listened to *Ulysses*, Penelope. The phenomenology of a single day. Life as a succession of such days.

MONDAY 25 JULY 2022 07:16

36 days without cigarettes and alcohol. I only hoot after four. The exercise is going well, but my knee has gotten worse these past few days. Perhaps it is the cold and rainy weather. If so, it's a pity I live in Ireland.

Lin made *xihongshi chao jidan mian*. I steamrolled Davey in a chess game and he was upset so I gave him a cuddle and we walked to the crossroad. We chatted, and I felt I learned a lot about him. He has a level head; more like Ralph than me, thank God. When we got home, he did a Chinese lesson, then played Master of Puppets on the Strat. Lin and I laughed to see the little dude rocking out so full of joy, proud and glowing.

TUESDAY 26 JULY 2022

I've worked out a system to deal with the knee. I bend it while laying on my back to attain a kneeling posture. I hope this is not damaging the knee. I got Davey to hold off on the guitar until I got meditation out of the way.

Afterwards I did a lot of snipping and sawing in the garden, tidying shaggy trees to above head height, as Chen Fu had advised all those years ago.

After dinner, Davey found a video on how to play the Bohemian Rhapsody solo. I went up to watch Stranger Things, and Lin did her Chinese Medicine class. When I came down Davey could play the solo. He said it was mind blowing. He hugged me and said I was the best dad in the world, and it felt like he meant it. Lin told me Davey said he had never been so happy as when learning to play the Bohemian Rhapsody solo.

FRIDAY 29 JULY 2022 07:49

I feel bad for leaving Lin to clean a big Ares shit. I filled the bucket and brought her the mop, made her a cup of tea that is going cold. It is raining, and it rained all night.

We did a car wash, because the car is covered in little bat shits. They live in the chimney. I told Davey they were faery poops.

. . .

SATURDAY 30 JULY 2022

Lin made chicken with cucumber and aubergine in *majiang*. Davey and I played chess. I had him under huge pressure in a corner, but then he pulled off a win very neatly. Afterwards he continued working on the Comfortably Numb solo. It's a pity we don't have friends to share our happiness with.

When Davey is back at school in September I will start writing again.

SUNDAY 31 JULY 2022

Davey beat me soundly at chess, then he played guitar. Lin was out gardening. I stripped ivy off the trees I didn't want to cut. The fragrance of Lin's roses filled the garden.

MONDAY 1 AUGUST 2022 07:16

It is a yellow weather warning. I see the white horses in the field through sheets of rain.

All Bran, granola, blueberry, banana, flax seed, chia seed. Gilenya, mood medicine, enzyme, probiotic, vitamin D, fish oil.

Every day when I start my exercise I feel that I might not be able to manage it, but once I get going I feel good. Sun salutation, pushups with kneeling meditation, floor stretch, open leg stretch, repeat sun salutation, pushups and kneeling meditation, strengthening exercises for legs, and a couple of dumbbell sets. Finish with meditation.

FRIDAY 5 AUGUST 2022 07:46

I was thinking about how to save the last of the money, that there was no more coming in. We need jobs, though there is something beautiful and pure about our disconnection from the world.

SATURDAY 6 AUGUST 2022 07:40

When Lin woke I brought up her citizenship application and us both getting jobs. We agreed that when Davey went back to school in September we would go to the welfare office and see if they could help us.

THURSDAY 18 AUGUST 2022 07:29

Raindrops on the window; a purple sky above the fields; sunshine flooding from behind. Lin sends messages with a stony face, considering what to do when her sister dies.

We went to the library. They didn't have *Swan's Way*, but I found *Poguemahone*, by Patrick McCabe.

. . .

FRIDAY 19 AUGUST 2022

I saw a photo of all Scarlet's people at her place and felt resentful of their health and good cheer. Warnock had his shirt off and was looking strong and healthy. I disdained to press the like button. I also resented Darby saying he would drop by with some weed yesterday but never did. I feel like I am begging now. I think I can cope without the weed, and maybe it would be for the best, but ….

Lin is planning a prayer group for her sister through a Buddhist friend. They still haven't told her she is dying, but she must realise by now.

SUNDAY 21 AUGUST 2022 07:32

While Lin did a long meditation, I hooted with abandon, and walked around in a fog. Then, while doing my exercises, I discovered a chakra meditation that I hoped to get to know better. I was coming up from the lower parts, the root, toward the crown, and the space above the head.

We met the weather guy on our walk at Dangan. I described the day as perfect and he agreed wholeheartedly. When we got home we walked round the garden, and each ate one of our apples.

MONDAY 22 AUGUST 2022

I had a hoot, then did my meditation. I played the chakra chanting, and as I moved up through the chakras, I felt energies unravelling. By the time I got to the chakra above my head, I felt a burst of light glowing above me. When the chanting finished I stayed in the kneeling posture for some time.

Davey was grouchy with hay fever at Dangan, but he understood what Lin meant by negative energy, and settled. When we got back to the car, Ares went into a bush, pulled out a pigeon, and jumped into the car, blood and guts dripping from his mouth. He growled when we tried to pull the pigeon free. We got him out of the car, and Lin pried what was left of the pigeon out of his mouth. Ares was left in his room for the rest of the day.

Lin was busy all day with messages and phone calls to her family. They were trying to figure out what to do with the sister's belongings. They won't give Liu Hao money now, because he is incorrigible. The police want to put him in prison for a year.

I listened to *Swan's Way*; drifted in and out of consciousness.

THURSDAY 25 AUGUST 2022 07:14

Lin has been up meditating for over an hour. The weather beams blue, green, and gold.

After a cup of coffee and a hoot I started my meditation. I took my time and went deep. I had another hoot at the midway point and put on Om chanting.

Lin set up an Old Person Monitoring System for her sister and her mom and dad. I think this could give her some peace of mind.

At Dangan I had to take a few deep breaths to ground myself, push through the pain.

FRIDAY 26 AUGUST 2022 08:14

Lin has already taken Ares for a walk. I can hear her talking to her mom about Pure Land.

I had a few hoots, then did my yoga meditation. I tried to focus closely enough to catch the instant of now, to surf its swell into forever. As well this moment as the next: they are all one.

I played Boston on the drive to Dangan. Davey liked the second song, Peace of Mind, so now he is learning how to play it. Later, when I took Davey down to his room, he hugged me and said you and me have so much in common, we like the same music, we like D&D, you are my best friend.

I went back down to my room and read *Poguemahone* but couldn't sleep, as my leg was jumping. I went down for a bowl of cereal. I heard daddy, and there was Davey. He couldn't sleep either, he said, and he pulled up a chair beside me. I took him back up to bed, and lay down beside him. I think Peace of Mind is a good favourite song.

SATURDAY 27 AUGUST 2022 08:24 .

Meditation went well, coming up from the root, unravelling channels, stretching them up toward the crown, letting the crown blaze. Davey was practising Peace of Mind. I asked Lin to join me. I felt she needed some mediation. She looked flustered.

We talked to her family. Her mom and dad seem lovely if you didn't know the dark secrets. I saw her sister but couldn't talk to her. She seems alien, like someone already gone. Sick bed; bed of death. Poor people. At Dangan Davey chatted away, sometimes holding my hand, sliding his fingers between mine.

Lin and I walked round the garden, experiencing the subtle scent of the roses. I have learned that it is not simply a question of some roses having more fragrance than others; there are times and weathers that make roses more or less fragrant. Colours translate into scent.

SUNDAY 28 AUGUST 2022 06:55

I dreamed that Lin and I had been infiltrated by spirits, and we had to fight to expel or accommodate alien energy.

TUESDAY 30 AUGUST 2022 06:42

Sore lower back and legs make me feel like a man made of wood. I'm hoping no weed will clear this up. I am so cranky these days, and keep falling into panic. Kitty sits on the wall by the pink gate, surveying her domain.

Lin had a debate with the sister-in-law about telling the sister she is dying. She is at the phone again this morning. It is a full time job. She is reading *The Tibetan Book of Living and Dying*. The meditation in preparation for death is like the chakra meditation I am using, moving up the body, helping the energy flow up and out through the top, the solar anus. Davey commented you guys are really getting into this Buddhism stuff.

WEDNESDAY 31 AUGUST 2022

I'm having the same lower back/kidney pain that I had at the start of this diary. I still can't figure out what triggers it. My mood has been bad, and I have been fighting with Davey. One of our battles had Ares jumping up at me. It was chaos: tears, roars, snapping, and snarling.

FRIDAY 2 SEPTEMBER 2022 07:28

I didn't take an amitriptyline, and I slept well last night. My kidney is still very sore, but I am coping better with it now. I have learned to float atop the pain. When they got home from hurling, I had a towel waiting for Davey, and put it over his shoulders. I felt sorry for him out in that freezing rain, but he was happy. He had a shower then played guitar. I read *Poguemahone* in bed. Lin asked me the colours of the chakras, and I googled. Red, the lowest vibration, is the root. 480-484 Hzs.

SATURDAY 3 SEPTEMBER 2022 07:48

Golden sun lights the grass. Lin is already up, doing yoga.

My routine was difficult but I completed the whole cycle. During meditation I found myself smiling without thinking about it, recalling Davey's face the night before.

SUNDAY 4 SEPTEMBER 2022 07:37

I was tossing and turning at two, so I looked at my phone for a while. Lin was reading *The Tibetan Book of Living and Dying* in Chinese on Kindle. She got up at 5:30 to meditate.

At Dangan we were coming up to another Bernese on a lead, and Ares attacked. It was savage and dangerous. Lin tried to get in and grab him but couldn't. Eventually I seized him by the scruff. The man had been very brave to stand his ground holding his dog's lead. I apologised profusely. We decided that we must neuter Ares as soon as possible.

MONDAY 5 SEPTEMBER 2022

I had a big hoot, put on Reiki music, and did my yoga meditation. When I moved up to the crown, I saw a flower blooming above me. Saw? Not exactly.

At Dangan Ares ran around happily, unaware of his impending surgery.

TUESDAY 6 SEPTEMBER 2022

I dreamed I was hosting an Aihua party. It was a let down because there was no beer. I had gathered scraps of paper in my pockets, took them out in clumps. I tried to assemble the damp writing on Chen Fu's bed.

Lin trimmed my beard and put my hair in a ponytail. I brushed my teeth, washed my face, and got dressed. Davey played guitar, then beat me at chess.

Davey and Lin seem not to realise that it's my birthday. I don't care that it is my birthday, though facebook has me thinking about the 40th anniversary of my high school graduation. There won't be many of us left in ten years.

WEDNESDAY 7 SEPTEMBER 2022

I checked birthday greetings on facebook before I got up. Lin and Davey had forgotten, but I reminded them so it wouldn't be awkward. We took Davey to school and Ares to the vet, though we had to go back because he wouldn't budge. He weighs about 60 kg, so there wasn't much they could do when he refused. They got us to muzzle him, and when the vet injected him his back legs began to give, and his tongue lolled. We stroked him and spoke lovingly until he collapsed; they carried him in and left him on the floor.

In the late afternoon, Lin brought Ares home, and he was still sleeping in the back of the car. It was difficult to get him out of the back and laying on the tarmac. We put the cone on his head, then slid a blanket under him and tried to stretcher him, but it didn't work. I hunched over him and tried to walk him leg by leg. He snapped at my hand, and when I stepped back he snarled, and then launched at me, clamped onto my arm. Lin yelled no no no. It didn't hurt but I knew it was bad. Davey followed me around asking are you OK. The blood soaked my jumper on both sides of my forearm.

I wanted a cigarette. I decided that I would go to the hospital and Lin would follow. I stopped at the little shop, got a pack of smokes, and had one immediately.

I drove to the hospital, found a place to park, then went into Emergency. I grabbed a mask from a box at the entry. There were girls being checked in, so I had another cig. Inside I paced and sighed. Lin arrived, having hitchhiked. They sent me to emergency surgery. The corridor was full of people waiting. I found a seat near the office. I was starting to feel pain, so I got a nurse to give me pain killers. Lin brought me *The Tibetan Book of Living and Dying*, but the trials of the soul after death freaked me out. I chatted to Davey on Lin's phone. I sent Lin home but she kept coming back. I don't think she slept.

A doctor washed and bandaged the puncture wounds, gave me a sling to keep my arm elevated, and injected me with penicillin. I sat all night on a plastic chair, holding my arm up over my head so that it wouldn't compartmentalise, as the doctor had put it. I felt that my meditation and breathing could keep me strong, but toward morning, I couldn't count my breath any longer. I snuck into a little courtyard again and again to smoke. At around six I told a nurse I couldn't stick it anymore. She couldn't do anything for me. They told me I needed to wait for Plastics at 7:30.

THURSDAY 8 SEPTEMBER 2022

A doctor arrived at 7:30. He washed my wound and told me I might need to stay 48 hours as my status as immunosuppressed made infection dangerous. My morale crashed at the idea of having to stay two days and nights in the chair in the hall.

Lin was there when the Senior Plastics Guy arrived. He said they would give me an intravenous dose of penicillin and send me home. A young doctor came down and gave me a prescription for penicillin pills and paracetamol, then sent me away, though I had to wait for Aideen to take the needle out. She made a balls of it and left a black bruise.

I walked past Ares gingerly, as though he were a bear trap. I went up to lay down but was too tired to sleep. I held up my arm, breathed in, breathed out. The queen of England died.

Lin fed Ares chicken by hand, trying to get him to take medicine. When she forced it into his mouth, he growled and went for her. I slid a stool in front of him. Lin screamed and ran. He sat in the middle of the kitchen and we didn't dare go near him.

We agreed he couldn't stay with us. Lin was heartbroken.I said the only ones are we three. We three are the ones to stay together and protect one another.

FRIDAY 9 SEPTEMBER 2022

I drank two cups of coffee while catching up on the diary. I had a quick breakfast and my pills, then it was time to take Davey to school and go to hospital. Lin parked and Davey went in. When we tried to reverse, the brakes locked and we couldn't move. We fiddled with it but made no headway. I googled the problem without success. Lin told me Darby had arrived and I asked him for a lift. He dropped off Darcy first. He looked like a very good man leading his little girl in by the hand.

I got out at the hospital. The lady at reception was kind, and got another lady to take me down to in-patients, where a doctor and a nurse changed my bandage and had a look. He said there was no big problem and told me to stay on the antibiotics.

Lin was still with the car outside Davey's school. I waited for a taxi out front, where I bummed a cigarette from a guy who wasn't too happy to part with one. When I got back to Lin she was on the phone paying for a new AA membership. We talked to the vet about what we should do with Ares. She thought we should put him down. The cab driver asked what if he goes for a kid? Lin cried.

I went out to the stone circle and smoked a reefer. It made me feel like my mind was on fire. I walked down to O'Toole's garage and talked to Matty. I had the opportunity to slip in Drink deeply at the Pierian Spring or drink not at all. I also had a chance to say god willing. I blabbered to Lin while we ate fried rice. I had so many ideas. I saw so many symmetries; so many patterns and reasons. Lin listened but grew tired of it. It is all gone now.

I cleaned up the kitchen. I was tired, but I didn't want to rest. I called Des and cancelled Davey's guitar lesson. He sent me the number of a spiritual healer in Westside. When Davey got home, I went out and thanked Declan for collecting him. I had a super philosophical chat with Davey, and he was with me the whole way. We finished with him googling optical illusions.

Lin let Ares stay in, against my wishes. Davey and I are scared of him and his big, clattering head.

I felt proud of myself for having been so clever that day. The mission is to unlock this cleverness when I am not high. This may be the job of freeing the chakras.

SATURDAY 10 SEPTEMBER 2022 08:27

I slept well, and now it's damp and rainy, so Kitty is in, even though she has worms. Ares is on the red carpet with his big awkward cone, Lin on the red sofa with her computer, and Davey in the living room playing Freebird with the slide thing we got him yesterday.

My arm hurts when I type, but I keep on. It took a while to get back into the swing of my yoga meditation, but I was able to do the whole routine. I took my time and luxuriated in the process ending with a guided chakra meditation.

Lin wants to put the fish in the river. *Fang sheng*. We went out to the stone circle to gather apples for me to stew later.

I bought a pack of cigarettes and rolled a few joints. Today we are housebound. We will have a walk down the road. Tomorrow I will be pure again.

SUNDAY 11 SEPTEMBER 2022

I have been having complicated dreams. I can remember bits of them while I am still in bed, but then my memory washes clean.

It rained all day, and I hooted all day. Lin and I meditated with the chakra chanting.

Davey and I washed and sliced apples. He made a batter, and I added cinnamon, nuts and raisins. We put it in the oven and it became a thing of beauty. Davey won a game of chess with a tidy checkmate. After dinner Davey learned the second solo from Sultans.

TUESDAY 13 SEPTEMBER 2022 AT 12:00

My arm was swollen, probably from exercise, and not keeping it in the posture they suggested, so I spent most of the day in bed. Willow called to say she loved me.

When I came down the house was messy, and I started to clean up grumpily, exasperating Lin with my petulance. She made rice and veg, and I ate with her in silence, then apologised.

After dinner we had a walk down the road and met Peter. He said the car part was delayed because of the queen's funeral.

THURSDAY 15 SEPTEMBER 2022

I did a guided meditation, then I moved and breathed with meditation music. I was careful of my arm. We went for a walk down the little boreen we discovered the day before. It didn't go far before it was stopped by a farmer's field. I missed calls from Willow, so I called her back and we had a nice chat. She is kind to me, like a mother.

I felt fear, worry, and anxiety pull one way, while hunger and desire pulled the other. I wanted a joint. While Lin was in Dunnes, I got a pack of cigarettes. I called a cab and he was waiting for us as we came out. The driver was a big guy with a painful life story. We stayed in our drive while he finished– his daughter kept trying to kill herself, and he had stopped her twice. He said I can't do it a third time. Lin wondered how I would respond. I said you may have to do it a third time, Joe, that may be the cross you have to bear. He was moved, and he shook my hand.

I got some weed from Lin and smoked a joint. I realised how Lin balanced my mind. It has often seemed that my life has been laid out perfectly before me, and that she is exactly the person I need to balance my excesses. We had a great chat about chakras, lines of force, life energy.

Davey won a tight game of chess, then he played Comfortably Numb. As we got ready for bed, I gave a big Blakean spiel about how school is just a way of managing and assimilating kids. Davey looked at me with respect while Lin slapped me softly, telling me to shut up.

I finished *Poguemahone*, then started again from the beginning. It is circular, like *Finnegan's Wake*.

FRIDAY 16 SEPTEMBER 2022 07:59

Liu Hao called Lin to tell her that something was wrong with her sister's eyes. He is 16, his father dead, his mother dying in front of him, and in trouble with the law. The fog is a white wall between me and the hills beyond.

After a few hoots I called a cab, and Ollie showed up before long. I smoked a few cigarettes outside, then went in and found Plastics at Outpatients. While I waited I did a chakra run up the spine, and some controlled breathing.

They called me in and changed my bandage. They told me I was fine and didn't need to come in again. I passed a Chinese nurse, and asked *ni hui shou zhongwen ma?* She said *hui*, and I said *ni tai bang le*. I chatted Ollie's ear off on the drive home.

I hooted in earnest for the rest of the day: in the pink chair behind the soccer net, and in the shade at the edge of the trees. I put on meditation music while I made cherry tomato spaghetti sauce, and Lin and I meditated while it simmered.

Lin walked the eight kilometres to Davey's school down the back roads.

I kept meaning to lay down but instead smoked reefer after reefer, and ended up responding to an online solicitation for volunteers to teach English to Ukrainian refugees.

SATURDAY 17 SEPTEMBER 2022 08:21

I had a short chat with Ralph after breakfast. It was nice; I hope we can talk again. I told him about some of the things I have suffered recently, and he said he had friends coming over.

I had cigarettes on my mind. I was petulant and fought with Lin, looking for an excuse to get cigarettes. I told her to give me the marijuana, and I drove to the little shop to get a pack. When I got home, I started hooting. Davey went up and played PS4. I went into the Zen room where Lin was doing meditation. I apologised and did my routine.

Davey and I took a walk down the road, and played chess when we got back. It was hard fought but I won with a tidy checkmate. I opened the bottle of wine Lin got for the stew. It was nice to have a glass of wine. I kept hooting. Lin was always reminding me that intoxicants are not good for the chi, and the flow of energy along the chakras. I took solace in the belief that I could free myself from these things and live a pure life, volunteer for things, get involved in the world at large. I can't present myself publicly when I am constantly stoned, and in constant anxiety. I want to be clear and at ease.

Lin made a Chinese dinner. I had a chat with Davey about Romantic Philosophy. He gets most things I say to him. Afterwards we had a walk in the garden. I was pretty wrecked. Liu Hao called Lin. Her sister was speaking incoherently. I took Davey up to bed. Lin was on the phone when we went up.

SUNDAY 18 SEPTEMBER 2022 07:35

When I woke at four, Lin was not in bed. I went down and she told me her sister was gone. She had been speaking incoherently, and when they told her to go to sleep she said she was already sleeping. They turned off the light to let her sleep. Her breathing was laboured, and then it stopped.

I told Lin to do nothing, that Davey and I would look after things, and she should just relax. She hadn't slept all night.

According to the principles of *The Tibetan Book of Living and Dying*, Lin will keep a 49 day vigil, to help guide her sister's soul past this incarnation. We meditated together. I went up through the chakras. At the green chakra I summoned love. At the crown, I saw Lin's sister's smile, her laughter, in white light above my head. I became nothing; became her; wished her on.

I organised salad and toast for lunch. Lin went up to lay down. I worked on a stew all day. I had a glass of wine. Davey played guitar, then we had a tight game of chess. I was angling for a checkmate, but he broke me down, and I conceded when he had more pawns remaining. I took Davey up to bed, and sat in his room for a bit. I enjoy speaking with him. I feel I can give him a strong intellectual foundation through conversation.

I lay in bed and considered my morning prayer, brought up from the green chakra to the crown chakra. When I became nothing I saw above me, in the white violet light, Lin's sister's laugh, and her smile. I tried to become this laughter and this light, shared with all life, and I prayed and tried to let her life become all light. I tried to be what I shared with her, in pure love. Her strong brave laughter and her defiant smile. Gone now: pass by.

I see Lin walking past the pink gate with Ares on the lead, her face far away.

MONDAY 19 SEPTEMBER 2022 07:40

I have been having dreams I can not remember, but which leave an impression of heavy, knotted coils. Lin fell asleep on the sofa waiting to be called by her family in Heilongjiang. It is a soft, dim morning.

Lin meditated beside me. The meditation was strong. I did a chakra and a prayer for Lin's sister. We must look at life as though we live one another's lives.

I didn't smoke yesterday, didn't feel the need.

TUESDAY 20 SEPTEMBER 2022 07:36

There is subtle light on the field across from me, but above is a blue wash of raincloud.

Lin hasn't slept in two nights, and wasn't sleeping well before that. Her brother and his wife had had it with the mom, and were trying to relinquish responsibility. Mom was on the warpath too.

I renewed *Poguemahone* then had a look round. Davey grabbed a big print *Fellowship of the Ring*; a beautiful fat book.

WEDNESDAY 21 SEPTEMBER 2022 08:01

Rain spatters on the window on this dark, mournful day. I am smoking again. Such an awful thing to have happened. I'd been so buoyant and at ease.

We had a simple dinner. I sliced and toasted sourdough. While eating, Lin said: I'm back. I was so relieved. I wished I could have said the same thing, sitting in my cloud of gloom.

After dinner, Davey and Lin went to soccer and hurling. When they got home, Davey played along to Comfortably Numb. I took him to his room and chatted a bit. When Lin came to give him water I got up to leave and Davey said Daddy is making his escape, so I sat down again.

Back in our bed, I kissed Lin many times, and she thought I was trying to seduce her, but that was not in my mind. Chen Xi will stay with us for two weeks before returning to China.

THURSDAY 22 SEPTEMBER 2022

I started with a binaural sound for the sacral chakra. After I finished my first sets, I hooted again, put on sound for the crown chakra, and inhabited the space above my crown in shimmering violet/white. Aaaaaaaaaaaah.

Lin took Davey to bed and gave me a kiss before she went back downstairs to read a prayer I think.

FRIDAY 23 SEPTEMBER 2022

Jobin, the physiotherapist, gave me exercises to maintain the strength in my hip, which he thinks is the main problem. I think he indicated belief in the power of meditation and the ability of someone to heal himself, even if a thousand others couldn't.

. . .

MONDAY 26 SEPTEMBER 2022

Lin gets up to meditate every day at four. She keeps two candles lit in the Zen room at all times. She chants Dharma.

FRIDAY 30 SEPTEMBER 2022 08:27

Lin was having a bad dream so I held her. It is a damp, orangy morning, with clouds tumbling over the hills.

MONDAY 3 OCTOBER 2022

Lin got up at 5:30 to read Dharma. Typing is difficult this morning. I am confused about my smoking habit, the need and the panic. My hands are cold.

In the car taking Davey to school, I convinced myself that I could buy a pack and then throw it out after my exercises. I dropped Davey off, waited a few minutes for the shopkeeper to arrive, got a pack and smoked one immediately, as though my life depended on it. When I got home, I hooted and did my physio exercise. Then I hooted and did yoga mediation with the chakra chanting track.

At one point on our walk at Dangan Ares was dragging Lin prone across the pitch by the lead. Willow called and we spoke about the past.

. . .

WEDNESDAY 5 OCTOBER 2022 07:45

I probably miss the important parts of each day in my diary. Little sparks of wonder. We saw so many fish at Dangan. When I finished my mediation and opened my eyes, the world was sodden, dark and rich in meaning.

FRIDAY 7 OCTOBER 2022

Lin dropped me off in front of Melania the Healer's home. I waited out front for her to call me in. She said she had seen four spirits around me when I was looking for her house. She said my third eye was to the left, my sacral area to the right. She said I smoke because I am in pain, and that I shouldn't beat myself up about it. If you want to eliminate something, let it flourish.

I went up to lay down after lunch. I heard Lin's mom heartbroke crying; no matter what Lin said, her mom couldn't stop sobbing. I read *Poguemahone*, then looked at my phone. Greg said it was a pity that I didn't make more of an effort to publish my poetry back in the day. He wanted to let a friend of his read *A Man without Talent*.

I need to exercise this morning. I feel dread at the thought of Saturday yawning in front of me, a low-level terror. I will smoke too much.

. . .

SUNDAY 9 OCTOBER 2022

I snuck in to get a pack of cigarettes with the milk. Lin and I are distant, though there is no animosity. She is focussed on her meditation, reading the Dharma, and her vigil for her sister. She is different now. She has stopped drinking and committed to Buddhism.

MONDAY 10 OCTOBER 2022 07:39

I had a bath and washed my hair for the first time since the dog bit me. I wake up each morning expecting news of nuclear war, but it's just the usual Russian cruelty and brutality.

I need to make some phone calls for Chen Xi, help her book a Covid test.

The 40th reunion of my high school class is all over facebook. It makes me question myself, my value as a person, the life I have lived. Makes me feel empty, detached from the world.

TUESDAY 11 OCTOBER 2022

After dinner I went up and watched Ozark for an hour. When I came down Davey was learning Van Halen, and Lin was cleaning up for Chen Xi's arrival on Saturday. Davey and I went up and played Civ.

FRIDAY 14 OCTOBER 2022 05:13

That the symptoms are back is my own fault. Darby gave me some weed last night. There is no moderation with me.

I felt empty, floating in nothing. Lin went to get Davey. I smoked and watched Karen videos. There was nothing I needed or wanted to do, nothing meaningful anywhere.

I took Davey to Des for his guitar lesson, then walked down to the windsurfing bay. It was a scene of beauty, but it didn't interest me. I looked for a moment, tried to feel something, then hobbled back and sat in the car, eating crisps and looking at my phone.

Des and Davey played Sultans of the Swing. Afterwards Des and I talked about having a beer one day. Before bed Davey hugged me and held me tight. I pulled him close, pressing away indifference.

SATURDAY 15 OCTOBER 2022 AT 06:56

It is black out but not raining. There are stars in the quiet sky. Chen Xi is down in her room.

I got very bloody stoned first thing. I had the idea that I should use the diary as a source for finishing my book. I saved it as a PDF, but the file was so gigantic it crashed my computer. It is a huge document, two million words. I emailed it to Greg to ask if he might upload it to google. I thought maybe if I took out the photos, and gave it a serious editing, I might have something. *Portrait*, I explained to Lin, ends with a diary. Lin wasn't happy to see me stoned again. She said I sounded like I was drunk.

Davey and I played Civilisation, and then I went to lay down. After a while, I called Davey in, and he lay beside me. It rained more heavily than I have ever seen, and we propped our pillows up on the bed and watched it like TV. I worried about Lin on the road.

We heard the door open and went down. Chen Xi and I drank wine. Davey played guitar but Chen Xi wasn't listening, she was speaking critically about the Chinese government. I know Lin felt challenged; it is unlike her to abide such bombast.

I hooted like gangbusters, then said to Chen Xi I needed to watch TV and excused myself with numerous intermissions for just one more joint. Lin tried to take away my last swallow of wine and I said are you mad, woman, that's my favourite bit.

SUNDAY 16 OCTOBER 2022 07:47

The treetops sway, rain specks the windows.

I hooted with abandon, finished Darby's weed. I made my diary entry, then looked back through this Time Machine. I ate my breakfast and swallowed my pills. Lin went shopping, so I called Chen Xi in, and we listened to the chakra chant together while doing yoga meditation. Lin got home and unpacked the groceries, then we all went for a walk at Dangan.

Later Davey and I played Civ. When we came down, Lin was making cabbage soup, and Chen Xi was exercising in the Zen room.

MONDAY 17 OCTOBER 2022 07:52

Chen Xi is doing face exercises at the dining table; Davey is just coming down.

We went into town so Chen Xi could change money. Lin took Davey's Strat to the shop looking cool in her docs, sunglasses and cap. I stayed in the bank with Chen Xi. The guy knew right away what was wrong; he raised the bottom string from 1mm to 1.4mm. Afterwards we had coffee at McCambridges.

Davey was thrilled to be able to bend the skinny string again. I sat on the green sofa and enjoyed the company.

FRIDAY 21 OCTOBER 2022

Chen Xi was doing yoga so didn't want lunch. I made beans on cheese on toast for Davey and me.

I opened a bottle of wine and drank it with Chen Xi. We talked about Buddhism, and our shared beliefs. I urged Chen Xi to get a *guqin* and learn how to play it, to bring music into her Zen routine. We opened another bottle of wine. Lin and Davey went to the other room to play with the *guzheng*. I spoke straight with Chen Xi about my worries for her, and when I told her how much I cared about her, she cried and left the room. Lin made dinner, and I went down and got Chen Xi to come back.

Davey played New Dawn Fades and I sang along with passion. We went up and started a new game of Civ. When we came down Chen Xi was in bed. The simple things she wanted from life had not worked out for her. I wished I could make it up to her, but knew I could not, and what are regrets good for anyways? We need to find a Zen peace. Love. Kindness. I told Chen Xi I had been her husband wife daughter sister grandmother over a thousand lives. I wanted to help her but she said with tears in her eyes she wanted to find her soulmate.

SATURDAY 22 OCTOBER 2022 08:24

I had a sleepless night with a hypersensitive leg and aching balls, so I took one of the super painkillers. It is so depressing to think these devastated balls are mine. It is dim, rainy and still, with mist on the hills beyond. Lin is having a shower; the others are asleep.

Chen Xi seemed to have forgotten most of what was said the night before; she was laughing and in good spirits. I told her that what I said might have been clumsy, but I said it because I cared about her. I told her about seeing a video of Hu Jin Tao being led out of the Party conference. He was the leader during the golden years of China, the days of One World One Dream. This was a clear sign that it is over, and not coming back.

Lin prepared hotpot, and we had a Chinese style dinner, with great chat over the table. Chen Xi fits in with us so well. We all cleaned up together, laughing.

SUNDAY 23 OCTOBER 2022

Chen Xi joined me as I did my yoga meditation. It was nice to have her in the room. It is good to meditate with another person, to share energy.

I tidied up and vacuumed. Lin got home and unpacked groceries. I chatted on the phone with Eoin about meditation and Buddhism. He will visit soon.

Chen Xi vacuumed the Zen room, and then the stone room, full of the debris of my smoking paraphernalia. I prepared a couple of frozen pizzas for lunch, and started a beef stew that would simmer all day.

It was too rainy to take Ares for a walk for the third successive day, so Davey and I drove to the little shop for wine and cigarettes. We listened to a live version of Sultans of Swing. Such beautiful guitar.

Lin put vegetables in the beef stew. I added wine, and Chen Xi and I drank the rest.

MONDAY 24 OCTOBER 2022

I took Davey to school. We listened to Comfortably Numb, *Live at Pompeii*.

When I got home Chen Xi was having a problem on the phone. The money to her dad and Tan had been sent back because it was 100 RMB over the limit. I expected her to freak out, but she handled it well. In fact, she was laughing.

I did my yoga. Lin prepared avocado, leaves, and toast for lunch. I began the cherry tomato spaghetti sauce. We were happy and laughing.

I got the cherry tomatoes going and then I went up and lay down. I didn't come down until after Davey was home.

When Chen Xi went for a walk, I reminded her to put on a reflective jacket.

TUESDAY 25 OCTOBER 2022 09:26

I didn't sleep well. I am uncomfortable when I lay on either side. The hips. I took two painkillers before I went up; no result. I bore the discomfort and then went down and had tea and toast with Karen videos on youtube. Lin came down, and we went up again together.

At half one, Kitty scratched at our bed. Lin went down to put her out and didn't come back up.

I am still smoking like gangbusters–almost a pack yesterday. It is dim, and the trees shake their pagan rattles.

Before I took Davey to school, Lin said that as it was an eclipse we should all meditate together. At ten we put on the chakra chanting, and each did our thing. I had a good, deep meditation. Chen Xi continued until she answered her phone, and found that they had sent back her third money transfer. That was now three out of four transfers returned. She felt dizzy and nauseous.

Lin and I walked in the eclipse, but didn't really notice anything out of the ordinary. We did the whole walk. The faith healer called to make another appointment this Friday.

The heating guy worked on the plumbing system. I felt proud of my team. Ares was barking savagely in the library, and Chen Xi, Lin and I were speaking in Chinese and in English about meditation techniques and Buddhism. I got a message from Eoin saying he was coming over. Lin put out the Chinese tea set. We had a great discussion about Buddhism and meditation. Eoin is very knowledgeable about this, as are Lin and Chen Xi. It was a powerful conversation, and in the end Eoin closed his eyes, and the three of us started to worry that he had lost himself, but then we realised he was trying to heal me.

There was a message from Greg, conveying his friend's response to my story. It was positive, and this has given me some much needed encouragement.

We got ready for bed. I was given kisses and then Lin took Davey down to his room. He finished *Fellowship of the Ring* last night. I will go to the library and get him *Two Towers* today.

How long will the money last, and what happens after?

WEDNESDAY 26 OCTOBER 2022 07:35

Lin and I switched sides of the bed. My side had become a deep crater. Lin seems happy with the arrangement. At one point the palms of our feet pressed together. Her skin was smooth like a baby's.

Lin made noodles. I called Chen Xi out of her room and we ate together. There was good spirit at the table.

Three of the four money transfers Chen Xi made were refused, but they haven't reappeared in her account. She is under a lot of pressure, but her character is much improved and she is maintaining her humour. She helped me prepare a heating pad for my hip.

. . .

FRIDAY 28 OCTOBER 2022

Lin and Chen Xi are chatting in Chinese, and Davey is playing guitar. The animals are in. It rained heavily last night and it is still raining. My trousers are damp from having sat in the rain with coffee and a cigarette. I have a lot to write today.

Diary, cereal and pills, brushing of teeth, change of underwear and t-shirt. Davey was dressed as a plague doctor for Halloween. We left for school a bit early so I could get to the appointment with Melania on time.

I played Sweet Child O Mine loud. At the bottom of the road I saw a guy waiting for a lift. I picked him up. Omar was a foreign student at NUIG, studying International Development. He was pleasant, soft spoken, and humble. I let him off by Agnes the crossing lady.

Davey got out and I drove to Melania's place. I parked nearby and had a cigarette. Someone came out and drove away. I went in. She got me to sit and reclined the chair so I was lying down, then put a blanket over me. She asked me how I was and I said I am always keeping a brave face for Lin, Davey and Chen Xi, but I am in constant pain, and it is very difficult. She advised me to take milk of magnesia, vitamins, and protein powder.

She told me I was going to cut ties with someone today. I

told her I valued my past, that I always wrote about it, and she told me I wouldn't cut ties of love, only ties that held me back, that this would help me with my writing.

She got me to close my eyes and relax, and then started a guided meditation. While it played she touched my chakras, first around my head and neck, and then my belly. She breathed on my forehead.

I saw everything vividly and spontaneously. I was instructed to gather my regrets into a ball. I knew what this meant immediately, and a flood of small regrets, memories that made me stop and shudder, too many to enumerate, came at me. I was told to see these regrets as a black ball of iron, chained to my ankle. The archangel Michael appeared, and cut this chain with a flashing blue sword. The black ball floated above me and resolved itself in violet light.

I was asked to think of someone I wanted to cut ties with. I had thought of Chen Xi or my father before we started, but my mother's ghost appeared clearly and definitively. She stood or floated before me in her wretched nightgown. I was asked to visualise the ties that held her to me, and I saw heavy iron chains. Asked where these connected to me I found it was my solar plexus chakra, yellow. The archangel cut these chains with his blue flashing sword.

The chains were thrown into a fire. I stepped toward this fire and was instructed to undress. I wore the green rugby pants and orange muscle shirt that I wore when I was eighteen or twenty, around the time my mother died. I threw these clothes in the fire, then stepped toward a stream of glittering starlight, went in and washed myself.

I was called out to a green space, and felt the grass beneath my feet. I expressed my freedom by dancing and doing somersaults. The archangel Michael approached with angular face, gave me a white gown, cool and soft, a sword and a shield and directed me to speak truly and justly. Lady Fate gave me a sapphire ring, which I put on the largest finger on my left hand. When I need strength I am to touch this finger.

There was more I can't remember but pieces came back to me through the day, not as memories but as understandings. I went out and got in the car. As I got to the first turn up out of the crescent, four or six gardai armed response units pulled up in front of me, and maybe 15 gardai in black helmets and body armour jumped out of the cars with machine guns. They ran into a house a few doors down. I stayed a moment to see what was happening. A car pulled up and a guy with blue gloves jumped out and followed them into the house. I drove home.

When I got home Chen Xi had gone for a walk. Lin made me tea and I told her what had happened. She listened closely. Lin and I went for a walk with Ares, and had a great chat. She wants to do the meditation retreat in April. Ten days meditating from 4 am to 9 pm. It would be very tough, much more than I could ever manage. I told her we support her. I told her that I had always thought I had courage because of the way I fought and risked my life so often, but that this wasn't courage it was wildness and despair. I understood now that my real lacking in courage was my inability to risk sending my writing out to be published, and that if I wanted to establish my courage this is what I would need to do.

When we got in the car, I realised I needed to speak with Chen Xi. I asked Lin to take Davey to his guitar lesson, and offered to cook dinner. We decided on quiche. I would share the four tins of Guinness with Chen Xi while Lin and Davey were at guitar.

When we got home I tidied, and Lin chatted to her mom. Chen Xi came out and I prepared lunch, then went upstairs and lay down. Lin and Davey went to guitar. Chen Xi was doing her face exercises. She wanted a cup of coffee. Then, she came over and we sat at the stone counter. I opened two tins of Guinness. She poured hers in a pint glass, and I drank mine from the tin.

I told her about the session with Melania while preparing quiche. I told her I know it sounds crazy, but I thought it had pragmatic psychological results. She said this wasn't crazy, it was something she believed in. We talked about our life together. I told her how many regrets I had for how I had ruined our marriage. I told her how much I worried about her and felt remorse, how I would always love her. It suddenly dawned on me what I needed to talk to Chen Xi about. I told her I wanted to put all these regrets in a ball and see them chained to my leg. Then I wanted, with her permission, to cut this, remove the regret and let only love remain. She agreed, and gave me a big hug.

Lin and Davey got home. We were such a happy family. Chen Xi and Lin chatted away in Chinese and I only got bits of it. Davey played guitar and looked at the iPad. Ares cuddled Lin rubbing his head against her, gazing up at her with love. Kitty glared at us all from the windowsill. I finished the quiche and we had dinner, then Davey and I went up and played Civ. When we came down Chen Xi was in bed. Lin was reading *Siddhartha* by Herman Hesse.

I woke when Lin was getting up to do her prayers, but held the water bottle against my stomach and slept again. Davey came in to get his trousers, but he didn't turn on the light so I kept sleeping. I heard Chen Xi talking to Lin. I came down and Lin had a coffee ready for me.

I had a smoke and my coffee outside in the rain, then I started on the diary.

There is a guy on Fetlife who wants to sell me some weed. Maybe I will get some, maybe I won't. I know I shouldn't. I am already smoking cigarettes with abandon–just dumped a massive heap of butts from last night in the black bin outside.

SATURDAY 29 OCTOBER 2022 07:25

Outside is grey and dim, deep green and sodden.

I saw an ad from Yando in a 402 Ireland group on Fetlife advertising high quality weed. The ad disappeared shortly after he posted it, but I managed to message him.

We arranged to meet midday in town. I told Lin I wanted to go for a walk on my own. When Yando asked for a meeting place, I suggested Dungeons and Donuts. I stood and waited, then I saw a guy who I figured must be him and we nodded at one another and walked down to the ATM at Lynch's Castle. Yando wore a cream toque, functional jacket, and Norse beard. He said he was from out Loughrea way. He described the weed in detail. Grown outdoors. He likes the smell of outdoor-grown best. I concurred amiably with everything he said. He ghostwrites celebrity diets, something like that. He used to work as a chemist but found it difficult as an autistic. I told him about my illness, about meditation, wellness, our garden, Lin becoming Buddhist. He gave me two quid for the parking metre. We got in my car and he produced a huge bag of buds and I gave him 150. He got out and walked toward an old war chariot, painted in desert camo.

When I got home I immediately got out of my face. Lin came down and made lunch. She was upset to see me stoned. Her back was very sore. Chen Xi was also shocked that I would do this. At lunch, I blabbered about meeting Yando. Lin and

Chen XI scowled, and Davey kept asking questions. I dug myself in deeper. I couldn't shut up.

I was away with the faeries. I played Civ with Davey until just before dinner. Lin and Chen Xi were grim, though they now and then saw the awful humour in it. They just asked me, dumbfounded, why I thought now was the time to go on another weed binge. Lin asked if the spiritual healer had advised me to get really stoned? They both laughed when I admitted, well not exactly.

I made no effort to help tidy up. I hooted, played guitar with Davey, then went up for more Civ. I had longboats and berserkers; I raided and pillaged. We played until almost 8. Davey felt a bit dizzy. He asked if playing so long was bad for you.

I expected Lin to be grouchy but her face was shining with smiles, so bright and alien. I took Davey down to his room. I didn't stay long as I had chatted to him all day.

Meditation yoga, bath. Play with Davey, guitar and Civ. Berzerkers and longboats. Brilliant. I have a World Congress Edict to neutralise Cree preachers. I will fill my coffers with gold.

SUNDAY 30 OCTOBER 2022 07:14

I slept perfectly last night, the first time in ages I didn't need to get up during the night. I have soreness this morning, but

I can float atop the pain. The sky is steely above the black hills, between a weave of branches.

We parked at the Claddagh, went to Quay Kitchen. We sat out front at wobbly tables. It was fun to see all the people. I got a Guinness, then hurried away for cigarettes, at the corner of Druid Lane.

The sauces were excellent. Lin was quiet. Chen Xi ordered two desserts, and we ate them together. Davey was excited to eat desert, as we never do this.

We walked down the town. It was difficult for me to manoeuvre, but Davey helped me along. I had a heavy deadness in my back and shoulders. We got to Eyre Square, turned around and walked back. At the car we noticed stars and a crescent moon.

MONDAY 31 OCTOBER 2022

Chen Xi is stressed about trying to make her bank transfers again. She has a few very tough days ahead of her, jumping through hoops.

She leaves us for Dublin tomorrow. She will spend a day and half a night there, then on to Paris, then quarantine in Beijing. She has promised me that if she needs to put a stool through a window she will call me first.

TUESDAY 1 NOVEMBER 2022

I have a hundred new pains and spreading numbness. I must stop smoking immediately, he says before going out for the third reefer.

It is black and cold. I said goodbye to Chen Xi fifteen minutes ago, and Lin drove her to the bus station for the 5:15 to Dublin.

We had a decent goodbye. Our friendship is deep and true. Money in the bank as she put it.

Davey said goodbye to Chen Xi very well last night. I was proud of him. I hope there can always be love between them.

Lin will be back soon. After breakfastI hope to go back to bed. I don't feel right.

THURSDAY 3 NOVEMBER 2022 08:31

I slept well last night, and don't feel as bad this morning as I have the past few days, though my body still surges with pain. It is bright out for a Galway November.

It was difficult but I persevered with my physio exercises. Halfway through I made a drink with protein powder.

I vacuumed, then we went for a walk at Dangan. Lin walked behind us. She has a sore back from Ares pulling at the lead.

Davey and I were speaking about Civ, nuclear and astrophysics. When we got into the car, Lin started crying. I thought maybe it was because she had nearly completed the 49 day vigil for her sister. I think she didn't really know why she was crying.

I thought about teaching Fluentify, about finishing my story, about going into the welfare office and seeing if they could help me get a job.

FRIDAY 4 NOVEMBER 2022

Yesterday morning I did my diary, had my cereal and pills, then thought about transforming my diary into the second book of my story. It is a very big job, and I'm not sure how to handle it. I will have to set a time for work each day. So busy now with exercise and walking Ares. If I started getting up at six I could squeeze in a bit before Davey went to school. I don't think I could do it in the afternoon or evening. I will have to stop writing the diary to make time.

SATURDAY 5 NOVEMBER 2022 07:10

I slept very well. There is a wine glass from last night on my desk, and it is still mostly dark out. It was raining last night but now it is still.

Yesterday Lin finished the 49 day vigil for her sister's soul. She kept a candle lit, prayed and read Dharma every day. She didn't drink or eat meat. I think she will stop drinking for good.

I started compiling pieces for the second book of *A Man without Talent*.

Lin was meditating. I did a sun salutation and kneeling meditation beside her. She asked me What will I do When I Wake Up?

We went for a walk at Dangan. I walked well and had a good chat with Davey. It was a beautiful morning. The water was so smooth.

I hooted myself silly. When they left for football, I finished the bottle of wine while mining the diary. I don't know for sure how this will work, but I have a *modus operandi*.

Learning consists of daily accumulation. The path of the Dao consists of daily diminishment. Two million words. I will strip this to the core, leave only what is precious to me. *That which thou lovest well remains. The rest is dross.*

When they got home we had dinner. Afterwards Davey and I went up and played Civ. It is getting near the end. When I am ready, he will annihilate me with nukes, then we will start a new game. My little buddy is back at school tomorrow.

I filled the hot water bottle and two mugs of warm water, then went up. Lin put the animals out.

We all cuddled on the bed. I was given kisses, and Davey told me I am The Best Daddy in the World.

Lin took Davey down to his room. When she returned, she kissed me again.

Printed in Great Britain
by Amazon